Winds propelled by the cloudsteeds' vast wings pounded as Jarrod and Martin clung to the icy mountainside; they felt themselves being pried loose.

"Keep going!" Jarrod yelled. "They'll kill us if we stay here!" He pushed at Martin's shoulder and she moved at once. A cloudsteed dropped toward them, lashing out with a sharp, horny hoof. They flung themselves forward and were only aware of the next attack when the force of the horse's wings slammed them into the rocks.

"On, on, on, on, on!" Jarrod screamed as he surged for the cave that meant survival. He caught Martin with one arm and hurled her forward to safety as flying shadows cut across their path.

The winged horses continued to circle even as they sprawled on the cave floor, chests heaving.

"I-I thought," Martin gasped, "that cloud-steeds were supposed to be man's noblest allies . . ."

"Unless," Jarrod stared at the huge forms, "they're protecting something . . . Guarding the unicorn . . ."

THE UNICORN QUEST

JOHN LEE

A TOM·DOHERTY ASSOCIATES BOOK

THE UNICORN QUEST

Copyright © 1986 by John Lee

First printing: February 1986

A TOR Book

Published by Tom Doherty Associates
49 West 24 Street
New York, N.Y. 10010

Cartographer: Nancy Westheimer

ISBN: 0-812-54400-5
CAN. ED.: 0-812-54401-3

Printed in the United States of America

0 9 8 7 6 5 4 3 2 1

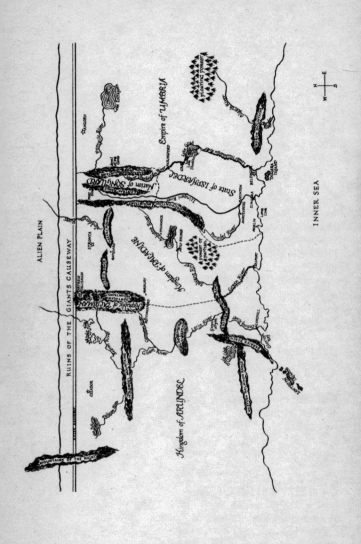

CHAPTER I

"STRAND SHALL HAVE NO HISTORY UNTIL IT HAS BEEN CLEANSED and can be called ours again." That was the adage every child had learned in Dameschool, a precept that had been in force for centuries. There were the songs of minstrels, but no histories. The great deeds of war were rhymed, but never catalogued and it made Jarrod Courtak wonder what he was doing behind the specially installed desk in the gallery of Celador's Great Hall. This was undeniably an historic occasion. Oh, there had been Conclaves aplenty before, but never one attended by the Untalented. No matter how powerful a Lord Temporal might be, if they could not make Magic they could not attend. Yet there they all were, filing across the floor with their entourages.

The Magisters of the Collegium had vied for places in the Hall with all the ruthless guile of schoolboys, but it was he, not even a senior student, who was to keep this unlikely record. It had made him even more unpopular than usual. It was, he had quickly found, a decidedly mixed blessing to be known as a Mage's protégé. The Dean of the Collegium had told him, somewhat sourly, that the record was needed for the Archmage's Archive and that he had been picked to describe the proceedings because of his memory and because he wrote a fair hand. His fellow students, and many of the Magisters, had muttered about favoritism. He sighed and whittled the nib planes of the clern-feather quills and laid them neatly beside the sandbox.

5

He gazed moodily past the inkhorn at the living kaleidoscope. The morning sun streamed down through the stained-glass windows and threw black-bordered pools of color on the crowd below. The three central chandeliers glowed with the borrowed light, but did little to illuminate the controlled riot of fan tracery that grew out of the capitals. He craned forward to look down on the three columns of backless benches that marched on the dais that spanned the far end of the room. Should he put all that down? Better do it and take it out later if they didn't like it. He selected a quill. Start with the dais and work backwards.

There were five figures sitting immobile and inward-seeing in carved and canopied chairs. The High Council of Magic sat, accoutered and in public state, but utterly withdrawn. In the center, as was proper, was Ragnor, Archmage and Mage of Arundel, clad in the full regalia of Power. Jarrod stared at him and the pen stopped its track across the vellum scroll as his eyes became drawn into the patterns of force. Limned in gold and silver runes, they shifted and ran across the robe as if they had a life of their own. He tore his eyes free and the hand resumed, noting that the Archmage's long, straight hair had gone white. The forehead was high and had been made higher by the passing years: the face was oval, would be mobile, and was seined by time and Magic. The sapphire biretta, outward symbol of the Mageship of Arundel, sparkled. The heavily wrought Chain of the Archmages hung from his neck to the folds of his lap. Jarrod scanned him once more and then moved on.

To the right was his mentor, Greylock, Mage of Paladine and Keeper of the Place of Power. The youth felt a surge of contradictory emotions. Greylock was the closest thing to a father that he had ever had. It had been months since he had seen the man. Back to the business at hand.

The hair was iron grey and curly, topping a heavy, square-jawed face. The lines were set and serious. He wore deep green with cabalistic symbols etched across in black. His circlet was of lowly diamonds, but the cheap stones only served to emphasize the importance of the wearer. That was one trick, Jarrod thought ruefully, that I'll never be able to learn from him.

On the Archmage's left, on the Throne of Kings, which was said to have been hewn from a single, grandfather robur by the first of her line, sat Arabella of Arundel. The Princess Regnant's blond hair was piled up in artful simplicity, accentuating the graceful neck and the sureness in the set of the young shoulders. Beside her, encushioned, was the ruby Crown of State, but she sat on the Council not by virtue of her rank, but because she was a truly remarkable thaumaturge.

Beyond her was the Chief Warlock of Talisman, looking so old and frail in his great big chair that it seemed impossible that he would make it back from wherever sleep, or his meditations, had taken him. At the other end, completing the quintet, was Naxania of Paladine. Jarrod's hand hesitated and hovered above the parchment.

He knew a lot about Naxania. She was the daughter of his King and he had grown up in their palace at Stronta. Should he say that her older brother's recent embrace of Umbrian ways, complete with mechanical workshops and a Chapel of the Mother, had made her even more sharp-tongued? No, better not. It had no bearing on this occasion. Stick to descriptions. She was as pale as milk, with raven hair caught up by rune-scored combs. She was older than Arabella, but not yet out of her twenties. She was accounted beautiful, despite what Jarrod considered the meanness of her mouth. These five were the highest of sorcery's High Council.

Before their feet, the Lords Temporal shifted and buzzed. At the front, though carefully separated by the width of the chamber, sat Robarth Strongsword, Naxania's father, with his son, the Prince Justinex, and, at the center of a curious vortex of stillness, Varodias the Tenth, at the behest of the Mother, Emperor of all the Umbrians and Elector of Andrium.

Robarth, who, people said, loved wenching only slightly less than warfare, was jocosely at ease with his nobles, but there was a circle of space around Varodias. Robarth lounged and laughed, but the Emperor sat rigid and straightened by his dignity, his back turned slightly to the wall. An errant shaft of sunlight struck amber shards from the polished cabrion that sat on a cascade of ecru silk at the base of his throat. The scatter threw speckles of gold over the hooded falcon that stood, taut and motionless, on a stand close beside the gloved hand.

Between and behind the two monarchs were a mixture of

noblemen, Holdmasters and Commanders, but two groups stood out. The most noticeable and powerless were the fierce and hirsute mountain chiefs of Songuard. They wore the traditional bright and boldly patterned cloth of their peoples over their leather armor. Though they seldom met amicably in their own land, they clustered together now, uneasy in the presence of so many people and so much finery.

Up and down the aisles and into the rows moved the Oligarchs of Isphardel, patting a shoulder here, shaking a hand there, bowing low in quiet conversation. The traders of the world dressed the part and seemed to know everybody. The exotic splendor of their fur-trimmed silks was matched only by the windows for variety and hue. Vivid turbans bobbed as they wove their way around the room. Cornucopious sleeves curved and dipped, pomanders were held discreetly to the nose. From time to time notebooks appeared and orders were taken, proof of the power of commerce, even here, where Magic ruled supreme. Jarrod stopped writing and sat up and stretched. There, he thought, that covers all the national groups. He read through what he had written and made some corrections.

It was not possible to isolate the moment of change, but, between breath and heartbeat, the Councilors were present. They emerged as one from whatever regions they had been inhabiting and their presence was palpable. Feet shifted and benches creaked. Men cleared their throats and, at the back of the Hall, nervous laughter broke out and was quickly suppressed. The Archmage rose awkwardly into the growing tension, levering himself upward with his Staff. Then he lifted it and brought it down, ringingly, thrice.

He was a tall, thin man, but he stooped somewhat and looked shorter than the almost eight feet of his height. It was obvious, even to those who did not know him, that he had been practicing drastic necromancy of late. The spritely strength that had always marked him had been leached away. There was a spiritual pallor about him and Jarrod tried to remember, as he readied himself to write, the last time that he had appeared in public.

"Majesties, Great Lords, colleagues, friends." The Archmage's voice quavered, but he spoke strongly, in the formal mode and in perfect and unaccented Common. "My thanks to you all for coming. I am sensible of the sacrifices that some of you have had to make and I am grateful. I have summoned this exceptional Conclave for the gravest of reasons and I assure you that I would not have called you away from the defense of your realms and your other vital enterprises had I not feared for our very existence." He paused briefly, eyes scanning the crowd.

"Oh I know that there has been war for time out of mind and time out of memory. Who among us does not know that those Others seek to annihilate us and all that we have done, all that we have grown. They have always been bent on replacing the sweetness of our own air with the corruption that they breathe. But now, ah now, we may founder at last." He paused again and let them hang. "You are here," he said slowly, "because the inadmissible is imminent.

"Hear me, O Princes, and harken to me, most fierce and peremptory lords." The voice gained force and organed out. "Likewise give heed to me all ye who control the destiny of this our world." The tip of the Staff slammed down against the hollow wood beneath him and he waited as the sound reverberated into silence.

"Some months ago, while I was conducting experiments in search of the Final Spell, I stumbled upon a new line of endeavor. It has occupied me ever since. I have discovered the secrets of the future." His left hand waved as the hubbub rose up and fell away. The others on the dais sat as still as basilisks.

"I have not the strength, nor, in truth, the inclination to repeat the spell successfully and I very much doubt that even my friend Greylock has the power, as yet, to break through the closely woven fabric of time. I do not know how far I saw, or even if it was a future continuous from our now that I witnessed, but what I saw was enough. Lords of Creation, it was enough! Those glimpses brought me sorrow, they brought me anguish and anger. What I saw was war. Nay, nay," and the hand waved dismissively, "not the kind of war that has girdled us for so long; not the ordinary violence that has been both swaddling and cerement to our brief existence; but bloody onslaught, death, destruction, weapons of hideous power never seen before nor thought on. Oh harrow! Harrow!"

The head bowed at the memory and the long, white hair

swung forward. When he had composed himself he said, in a low voice that made those at the back strain forward to hear,

"Everything will change. To a certain extent, the effects of this never-ending conflict have been limited by our inability to take the war to the enemy and their inability to survive in our air. We know so little about them because the merest touch of it withers them away to dust. They are fearfully handicapped by their protective sheathing and the pipes they need to keep breathing, but all that will change."

The voice rose again and reacquired compulsion. "You Princes and Governors, know that your provinces shall be the seat of ravagement and ruin. You Captains and Commanders, know that all your knowledge and all your skill will be for naught. The enemy shall invade us all—*un-en-cumbered*—wheresoever they will. Not a hose to be seen."

Murmurs of disbelief erupted and the Archmage drew from his robes the stone Errethon. It filled the upstretched hand and slowly roused itself to color until it glowed incarnadine. Truth had been spoken and the sight of it quieted the listeners. The Archmage turned in the silence and urged the Mage of Paladine to his feet as he laid his Staff on the floor beside the chair. As he rose, it was apparent that Greylock was short for a wizard, no more than an inch or two above the average. Both men stepped forward, standing out sharply against the blue curtain that spanned the apse behind them. It hid both exits and the massive water clock. Time had been banished.

"My friends, while I cannot pierce that shroud again, the message of my visions was clear and urgent. Mere words are not enough to convey to you the magnitude of the task that confronts us beyond tomorrow's corner. Comprehension requires sight. I have determined to use the assistance of the Mage of Paladine and, through him, the strength of the Ring of the Keepers to show unto you the things that have assailed my eyes and my heart. Those among you who know that your stomachs do not take quietly to battlefields had best depart. In the days to come it will be held no shame against you that you knew yourselves well enough to be wise. This too I have seen."

There was hesitation and a few, furtive departures, but, for the most part, attention was riveted on the stage. The Archmage unfastened the chain that he wore as a badge of office and held the ends out toward Greylock. The younger man slipped the ring from his finger and hooked it over one half of the clasp. When the circle was closed again, both men turned sideways and stood back to back. They lifted the chain over their heads and settled it around their shoulders. Slowly and quietly, their hands tracing patterns of Power before them, they began to intone.

Little by little, the air around them began to darken and rise in a thinly swirling column. It gained substance and opacity until neither man could be seen, though the mounting murmur of voices from within could clearly be heard. The column spread out until a broad, black cloud covered the dais and rolled toward the vaulted ceiling. Inside it, lighter patches flickered into being, faded and flickered up again. The chanting rose in volume and intensity and the paler areas shifted, coalesced and gradually began to form a picture.

Most of those that sat in the Great Hall were at a loss to grasp what they were seeing until, with a vertiginous lurch, they realized that they were looking down at a section of the Upper Causeway. It was like looking down from the back of a cloudsteed. They saw the ruins of the Giants' Causeway stretching away from its foot, but they did not run far. The alien atmosphere lapped at its tumbled edges. From out that atmosphere blotchy pods extruded and exploded against the Northern face of the wall. The seamless blocks of stone became covered with slime and projectiles began to burst wetly on the broad surface of the roadway itself. As the viewpoint slid disconcertingly down toward the ground, there seemed to be something wrong with the battlements and then came the shocked realization that they were melting. Stone was flaking and sifting down and the outer surface seemed alive. The security of a lifetime began to look like sealing wax left too long in the sun.

Gaping holes began to appear in the near side of the Causeway and then a whole section slid into dust and rubble. The smoke of stonedust hung in the air for an impossible time and men milled helplessly before they turned and fled from the reality of that corrosive ether. Machines heaved themselves out of the leaden fog that had filled the jagged-sided fissure, like turtles from the sea. The defenses that had preserved the world for generations, mankind's greatest feat of building, had been broached and broken. A despairing moan was wrenched from a corner of the Hall. The watchers sat rooted to their benches with bile rising in their throats. The images within the black cloud sped implacably on.

The forces of Strand were not impotent and, as the range of view deepened, they could be seen moving into perimeter position. A squadron of cloudsteeds climbed the sky. The machines crawled through the torn masonry, beetles from a rotted wainscotting, followed by figures in protective suits. The suits looked familiar, but now each was independently mobile. They swung out and took up places between the vehicles. There were no lines to supply them with stuff to breathe and yet they moved easily as they brought strange new weapons to bear. Fire, or light, or both, flamed forth, scything through armor as easily as through bone and sinew. It cut down warriors, warcats, horses, anything it touched. The screams of the dying tore at the watchers' ears and rang around the insides of their heads. There was slaughter, slaughter on all sides, until the mind could absorb no more. No matter how visceral the longing to be shut of them, the pictures continued.

Men and beasts became too mired in blood to crawl away to die. The unwilling audience watched as the abnormal vapors welled out and up, covering the enemy and reaching out to engulf the survivors. They saw skin purple, blister and break. They saw foliage wilt and die as well, but the plants could not scream as the men and animals did. It was impossible to tell from those sounds of extremity which was which.

Still they watched, the cords of the neck strained taut, the eyes flinching like a dog before a whipping and, like the dog, compelled to gaze upon the coming pain. Their attention was commanded by the moiling suppuration visible in that monstrous cloud of vision. Jarrod, quill quite forgot, fought to look away and became aware of moans forced, willy-nilly, from throats dry with horror. The inescapable image ahead was clear enough for him to distinguish faces and they were faces that he knew.

Tears filled his eyes and forced the horror out of focus. Think about something else, he said to himself as his stomach rebelled dangerously. He wasn't going to shame himself in front of all of these people by being sick. Think of something pleasant. Think of growing up in Stronta. Try to remember the sense of finally belonging when you had been transferred from Dameschool to Greylock's tutelage. He had been awed, of course. After all, the Mage of Paladine was a figure of enormous power and mystery, but the man had been kindly; gruff, but kindly. For the first time in his life he had felt that he fitted in. He squeezed his eyes shut and hugged the memory to himself, but the Archmage and his reconstructed vision were too strong for him. Sound intruded first and then his eyelids opened themselves.

The shadow scene had changed. He was high in the air once more, but now they were over Paladine's ancient enigma, the Place of Power, well beyond the walls of Stronta and the Great Mind Maze. The ground was all too familiar to Jarrod, but he seized eagerly on the fact that no fighting was going on. He knew the respite would be brief for, as the impressions grew closer and more distinct, it was obvious that battle was impending. Light seeped up the Eastern sky, revealing a large force of Paladinian levies ranged on and beyond the Upper Causeway. The Maze Gate was open, but here at least the Causeway above it was still unblemished, could still carry six chariots abreast. Before it was a battalion of warcats, their warriors by their sleek sides. They were a proud and fearsome sight, those warcats, standing half the height of a man, with the rising sun gleaming on the tawny fur and sliding across the darker spots that dappled their hides.

The warcat warriors were dressed in the lightest of armor, needing all the speed they could muster to fight alongside such swift and nimble allies. No words were spoken, but Jarrod knew that thoughts, plans and reassurances were flying from warcat to warrior and back. To those outside this elite and self-contained force, it seemed unnatural and there was constant speculation as to who controlled whom. Jarrod thought it wonderful and had always had a hankering to be one of them.

Atop the Upper Causeway, commanding the conventional forces from above, Robarth Strongsword's brother, Naxus, Prince of Paladine and Margrave of Thannock, cut an arresting figure astride his black charger. It was the one place where he felt taller than his brother and the man seemed to strut in the saddle. About a league away the ominous curtain hung and bellied. Below him the troops waited.

For those in the Great Hall the painless interval of wondering was brief. From the murk at the back of the conjured cloud there lumbered a heavily armored box on belt-connected wheels. The warcats growled and their tails switched, the black horse reared and the men readied themselves. More and more of the blocky constructs inched forth like scaleworms on rain-fresh earth. For a beat the two lines faced each other and then, faster than the eye could follow, something lashed out from one of the vehicles and the Prince's headless body toppled slowly from the charger, staining the terrified animal's flank an even darker hue as it fell. As if it had been a signal, beams of the hot light shot out and the lofty chamber echoed anew with tormented shrieks of unendurable pain. The flesh charred and smoked wherever the beams touched. Maddened cats, their fur afire, rushed at the enemy. Those that got through slashed futilely at the metal protecting the unreachable foe. They died by the score in a welter of blood, entrails and agony, and their partners died with them.

The wail of a woman's shocked outrage threaded the space from the platform, proving, for those who cared to heed, that those on the dais could see what transpired, even if they could not be seen. As if in response, the scene flickered and changed. The picture sharpened once more upon the Upper Causeway, but a lot further East. This time they were undoubtedly at Angorn, capital of Umbria and seat of Varodias' home Electorate. Lined up on the far lip were several spindly towers, topped by rapidly revolving vanes. The bases of the towers were wreathed in billowing smoke and, for a moment, it looked as if, here too, the enemy atmosphere had encroached. Then the startled gaze took in the sooty boilers that were providing the motive power.

There was an instant buzz of comment from the Elector-Scientists as all their suspicions of Magical chicanery in these presentations vanished. There were those among them who had been working, secretly and fruitlessly, on just such machines. They strained forward to a man to take in every possible detail. The gorge-filling sights and sounds of the previous minutes were effortlessly banished by the itch of research. What was more important to those who were not citizens of the Empire was that the tattered arras of fume was being held at bay.

The angle of vision shifted again, despite cries in both Umbrian and Common for a little more time. Now the gathered watchers were above the evil brew and looked queasily across it at an unending string of white-clad peaks. They were known to only a handful on Strand and none of them were in the Great Hall. A formation of machines moved in from the edge of the vision and most assumed that these were yet more examples of the foe's ever-expanding arsenal of terror. Then some trick brought them closer and men could be seen within. The contraptions they rode in were held aloft by a blur of motion above them and they trailed plumes of white smoke behind. Shafts of light speared up so suddenly that Jarrod gasped. They groped across the clear heavens like a blind man's fingers and when they found their prey the conflagration was instantaneous. Machine after machine burst apart or canted drunkenly and slid down to destruction. The spectators seemed to fly forward themselves and could now see the desperation and the sweating faces of the men who wrestled with controls and the twisted mouths of those who flailed unavailingly at burning clothing. They watched the panic that sent some of the untouched remnant colliding with their fellows, achieving, as they spiralled lopsidedly to doom, what the foe had failed to do.

The dark cloud spanning the dais boiled lumpishly and pieces of action jerked randomly across it. Jarrod leaned forward with the rest, eyelids unmoving, mouth hanging agape and the breath panting shortly in and out. The tension was screwed tighter as the snippets revealed the deaths of so many. Would he be one of them? He knew that there must be those around him who were witnessing their own, and not all of them ended as nobly as they would have wished. The pictures grew more fragmented, the changes more spasmodic and arbitrary until a wild, uncontrolled, ululation of grief sliced through the bond of fixation. They were shudderingly back in the present. The cloud writhed, withered and withdrew to reveal both Mages, still joined at the neck by the chain, sprawled across the boards.

The strongest men of Strand sat helpless, gripped by the phantasmagoria, nailed to their seats by the wanton horror they had witnessed. Attendants appeared from behind the blue curtain and hovered uncertainly at the sides of the platform until the Princesses, the first to recover their wits, galvanized them to attend to the Mages. It was hot in the unheated Hall and the stench was appalling, but still the Conclave sat and many among them wept. They had seen friends and relatives perish without benefit of valor and noble gestures made pointless. Their self-assurance was in splinters on the flagstones of despair and they knew the future to be lorn and harsh past the mending of any minstrelsy.

Jarrod could not write, indeed had not written since the speech had ended and the havoc begun. There would be time enough to write and he knew he could not forget what he had seen, knew he would see it again. And again. All he wanted to do now was to go somewhere private and be sick. His teeth were curdled and furred and the aftertaste of bile made his throat acrid. He knew that to make it down the stairs he would have to begin with simple things, like packing up his instruments without spilling the ink. That done, he began to shake. Around him the benches scraped and men lurched and stumbled. On the dais the two greatest practitioners of his art were carried away. He saw none of it. He finally marshalled himself and, tucking his writing box under his arm, descended the gallery stairs under rigid control, despite the jostle of men. He maintained it through the jewelled light and out through the side door to the reassurance of an untramelled sun. Then he broke and fled through the courts and gardens to the safety of his room.

In the deserted Great Hall, the flags of battles past, lost and won, that had been hung upon the pillars to flutter bravely in the draughts and to make the Lords Temporal feel more at home in that most potent seat of sorcery, now hung forlorn and pitifully brash. The waterclock behind the empty dais, revealed once more by the swarming servants, trickled down to the midday hour. The banners served now as gaudy reminders of heartaches to come. In the many towers and courts of Celador, the powerful and the meek sought relief and, for once, it was a great advantage not to be numbered among the mighty.

CHAPTER II

THE GREAT HALL SOARING UP TO THE DELICATE STONE CANOPY in serene perpendicular beauty, remained impervious to the moods of men. Trestle tables had been set up and food laid out, just as it had been in the servants' halls, but the cooks had striven to little purpose that morning. The great had no thoughts of eating and the servants were kept too busy to do more than snatch a bite between errands. There would be an oversupply of broken meats come nightfall. A fair number of those who had been in the Great Hall had taken to the saddle to cleanse their minds, but there was much calling for wine. Some sought the comfort of company and huddled with their fellows beside the fish ponds, or among the beds of simples in the Collegium's broad gardens; but most looked to solitude for their easement.

That particular luxury was, as usual, denied to their leaders. They were supported and circumscribed by the need to set an example. The exigencies of administration required that they return home as soon as possible and, all unaware of the content of the Archmage's discourse, they had scheduled a Council of War for later that same day. Pride and their stations ensured that none would ask for a postponement. Besides, there was too much to be taken care of. The rulers of Strand headed for the cote towers where their bunglebirds were housed.

Even the Umbrians used bunglebirds, although they had proved to their own satisfaction that they were technically incapable of

17

flight. In the Empire's defense it must be admitted that they were a very unlikely binding for the fabric of the world, with their ragged, round bodies and constantly moulting blue-grey feathers. Most of them merely repeated messages with blithe disregard for sense or punctuation, but there were those that were articulate. A few that worked for the same person constantly came to have voices indistinguishable from their owners. Their coloring and their lurching, ungainly flight made them almost impossible to bring down and, given their strong homing instincts, they seldom went astray in aught but memory. They had drawbacks. They were messy, they shed and they were forever hungry. It took three years to train one to carry a twenty word message reliably and even then, if given more than one message a sennight, they were almost certain to get things garbled.

The legends say that this was not always so. Time was when the bunglebirds could think for themselves and only served man because it pleased them and because they were too lazy to search for food. If ballads are to be believed, then, in the days when Errathuel was young, the chiefest of them was celebrated for his wit and made much of by humankind. He began to believe his flatterers, and so puffed up did he become that he challenged the first and greatest of the Archmages to a matching of the minds. Such was his vainglory, that he wagered the servitude of all his kind. He lost. Now his descendants were lumbering off tower tops at man's behest.

Across the gardens and the pleached walks, the Collegium, in its turn, prepared for a meeting of the High Council. The library was dusted and polished and the timeworn, ivorywood table was beeswaxed and buffed until it flowed with reflections. Chairs were brought out from book-lined alcoves and placed, expectantly, about it. There were ten of them.

As the water level reached the fourteenth hour, the first five were filled by the Collegium's contingent. Dean Sumner and his Department Heads poured themselves glasses of chai and sat chatting in muted tones. Arabella was next, dressed in quiet red with deeper blushstones than she had worn in the morning at throat and buckle. The Chief Warlock of Talisman wandered somewhat absently in and latched onto the Princess Regnant with evident relief. Naxania of Paladine was not far behind. She had worn a cloak over her dark blue gown for the short journey from the palace and made a great business of doffing it and finding a suitable bookcase to drape it over. They took their places and waited. At last, the two Mages were escorted into the room and eased into the two vacant chairs at the head of the table.

"Are you all here?" The Archmage's voice was querulous and he looked brittle and dessicated. "I don't know why I feel so awkward. We are among friends here, Greylock and I, and you all know that we haven't been able to see since the Conclave. I know that this will pass and yet I feel uncomfortable."

"You must not distress yourself on my account, my friend," Greylock said as he settled back into his chair. "I may not be able to see now, but I was also spared this morning's sights and for that I am grateful. Besides," and his left hand groped out toward the oblivious Archmage, "you promised me that I'd be able to see in a few days." Ragnor's head turned toward his companion's voice.

"Didn't foresee it though. Never mind; we don't have the luxury of time, so we've got to get on with it as we are." He hesitated and his head swivelled seekingly.

"Your Royal Highnesses." There was a hint of a question in the address. "I must apologize for subjecting you to so much unpleasantness . . ."

"Because we are women, Archmage?" Naxania's voice cut across him. "I do assure you that we coped better with those sights than any of the men in the Great Hall."

"I am much relieved to hear that, your Royal Highness." The Archmage inclined his head in her direction. "Now, I don't know what the strategists are going to decide, but I do know that we've got to come up with something effective and we've got to do it quickly. The major thing, of course, is to stop the enemy. If we don't, it'll be the end of our world. But it's got to be Magic that does it. If the conventional forces pull it off, the future of Magic will still be in jeopardy.

"People aren't impressed by things running smoothly, not that that'll go on for much longer. We're losing support every year as it is. Rural sorcerers are having difficulty collecting the tithe, the Maternites are gaining converts everywhere and the old, local gods are making a come-back. I'm sure you've heard some of the recent ballads. It's up to us, to the ten of us sitting here to defend our art and preserve our Discipline.'' He sat back in his chair and his shoulders drooped.

''What more can we do, Archmage?'' The question came from Dean Sumner, a thin, grim raven of a man in his conspicuously threadbare black robe. The mouth was pinched with ambition unsublimated and unfulfilled. ''Even if we came up with the Great Spell, you no longer have the strength to perform it,'' he added.

''I know, Sumner. I know. D'you think in this state that I need a reminder?'' The voice was sharp. The Archmage stopped himself and sighed. ''I'm sorry. I grow hasty in my fatigue and that solves nothing.'' He paused again. ''Well, I'll tell you one thing we'll have to do, though I don't for the life of me see how we're going to do it. We have to push that atmosphere back a good long way. They're independently mobile now, or they will be. You all saw that. You also saw how good we were at stopping them. So, if we push their bases back, we might put them out of range as it were. Any suggestions?''

''But Archmage,'' Arabella said gently, ''we shan't be able to do it. If we could, it would have been in the vision.''

''I know, my dear. I know. I have never wanted to be proven wrong, but I do now. I would gladly give up what's left of my life to be wrong.'' His words were tinged with the sadness and weariness that were apparent in his face. The head came up slowly. ''Any suggestions?'' he asked again.

''If we wait for the Winter storms,'' the Chief Weather Controller ventured hesitantly, ''providing we have a really bad Winter and if all of us, if all of us pitch in, we might be able to shift them back.''

Greylock shook his head ruefully. ''It's never really worked, Mydon. You know that better than anyone. You also know the kind of damage the backflow can do. I'd as lief not do their work for them. No, there are some practical things that we can do, albeit minor ones. We'll obviously need more Wisewomen, and, from what I hear, there'll be new types of wounds to treat. That'll mean special training for them. We'll have to order the planting of a lot more clypsidra to cope with the burns and they'd best boil up a lot of fever tree bark. I think it would probably be best if Weather Control . . ." The Mage went on talking, but only Ragnor paid him heed. The rest of the Council was staring at Naxania.

The Princess of Paladine was sitting very straight on the edge of her chair, as if revisited by the backboards of her youth. The neck arched up and the small gold crown in the mass of black hair caught the light as the head tipped back and the mouth fell open. She braced herself against the arms of the chair, elbows out, as if trying to rise, but the only things that moved were her eyelids. They slipped shut. A tendril of hair swung loose. There were noises from the throat that finally silenced Greylock. There was a sort of liquescent gargle and then, slowly, almost unwillingly, she began to declaim.

> *"When Time's only coffer has opened its lid*
> *And unicorns are by a young man led,*
> *When mankind for power has exhausted its bid*
> *And Strand of its best and its bravest is bled;*
> *When heavens hang heavy and both moons are hid,*
> *The Ancient shall rise from its slumbering bed."*

The head lolled and then fell forward and a dark tide of hair tumbled over it. The crownlet, all untethered, fell to the muffling rushes.

"What is that? What's happening? Will someone, for the Love of Lore, tell me what's going on."

"Are you alright, your Highness?" Both Mages spoke at once and were answered by the Dean, who was up and leaning over her.

"It's the Princess Naxania, Sir. She seems to be in a trance of some sort. She's breathing easily and the pulse is normal. Ah, here she comes." He chaffed her wrists as the others eased her body back into the propriety of her chair. Her lashes fluttered and she groaned softly.

"Easy, Highness, easy there. It's alright now." His voice was surprisingly gentle as he soothed her back to consciousness. Her body shivered convulsively and the eyes shot open, disorientation and fright in the start of them. She drew a long, shuddering breath, fighting for self-control. Her pallor had become chalk white and she swallowed several times before trying to speak.

"I'm sorry," she said, falling back on a royal voice honed by tradition and garden parties. "I've no idea where that came from. It's most peculiar. I was compelled to say it; really most unpleasant. I have absolutely no idea what it meant." She shook her crownless head in bewilderment.

"Can you remember what you said?" the Archmage asked into the silence.

"Yes, I think so."

"Good, then say it again."

The Princess brushed her hair back with her hands and repeated the verse in slow and measured tones.

"Well," said the Archmage when she was finished, "I don't know who your friend is, but he's a rotten poet. Anyone have any notions as to what this is all about?"

"Are you sure that you have it right, Highness?" The questioner, once again, was Sumner.

"My good Dean, I have repeated it twice." The man drew back at the rebuke and resumed his seat.

"All the tales that I can recall refer to an affinity between unicorns and virgin girls, ma'am. I merely wished to make sure." He sniffed. The Archmage came to his aid.

"Think we should act on this, er, this piece of doggerel, Sumner?"

"Given the circumstances that you brought forth so vividly in the Great Hall, Archmage, can we afford not to?"

"No, Sumner, I don't suppose we can. What we have to do is play all the wild cards we can and hope that the Gods of the Odds give us a trump. And this certainly is a wild card." He gave a pleased snort of laughter. "I think we should keep quiet about it though. I mean, if this gets out and nothing comes of it, begging your Highness' pardon, we shan't exactly have struck a resounding blow for the good name of Magic, shall we?"

"I think the good Dean is right," Arabella interposed quickly. "For whatever reason, we have been vouchsafed a great gift and we have no choice but to accept it. It does appear, however, that the language would do justice to the pronouncements of the

Oracle Damfino. We should do well to take precautions against
too easy an interpretation.''

"What do you suggest, my Liege Lady?" The Archmage's
voice held affectionate approval.

"To be on the safe side, I think we should send both a young
man and a young woman, and I think that both of them should
be virgins.''

"Your Royal Highness," the Archmage had switched into the
formal mode, "I observe," and irony underscored the verb,
"that the will of this Council in the matter of the Unicorn Verse
that has come to us through our sister of Paladine is that we send
forth an expedition to hunt out this mythical beast. It is further
agreed that the party shall consist of one young male and one
young female, both of whom are to be in, ah, a state approaching purity." The blank eyes swept around the table. "Does
anyone say me nay?" He waited.

"Right then." He was back in the vernacular and the room
relaxed. "I think that one, or both, of them ought to be Talented
and we can't pick anyone vital to the war effort." He was
plainly pleased, but the tiredness showed in the slackness of his
body. At his right, Greylock's knuckles were white as he strained
for control.

"Right then," he said again, swaying slightly as he leaned
forward, "if there's no further pressing business, the Mage of
Paladine and I have to get back to bed. I'd like you to think
about candidates for this search party. You all know where my
rooms are." There was silence. "Adjourned," he said with
evident relief.

The men and women to whom the Archmage had referred as
"the strategists" were subdued as they climbed the treads to the
Great High Presence Chamber. The room that greeted them was
immense. It occupied the top two floors of the West side of the
court, at right angles to the Great Hall and connected to it by the
staircase they had climbed. They represented all of the countries,
although there were no Songeans present. The defense of Songuard
was financed by Isphardel which, being a mercantile and maritime power with no direct access to the enemy, preferred to
spend its money rather than its citizens. To that end, they paid
for the outfitting and upkeep of an Umbrian garrison at Fort

Bandor and knew they had the best of the bargain. When it came
to military logistics and disbursements, however, the Isphardi
representative had no equal.

Arabella of Arundel emerged through the doorway from the
Royal Apartments as the last of the generals took his place. Her
hand went involuntarily to the stones at her throat as she reflected wryly that there were advantages in everything. The crisis
and the sights of the morning meant that she wouldn't have to
fend off ambitious suitors or Prince Justinex' more insidious
suggestions. She inclined gravely to the Umbrian Emperor as she
approached the ellipse of carved chairs, each with its cloth of
state, and was grateful, once again, that he was married.

There was a feral quality about Varodias that disturbed her. It
was as if his emotions and reasonings were governed by a
completely different set of rules, ones that were, perhaps, just as
valid as her own, but far more savage and unpredictable. His
answering smile was as welcoming as cold gruel, but hers did
not falter. Thank goodness he hasn't brought his hawk, she
thought, as she moved to acknowledge the King of Paladine. As
ruler of the host country, she took her seat in the center.

"Majesties, Excellency," and she smiled again as she nodded
to the Oligarch Olivderval, the only other woman in the room.
"Lords all, I give you good day. To those of you I have not yet
had a chance to greet, be welcome to Celador, though I could
wish the occasion a more pleasant one." She paused and inclined to right and to left.

"The Archmage and the Mage of Paladine, as you might
expect, are not able to join us, but I shall do my best to answer
for matters Magical. Meantime, there is much to discuss and
more to be done." She caught Robarth Strongsword's eye and
added smoothly, "What says my neighbor Paladine?"

Robarth looked at her appreciatively. "Well, first off, my
brother sends his apologies to you all. He wanted to come, but I
forbade it. It's difficult enough as it is." He glared round, defying
the sympathy he was afraid to find. "One of the things I say,"
he resumed, "and not for the first time, mind you," he added
with a grim little smile of self-knowledge, "is that we have all
grown too lax. We've all sustained losses in the past, but we've
never really believed that the offal would ever, could ever, attack

us in depth. They hadn't the capacity to maintain a long sortie, luckily for us. Well, that's all changed and we're goin' to have to change too. Right rapidly. We've let things go too far." His eyebrows rose and he looked from side to side. "Lodgin's," he said slowly, "have bin built along the insides of castle walls, even here. The upper chambers of most of our towers have fine, big windows nowadays. It won't do. It simply will not do. And another thin'. We keep too many retainers. There are too many people livin' in the fortresses for any of us to withstand a long siege. And we have to think in those terms now. We must return to the ways of our forebears, that's what I say. We grow too soft."

"Ah, too true, my brother." The Emperor gave three or four quick nods and his thin, humorless smile. "Though the Empire seemed to hold its own in this morning's display. Not so?"

"The Empire is, as always, to be congratulated on some impressive technical feats, attributable, I am sure, to your Imperial Majesty's inspiring leadership," Borr Sarad, the Thane of Talisman, interposed with his customary diplomacy. As the elected ruler of a tiny country that was sandwiched between powerful neighbors, he was a practiced peace-keeper. "This new mobility of theirs is, nevertheless, a threat to us all."

"To say nothin' of their weaponry. The warcats were quite useless. Sorry Borr," and Robarth's left hand gestured placatingly at the Thane, "but you know it's true."

"We'll retrain them," the Thane replied, with a trace of heat.

"But you won't." The flat contradiction came from the Oligarch. The Isphardi sat back in her chair and looked at them. "We all saw that this morning. That, we are to believe, is the future. It could, of course, be in the very near future, before you have had time to devise new tactics. Naturally, my Lord, I should prefer to think that your animal battalions are going to be slow to adapt."

She sat quite still, dumpy and dispassionate, too small for her seat, but not in the least diminished by its bulk. An uncomfortable silence grew and was broken by a voice new to most of the people in the Chamber. Silence, like the surface of a pond, invites the breaking of its stillness and the voice that rippled out to them sang with the accent of the Southern Marches of Arundel.

"If you will excuse me, the Farrod will not handle this well at all. You cannot blame them. Pull them out of their fields and confront them with an enemy that throws fire around and they'll bolt." Darius, Holdmaster of Gwyndryth, had risen to his feet, oblivious to the company. He paced about before them as he spoke.

"To most of them it will be as if the foreigners have mastered Magic overnight. Now, if we work new tactics out in advance and then call them out for intensive retraining, instead of for combat, they will stand a better chance later on." His demeanor was quiet and grave and he moved lightly on his feet, belying his build. It was as if he were thinking aloud, as indeed he was. "From what I saw, we may even be able to achieve encirclement. Any time we've tried that, we've ended up trapped between them and their muck, and you all know what that means." All traces of an attempt to harness his speech to the formal mode had vanished.

"The pictures didn't show, or at least I couldn't make out, how long they could stay out of their own stuff without stocking up on something new to breathe. I didn't see anything resupplying them, so if we could get behind them, we could probably hold them off until they ran out." He paused and looked up and seemed to notice, for the first time, that he was on his feet. He moved his formidable bulk back to his chair and sat, abashed at his involuntary boldness. Slowly his face began to take on the color of his hair. Several men spoke at once then and the discussion became general and the debate more technical.

Darius let his eyes wander to the window. The Archmage's rooms atop a tower in the middle of Magicians' Court snagged his attention. The square windows were outlined in raised stone. The outside staircases that wishboned up the surrounding buildings contrasted starkly with the keep-like tower. At its foot, out of the Holdmaster's sight, and long after he had left the Presence Chamber, a cursing figure in a sedan chair emerged, unstoically borne by four brown-robed Apprentices. Impervious to imprecation, they headed toward a ground floor entrance between one of the arching stairways.

"I said gently, you Talentless spawn! You bounce me around

like a strapful of books.'' The Archmage extricated himself from the chair and steadied himself on a short crook.

"Adran? Are you here?"

"Oh yes. I'm wise enough to stay in bed. Over here,'' Greylock added. "I still can't see you, so I don't know what direction that would be.''

"Well don't just stand there, you gormless excuses for Sorcerers. Take me over there. Get me a chair and then clear off out of here until I howl for you again.''

Ragnor was feeling much recovered. When he had settled himself and they were alone, he reached out to touch Greylock and orient himself.

"You know how I know I'm getting old?'' he asked rhetorically. "I can't frighten them any more. Time was when I could induce terror. Nowadays they just smile and say to themselves, 'Oh, there goes old Ragnor again.' It irks me, stupid as that may sound.''

"Can you see?'' the Mage of Paladine asked abruptly.

"No. Not yet, but it'll come. Shouldn't be too long.''

"Then what is so important that it brings you to, er, to visit me in such a condition?''

"What brings? . . . Oh, I forgot. You didn't see any of it, did you? No matter. You know what the situation is. We've got to move fast.''

"That much I've gathered.''

"Very well then, how much trust d'you put in that verse?''

"In what way?''

"Well, that young Princess of yours is an ambitious little package.''

"I couldn't see anything, of course, but I don't think she would, um, she wouldn't invent anything like that.''

"You sure?''

"Reasonably. I've known her since she was born and I assisted with her training. I don't know if what she said has meaning for us, but I'm sure it was as much of a surprise to her as it was to the rest of us.''

"I thought as much, but I wanted to be sure.'' The Archmage sighed and then added, "What are we going to do about it?''

Both men sat silent, looking toward, but not at each other

while the croprain pattered at the window and the light died. Ragnor had dismissed the boys, so there was no one to light the tapers or the oil lamps, but, for the two of them, there was no change in the quality of the darkness that they shared. There was a crepitation of floorboards and an answering crackle from the dying fire before Greylock asked,

"Have you heard from the other Council members?"

"Oh yes. They've been coming all afternoon. Haven't been able to get any rest at all. Sumner has several candidates and wants to set up an exam." He snorted. "If we waited for him, we'd have to hope the creature had offspring. Arabella has a suggestion for the girl that sounds promising. Daughter of one of the March Lords—Darius of something unpronounceable."

"I don't know any of them. Why her?"

"From what I can gather, her father made rather an impressive showing at the Council of War. He even managed to hit it off with Varodias, and you know how often that happens. Seems the Emperor invited him back to Angorn as an official observer. Naturally the Princess had no choice but to agree. While performing this unique function for the realm, he will be leaving behind, d'you see, this willful, virgin daughter. And so, my dear Adran. . . ." And the fingers of his right hand circled unseen.

"Is she Talented?"

"Not as far as I know, no."

"Well then?"

"All it means," said the Archmage, "is that the boy will have to be a Magician and, since the verse plainly says, 'a young man,' that's entirely as it should be. All we have to do now is to decide on the male. What about that boy of yours?"

"Which one? Courtak?"

"That's the one."

"I do wish you'd stop talking about him like that. You make him sound like my bastard."

"I meant nothing by it," Ragnor said placatingly, surprised at the sharpness of his colleague's tone. "It's just that you've brought him up since he was very young, haven't you?"

"He was brought to me when he was about seven," Greylock said and shifted his position on the four-poster. "He had the Talent, that was obvious. All you had to do was look at him; and he had this extraordinary memory. I couldn't resist the temptation to develop that kind of potential." The tone had softened, become nostalgic. "To begin the training at such an impressionable age. I was cautious though. I held him back. I've made him very jealous of his strength, very careful about expending it."

"Most wise, I have no doubt, but is he up to this?"

"More so than he would think, I should say. It might be very good for him. I could wish he had a little more confidence in himself, but he's sound. Still, I don't know. Where does one look for a unicorn? Not in Umbria surely?"

"No, not there. Not if it's to be of any help to us. But close to there maybe. One would have to say that it's an unlikely direction. If it's in the Unknown Lands, we're as good as lost, so we might as well look in our own unlikely places first. Got any ideas?" The Archmage lifted his sightless head and, squaring his shoulders, moved, buttock by buttock, back into his chair. The silence grew thin.

"Somewhere in the Eastern mountains of Songuard would seem as good a bet as any." The grudging voice was Greylock's.

"D'you think you could handle their training?"

"Well, I think I'm capable of . . ."

"Oh good. That's settled then. The girl's here with her father. She's twenty and her father'll be agreeable, or so Arabella says. Where's your, er sorry, where's the Courtak boy?"

"He's in school at the Collegium. But what will the rest of the Council say? You move so fast. We talk for ten minutes and you sound as if everything had been decided. You always do this. How can you be so sure?"

The Archmage smiled and shook his head. "It's simple, Adran. They have our vote. Arabella's candidate has been picked, so she'll support ours. Courtak, if I'm not mistaken, is a ward of Robarth Strongsword and the girl is the daughter of an Arunic Lord who is about to become even more notable. I can't see the Chief Warlock objecting to anything. Sumner is the key—his nominees are being overlooked, every one of them. However," and here a grin of the purest mischief animated the rumpled features, "you just told me that the young man is a student at the Collegium. Now, how could the good Dean object if the matter were put to him by the Mage of Paladine, especially when the boy is one of his own flock?''

"Ragnor . . ."

"Why don't we see if we can't get the young people together at that ball they're insisting on holding. It would be better if they liked each other.'' He paused and then said gently, "It would be good for his development, Adran.''

"It would be best if you approached Sumner," Greylock said resignedly. "I'd be suspected of bias.''

Three courts away, the windows of the Great Hall, dull from the outside in the daytime, glowed outward now in splendor. Their colors were muted, but they shone with increased subtlety. Inside, the tables had all been pushed back and the food-fouled rushes swept away. There were groups of padded chairs on the dais and an arras hung across the stairway to the Presence Chamber. The flags were gone and the pillars' nakedness had been covered with fluted damask, so that they looked as if they had been carved from old alabaster. The inset windows were swagged by curtains, the better to lend discretion to an amorous encounter. Clean-burning links leaned out of the walls at intervals, creating pools of truth in the otherwise flattering lighting provided by the chandeliers. In the hanging gallery where Jarrod Courtak had so lately sat, musicians played a lively air.

He himself now stood in the doorway, feeling nervous, but looking every inch the courtier. The brown robe was gone and its absence revealed that he was tall and slim with unexpectedly broad shoulders. He carried his one suit of party clothes well. The colors were a trifle somber for his evident youth, but he looked elegant in the dark red velvet doublet, which was slashed on the sleeves and the outer thigh with grey silk. There was a froth of lace at the throat and cuffs, and the calves were well turned in the hose. He had admired the top part of himself while he was brushing his curly, black hair, but there was nowhere in the Collegium where he could have seen himself complete.

He had objected when he was ordered to go to the ball. He had pleaded that he was not recovered from the vision and that he could not dance. Both were true, but he was told that it was time he grew up. He had argued that his clothes weren't good enough for a royal occasion and that he had no time to get ready. He was advised, acidly, to hurry and do what he was told.

He stood watching from the doorside, wondering why he was there and unwilling to commit himself to the festivities. He noted that there was a light, almost defiant atmosphere in the Hall. Ladies, in all their finery, were openly flirtatious. The men were as lavishly clad and inclined to gallantry. The royal party was not in evidence, but there were couples dancing the courante nevertheless. Still feeling insecure, he pushed himself off the wall and made his way down to the buttery to get a drink. He was uneasily aware as he progressed that he was being eyed appreciatively by members of both sexes. It was as if there was a moratorium on propriety and it made him feel even more out of place.

He collected his ale and, flagon in hand, turned back toward the doors and found himself as rootbound as he had been in the morning. A man and a much younger woman had just come in and were standing where he had stood. His eyes ignored the man and fastened on his companion. She had hair to the shoulders the color of red gold and a very pale face. The dress was a deep yellow and, as she turned toward her partner, green seemed to run across it as the folds swung and reformed. The man said something to her and the head went back in an unheard peal of laughter. Jarrod envied the man.

His concentration was broken by a fanfare that brought silence. He turned and watched as the Princess Regnant and her party entered, preceded by musicians playing a brisk progress. They ranged themselves for inspection, chatting the while, until the strains of the Royal Gavotte emerged from the gallery. Robarth Strongsword led out Arabella, while Justinex glowered, and Varodias, shorter than his partner by half a head, despite his heels, took the floor with the Princess Naxania. As they danced down the center of the Great Hall, other couples joined them until the room was filled with a dazzling flow. Silks and satins swirled, capes cut dashing semicircles as feet in pointed slippers and buckled shoes executed the intricate steps.

Jarrod, mindful of his height, moved against the wall and stayed at the back looking out over heads. He finished his ale slowly and then went back for more. He intercepted some encouraging glances, but couldn't muster the courage to take advantage of them. He cursed himself for being so lack-willed and vowed that he would learn how to dance. He caught sight of the girl in the yellow dress once or twice, dancing with different men.

The room filled up and he moved sideways, holding his ale aloft, until he came to an unoccupied embrasure. He sat there watching backs and shoes, feeling safe and sipping his beer.

A pair of gold and green slippers came to a halt in the corner of his eye and a rich voice said, "Why thank you, Sir, I do admit that I could do with a rest. One gets so warm while dancing."

He looked up into a gleeful smile and gooseberry green eyes that sparkled with gentle malice. He bolted awkwardly to his feet and despairingly heard himself say, "Oh. Er yes, yes. I mean . . ."

"How kind of you to share your privacy and your seat with me." The girl in the yellow dress cut in effortlessly as she sat down and patted the cushion beside her. "You must forgive me for being so bold, but there really isn't anywhere else to sit down. The benches are all filled with stiff, old biddies looking hard for something, or someone, to disapprove of."

She paused and looked sideways at him as he perched himself on the edge of the seat. If you don't say something, she'll get up and leave, he thought, but nothing reached his mouth. Undaunted by his continuing silence, she added, "I'm Marianna of Gwyndryth, by the way."

"Oh. Er, how d'you do. I'm very pleased to meet you."

"And what's your name?" she prompted.

"Oh. I'm sorry. It's, er, Jarrod Courtak and I'm at the Collegium, though I'm actually from Stronta. That's the capital of Paladine." He knew he was rattling and shut his mouth abruptly.

"So I had heard. So you're at the Collegium. Then you must be a Magician? Were you at the Conclave?"

"Yes. Yes I was," he said, trying to sound offhand.

"Daddy was, too, and he said it was pretty grim."

"Yes it was." Jarrod was beginning to relax. "It was the worst thing I've ever seen in my whole life."

"That long?" Her eyebrows rose mockingly and Jarrod's

spirits sank again. She pulled the corners of her mouth down against a smile. "I'm sorry, but I just couldn't resist. You were looking so solemn." The smile escaped and lit her face. Jarrod, warmed, grinned back.

"Look, can I get you something? A drink or anything?" he asked in a belated rush of manners.

"A glass of wine wouldn't be a bad idea. Would you mind?"

"Not at all. It'll only take a minute." He looked at her for a long beat and added, "I'll be right back." He rose and plunged between shoulders in search of the buttery.

His head was full of sudden thoughts and quickly suppressed hopes as he sidestepped and elbowed through the multicolored crowd. Ladies past the bloom of youth sat and hoped that the compliment of candlelight would serve them just as well. Unattached men eyed them weighingly and decided that they could wait. In the middle of it all, elation came and went in Jarrod and his pulse seemed to be keeping pace with the lilting music.

A drink in either hand, he made his way back to where he had left her, trying not to spill them and wondering what he was going to talk about to this sophisticated woman. He reached the window seat, but she was gone. He pushed his way to the next embrasure, just in case he had misremembered, but found an entwined couple and retreated. He told himself that a friend had asked her to dance and that she would return for her wine when this dance was over. Or the next one. He stood there a long time, a drink in his left hand and his right, feeling increasingly foolish and conspicuous. Finally, he drank his ale and then, angrily, the wine. Then he left.

In a well-appointed apartment in one of the side courts, Marianna of Gwyndryth confronted her father. Her head and her color were high.

"I don't care," she said blazingly. "I went to the trouble of finding him and I tried. I really tried. He's hopeless. He's a child. He couldn't find Songuard, let alone a unicorn."

Her father bulked over her and looked at her steadily. He was used to these kinds of arguments, though he rarely won them. This one he did not intend to lose.

"You're going and he's it and that's that," he said, his Arunic made comfortable by his country burr. "We're being done a very great honor, the both of us.'' His daughter answered in the same language, although her accent had been polished away.

''But father . . .''

''Don't you 'but father' me. You can't wheedle round me this time. I'm going to Umbria as an Observer and you're going hunting for a unicorn with yon Courtak lad and that's all there is to it.'' He looked at her sternly, expecting a challenge, but all he got was a look of rebellious acquiescence.

''There is one other thing,'' he began more gently. ''There was a condition and I said, I said that . . .'' He broke off uneasily. ''I mean, I know that you. . . . Oh, never mind. Come, give us a kiss and off to bed with you. It's been a long day. There. Goodnight, poppet. We'll talk again in the morning.''

The last of the late night fires was banked and tapers were extinguished all over Celador, save in the Great Hall, where men on ladders busied themselves taking down fabric and soskia boughs. They were bringing back reality for the morrow.

CHAPTER III

THE MORNING OF DEPARTURE WAS NEWLY WASHED AND POLISHED as the Magicians of Paladine and their attendants rode through the tall, intricately wrought outer gates of Celador, their protective inscriptions already growing faint with age. As they clattered down the road into the countryside, a battalion of cloudsteeds wheeled in complicated formations overhead, an unneeded reminder of the reason for the journey. They passed through the groves at the bottom of the hill and set off across the waterlatticed, flat, green land. To their right, coppices of fever trees screened the training grounds of the warcats. There was nothing to be seen or heard, but the horses, nostrils flaring, rolled their eyes uneasily and moved in nervous diagonals.

Well they might, for warcats were a mutant breed. They had strayed early into the Barrier Lands and when mankind had caught up with them again they had changed. They had grown beyond recognition and had developed a streak of rage and a cunning that made them greatly to be feared. They did not turn on their former friends, however, but brought to them yet another attribute born of the Barrier Lands. In the early part of every year females bring their litters to Holdings and hamlets. There they wait for the young ones to gather. 'For every cub, a boy who hears' is an old and worn phrase, but a true one nonetheless. The bond formed then is for life and neither partner long survives the other. On the rare occasions when they come into contact with the rest of the world, they make them feel uncomfortable.

Most of the warcat battalions, as well as the cloudsteed units, were trained in Talisman and it was thither that the train was headed. The Princess had reasserted her secular precedence now that the Conclave was over and rode in the van with her bodyguard. The center of the line was grouped around the Mage who, for pride's sake and because the sun was gentle and the early air nipping, rode a barbary mare. She was old now and greyer than a dapple should be, but she still carried her master with a high-stepping arrogance. A leather litter, borne between two skewbalds, trotted unevenly behind the cloud of homebound Magicians. Courtak rode in the back of the column with the retainers and the baggage. Behind them, languid in their self-assurance, rode the rear guard.

Bouncing along in his hitched-up brown robe, Courtak eased his unfamiliar and skittish mount into a trot and tried to assemble his recent past into a coherent pattern. It was all happening too fast. He was being numbed by events and he wanted time; time to grieve for the death he'd seen, time to assimilate, time to find out what he was getting himself into. What he was being pushed into. The rest of him was happy. He was out, he was away. The Collegium was behind him and he didn't have to deal with that any more. He felt released and swallowed the morning in a gulp. It was a beautiful day, the blood was rising as it always did when things turned green again, and the future beckoned as seductively as a Zingaran dancing girl.

The chafe of his saddle had begun to diminish his pleasure by the time the advance guard swung South at the second major fork. They took the longer, harder, but safer road through Talisman rather than the one that ran on toward the Upper Causeway. There were a number in the procession who had seen the Archmage's vision and each was grateful for the distance and for the rock that would be between them and the Others. The ravelling cavalcade crossed the Meander twice more as it headed toward the arcing sun.

They pushed hard past groups of women planting rice and, as if challenged by this unshared toil, ate in the saddle in lieu of taking a midday break. Jarrod had counted on a midday halt and began to think longingly of cushions. There was one pause when Greylock, exhausted past stubbornness, was taken from the mare's back and transferred into the litter. Aside from that they walked and trotted monotonously on, the sameness of the view throwing the riders increasingly into their own minds for diversion. The heavy scents of wetland and germination assailed the nostrils and then dulled them. Spittle began to fleck the chests and shoulders of the horses and they blew gently. Courtak ached past caring and tried to hurry the sun down behind his back some time before the Princess called a halt. That, though, did not mean a rest for him.

Naxania travelled with a household of twenty, the Mage had twelve of his assistants with him and there were a dozen more teachers and pupils from the Collegium. Add to that a hundred cavalrymen and a great deal of firewood had to be collected and a backbreaking amount of water drawn, first for the horses and then for the dinner. They were camped in a break of nurse trees and, before taking their turn with the buckets, Jarrod and the other Talented paced the borders, laying down spells of safety. He did his best to attune himself with the solid boundaries of the area so that he could help with the setting of the watchward, but his legs were not quite his own and his concentration wandered the aimless corridors of discomfort.

He completed his tour with teeth gritted and lips pulled in, but he could walk without staggering. He headed off in search of a bucket and found one by the picket line. He gave his horse a nosebag before going awkwardly to the stream on the other side of the roadway. He bent to fill it and knew he had begun to stiffen up. He groaned at the thought of the night's hard ground. Beside him a young page hooked two full buckets to a yoke and struggled to straighten under the load.

"Oof," he said, "if I'd realized that pages have to get the water for the Princess' whole party, servants and all, I'd never have picked this for a disguise." The voice was familiar and Jarrod looked round questioningly at the stranger.

"I'm not at all sure that I'm flattered by the success of my impersonation. Just a few days ago you couldn't wait to get me wine. Now you don't even know who I am." The mouth pursed self-mockingly and green eyes darted sideways at him.

"But you're . . ."

"How did you guess?"

He missed the mockery and replied seriously, "The eyes, I think. But what are you doing here?" he asked. "And like that?" He gestured up and down.

"Well, it's supposed to be a secret isn't it? And I'm not Paladinian. Can you think of a better way of getting me through unnoticed? No one looks at pages." Naxania's latest acquisition settled the bar across shoulders that were none too wide and went, bent and quick, toward the glade where the silken travelling tent had been erected.

Jarrod's mind flailed as he lugged the heavy wooden bucket back to his waiting horse. As the animal drank in noisy absorption he began to rub him down while his mind juggled a lot of important questions. They looped and circled around the trouser-clad figure of Marianna of Gwyndryth and the idea that there was a secret that they held in common. The slight of their last encounter had rankled, but it was scrubbed away now by speculation. He finished off the horse and went and got it some more bran. When he saw that its head was well down, he went over to see if he could be of some use in getting supper ready. The riding and the air had given him an appetite to match the ache in other parts of his body.

The following day dawned cloudless and windless, as do all the days in planting and harvest seasons in the Magical Lands. There had been wind in the night to clear the skies and the grass sported the vividness of a child's coloring book. The Magicians in the group had been the first up, while the world was dark and its details undetectable, and had sat, separate and removed from each other and their surroundings, performing their morning rituals. The morning made, Courtak fed his horse, gathered firewood and decided to skip shaving, aware that no one would notice for at least another day. His mind wandered back to Marianna and he suddenly wanted very much to look older. Perhaps, he speculated, he should just let his moustache grow?

There was scant time for daydreaming. The tent was struck, the kettles were scoured and loaded onto one of the wagons, horses were saddled, girths cinched and bedrolls strapped on.

The fires hissed and spat at their quenching as the van moved off.

The cortege strung itself together and headed for the mountains that had delayed daybreak. The character of the countryside began to vary as meadows edged into prominence and irrigation ditches began to run atop earthworks that also served to keep the animals from straying. The fields were increasingly dotted with the brown and white and black shapes of kina. The column was halted once as a seemingly endless herd of milch kina ambled in front of it. They sat astride their horses waiting, while a new breeze made the slender, curving tops of the quandry trees that lined the road twist and turn in animated disbelief.

When they moved on again, the agitation of the questioning treetops was echoed by chattering flocks of speckled hedgehoppers that joined them in pilgrimage from field to field. The small grey and brown creatures swooped to the lower branches and perched, eyeing the passers-by with heads cocked. Having made up their minds, they flew on, gossiping furiously, to the next meadow to exchange information and argue with their neighbors, who then came to verify matters for themselves. Just as no farm is without its mousels, no field seems devoid of hedgehoppers, a fact that farmers look upon as a decidedly mixed blessing.

To Jarrod's relief, there was a brief halt at midday. He had become accustomed to the discomfort and had adjusted to the horse's gait, but he relished the chance to lean against a tree and watch for the Princess' newest page. He caught no glimpse of her. She remained an intriguing and attractive enigma.

The animals were watered and allowed to graze for a while and then the group, with the Mage back in the litter, pushed on. They crossed the final oxbow of the Meander and headed for the foothills that marked the Tallic border.

The route ran well South of the Fortress Talisman, up into the Dortagen Mountains toward the passes that gave onto Paladine. The weather-polished summits of the central spine gleamed in the powerless sunshine. Time had begun to soften the outlines of the quarries that pocked their flanks, abandoned since the Causeway was completed, but slashes of white, like the remnants of a long-healed wound, still jarred the eye. The road, in immaculate repair now, unskeined upward and the air became as cool and

crisp as a new-bitten apple. There was already evidence of the
year's first hay crop, testament to the ingenuity of the farmers of
Talisman who covered their productive land with sacking against
the cold of night.

Dry stone walls outlined the arable patches but their presence
was diminished by the solid clusters of cinder trees that marched,
in broken formation, toward the peaks, windward of the corn to
come. Later in the year there would be staggered swatches of
gold to light up the mountainsides, but now the cinder trees had
no competition. They have a magic of their own, with feathery,
dark grey leaves that look as if they had been sifted down onto
the branches instead of growing out of them. The undersides are
deep silver and, when the wind puffs at the closely packed
foliage, it is as if gigantic bellows were blowing the ashes of all
the night fires into the air. The gust gone, they settle gently
down, like soot on Umbrian roofs.

The company urged their mounts up the steepening incline and
whips cracked from the wagons in the rear as the carefully
tended farms with their stolid people dropped from view. In their
stead a broader, more spectacular panorama unrolled. Drivers
cursed and plied their whips again as they negotiated cuphook
turns, but they took the time to look back out over Arundel to the
artificial hill, crowned and covered by the palace, from whence
they had come. Their spirits lifted as they climbed. The sun
warmed their shoulders and, in those keen airs, the brightness of
new-sprung leaf and blade was as sharp as a pang of joy. It was
difficult not to be enamored of life and its possibilities.

The road began increasingly to wind through rock as they
reached for the beacon fires and the passes above. High-living
firs with arthritic roots fought a silent battle to cling to the
fissured stone and, now and again, water welled out of the
mountainside and rivuletted down beside them. Horned sheep
watched superciliously from crags as breathing became labored
in the thin, dry air. The knowledge of a posting inn at the mouth
of the col ahead made the ensuing hour bearable for the humans,
but brought no easement to the beasts. The ermine-clad peak
looked impassively down on them all.

What few rooms the inn possessed were taken over by the
Princess and by Greylock. The soldiers occupied the stables and

the rest hauled themselves off the road on either side of the squat building. Cloaks materialized from saddlebags and the Magical contingent paced and intoned. Walking was a lot easier for Jarrod this time but his concentration still left something to be desired. Duty done, he went for water, shuffling automatically forward as his turn notched closer.

"It seems that every time I come across you, you are withdrawn from the world. Is that part of being a Magician?" The voice startled him out of his reverie.

"No. Just part of being saddle sore. I didn't expect to see you tonight," he added, changing tack and trying to sound as nonchalant as he could. He was convinced it sounded surly so he added hastily, "I mean, er, I expected you to be at the inn."

"No. Her Royal Highness," and there was tartness in the title, "has decided to sample the local fare, so the kitchen help has been dismissed for the night."

"Oh. Well then, you're welcome to join me for supper if you want. That is, if you don't have any other plans." He surprised himself with his boldness, but he was prepared to retreat rapidly if he sensed disapproval.

"How nice of you," she said politely, and the smile that followed made him feel almost poised. "But," she added, "on one condition."

"What?" His poise had deserted him as suddenly as it had arrived.

"You must promise to stop staring at me like that. You're beginning to make me feel quite nervous." She flashed another smile up at him and he felt the heat floodrace up from the base of his throat into the roots of his hair; he was desperately grateful for the red cast of the dusk.

"I'm sorry," she said, putting a hand on his sleeve, "I shouldn't have said that. It's just that at home I have to maintain my distance with young men and it gets to be a bit of a habit. Here, give me part of that handle. It'll be easier up the slope that way." They carried the bucket back to the lines of horses in silence. He thanked her and she waited while he tended to his mount and collected himself.

"There," he said finally, his breath steaming out as he straightened up, "that does it." He patted the horse and walked over to where she stood in unaccustomed patience. She had decided to get to know this boy, and she was determined to see it through.

She turned as he came up and said, "Let's go to the fire. I'm starting to feel very cold." She tugged at her cap and linked an arm through his, feeling it tense as she did so. She smiled to herself. She poked gentle fun at the fact that he could only eat standing up or lying on his side. She told a couple of disrespectful stories about the Princess Naxania and asked a respectful question or two about the Collegium. By the time they had mopped up the last of the gravy she had the young man talking easily.

He got up wincingly from the cloak they shared and fetched more wood. They sat in companionable silence for a while, she, chin on her knees, staring at the flames and he, lying propped up on one elbow, doing his best not to stare at her. It was he who broke out into speech first.

"I don't understand why you're playing at being Naxania's page. I mean, you're a Lady. I don't mean to pry or anything, but . . ."

"Of course you do," she interrupted, "but that's all right. How much do you know?"

"What about?"

She gave him a sharp look. "Have you talked to Greylock?"

"Yes." His voice was instantly guarded.

"Well?"

"He told me he had some sort of job for me." He was beginning to feel uneasy again and wished he'd never started asking questions.

"And?" she pressed.

"Well, it's sort of secret."

She gave him another appraising look, but this one lasted longer. "It's much the same for me," she said at last. "Mine's connected with the war effort and they don't want people to know about it. Dressing as a page was my idea really. I despise riding sidesaddle." She tilted her head back and laughed wryly at herself. There was silence again as they watched the nightmoon shoulder its way out of obscurity and upstage the stars.

"Tell me about you," she said languidly, turning her head over her right shoulder to look at his shadowed face.

"There isn't much to tell and what there is isn't very interesting," he said defensively.

"Are you looking to be coaxed then?" The firelight leaped off her teeth as she grinned.

"No, of course not. It's just that I haven't done anything yet." His voice was tight.

"What do you want to do?"

"One day I'm going to be a great Magician." The words were spaced, but the voice was uniformly fierce.

"Well, the world could certainly do with one," she said, taken aback by his sudden vehemence. "I mean no disrespect," she added hastily, "to the Archmage or to Greylock."

"That's all right. I just got carried away." He felt awkward with her again and was relieved when she said that it was time for her to get back. He watched her go until he lost her silhouette in the darkness, then he rummaged in his saddlebag for his soap and his orange stick and limped stiffly downhill to the stream. He slept sweetly that night, despite his aches and pains.

She made concentration difficult for him in the morning, but he felt ridiculously well and very alive. When he got into the saddle he was delighted to find that the lower half of him was toughening up. He felt like cantering, but the party wound its way sedately through the pass, past the matching posting inn on the other side, and downward toward the border with Paladine. The cinder trees marched up to meet them, protecting the rotation of crops in the immaculate quiltwork of the fields. On this side of the mountain the flat and unmelodious clanging of belled kina competed with the creaking of the wagons and the curses of the drivers. They entered a belt of firs and fireblanket trees and, when they finally emerged, their homeland was laid out before them.

They made their way around Lake Sidron and the Upper Causeway came into sight once more on their left. In front of them, the solid bump on the horizon was Stronta. Memory invested it with a star shape and the eye strove to match the memory. There were mills on the mountainside now, their wheels in the headlong streams, and down on the plain below the moving white shapes cropped to provide the cloth they worked on. There were similarities in the fertile carpet that lay rumpled far below their stirruped feet with the plains they had left two days before, but the variations in the patterns were as distinct as Songean tribal motifs. Farm complexes and wool stations rang changes in the landscape, as did the carding pits and the occasional fuller's yard.

Jarrod looked out across the land he loved and felt that he could reach out and touch the flax fields and the shining surfaces of the retting ponds that sat and waited for the flax to die. If he just stretched out his hand, his fingers could caress the castles and the crennelated manors, read with a blind man's fingers the stories of tanneries and hot-tempered smithies and encounter and absorb the peace of long abandoned belfreys whose brazen warnings would clapper soon again. It all seemed beautiful to him and his heart went out to it, wrung by the vulnerability of foreknowledge.

By the time they had descended to the plains, the ravelins and bastions of Stronta had surrendered the haze of distance and come clear. Courtak was sitting easy in the saddle. He had regained pretentions to style and rode with erect pride into the triangle of walls that led to the gate tower. Those star points had always been an architectural extravagance. They dominated a flat landscape that had not felt the hot breath of siege, but they seemed very necessary to Jarrod now as he clattered into the cool and shadowed security of the castle. The wardcorn's trumpet rang out in welcome.

Jarrod dismounted at the stables and stood uncertainly, with his saddlebags slung over his shoulder, while chickens pecked around his feet. He assumed that he would be sleeping at The Outpost, but no one had given him specific instructions. He had been consigned to the baggage train and forgotten and it made him resentful. He hefted the bags to the other shoulder and set out for the Maze Gate. He strode as if he had a purpose in mind, but was halted by the sound of his name.

"Ay! Jarrod! Slow down will you." The caller was Tokamo, his one real friend. The friendship had undergone strain when the Mage had allowed the tubby young man who now came skidding around a rooster and his flock of favorites to leave for the Collegium. Jarrod had been kept at Stronta. It had been Tokamo who had made the effort to keep the friendship going and now there was a deep affection between them that they were only capable of expressing through gruffness and the punching of arms and shoulders.

"All right Jarrod, what's going on?" His gown was mired from the journey and his face was pink from the exertion of catching up. The eyes twinkled with curiosity.

"You tell me, Tok. You're the one who rode with Greylock's party." Jarrod heard the pettiness in his voice and was annoyed at himself.

"Well, something must be up," the other boy replied, ignoring the tone, "or Greylock wouldn't have sent me haring after you."

The trilled R's of the Pallic tongue soothed Jarrod and he relaxed into a smile. "You going to tell me why he sent you, or do I have to guess?"

"He said you'd be sleeping in your old room in his tower and that you're to present yourself after supper. That's all I know. I thought something important must be going on."

"Beats me," Jarrod said, regretting the untruth as he uttered it. "I expect I'll find out after supper." They moved out of the way of incoming horsemen and resumed their walk to the North Gate. It was the only one in Stronta that was always open, despite the fact that it faced the distant, enemy-held territory. It was a safe enough gesture, since it was protected by the Great Maze that only the Talented could cross.

Tokamo picked up the conversation. "You haven't told me what it was like at the Conclave," he said.

"I know. I just haven't been able to face it again. Talking about it means having to remember and I'm trying very hard not to."

"Was it as bad as they say?"

"I don't know what they say, but I'll wager it was worse. Honestly Tok, do I really have to start again now?"

"Course not. It's just that you're the only person I know who was there."

"Give us a bit more time, that's all," Jarrod said as they passed through the gate.

The Maze, like so many other things on Strand, was said to have been created by Errathuel. Anything old and not entirely understood was automatically credited to the first Archmage. There was more room for doubt here than elsewhere, though, because the Place of Power was immeasurably older than Stronta and the Maze might well have been intended to defend it rather than the fortress. If one could look into it and hold one's focus long enough, it would become apparent that all that was there was the disappointment of rough grassland. But holding the gaze steady was impossible. Something always caused the eye to skitter and conjure up an imprecise opacity.

Once the area was entered, the Maze took its form from the mind of the trespasser. Whatever the instinct thought of as impenetrable or baffling appeared before and around all who ventured in. Those with the Talent won through effortlessly, but those who lacked it found themselves back where they started. Some bore the marks of the thickets and briars that had sprung up between one place and the next; others had confronted looping skeins of gold and silver tied inextricably together, or smooth, high walls as unending as the Upper Causeway. It was darkness, it was fog, it was an ocean of fleece, it was frustration and it was the first test in a Magician's life.

Custom dictated that aspirants wait until their tenth birthday had been marked before trying to cross. For the very young, it was a place where monsters dwelled and where bad little boys were sent. But for generations the venturesome young of Stronta had dared each other into the Maze well before they turned ten. Each succeeding group thought itself the first to be so bold, and wise parents, remembering that the preparations had been the best part, ignored the feverish symptoms of a coming attempt. Jarrod had tried when he was eight, and his elation at finding himself looking back toward the palace from the far side was quickly tempered by a long, lingering dread that Greylock would find out about it. He had been the only person with the slightest doubt about his Talent and there had been a part of him that had hoped that he would fail. He had had a fierce desire to be ordinary, but the Great Maze had set him apart then as it set Tokamo and him apart now.

They crossed in comfortable separation and emerged unscathed by deception. They crossed the bumpy patch of ground before The Outpost and Jarrod noticed that a new stable block had been built since he had been gone so that an el now enclosed the gardens and the fish pond. The trees looked no taller to him, but he realized that they must have grown. Behind them were two fat towers, linked by a squarely crennelated hall, and thither the two trudged, lugging their baggage. The right-hand tower, which was their destination, was the taller of the two and its top floor reflected the light of the setting sun.

Nothing had changed in the room. The walls looked pink in the evening light, but nothing could beautify the plain cot he could no longer stretch out comfortably on, nor the unpainted bookshelf holding books he thought he had abandoned two years before. The splintery clothes box with old initials carved on its lid was in its accustomed spot. The same, much abused table sat under the window, which was still too high for the seated student to see out of. The heavy, wooden shutters were folded back now, but the inevitable bucket of wet clay to seal them against the Others' air sat to the right of the table. The little bench was under it, but the cushion he had stolen from the castle had disappeared.

Jarrod smiled and sighed ruefully as he looked around him. It was as ugly and uncomfortable as ever. It had seemed, at times, to embody all the frustrations he had felt, but, after two years at the Collegium, it felt like home. He unpacked and automatically went downstairs to the adjoining hall to help set up the trestle tables for dinner.

The food had not improved while he had been gone, but he gave a hand with the clearing and conscientiously reminded the steward that he was available to the kitchen roster once more. He went back to his room to wait the habitual half hour before he made his way up to the Mage's quarters. He moved the table aside and stood looking toward the mountains he had so lately crossed. He let the pent up questions purl through his head. He found no answers, but the speculation hurried the time along and, when the visiting hour arrived, his mood was one of anticipation.

One was as liable at that time of night to find Greylock at work on the top floor as in his rooms on the floor below, but that evening the Mage was sitting in the small, shelved and panelled cabinet. As Jarrod entered, the old man was rummaging among untidy heaps of scrolls and books of bound parchment. He looked up and over his shoulder.

"Heard you at the bottom of the stairs, lad. My ears still have their new sharpness, even though my eyes are back to normal, and besides," he added, straightening up and smiling warmly, "you still scrape your feet on the steps." He stood and looked at the youth for a long, fond beat and then gestured to a chair on the other side of the fireplace.

"Sit yourself, lad, sit yourself. Oh, and welcome home. It's good to have you back."

"Thank you, Sir."

The lanky form folded down into the slightly larger guest chair as the older man looked around at the spilling shelves and said, "No matter what else you do before you leave, you're going to have to straighten this room out for me. I haven't been able to find anybody who could do it properly since you left. No one else remembers where everything should go, least of all me. I must admit that I got spoiled with you around." They both smiled at the memories evoked and settled themselves a little more comfortably in the wishbone-legged and leather-backed chairs, their feet thrusting toward the fire.

"Well now, about this matter of the unicorn . . ." Greylock said with unaccustomed hesitancy.

"Yes. I was rather wondering about that. You only told me that I'd been picked to find one."

"I should think you have been. The whole thing is most peculiar. These are remarkable times, lad, remarkable times. Anyway, the Council of Magic was meeting to discuss what to do about the things that Ragnor had shown us when Naxania was possessed, or used, by someone or something. She suddenly went into a deep trance and out came this verse. I've got it down here somewhere," he said, burrowing into the sleeves of his gown. "Ah yes, here we are. Now, where are my spectacles? Oh, thank you." He peered at the grubby sheet of paper and then read aloud.

"There you are," he said when he was finished. "That's all there was, but we can't afford to overlook anything that might get us through the days ahead. We're taking it seriously. You, of course, are the 'young man.' "

He paused, waiting for a reaction, and when none was forthcoming, continued. "There were a number of reasons why we picked you. You're the right age, you have the Talent and, for what it's worth, I think you'll make a fine Magician one day." He paused again. "Then there's the business of being a . . . of not having had, er, you know what I mean." The Mage plunged on to cover his fluster. "Some of the Council felt that the verse might be wrong because the legends and stories always seem to associate unicorns with young girls and, since we can't take any chances, we decided to send two of you. You and a girl."

Jarrod sat very still as a great many things suddenly fell into place. The Mage watched him shrewdly, surprised at his continuing impassivity. "She is Arunic and a little older than you I think. She has no Talent, as far as we know, but she, er, she fills all the other qualifications. Her name's . . ."

"Marianna of Gwyndryth," Jarrod finished.

"Ah. So you've met her, have you? So much the better. You'll be training together and you're going to have to depend on each other out in the wilderness, so I hope the two of you got on." He cocked his head sideways and looked at the boy, but Jarrod still sat looking at the fire, his long legs stretched out in front of him.

"There must be a lot of questions milling about in that head of yours. I probably shan't be able to answer all of them, but I'll do my best." Greylock's tone had become avuncular in response to the boy's lack of reaction. Jarrod sat up slowly and turned to look at the man who had guided his life.

"I did some thinking on the trip. There wasn't anything else to do," and the youngster managed a lopsided grin to mask the hurt he had felt at being left back with the baggage. "I really don't know anything about unicorns, except as heraldic figures. I know they are supposed to be partial to maidens, but that's about it."

"That's about all anybody knows. That and the fact that they are supposed to bring harmony. The Isphardis will occasionally trade something that they say is a unicorn's horn—I've seen one of those myself—but that's about the extent of it."

"D'you think they really do exist?" Jarrod asked, hating the uncertainty that crept into his voice.

"With things as they are, or rather as they will be, we have to believe. We have no choice." The Mage sought to force conviction on the younger man. There was a silence and the noises of the fire were loud in it.

"Where am I supposed to look for it?" The voice was matter-of-fact and Greylock gave a little inward sigh of relief.

"The Council felt that the animal would be in a remote and fairly inaccessible spot."

"The Unknown Lands?"

"No reason to think so, and if it's there, it might just as well not exist. No, Southwest Arundel or the Songean mountains, the Saradondas, would be the best bets. I cannot believe that they would live in the Empire." The last was said with finality. Jarrod rose and put another log on.

"Do we know where the Isphardis found the horns?" he asked as he straightened up. He stayed standing, with his back to the fire and his hands spread wide behind him, looking down at his mentor. The face was still pale, even in the ruddiness cast by the catching wood.

"I asked that rascal Alexopol when he came to pay his respects. He gave me that line about the sea being their greatest source of riches. They do so love to be mysterious. It made me think, though, that we ought to start with the Saradondas." He smiled, pleased that the boy and he had reasoned alike.

"Did the verse come out in Common?"

"Yes. Why?"

"Any accent?"

"Oh, I see. No. It sounded just the way the Princess usually does when she speaks Common. Sorry, no clues there I'm afraid."

"Shouldn't it be the Princess who goes along? I mean, she's the one who's susceptible to whatever it is."

"Good point, lad, but there are a couple of good reasons why she can't. Politics is one, of course. This is a Magical expedition, not a Paladinian one. Besides, can you really see Her Royal Highness scrambling around mountains and living off the land?" They both smiled broadly at the pictures it conjured up. "No," Greylock said. "It's got to be the Gwyndryth girl. I've asked her over tomorrow and I'd like you here at eleven. I know there's a lot more to discuss but I'm too tired now." He looked up and the smile was tremulous. "On your way down, would you tell the duty boy that I'm ready to go to bed now?"

"Yes, of course, Sir," Jarrod said with a quick stab of concern. "Is there anything I can get you?"

"No thank you, lad. You'd best be to bed yourself. It's been a long day for all of us."

"Very well, Sir, I'll see you in the morning."

"Good night, lad," the Mage said softly as the door closed. He sagged back in the chair, allowing the desolate weariness to show at last.

CHAPTER IV

BEFORE THE SUN WAS ROUSED FROM SLUMBER, JARROD HAD discovered the pleasure of performing his daily exercises amid familiar surroundings. It was a setting that he had never thought of as conducive to relaxed concentration. Yet, as he settled with obsessive, but involuntary precision onto the same spot he had occupied since that first, far-off morning, he was suffused with comfortable certainty. The Making of the Day welled up as fresh and meaningful as he had always known that it was meant to be. When he had hoisted up the sun, he felt buoyant and optimistic and ready for anything, even Marianna. There was a spring in his step as he climbed up for his appointment.

The scent of Greylock's work chamber coiled down the stairs to greet him. It was at once heavy and dry, with a solid underpinning of old parchment, herbs and the confinement of unopened windows. Then the separate strands teased his nose, demanding identification. Burning tallow and wood smoke for a certainty; some sort of potion that called for a lot of jothonium. He paused on the landing and stuck his head through the open door.

It was a big room and took up the whole of the top of the Tower. The first impression it created was of air and light and the second of crammed and barely contained activity. The former came from the wide set of windows that seemed to constitute most of the walls and the latter from the vials, retorts, boxes, manuscripts, bottles, burners, braziers and piles of paper. It was the kind of room in which the extraordinary was an everyday occurrence. That feeling was heightened by the tensions of an energy that tweaked the edges of the mind. Through the expanse of paned glass, the Upper Causeway seemed very near. Nearer still were the upthrusting bulks of the Place of Power.

Marianna of Gwyndryth looked completely out of place as she sat talking with the Mage. Her costume was neat and muted, but the sunlight burnished her hair and made it glow.

"Come in, lad. Come in," the wizard said without turning. "Get yourself a stool and join us. We were just talking about you." They waited until he came over.

"I understand that you two know each other, so we can dispense with introductions." Greylock smiled benignly from one to the other. Marianna inclined her head and Jarrod followed suit, turning his palms out with formality before he sat down.

"I've filled Marianna in on the background," Greylock said to him, "and she understands the need for secrecy. In fact she came up with an excellent idea. She thinks it would be easier and attract less attention if she stayed dressed like a man. She's even prepared to give up all that lovely hair." He looked at her and smiled. Jarrod said nothing.

"Now," Greylock said, sitting forward and wagging blunt forefingers at both of them, "the two of you are going to have to learn to work together in rough country. You're going to have to be totally self-sufficient." He turned his head toward Jarrod. "And I don't want you using Magic, young man, unless there's absolutely no other way out." Courtak's eyebrows shot up. "I know, lad, I know, but the less attention you draw to yourself the better, and you know how people are when a Magician shows up.

"First off, I'm going to give you a couple of days to get your equipment together and get to know each other a bit better and then I'm sending you off to the Assaras for some mountain climbing and some practice in living off the land. I've laid on an instructor, you'll meet him this afternoon, and he'll tell you what you'll need." He paused and looked from one to the other but he learned nothing.

"I think that's all for the moment. Any questions?" There

was a mute shaking of heads. "Good. Off you go then, and good luck."

The Mage was abruptly dismissive. His two visitors rose dutifully and Jarrod carried the stool back to the long, cluttered table. He turned back in time to see Marianna drop a deferential curtsey that didn't look right in trousers and went and held the door for her.

He was angry, the morning's mood worn quite away, and, as he spiralled down the stairs behind her he said, "You knew all the time, didn't you?" There was resentment in the voice. He felt that he had been made a fool of.

"My father told me the day of the dance." The noncommittal voice bounced up the curving stone. She did not turn her head but concentrated on the placement of her feet.

"Why didn't you say anything?"

"I didn't know what, if anything, you'd been told and I felt that if you didn't know, it was hardly my place to break the news." She was freezingly polite. They continued round in silence until they reached the landing below Greylock's apartment.

"My room's on this floor."

"How convenient for you." She turned and smiled a smile that died too quickly ever to reach the eyes. "Since I can't get through the Maze, I'll have to ride all the way round. Which reminds me, if I'm to get back in time for lunch I'll have to hurry. I'll meet you inside the Maze Gate in three hours." The smile flicked out again and she was gone. As he walked down the narrow corridor to his room, Jarrod felt foolish and uncomfortable. He didn't think he was going to enjoy this hunt at all.

His fears were amply justified in the following weeks as Marianna, or Martin, as she had become, proved more adept at almost everything than he. When they were alone she assumed command as if by right and he could not gainsay her. He felt galled and diminished and clung to his one remaining buttress of pride, his skill with the bow. Practice gradually begot acceptance and hard and continuous work gave no time for resentment. Resentment, nevertheless, was there.

The first time that they rode South to the mountains they passed units of the Farrod making their way toward the palace with the unenthusiastic tread of men called untimely from their fields. When they returned, tired, scraped and bruised, they had to detour around the town of tents that had gone up to house the full mustering. Hobbled horses grazed at the fringes of the camp and, as they circled round to their respective stables, their eyes stung in the waft of smoke from the cooking fires. Gossip, endemic to courts and armies alike, needs an ignorant audience to thrive, and they were severally regaled with the story of Robarth Strongsword's fall. The kindly and the loyal said that his horse had stumbled and thrown him; everybody else said that if he had spent less time with his whore and more with his horse he wouldn't have fallen off. The only point of total agreement was that he had broken his leg, in how many places depended on who was telling the story.

Jarrod began a routine that consisted of weapons training with the Farrod in the mornings and lessons in Magic in the afternoon. He found that the King's accident had done nothing to improve the morale of the men he had seen trudging North two weeks before. The work-outs were dour and unalleviated by the bawdy humor that usually makes practice bearable. It felt strange to be taking lessons from Greylock again after two years away at school. The lessons were quite different, but he felt that he had been sent back to an earlier class. His progress was interrupted by what he thought of as exercises in survival and humility on the weekends, but, as iteration toughened him, the blisters calloused over and the body hardened. He gradually acquired confidence in his new-won skills.

A month passed around the two young people and the pace of life quickened with the season. Prince Naxus, eager in his new command, drove the troops with a zeal they did not match. Rumor of the sights of Celador had spread, but if Naxus paid the portent any heed he did not show it. Courtak ceased to attend weapons practice and began to learn shapechanging from the Mage instead. At least he would eventually learn shapechanging, for the early parts were confined to the work chamber and were grisly in the extreme. It entailed examining the inner structure of the creature whose shape he would one day assume. His work apron became bloodstained past the ministrations of any laundress as he painstakingly dissected each animal, layer by layer, from skin to stomach lining. It was delicate and disgusting work and it was only the beginning. The next step was to assume control of a living example and learn from it the workings of the flesh so antipathetically committed to memory. To absorb the instincts of a bird or vole, to comprehend the ferocity of a stoat or the mating drives of a loupe in the fish pond was the hardest thing he had ever tried to do and, more often than not, he failed.

Greylock brooked no failure. The Mage pushed him mercilessly until Jarrod felt that the man was trying to pour all of his art and knowledge into him. He felt that one of these days he would break open and leak spells and lore in all directions. Rebellion began to build up in him, but, before it could crest, the rote of lessons was abruptly interrupted. Martin and he were summoned and told to prepare to leave the following morning for a fortnight's stay in the Caddis Mountains. It was to be their final test and they were going alone. Martin said that she was eager to get to the search itself and Jarrod matched her outwardly in enthusiasm. Inwardly, he felt rushed and unready and wondered why they had been given so little warning.

The Mage was no less prey to doubt as he stood in his aerie in the early light and watched the two ride out. He knew that battle was coming and, while he would have welcomed Courtak's help, he was afraid that this was the fight that would be lost. He could not place the mission in jeopardy, so he watched them until they had disappeared behind the fortified point before he turned back to his preparations. His skin prickled from the inside and his eyes were filled with the immanence of sight known but not experienced. Below it lay the fear that he would go blind again. The feelings of tension, the sudden tremors of the skin and the steadily tightening muscles at the base of his neck had increased over the past three days and he had dared delay no longer. He hoped for a little more time to build his strength in spite of the denials that his body gave him. He dismissed the two riders from his mind and started to ply a pestle and mortar.

While Greylock brooded and prepared, the two slight figures cantered down the road to Gapguard, The Sentinel of the South as men called it.

The pair looked of an age now that Martin had cut her hair, but she continued to order Jarrod around with all the assurance that three years seniority gives at that time of life.

She turned toward him in the saddle and said across the wind, "Ever ridden bareback?"

"Never."

"You ought to practice. What if you lost your saddle?"

"You're crazy. If I didn't have stirrups this animal would just walk out from under me."

Martin grinned. "Comes of having legs like a clern," she yelled over the hoofbeats and kicked her mount ahead.

Jarrod was grinning too. Green was returning to the world and that always made him feel good. Marianna, no Martin, he corrected himself, was being nice for a change. Well-being coursed through him. It was good to be alive and riding through the barred sunshine. The birds were back from Southern wintering and the royal forest was filled with calls of warning and seduction. The day was soft and there were times when the sun, the intoxication of the air and the rhythm of the animal made him feel that he and his mount were one. During those times he knew that he would find a unicorn and bring it safely home.

After a sennight in the Caddis he was a deal less sure. The bright, new green of the plain was nowhere in evidence. There was snow and there was drenching fog that got them lost. The lower slopes had been runnelled by streams too small to make their way onto the maps, but there had been no need to rope themselves together. He thought apprehensively of the Saradondas as he bellied his way along a slim ledge. Martin was leading confidently and Jarrod realized how easily he had come to depend on her. He had no problem thinking of Martin as another boy during the daytime. It was different at night.

The weather cut conversation down to a minimum and most of what speech there was was confined to cursing at the conditions and the cold food. What wood they found was too wet to burn. Jarrod was surprised to find that Martin was a fluent curser when the mood took her. It was a side that she had never shown when the guide was there and, though he tried to list it among Martin's other accomplishments, it jarred him. Not that they were without causes for imprecations. The mountain they were on presented problems enough as they scrambled up and it was a relief when the local weather controller gave them some warm, blue days. They started the ice thawing and caused a thousand new noises.

Fear of avalanche died away after the third day and Martin announced she was going hunting and that she would prefer to do it alone. Jarrod felt a little hurt at being excluded but, mostly, he felt relieved that he didn't have to go.

"Don't spend the whole day basking in the sun," Martin said good-naturedly. "Your bowstring ought to be dry by now."

"Try bringing back something edible for a change," Jarrod called after the retreating back.

He sat back, hands behind his head, watching the raptors circle the foothills in search of the unwary. He followed them as they floated on outstretched pinions and rode the currents insolently and in beauty. He remembered the sinewy system beneath the feathers and set himself to visualize them in the motions of flight. He began to follow a young male sauntering out over the valley and tried to experience the tension and stress caused by the wind when it met an immobile wing. He synchronized the anatomical creature in his head with the movements of the kester hawk and, in time, became adept. He could even anticipate the shift in angle of the flexible wingtip.

He wondered how the bird must feel on a day such as this and knew the sun on his back and the flutter of the feathers on the edges of the wings. He saw the world as a map, with every detail sharp and clear, and was consumed by a fury of hunger, barely harnessed by an icy patience. Underlying it all was a joy at being on the wing again, being able to see the ground below and the inevitable prey. He knew the exaltation of the hunt and the need to kill. Very soon he would kill.

He tilted his body and opened the tailfeathers slightly so that he could rise with circular swiftness on the draft of warm air. The amazement he felt at being able to see details on the bottomland below as clearly as he had before was foreign to the hawk's consciousness and, in an instant, the unity was gone. Jarrod was now aware that he was controlling the bird. He had maintained the shape but the reflexes were no longer his. He tested his control. His feet ended in the lethal curvature of talons and he flexed them to reassure himself. His arms were feathered and fingerless, but they answered to his commands. He had control, but the body's true owner, though dispossessed, was still on the premises.

Jarrod knew that if he didn't satisfy the craving for food that invaded him and made all other thoughts seem irrelevant, he would have a mutiny to deal with. He banked back toward the wooded hills below and discovered that, now that his thoughts were not entirely hawk thoughts, he could enjoy the sensations of flight that his host took for granted. He wheeled and swooped in the morning sun, smelling the changes in the temperature. He widened his angle across the wind as he passed over a tall outcropping of rock and watched his shadow race brokenly before him down the distant slopes.

His eye sensed movement that was not his own and knew it upon the instant as a very young groundwart. As he was thinking that the mother must be close by, his wings folded of their own accord and he plummeted straight down. A clear membrane slid down over his eyes and the small, hairless, snouted thing rooting obliviously below appeared to leap up at him. He tried desperately to unfurl the wings, but knew as he did so that there was no way he could pull out of that insane dive in time. The body he was in was not built to withstand impacts at that speed, not even if he managed to break their fall by hitting the groundwart. He had no opportunity to prepare himself to die before it was over and he found himself straining to lift away with the dead weight of his kill gripped securely in his talons. It was hard, determined work to beat a path through the unhelpful air.

He alighted at the foot of an old tree, lightning-blasted and Winter-bare, whose branches afforded a measure of protection from interlopers from above. He freed his claws from the sticky hide, cocked his head around for possible danger and then began ripping at the long-awaited meal. He tore with the wicked curve of his beak and gulped down gobbets that steamed, though the sun was high. He ate single-mindedly and without pause until he was sated and the small body on the soiled grass unrecognizable. He hopped stiffly to one side and began grooming himself while the circling scavengers made practice approaches to the remains, not quite daring to move in. Jarrod watched them with interest and a disdain that was not his own. Then, his preening completed, he rose heavily into the air and, sweeping deeply and strongly, he headed for the mountains. It didn't take him long to

find an updraft and he felt content and a little sleepy as he
spiralled aloft.

The Jarrod part responded to the mood with complacent satisfaction. Shapechanging wasn't that difficult after all. True, this
wasn't really shapechanging because his body was still on the
mountainside. At least he assumed his body was back there. He
suddenly very much wanted to see that body. He clamped control down firmly over his involuntary host and lifted them skyward while scanning the range with those incredible eyes. He
saw neither packs nor Martin. He flew back and forth searching
frantically and then, with a feeling of mounting panic, winged
Westward to the next mountain.

He spotted himself almost immediately, his mouth open and
his chin pointing to the heavens. He glided across the face of the
scarp toward the recumbent figure and tried to project himself
back into his body. Reason told him that he had never left it, but
reason wasn't doing him any good. He thrust his awareness
again at the long, dark shape below and, as he did so, his head
swivelled sharply around and he found himself flying away with
powerful strokes. In his eagerness to return he had lost control of
the kester and the hawk's consciousness had leaped in to reassert
itself.

He struck back wildly, but his partner was prepared this time
and the wings failed to obey him. He strained to slow the
movements but the muscles threw him off with ease. He withdrew and fought a battle for control of himself and this he won.
The mountain receded behind them and he refocussed his inner
eye on the avian structure and watched the intermeshing movements and the changes in secretions and circulation. He sought to
submerge himself in them and fuse with them and he was
rewarded. In phase once more, he tried to order their comings
and their goings and he found himself opposed.

The creature was not very intelligent, but it had an inviolable
regard for its own existence and it had no intention of surrender-
ing again. Jarrod marshalled his obduracy and when he struck
out again the wings faltered. The hawk put them into a long,
descending glide and maintained it stubbornly while its human
parasite hammered away at its will. Courtak continued his assault as the ground rose smoothly toward them and when he

sensed resistance weakening, pounced with savage glee and
knew for an instant that the wings were his own. He was jolted
out of them again. He grappled back at the fear-driven instinct
and the wings jerked spasmodically as they responded to conflicting commands. Fear rose in the young man as his kester
self began to tumble down the sky.

It gave him strength and he lashed out again. This time he was
not opposed and he regained his wings. He righted them and
soared away, making for a grove of trees. The blood was pounding as if he had made a difficult strike and brought off the kill.
Fierce exhilaration filled his conquered veins, but his human side
decided to perch a while and ensure that it could keep the upper
hand. As his pulse slowed to the rhythm of the downstroke, he
swung into a circle, looking for a sturdy and accessible branch.
Revolving in idling descent, he was surprised by a cloud of small
birds abandoning the security of the foliage. He thought that
something underneath had startled them until he realized that
they were aiming themselves at him.

Short, strident and repeated cries pierced up at him and he
changed course to avoid them, but found that he had underesti-
mated their combined fury. They were around him, swooping
and diving, and not all of them sheared off at the last minute.
Sharp little beaks stabbed through feathers and he lurched as pain
lanced through the tendons of his right wing. He was conscious
of a spreading numbness and the efforts of the hawk to take
control. He was being buffeted and chivvied from all sides and,
once again, from within. He fought to keep aloft and to escape
the frenzy of his tiny enemies, but there were too many problems
to cope with and not enough time or space. He was weakening
and being driven down. He knew fear and struck back at his
relentless attackers with beak and claw. There were fine droplets
of blood veiling the air and some of them were his. In a last,
desperate effort to escape and outfly them, he hurled his body
upward at his tormentors and was almost free when the outraged
hawk within burst from his weakening grasp and the world went
black.

He was down, there could be no doubt of that, and he was on
his back with his vitals exposed to the terrible needles of their
beaks. He knew that he had to move or they would surely finish

him. He did not want to die, not in the body of a bird. He struggled to right himself but his wings were somehow trapped beneath him and would not answer his need. His eyes darted skyward and encountered nothing more menacing than small, high clouds. They had left him then, content to abandon him to his scavenging cousins. Once more he struggled to turn over so that he might flop to cover. He heaved and rolled to his left and caught his wrist painfully under his hip. Wrist? His startled sight took in the contours of Martin's pack and relief poured through him and left him shaking. He collapsed and scanned the mercifully empty skies. He continued to shake but now it was because he was giggling feebly. He was himself.

He was claimed by the euphoria that was mingling with the residue of fright and lay in the sun and let the sweat dry on him. After a while he sat up cautiously and found that he was weak. He shaded his eyes and peered at the coppices below trying to spot some sign of his ordeal, but all was as it had been. He missed the kester hawk's keen vision and felt a pang of loss for the wonder of soaring, unaided, over the slow earth. He glanced up again and noticed that the sun was still shy of noon. He had only been a bird for an hour and yet he felt as if he had been sailing in the void for half a lifetime. It was a universe of Magic but not for Magicians.

CHAPTER V

FOR TWO FULL DAYS TROOPS SKIRTED THE OUTPOST WHERE Greylock labored. They gave the Place of Power a wide berth as they moved up to encampments behind the solid protection of the Causeway. Then, as reinforcements joined them, the first units deployed through the broadly arching gate. They crossed the rough tumble of the Giants' Causeway and bivouacked just out of bowshot of the oily, brown blanket that contained their enemy. The Farrod made its way, with commendable order, under the portcullises and took its place in the center of the shallow semicircle begun by the warcat battalions and the cavalry. They rested their pikes like stooks of corn and set about digging trenches and setting campfires. Once that was accomplished, they performed that other millennial military duty—they sat and waited. Four days passed in boredom and nervous jocularity and still the enemy did not appear.

The waiting was a special torment for Greylock. He went through books and scrolls in feverish haste, seeking for some way of averting the disaster that he feared would befall his country. On the fourth night he could stand his inner pain no longer. He rang the handbell on the small table by his chair and sent the duty boy for his robe and then for his crook. He needed help with the heavy robe and his frailty irritated him. Anyone who accomplishes Magic learns to cope with the body's betrayals, but it made surrender to the infirmities of age no easier. He

leaned heavily on the wooden stave and he took the stairs
slowly. He knew that he was badly in need of strength and he
went out into the night to borrow it. The boy followed him,
unbidden and unobserved.

The Mage entered the circle of the Place of Power. The boy
stopped well outside it, incapable of going in and half afraid to
stay where he was, tethered by his curiosity. He did not have
long to wait. He heard chanting and then his self-induced brav-
ery was rewarded with the sight of his Mage rising effortlessly
and unaided through the dark. He alit upon the closest, tallest
stele and stood outlined against the stars. The page, though he
was not cold, shook as Greylock tipped back his head and held
his arms out to the skies. The crook was grasped firmly in his
right hand and a glimmer was growing on the left.

There was silence, profound and exclusive. The grass was still
and not a beetle stirred. There was no linnet song nor soughing
wind that could disturb the living rigor. The figure on the
obsidian slab grew more solid to the boy's unblinking gaze. It
was as if it fed upon the countryside. Then, before he felt that he
had properly understood, the world was right again. His master
was striding toward him, carrying the Staff lightly by his side.
The radiance of his ring was matched by that of his face.

"Come along, boy," Greylock said, clapping him familiarly
on the shoulder, almost as if they were equals. "It's time we
both got some rest. Tell the Duty Master that I said you could
sleep in tomorrow."

Greylock's feeling of rapture lasted well into the morning and
then his monarch's voice boomed up the stairs to him. A royal
visit usually meant trouble and the opening salvo was not
encouraging.

"What d'you mean I can't see him? Flay me, d'you think I've
had meself carried all the way up here to be told I can't see him?
Get him!" Greylock met the youth on his way down and nodded
sympathetically to him. He entered his antechamber, his mind
rapidly going over possible problems.

"Be welcome, my Liege, and may fortune grant your subject
the ability to render you service." He bowed.

"Oh, go away with you, Greylock. Where can I rest these
splints?" The King was testy. The Mage led him and the four

tired footmen who bore him through to the bedchamber and motioned for them to prop him up against the bolsters. Robarth settled himself, dismissed his bearers with a wave of his hand and waited while the Mage drew up a chair.

"All right," he said, "when's it to be?"

"Any day now, Sire."

"You said that a sennight ago. You can do better than that. What do those prickles of yours say?"

Greylock gave a little smile at the word to disguise his wariness. "Nothing, I'm happy to say, Sire. They had reached the point where they were debilitating me, so I visited the Place of Power last night. It's strange, you know," he said with an easy familiarity bred of years as a counselor, "it's never been that bad before. Battle has always taken place before it got that painful. No, there's something odd going on out there. I don't know what it is, but I don't like it."

"But it's goin' to be soon, this fight?"

"Very soon."

"Is it the one . . . ?" and Strongsword let the question hang in the air.

"I didn't see what was projected," Greylock temporized. "All my energy went into Ragnor and I had none left for seeing. Afterwards, of course," he added wryly, "I couldn't see anything at all." His guard went down. He knew his monarch too well. "I don't honestly know the answer to that question and it bothers me. The Archmage told me that he had no way of measuring what time it was that he saw. He doesn't even know if he saw things in proper sequence. I don't know about you, but I haven't heard anything from any of the other countries, so I rather suspect that ours will be the first battle of the year. And they're early at that."

"You really think it's all goin' to come true?" This question was asked a trifle breathlessly.

"Oh yes." There was compassion in the Mage's voice. "No one could invent anything that detailed and, besides, Errethon awoke. Regrettably, Sire, I must advise you to expect the worst."

"Ha!" the King snorted as he elbowed himself into a more comfortable position. His injured leg was a white tube against the counterpane. "Not if my brother can help it."

"With respect, Sire . . ." Robarth cut him off.

"You didn't see it. Naxus rode Cromache in that benighted exhibition, the black mare he's always ridden. Well, he's killed her. Did it himself. Cried like a baby, but he did it. Now, what do you say to that, my good Mage?"

Greylock was alert again as the danger signals blared at him. Hope, too, inserted an insidious tendril. "That's very interesting," he said slowly. "He's deliberately changed the future that you all saw. One detail of it, at least. Whether or not it will be enough I don't know, but I sincerely hope that it will."

"I'll say aye to that, Sir Sorcerer, indeed I shall. I didn't like what I saw at Celador one little bit."

"Unless I misread you, Majesty," Greylock said, steering the conversation toward safety, "you didn't come this far, and so uncomfortably, to test my knowledge of time. You could have sent for me for that."

"Quite right. I've decided to pay you a visit." Robarth's tone was calmer.

"Evidently, Sire." Greylock risked a touch of irony.

"Oh, I intend to stay a while," the King said, with the beginnings of a smile. "I promised me brother that I wouldn't interfere and it's bad for morale for me to be seen like this." He gestured to the offending leg with distaste, his impatience obvious. "Now, I disapprove, as you very well know, of expanses of glass in fortified buildin's, but," he hesitated and harrumphed, "due to unforeseen circumstances, I find meself in need of the view provided by your top floor." He stopped and looked across at Greylock before adding, with a contriteness that touched the Mage, "It's too far for me to see anythin', I know that, but I'll get a feel of things. I'll be close at hand if I'm needed." He sighed. "Who'm I tryin' to convince? I just couldn't stand bein' stuck on top of that Causeway doin' nothin'."

"I know how you feel, Sire," Greylock replied quietly. "It is a hard thing for me to accept the inevitability of defeat. I am accustomed, as you are, to wielding power and affecting the outcome of events. I am haunted by the specter of, begging your pardon, being an ineffective onlooker as everything I hold most dear is destroyed." He sighed heavily. "Be that as it may, we shall both do everything we can to thwart the Archmage's prediction, and your Majesty must consider this as your abode for as long as it shall please you.''

"Just until the battle's over, old friend. I promise."

"It is an honor, Sire." He rose. "With your Majesty's permission, I'll call the men and have you installed upstairs. I'll need a little time to get the place prepared."

"No fussin', you hear me?" The royal forefinger jabbed out. "And Greylock," the look was level and compelling, "we'll win through. You mark me words. We always have."

"As your Majesty commands." The Mage bowed.

Robarth was installed in complaining state in front of the workshop windows and Greylock sent to the palace for Naxania. She would be of no help with her father, but he needed her for this particular battle. He called in Nazod, who had been in charge of weather control in Paladine since before Greylock became Mage, and ordered a storm for the morrow. He alerted Agar Thorden, his second in command, that he would be in charge of The Outpost the following day.

When Naxania arrived, Greylock gave her no chance to ask questions. He commandeered one of the smaller workrooms and set both Nazod and the Princess to work preparing the potions they would need for the ritual cleansing. He saw to the setting of the pentacle himself. The potions, specifics for endurance, were swallowed and herbs were consumed to clarify the memory and reinforce the will. That done, they entered the glowing lines and immersed themselves in the vigil of purification. Of all who spent the night under those roofs, only Robarth Strongsword slept.

They Made the Day, but there was no sun to see. Nazod's assistants had brought up clouds from the South during the night and kept them building overhead. Beneath that flocking the three strode out, each robed according to his station. Greylock wore the green and black that he had taken to Celador and carried his Staff. In the subdued light his diadem remained dormant and the Ring of the Keepers looked darkly ordinary. Naxania wore her hair unbound and the plain, unadorned blue gown of a Magician. Nazod, sustained by will and pride, kept pace with them. The emblems of his office were embroidered on his robe, but they were dulled by the lack of light.

They entered the Place of Power. The inurement of past performance made it routine and unexciting to all three of them, but there was nothing that could blunt the terror and elation of the ascent to the monolith's top. Greylock allowed them a moment to catch their breath. He turned to the Princess.

"Does it look anything like the vision?"

"No Sir," Naxania replied with unaccustomed meekness. She was selfbereft of rank and nothing more now than an adjunct to the Mage. "We saw most of it from above before. I think, though I can't be absolutely sure, that I saw us standing here." Greylock let that pass without comment. He looked at the old warlock.

"Eliahue, how fast can you call the storm down?"

"You know perfectly well that it takes about half a minute to charge the clouds and don't call me that." The Weather Controller was in a feisty and combative mood. The Mage heard the challenge and chose to ignore it.

"Sorry, Nazod," he said placatingly and turned back to Naxania.

"I have not prepared you for this, Highness, because I did not want to stir memories before I had to. However, if Ragnor and my intuition are right, this is the battle you saw at Celador. I know that it is not going to be pleasant, but I need to see through you. You are going to be my eyes on the other side of the Causeway. It is the only way that we can do any good." He put his left hand on her shoulder and looked her directly in the eyes. He saw the doubt and disinclination there and overrode them. She nodded in silent assent. He smiled at her then and held her fondly around the neck.

"Without you," he said softly, "I shall see as little this time as I did the last."

Naxania crossed her ankles and sank obediently to the stone. Greylock moved to stand behind her and faced out toward the Upper Causeway. As she began her descent into the remembrance of things to come, he peered forward anxiously to where men and galloping messengers were silhouetted against the implacable brown beyond. The knowledge of his office flowed into him from the forces sealed beneath his feet and his preternatural awareness took in a man on horseback, sword drawn and held aloft. The man brandished the weapon from time to time, at what, or in response to what, Greylock could neither see nor hear. He strained to see the color of the horse, but from his vantage point all the figures looked like paper puppets against a backdrop. All of them were black.

He glanced at the figure at his feet and began to repeat the words that his predecessor had taught him. It was a language that no other mortal spoke. He said the words quietly and they cosseted him with their familiarity. He began the round again and the dull, black jewel on his finger revealed inner fires. They broke forth slowly, as though emerging from the banking of a long night.

Soft tremors quaked across him as the power within him mounted. He reached out toward the Princess' mind and the memories that flickered there. She felt the touch and struggled to hold the vision still. With both hands upon the shaft, he raised his Staff above his head. The runes glittered and writhed along it and his shoulders shook.

"Wind!" he cried. "Nazod," the howl drew the name out beyond its length, "give me a wind! They come. I feel them coming." The words tore loose from his throat as he struggled to control the energies that were streaming into him in answer to his summoning and his need.

At his back, as if at his bidding, storm clouds mounted up and thunder growled. His robe began a dance of its own and, despite the shielding of his body, Naxania's hair flew like eelgrass on an ebbing tide. The stone in the ring blazed and he saw with two pairs of eyes. From above he watched a sudden light flash out and saw a severed head go down. The terror-stricken steed went bolting as the body toppled and dragged it along behind.

Reality now, or reality still to come? He closed his eyes and plunged more urgently into the woman's mind. There he saw the ugly, crawling boxes that dealt out death at such apalling distances. Description had not prepared him for this and he recoiled.

Once again, Naxus rode his horse across the 'Mage's inner sight and this time it was a chestnut. He waited, with horror crawling up his spine, until the insubstantial scythe gleaned the Prince. The bloodstained animal took off once more and the headless corpse bumped sickeningly along the paving stones.

In a consummation of hate and fury, Greylock hurled the wind

forward in an effort to dislodge the foreign air. From the rolling,
black clouds above his head he called down bolts of power to
excoriate the foe. He heaved the lightning cathartically at objects
he could only see in memories not his own. The high-held Staff
linked him with the fires that lurked amid the hovering rains and
he willed them at the enemy. The boxes crackled and all their
surfaces were alight with sparks, but they snouted on. They were
as contemptuous of his efforts as they were of the arrows that
bounced harmlessly away.

Naxania's concentration oscillated, unsettled by the readiness
of her mind to flinch from the detailed recall of so much that was
painful. To the Mage, it was as if his sight was moving in and
out of focus and he fought to steady her. It was not his only
fight. There was an enemy to turn back and the energies that
raged in his body to tame. It was too much. He could not hold
them all and when Naxania's mind went out like a taper in a
draft he thought he had gone blind again. He lurched against the
Princess' back and lowered his Staff instinctively to keep from
falling.

The blackness was shattered by an explosion of light that
flared across his retinas and left striations of red and yellow
behind. Slowly, sight faded back into being and he saw the
Causeway once more, but there were more pressing problems.
The filament that had connected him to the thunderheads had
snapped when the Staff had swung down and now they roared
and spat of their own accord. He sought to bind the elements
again and stopper up the skies. Without control they could harm
the men he could no longer see, but the rampaging of the storm
that Nazod had wrought was too great for him and passed
beyond his ability to restrain it. The angry voices of the clouds
made thought impossible and the rain began to fall in a stinging
pelt.

Naxania sat slumped at his feet and Nazod lay toppled at his
side. Greylock stood in the downpour, his body swinging lightly
with fatigue. There was an exalted and inappropriate smile on his
face. The intense joy that the performance of strong Magic
brought kept him upright, but, finally, his being shot through
with epiphany, he sat. The wind, as if bent upon dislodging
them, whooped and scoured at the stone. The fire in the ring,

responding to the Keeper's state, died grudgingly away. Broken phrases whispered still from between cracked lips, but they evoked no response.

All that had been seen in Celador's Great Hall had happened again as irresistibly as a nightmare that replays itself and from which there is no awakening. The carnage was no less painful for having been foreseen. Naxus had tried to change the future and had failed.

Beneath the anticipated and unnatural assault, the Farrod held for a while and then turned and ran for the Maze Gate. Hundreds died under the frantic feet of their comrades as they scrambled and fought to win their way under the portcullises. Those who had been in the front lines were decimated by the invaders. Never in Paladine's recall had so many of her men perished so ignominiously, their breastplates whole and their backs destroyed.

The intervention of wizardry had, in some ways, made matters worse. The storm had stampeded the horses and had made the warcats nervy and difficult to control. It had cut down on the cloudsteeds' losses because it kept them grounded, but that was not accounted an advantage. It was only after Greylock's failure that the elements came into their own. Driving rain had bounced whitely back as it riddled the surface of the plain. The engines of death began to slip and struggle in their progress, bogging down in slicked earth and corpses. Banded tracks slid from wheelmounts in the churn and whine of faltering machinery, but the Paladinian army still lacked the means of disposing of them. They hoped that whatever it was that the foe had to breathe would run out and thereby achieve what men could not. They were cheated even of that. The enemy emerged anew from behind their curtain and winched the battle wagons away into their own obscurity.

Magic did not go unscathed. The Mage was too far spent to get himself or his companions down. It took considerable courage on the part of the lesser Sorcerers to enter the power-lashed circle and tie ladders together for the perilous climb to their aid. The Princess was borne back to the Palace, where she drifted in and out of consciousness and made no sense in either state. Fevers, bred of the drenching and the defeat, laid many at The Outpost low. Wisewomen bustled about and herbs and simples were stripped from the garden.

Tents for the wounded and the maimed blossomed beyond their buildings and within the walls the Mage lay insensible for days. Around him the Talented worked and mourned, for the storm that had saved Stronta had been the last piece of summoning that Nazod would ever do. The stubborn heart in the frail body had cracked in the effort to oblige his master. They buried him with grief and honor and they did not put his first name on the stone.

CHAPTER VI

JARROD CANTERED BACK INTO THE AFTERMATH, PAST THE GUYROPED lines of the suffering that spread Westward from the fortress walls, and was angry that he had been sent away when there had been danger at home. Martin had turned off earlier to go into the castle. She was shocked by what she had seen. It was the closest that she had ever been to the war that occupied so much of her father's time and took him from her so frequently. It was a grisly introduction, but it moved her in unexpected ways that troubled her. She felt pity and regret, as was only natural, but she knew that excitement and disappointment were behind them. She had discovered that she was drawn to the glory of battle.

Jarrod had no such inclinations. He had seen too much of warfare for that, but he had never been around such outright defeat before. He was oppressed by the sullen faces and dejected miens, by the moans of pain coming from the tents. His mood plunged toward despair when, while unsaddling, he was told of Greylock's condition. He went directly to see the Mage's personal Wisewoman, knowing full well that he would be refused permission to see him. He had played this game with Diadra before and knew how much she enjoyed these brief intervals of power. It took him two days to get in.

The thresh of resentment that he had been nursing to dampen his concern turned to chaff when he saw the crinkled parchment of the skin. The raised delta of veins on the palsied hands that sat

upon the counterpane and danced in tuneless independence brought
tears to his eyes. Sorrow and relief flooded over him. His old
taskmaster looked attenuated, but Jarrod convinced himself that
the man would come back—just as he always had. His eyes felt
hot and his voice was not entirely steady when he broke the
silence.

"How are you, Sir?" The head on the pillow moved slightly,
but the lips stayed still. "We could have helped, you know. You
didn't have to do all this by yourself." He had meant it to sound
light and amusing, but it rang like an accusation in his ears.
Though the eyes stayed closed, a faint smile had appeared on the
Mage's face. When he replied the voice was shallow, but the
tone was warm. Jarrod bent to catch the words.

"You sound just like a mother. Scold, scold, scold." He
paused so long that Jarrod thought that he had gone back to
sleep, but then he said, "Not to worry. It just takes a little longer
when you get to be my age." He smiled to himself and went
away again. Jarrod waited by the bed awhile, savoring the
tenderness he felt and then went over to the grate and rearranged
the wood so that it burned briskly. He tiptoed out.

Greylock was sitting up in bed when Diadra let Jarrod in
again. He was still thin to the point of scrawniness and the color
in his cheeks looked as if it had been painted on. The skin was
loose and the eyes were lost in sockets grown too big for them. It
was hard to think of him as the stocky man he had been. The
flesh had dwindled down as if rendered by the Powers that had
possessed him. This was the price he paid for his earlier borrow-
ing. Jarrod sat down beside him and longed to take one of the
stubby, dessicated hands in his own, but he did not dare to.

"What was it like, Sir?" the boy asked finally.

"What was what like, lad? When will you learn to be precise?" The voice was hoarse, but Jarrod rejoiced in it. The man
was obviously getting better.

"The battle, Sir."

"Oh, the battle." There was a dry chuckle from the bed.
"You still mad at me for sending you away and making you
miss all the excitement?" He became serious again. "The battle.
Well, you saw most of it at Celador. Naxus changed his horse,

but it didn't make any difference. I've never seen a man die so many times. I saw it happen on the chariotway and then again and again in Naxania's mind. It kept popping back up. I had to use half my concentration to keep her mind still so that I could see what was going on beyond the Causeways." The voice ran down and the Mage was lost in his own thoughts.

"I did no good at all," he resumed, shaking his head. "It would have been better if I had stayed away altogether."

"That's not true and you know it. The enemy would have come clear through the Gate if you hadn't been there."

The Mage smiled gently at the heat of the rebuttal. "Nay, lad," he said, "that was more Nazod's doing than mine. Poor old friend, it was the death of him. Or I was." There was a silence that Jarrod dared not interrupt and then Greylock continued as if there had been no break. "But at least I got the euphoria back."

"Sir?"

"The feeling you get at the end of a long and difficult spell. It didn't happen to me at the Conclave. I thought it was gone for good. When Ragnor linked us, I called on our friends here to give me power so that I could funnel it into the Archmage. I felt them answer, but then everything went out. Well, not out exactly. It was as if I was suspended in a deep, grey fog. I couldn't see anything. Part of me knew that I was intoning a spell, but I had no physical sensation of doing so. Does that make any sense?" He paused to gnaw on it and then continued.

"It was quite awful. I rather imagine that that's what it's like to be entombed alive. I knew I wasn't dead, but I might just as well have been." The old man shuddered at the recollection and Jarrod bent forward and fussed with the counterpane.

"When I woke up again I was blind and there was no elation to sustain me; no reward for that terrifying experience." He was barely speaking above a whisper now. "Just weakness, helplessness and that unending grey. I think I'd rather be dead than go into that blankness again." The eyes closed and Jarrod knew that it was time to leave.

The following day Diadra came to get him. "He says he's going to give you lessons. I've told him he's not strong enough, but he'll not listen to me. Now, you see to it, young man, that you don't tire him out. I'll have to rely on you to have more sense than he does, though for my money, there's nowt to choose between you.'' She glared at the boy to emphasize her point. ''Upstairs with you then. The quicker you're up, the sooner you'll be down. And you'd best 'bide me, hear? Or you'll not be going up there for a good long while.''

Greylock was propped up once more, but he had regained his color and the introspective listlessness was gone. They both smiled as Diadra's parting imprecations clattered round their ears.

''She guards me as if I were her cub and treats me like a wayward child,'' the Mage said resignedly. ''Once, years ago, I was forced to use the Voice on her before the King could get in. Imagine that.'' He grinned in delighted reminiscence.

''I'm sorry, Sir, I don't follow you.''

''What? Oh I'm sorry. No, of course you don't. That's what you're here for. This afternoon you're going to learn about 'the Voice,' '' The noun was italicized. ''It's the best kept secret on the planet and I've no business teaching it to you. Still, these are very strange times and you'll probably need all the help you can get. ''Mind you,'' the Mage stopped and transfixed Jarrod with a well-remembered stare, ''it takes years to perfect. I'm still at it myself. Oh,'' he waved a hand dismissively, ''a word or two at a time isn't all that difficult, once you get the hang of it, but sustained speech is something else again.'' He settled back and looked up at his pupil speculatively, as if weighing his fitness for this new task.

''It's a way of pitching your voice with the same kind of exactness you use on your body when you go inside yourself. That's the level of precision it requires. You use the vocal cords the same way that you control your mind. It has differing effects on your listeners, depending on the way you pitch it. It can compel obedience and it can make people remember what you say, down to the last of their days.'' He paused again to see what kind of effect he was having on this particular audience.

''Obviously, it could be quite dangerous if it was misused. You must always be silent about it, deny its existence if need be. I can't put that too strongly. I'm breaking that vow this very minute and it bothers the watchdogs of my soul, but, under the circumstances, I feel that there's not much else I can do." His eyes sought Jarrod's and held them.

"I want you to swear, swear by your dead mother and the father you never knew, that you will keep faith on this." Jarrod was shaken by his vehemence and startled by the reference to his parents.

"I swear," he said hesitantly, "that I will never reveal this secret to anyone."

"Good enough, though there may come a time when you will have to pass your knowledge on." The tone was even and considered again. "These are dangerous and uncertain days. All my efforts could be ended before they have had a chance to flower, but I have reason to think that you will survive. I can't say the same thing for myself."

"Come on, Sir," Jarrod interrupted. "You mustn't say things like that. You're just depressed from . . ."

Greylock cut him off. "You don't know what I'm talking about, do you? Course you don't, how should you? Well, I suppose straight out is best." He paused and seemed to gather himself. "Very well then, I feel that you will succeed me as Mage and as Keeper. The two don't necessarily go together, but they always have." He stopped and watched surprise and disbelief chase across the open face opposite him. They were supplanted by incredulity and dawning hope.

"Don't you have anything to say?" the Mage asked gently.

"Er, no. I, er, wasn't . . . why me?" It burst from him.

"Because you have more potential than anyone I've ever come across." Greylock was matter-of-fact. "I've tried to give you a solid grounding and you've done well, I'll say that for you."

"Then why did you stop me from going to the Collegium for two whole years?" Jarrod had not meant the question to come out, but it was gone before he could stop it.

"Not because you weren't good enough. Surely you can't think that? The day they brought you to me, you couldn't have been more than six or seven, I knew that great demands were going to be made on you. I've tried to conserve your strength and your power. I've tried to build it as slowly and surely as possible." His lips pursed in an inward smile. "Bit of pride in it, too," he confessed. "I thought I could do every bit as good a job as Sumner and his crew. Still do." He looked quirkily at Jarrod. "I intend, by the way, to remain in possession of both posts for as long as I possibly can." A broad smile bloomed and the eyes twinkled.

"What about Thorden?" Jarrod demanded, shocked past the ability to field a sense of humor. "Everyone expects him to follow you. He's stood in for you for years."

"Ah yes, Agar." Greylock puffed out his cheeks. Then, "The truth is that he's a wonderful administrator; I'd be totally lost without him. He has a way with growing things and a knowledge of plants that's quite remarkable, but," and the word dragged, "he's an indifferent Magician. I must make sure," he added, more to himself than to Jarrod, "that the two of you become friends."

The voice trailed off and the Wizard was lost in an interior monologue. He roused himself and said briskly, "Lesson this afternoon and then we must purify you. In the last analysis, it is the Place of Power that decides who will represent it. I shall present you tonight to those who dwell there and I shall ask their approval of you as my successor. I think you will be, eventually, but the Place of Power will decide. It always has." With those words Jarrod's spirits quailed.

"Do you really think you are fit enough, Sir? I mean, you ought not to strain yourself so soon after, er after . . ."

"Don't worry, lad. You're the one as'll need strength. I shall have very little to do. Now, you better get along before Diadra runs amok." The Mage smiled at him, but Jarrod didn't feel in the least comforted.

He felt no better that evening. He had had no time to prepare; had no idea of what preparations he could have made had he had the time. He felt certain that he was going to let Greylock down. Then there was the Place of Power itself. His eyes darted involuntarily to the expanse of glass on the North wall. He, unlike the King before him, was thwarted by the dark and all the windows showed him were fractured likenesses of the room. His mind's eye simply removed the wall and summoned up the daunting monoliths sitting in unnatural symmetry on their flattened hillock. The Keeper had never allowed him into the Place and that had been one dictum that he had never had the slightest desire to disobey.

A sense of tingling emptiness started up under the bow of his ribcage as he moved, in answer to Greylock's indication, to the pentagon in the middle of the floor. He sat cross-legged beside it. He sat straight and moved his shoulders back and forth to ease the tension that had gripped his muscles. He had no need of the Mage's admonition to concentrate on the Place of Power for it filled his mind.

He fought the stomach-wrench of vertigo as a viewpoint that could never be his own moved him effortlessly around the moon-bleached perimeter. Three quarters of a gigantic circle were marked off by perfectly spaced pillars of rock. They were rectangular and at least six times the height of a Talented man. Each pair was capped by a gently curving granite slab, almost as long. They had looked like so many open doorways when he had seen them from the Tower's top, but, from above, the lintels presented a broken ring. All their surfaces were smooth beneath his extended view. Dimly perceivable and utterly incomprehensible patterns traced themselves from one side of the stone to the other. He knew instinctively that neither time nor Nature's crafty depredations could touch them. No moss, nor any lichen grew on them. They remained inviolable in their linked and massive dignity. Between upright and upright were fifty paces and between doorway and doorway fifty paces more. Nothing grew within save grass and stone.

Inside the circling embrace of those guardians were three very different blocks. They rose Southward like the first three steps of a stairway to the stars fit for the race that had built the Giants' Causeway. The first, furthest and lowest, stood in the gap that would have completed the pillared circle. It was a dull and mottled red. It looked as if blood had been spilt there for so long that the rock had finally accepted and absorbed the sacrifices. Behind it, in the center, was the second. It was milk white and untouched by age or stain—pure and pristine. The square top, shining in the nightmoonlight like a freshly polished table, was of an exact height with the crosspieces that surrounded it. The third and tallest, whereon the Mage and the Princess had wrought their unsuccessful best and where Nazod had died, was of an impenetrable ebon hue. It reflected neither moons nor sun. It rose, enigmatic, menacing, for a full hundred feet, a finger pointed in accusation at the sky.

Jarrod became aware of the Mage's voice and felt his body respond to the familiar cadence of the ritual. His sight was filled with the Place of Power, but he knew that he had stood up and was taking off his clothes. He was conscious of making an effort to fold them before Greylock's voice tugged him into the five-sided figure. His skin burned briefly as he crossed the line and continued to itch until the words came to completion. His eyes were his own again and he looked across the steady green line and inclined his head toward the celebrant. He took the hand that reached through for him and stepped out of the pentacle. The light flickered twice and was gone.

"Put your things back on and we'll be on our way." The Mage went over to the clothes press and got out his regalia. He donned it carefully, using the dark windows to set the diadem straight and then, crook tapping on every second step, they set out.

Purification had stilled the trepidation in him, but Jarrod felt it return with new vigor. He was thankful that Greylock made no attempt to converse and concentrated on his footing. The impersonal nightmoon turned the tufted grasses to silver and to black. It took over half an hour to get to the far side of the menhirs, half an hour during which Jarrod tried, unavailingly, to keep his mind still and calm. As they entered from the Causeway side, the corner of his eye caught the beginnings of a glow in his companion's ring. They cleared the stone that looked dappled with death.

He tried to walk with straight-legged courage, but his knees felt like signet wax just before the seal strikes down. Clouds scudded up and covered the moon. He stumbled and clenched his teeth to silence himself. There was a growing rebellion in his stomach. He kept dogged eyes on the ground and felt the muscles under his jaw jump with the strain. The last part of the trip seemed to be taking longer than the getting there and he was startled when he looked up and found himself in front of the swart block. He craned his neck and shivered as if frost still edged the night air. It blotted out the heavens. He stood by the

Mage's side in inky shadow. The Ring of the Keepers shone steady now and it was the only illumination.

"Come here and face me, lad." They were the first words that Greylock had spoken since they had left the work chamber, and they came as a shock. "That's right. Just there."

To Jarrod it seemed as if the Mage had grown taller, but his eyes were drawn by the light of the ring. He followed it upward as Greylock raised his arms and his crook aloft. He heard words that were meaningless and comforting, like old friends most cunningly disguised. They quickened his spirits and lifted his body up. He felt no surprise as he rose in the air. He felt assured. It was like being a small boy again and dreaming that he could fly.

His upward progress halted at the top of the stele and he drifted backwards and was settled gently on the level top. Above him, the clouds scurried on and, as if to keep his courage up, the nightmoon came back to keep him company. Presently, the head of the Keeper came into view on the far side of the white slab. The jewels in his circlet flashed as he came to rest in the middle of the white expanse. There were only fifty paces between them, but Jarrod, pushed past astonishment, felt that he had never seen the man before.

The Keeper of the Place of Power stood tall and regal. The runes of the Robe flowed unctuously and the stone on his left hand blazed about. Pale green fire surrounded the crook and the curving top uncurled itself. The Mage flung back his head and cried aloud and the diadem became a bright corona. Petillations of just bearable pain dashed across Jarrod's skin. Cold points of fire rippled over him as if he had been flung into an ice-encrusted bath. There was no invigorating afterglow. It was enough that it receded.

He was beginning to feel relieved when Greylock called again. He was shaken from within as force such as he had never known surged up through him, flinging his arms straight up at the sky. He knew that if his heart did not burst his head would, but, before either could sunder, the Keeper sent yet another invocation winging into the gathering maelstrom. Jarrod became a world that blew apart in flame and a most puissant joy. It was too much for him and the ensuing blackness was a balm.

He wakened to a sense of shame that deprived him of volition and it was some time before he knew that he was lying in the Mage's bed. He tried to sit up and was pushed back, so easily, by a pair of veined and spotted hands. Greylock, in a comfortable old gown, bent over him.

"Easy there. You'll be all right," he said, pulling the covers back up. "You did very well. Those that dwell in the Place that I pretend to be lord of approve of you. I knew they would." He was beaming.

"But I failed. After all you've done, I failed." The words came out as a wail of grief.

"Oh no, lad. No, no." The old man cackled, his normal chuckle quite transformed, "If there was a third call for me when I was presented, I never heard it. And I've been serving them, fairly well I like to think, for a long time now. No, no. They'll take you when the time comes. For now, we've both got to get some sleep and get our strength back as fast as we can."

Lassitude claimed Jarrod and he did not even have the strength to protest that he was usurping the Mage's bed. He did not hear him leave.

CHAPTER VII

"Up, sluggard! Up! if you're going to start every morning like this, I think I'll get me another travelling companion." Jarrod rose out of the depths of a fathomless sleep drawn by the voice he had come to know so well.

"Come on, you great, long streak of idleness, get up!" The voice was reinforced by an ungentle shaking. "I thought all Magicians, even baby ones, were supposed to be up very early, but you spend your time flat on your back. Come on, we've a ship to catch." Jarrod yawned and blinked.

"Ship?" he said groggily.

"Yes, a ship. In case you've forgotten, we're supposed to go off and hunt for a unicorn. While you've been lolling about in here these past few days, I've been working like an Umbrian to get the equipment together. I've got the horses saddled and most of the gear stowed, everything except your stuff, so get yourself going."

"Has Diadra . . . ?"

"Oh yes. She won't protect you any longer. Even she's finally admitted that you're a malingering good-for-nothing." Martin dodged the pillow.

"Well," Jarrod retorted, sitting up, "doesn't a man get any privacy?"

"Precious little from now on, but if it'll get you up any faster . . ." and the slim figure in leather trousers and boots made for the door. "And don't keep me hanging about down there. We've only got sixteen days to get to Seaport."

Jarrod scrambled out of bed and went down the passageway to wash, realizing as he did so that, yet again, he had failed to Make the Day. He had not woken before dawn once since that night at the Place of Power and he wondered guiltily if he would ever get back into the proper habit.

There was no time for introspection as he dressed hurriedly and collected his things. He tied them in a spare cloak, strapped his quiver on and slung his bow. He looked around the little room and felt, with a quiet pang, that this might be the last time that he saw it. He squared his shoulders, took a deep breath, and closed the door resolutely on his boyhood.

Martin was standing with Greylock at the bottom of the stairs when he emerged, squinting, into the early light. A little way beyond them a groom held two big chestnuts. The saddlebags on both were full, as were the houndbags slung beneath them.

"The one on the right's yours," Martin said, nodding in that direction.

When Jarrod returned from strapping his bundle behind the saddle, Greylock had moved up a couple of steps so that he was level with him. His smile was warm and confident and it embraced them both.

"My dear children," he said. The deep voice was husky and he stopped to clear his throat. "I have no speech to speed you and I really don't think you need one. You have been trained as well as anyone can be for a mission as strange as this one and I, for one, am certain that you will succeed. Besides, you need not take the word of an old Mage. The verse said 'when,' not 'if.' I shall wait here impatiently for your return and for a sight of the storied beast. Until then, my brave young men," and he looked at Martin's close-cropped hair and smiled at her, "may Fortune bring you safe journeying."

They showed their palms to him and bowed before turning to the horses. The groom held their heads while they mounted. Then they turned in the saddle and waved to the Mage. He raised his right hand in return and held it aloft until they had turned the corner of the stables.

Jarrod had been a little unsteady on his feet, but the saddle felt comfortable beneath him and the rising sun warmed his shoulders as they skirted the camps and the castle.

Once past Stronta they broke into the league-devouring canter that these Royal Post horses were bred for, but although they had left the encampments well behind them, Jarrod still thought that he heard muttering. He shook his head and dismissed it.

"Really only sixteen days?" he called over.

"Yes. There's a merchantman, Isphardi of course, leaving for Belengar on the 36th. Greylock's arranged passage."

"Think we'll make it?"

"We have to," Martin replied across her shoulder. "Shouldn't be too difficult on these animals. They can do fifty miles a day. Besides, Greylock's got it fixed so that we can change horses at the Royal Relays if we get too far behind. Useful friend that Mage of yours."

"What's in the houndbags?" Jarrod asked.

"Bunglebirds."

"Oh, so that's what it is. I thought I was hearing things."

"Knowing you, you probably were." She clapped her heels to her horse's flanks and surged ahead amid indignant complaints from below. The birds kept up an intermittent fuss for miles before lapsing into occasional unintelligible mumbling.

On the second morning Jarrod came awake in cold and darkness with an edge of anxiety in him. It was blunted by relief as he realized why he had woken. The stars were out on high, but there was no nightmoon to guide him as he unwound himself and went looking for a stream in the dim light. Afterwards, he settled with his back toward Songuard where, when he was a child, he had thought that the sun slept. With joyful concentration he Made the Day for the first time in a sennight.

The trip continued pleasantly and companionably. Jarrod had had his doubts about the venture, bulking large among them the feeling that Martin and he would not get along. He still had doubts, but Martin was proving to be an easy travelling companion. There was, however, one moment of loss and one of awkwardness.

The first came the night they camped on the far side of the Caddis Mountains. Martin had turned in early, but Jarrod stayed up by the fire and looked through the branches of the orchard where they had stopped. He searched the upper slopes for the telltale gleam that would mark one of the tiny weather stations. There was a part of him that had always hankered to go and live, lofty and alone, up where only the scarlet fireblanket trees grew. To be able to practice Magic, with no one to drive him and no responsibility other than to shepherd the clouds and control the weather, seemed to him the most enviable of lives. Now he knew that the unlikely adventure that they were embarked on had taken him beyond the possibility of the contemplative life.

The second occurred while they were riding through the region of the great estates where lone manor houses sat atop distant and commanding knolls. Martin broke a long, companionable silence.

"Courtak?" she said speculatively. "Are you related to . . ."

"Yes," Jarrod cut her off.

"This is the area where the family estates are, isn't it?" she continued unperturbed.

"I suppose so," he replied grudgingly.

"Don't you know?"

"No."

"Aren't you even curious?"

"No, I'm not." He was curt.

"I would be," Martin said, but she let the matter drop.

Jarrod left the silence alone. He felt ungracious, but he had stopped thinking about his family a long time ago. His grandfather had never made any attempt at contact, had made no offer of assistance when his father had died. Nor had the old Duke claimed the boy after his mother, weakened by childbirth and the loss of her husband, had followed her third son to the grave. Jarrod's uncle, Duke now in his turn, never came to court and Jarrod had grown toward manhood feeling no kinship with the clan. Talk of them, however, made him irritable, a symptom of the unacknowledged hurt below.

These minor moments of disenchantment did not last long in the face of continual exercise and pleasant weather and the two rode peaceably through kina country until strange new birds began to wheel in the sky. Martin identified them excitedly as sea birds and soon the noisy air began to smell bitter. Jarrod heard distant thunder, though the sky was blue, and looked inquiringly at Martin. She nodded and grinned delightedly. By common consent, they turned off the road and urged the horses through the scrubby brush until they topped a sandy rise. They reined in then and sat staring. They looked at each other, their eyes alight, and they went galloping through the thicketed swale down to the sunbound sea.

Jarrod pulled his mount up at the water's edge and let it stand, head down and blowing, with its feet in white froth. He stood up in his stirrups and gazed out in awe. He had known that the Inland Sea was big, but his imagination had not come close to this expanse. His mind opened up in appreciation of the subtlety in the constantly changing sameness. He sought to find the pattern underlying it, but could not. His eyes widened and he ceased to blink. He felt his powers of perception dilate as he concentrated and he glimpsed a structure of staggering complexity. He reached out toward it, but it eluded him with contemptuous ease. Jarrod withdrew, blinked and sat back in the saddle, shaking his head.

"What in the world was that about? You didn't even seem to be breathing." Martin's voice intruded on his awareness.

"It's quite wonderful," he replied. "I can't get near it. It's so, so vast. It has dances I can't even catch. Incredible. Quite incredible."

"Thank you very much. I'm so glad I asked." Martin shook her head in her turn. "Now, if you've quite finished seagazing, d'you think we could find Seaport before the daymoon sets?" She turned her horse and kicked it into a gallop along the seaweed-strewn beach.

They surrendered their horses at the Relay, coached and dispatched a bunglebird, hired a sedan chair for their gear, bought a cage for the remaining bird and set out to find the ship. She was a disappointment. The peeling paint on the gently moving stern proclaimed her to be the *Steady Wench*. Underneath that it said *Belengar*. Both were in the remains of an ornate script that must have been difficult to read when the paint was fresh. When it came to the figurehead at the other end, one could have wished that the paint had aged a little more.

The *Steady Wench* was a tubby three-master made of well bowed coran planks. There was a raised deck in the stern and

another, smaller one in the bow. Between them, interrupted by
the masts, a line of hatches gaped. She was a good four rods in
length and to Jarrod she looked like a bluebottle caught in a web.
Lines lashed her to the dock and the organized chaos of her
rigging reached to the tops of the masts. She rolled and dipped
now in a futile effort to get free that made the footing of the
sailors on the gangplank precarious. Along the swaying file of
men a steady stream of boxes, sacks and bales was passing.
Once aboard, they disappeared into the dark maws of the hold.

The two youths stood and watched the busy swarming as the
last of the cargo was laded. They finally mustered up the courage
to run the gauntlet of the gangway, lugging their belongings, and
stood uncertainly, trying to stay out of the way. They lingered
uncomfortably at the taffrail until a weather-beaten man in a
stained cocked hat and a frayed swallow-tailed coat threaded his
way expertly down from the poop deck and introduced himself
as Mr. Alsond, the First Officer. He took them in hand, summoned a sailor to take their gear aft and escorted them to meet
Captain Travert.

The Captain stood before the six foot wheel that shifted lazily
and griplessly on the final swell of the tide and watched the
activities in front of him unswervingly. He was less than a foot
taller than his wheel and he made his First Officer look dapper.
His dark blue uniform was splotched more darkly still in places
and the gold of the untidy epaulets was tinged with green. He
was bull-necked and bareheaded, with a mat of curly, speckled
hair in want of washing, and both his jowls and his chins had a
two-day growth of white stubble. The small, brown eyes were
darkly undercrescented, but they missed nothing.

"Welcome aboard," he said without turning his head. "I was
afraid you would be late. We shall be sailing on the third tide
and, if we get favorable winds, we should make Belengar in ten
days. Mr. Alsond will show you to your cabin. You'll be
opposite me, so I hope you'll be quiet."

That was all he said and, after a brief and speechless wait, the
First Officer led them away to a tiny cabin below. It had two
bunks, one atop the other, a table and chair that were bolted to
the floor and all of their packages. There was no room to move.

The lone bunglebird talked plaintively to itself in the confines of its new abode.

Jarrod bent over to get in and stayed bent over. He was only half listening when Alsond said, "Our orders are that you're not to be bothered and you'll not be. Your food'll be served in here and you'll get the same grog ration as the crew. If there's anythin' you need, you'd best come to me. Oh, and I'd steer clear of the Captain if I was you; 'e's not what you'd call a social man. Tide'll be ont' turn soon so, if there's nowt else, I'll be to my duties."

"Just one thing, Sir," Jarrod said hesitantly. "Would it be possible to keep him out on deck?" He pointed to the unwontedly quiet bunglebird.

"We can lash the cage aft, but you'd best bring it back down if the weather gets dirty." He picked up the cage and, with a brisk nod, departed. Feathers floated in his wake.

The two wayfarers sat on the bottom bunk and watched the light coming through the porthole stipple the surfaces it touched. It still seemed dark and cramped after so many days in the open.

"That man's Arunic," Martin said. "I could tell from his accent. He sounds just like the people at our lodge. That's the way the Coast people talk." There was silence for a space and then she said irritably, "Do you think this floor will stop moving around so much when we get out of harbor?" She tugged at the neck of her jerkin. "It's so bleeding hot," she added testily. "How can people stand this. It's like living in an unsteady cucumber frame."

"It'll cool off when we get out to sea."

"Let's go back up on deck. I think I'll suffocate if I have to stay here much longer."

"Well, at least you can stand up in this place," Jarrod said as he maneuvered into a crouch. "By the time we get to Belengar, I'm going to have lumps all over my head. And I don't know how I'm going to fit into that." He pointed at the upper berth.

They made their way to the port side and found that the gangplank was gone. When Jarrod looked over the side he noticed that the dock had dropped a couple of feet since they had boarded. He turned and leaned against the rail, savoring the iodine tang of the day and the experience of being on his first ship. He looked across the deck and out at the harbor. His sight was filled with vessels, moored, tethered or under sail, more of them than he had ever thought possible. He drew a deep breath and felt his excitement rising as if it was controlled by the tide.

They watched as barefoot sailors moved nimbly around in the ratlines and the foolhardy few walked out along the top spars. Orders were bellowed, men ran, lines were cast off and the capstan crew pushed against their spokes and broke into an anchor-raising chanty. They crossed to the starboard side and saw the thick chain come dripping from the water until the anchor broke the surface and swung up with mud clinging to its flukes. Ropes were coiled on the deck and the men standing in the sky shook down the topmost sails. The *Steady Wench* turned slowly from the bollard-lined quay and took the top of the tide through bobbing lighters and barquentines. They passed ten-oared dories skedaddling across the chop and made the harbor mouth. Then the mole was behind her as she slid away on the ebb.

Martin soon went below, but Jarrod stayed to see the sails belly and fill as they tacked across the Sou'Westerly that whitecapped the long estuary. The roofs of Seaport grew smaller every time they heeled over and came about and, before too long, the outlines of the land began to smudge. It had faded away completely when Martin rejoined him. The tan that had taken her so long to acquire looked artificial and, despite the breeze, there were beads of perspiration on her brow.

"It won't stay still," was all she could get out before doubling up over the rail. She stayed hanging there for the next hour, swearing weakly at Jarrod's ineffectual efforts to help. At length, she allowed herself to be led back to the cabin and crawled into the lower bunk. She let Jarrod take her boots off, moaning gently through tight lips, but would suffer no further ministrations.

"This is humiliating," she said and turned to the wall and drew up her knees.

The following sennight was filled for Jarrod with new sensations and the old feeling of loneliness in the midst of men. He adapted easily to the constant and contrary motion and found it impossible to empathize with Martin's endless misery. He felt guilty that the nap of his compassion had worn too quickly to the threads, but he slept on deck as often as he could. Even the

bunglebird was better company. He had had romantic daydreams
of winning Marianna's love by rescuing her from peril and
nursing her back to health and enduring gratitude, but he found
that reality and his imagination had little in common.

He spent long hours instead staring at the endless vistas of
water, bewitched by the sea and its range of uncatchable facets.
The ship, which had seemed so big when he had first seen her,
had shrunk to insignificance in the folds of that benign lap. He
sat at the bowsprit's root through entire watches, staring out past
the eponymous wench, with the spray sheeting by on either side
of him. He liked the soft nights even better. Then the bow wave
danced with pale fire beneath the celestial rondo of unfamiliar
stars. On such nights it was easy to believe in unicorns and the
fey folk; but there were other nights to come that would be more
suited to the hobgoblins and afreets of childhood.

The wind quartered and then shifted again to oppose them
from the East. The ship tacked ever more broadly against it as it
brought in the clouds and hid the sun. The sea got up and the
Steady Wench pitched in response. The bunglebird was banished
below decks and Martin's precarious recovery was abruptly reversed. It had a different effect on Jarrod. When the bad weather
set in and stayed, it annoyed him. He had known, intellectually,
that the weather could not be managed so far from land and he
had automatically discounted the absence of the nightly croprains,
but he was not emotionally prepared for the willful unpredictabil-
ity of the rain squalls. The disobedience offended his sense of
order. He longed to bring the wind under his control, if only to
assuage his sense of insult, but he heeded Greylock's injunction.
The itch of temptation grew more severe as the storm mounted
and tossed the ship hither and thither, making her belie her
name.

Ropes were strung along the deck and Captain Travert spent
more and more time on the poop deck. The ship was no longer
insignificant: she was gallant and indomitable, but she was also
losing way. The water was constantly ugly now, molten slate
with a broken crust of white. It washed over the midships as the
figurehead dived down ever steeper slopes. A lone petrel flew in
windblown warning and the Captain, as if in acknowledgement,

put about and fled before the overtaking tempest, the jib his only canvas out.

The sea anchors were heaved overboard and, with the wind behind them, the motion was easier. It did nothing to lessen Martin's agonies. Jarrod, confined more often than not to the cabin, had become inured to them, but, on a morning indistinguishable from the night before, he was jolted out of his torpor by a sensation of intense unease. He thought for a moment that he had finally succumbed to sea sickness, but then he knew, though he had never experienced it before, that somewhere there was machinery working. He could hear the wind howling in the rigging, even here in his bunk, and, between that and the groan and creak of laboring timber, there was no way that he could untangle a new strand of sound.

He lay there trying to regulate his breathing so that he could stem the rising tide of discomfort. When he was satisfied with his control, he moved his mind through the ship in search of wrongness. In the bowels, he felt a beat that should not have been there and tried to encompass it. His mind's eye became cloudy and the patterns dissolved and ran. Jarrod pulled back in panic and resurfaced, gulping for air. He was consumed with a desire to know what had stopped him and it drove him out of the bunk and up onto the deck. He slitted his eyes against the wind and scanned it. It was awash and, above it, the naked rigging thrummed.

His need sent him clawing for a rope. He was drenched to the skin in seconds, but that was of no concern to him. He pulled his way, hand over hand, obeisant to the wind and battered by the waves that sluiced up over his knees. He crabbed past the forward hatches and flung himself at the fo'castle door. He fought the swirling, spume-freighted wind for control of it and gradually strained the thick wood open. He edged his way around it and the thwarted gale slammed the door behind him and knocked him to the floor.

"What's the matter then? My cabin not good enough for you?" Alsond reached down and helped him to his feet. "You all right, boy?" The second question was sharp as the man looked into his eyes. Jarrod ignored both the humor and the concern.

"Where are the machines?" His voice was hoarse with salt and urgency.

"Machines? The bilge pumps are workin', but that's all." He looked up at the Paladinian suspiciously. "What's that to you?"

"What do they do?" He forced his breathing to be deep and even and his voice and control had returned.

"Do? They keep us afloat, that's what they do." There was a look of growing speculation on Alsond's face. "Feel 'em, do you?" he asked.

"Yes," Jarrod admitted grudgingly.

"Only people I ever 'eard of as does that are wizards. You a wizard, boy?" They were held in close together by the confines of the narrow passage and Jarrod began to feel trapped. The habit of truth made his admission automatic.

"I'm only an Apprentice," he said defensively.

"An Apprentice, huh? Can you do that weather control stuff?"

"We all can." Jarrod was stung by his tone.

"You any good at it?" Jarrod felt the tension building.

"I passed all the tests," he said stiffly.

"Then why didn't you say so before?" The query was couched in a barely suppressed shout and Jarrod felt his own anger mounting in response.

"I am not allowed to." His tone was cold.

"Whadda you mean, you're not allowed to?" The Arunic accent was thickening.

"The Mage of Paladine forbad me," Jarrod retorted.

"Oh, 'e did, did 'e?" Alsond's control, sapped by the storm and lack of sleep, was eroding fast. "Well, let me tell you somethin', young man, that Motherless Mage of yorn isn't goin' to drown and you are, along of the rest of us." He crowded Jarrod back against the wall. "What are you goin' to do about it?" A hand reached out and grabbed the front of his sodden jacket and Alsond thrust a demanding face up at him.

"Let go of me." The words were spoken very softly and each was separately spaced. Water dripped from Jarrod and pooled around his feet, but there was something about him that made the First Officer let go and take a step back. Jarrod shook himself and droplets flew about. "That's better." He was rejoicing inwardly at the success of his first use of the Voice. "All right,

I'll try, but I can't do it with all those machines on.'' Now that his adrenalin level had dropped, the machines were a hurtful persistence in his flesh once more.

"How long is this goin' to take?" Alsond's response to authority was immediate.

"I don't know. It's not exactly easy to concentrate out there. I'll need at least an hour to prepare. I'll need as much quiet as I can get, so I'd better use the Captain's cabin."

"You'd better do what?" The seaman was flabbergasted. "You can't do that."

"Look," said Jarrod, with a patience he did not feel, "I don't know if I can do you any good at all. I can't control the sea, I already know that, but I might be able to do something about the wind. I'm prepared to try, but if you want this thing done at all, you'll do it my way."

"Well," Alsond said, his anger drained by the change in the young man in front of him, "I'll have to ask the Captain. Why don't we put you in the mess until I get back. You look as if you could do with a shot of grog."

Jarrod smiled for the first time in a long while. "You don't know how badly I regret having to turn that offer down, but if I'm to do Magic soon, I don't dare. If the Captain says no and those things have to stay on," he added in a burst of candor, "you'll probably have to feed me a lot of that stuff." Jarrod followed him gratefully through a door and sank down on one of the benches.

What he felt, more than anything else, was relief. He was going to be able to express himself again. Magic was, when all was weighed and sifted, what he had been born to do. He had not realized until that moment how irksome the ban had been. His hand had been forced and he felt free to summon any help he could reach. He settled his shoulders comfortably and went within himself. When he reemerged, the Captain and the First Officer were standing and staring at him with a fascination that was touched with fear.

Jarrod rose with lithe assurance, the dignity of his calling upon him. There was no trace of the adolescent who was not quite comfortable in his own skin, and neither of the men who faced him could bring themselves to speak. It was Jarrod's first encounter with the superstition that clings to the Talented among those who have few dealings with them.

"Well?" he demanded, more brusquely than he had intended. The Captain stood his ground. He had lost considerable weight during his vigils and his face sagged with the privation.

"If your honor would consent, I'd be glad to surrender my cabin. I'm afraid we'll be driven onto the rocks if this keeps up. To tell you the truth," he said with a shrug of frustration, "I'm not even sure where we are."

"I'll do my best," Jarrod said gently, "but I'll need your help. The pumps will have to be shut off from the time I go into your cabin until I'm finished with the spell. That I'll have to do on deck. I'll need some oilskins and someone's going to have to tie me to the mainmast when I'm ready. Other than that, I want to be left completely alone."

"Anything you want." The Captain gave another weary shrug. "And who knows? it might even do some good."

Jarrod dried and changed in the Captain's cabin. The last of his jumpiness had gone, which told him that the machines had been silenced. He chewed some soggy timothy leaves from his pack and blocked out the noises around him before he allowed the simple to take him into relaxation and recall. He came alert again an hour later, donned the oilskins and, bracing himself against the walls, made his way to the door at the bottom of the brief companionway.

The noise of the wind took him by surprise, so, too, did a sudden rush of water down the stairs as the ship wallowed up out of a trough. He emerged on deck in time to see the mizzenmast bend to an impossible angle and then split and splinter with a sound like the cry of a coursed stag as it founders. Jarrod watched it fall and, even though it seemed aimed at him by the hurricane, felt only the detachment that his preparations had induced. The mast, festooned with a writhe of rigging, crashed through the rail to his right, snapping the wood like kindling. Sailors poured onto the treacherous deck and swarmed over it, hacking away with axes and knives. Fast as they were, the weather was quicker and the ship was slewed round to port, threatening to go broadside on.

To watching eyes, and there were eyes that watched, the

young Magician appeared quite unconcerned as he picked his way over the debris toward the bow. He clung to wood or rope whenever the sea washed in, turning his head to catch a breath. His ears ached and his eyes stung, but he pulled himself onward until someone shook him by the shoulder. He saw the First Officer's lips move as he bent toward him, but the wind tore the words away.

He leaned down to the man's ear and screamed, "Tie me to the mast!" He screamed again until he saw Alsond nod. An unanticipated wave hurled them to their knees. When it had run off into the scuppers, Jarrod crawled to the center of the deck and clung to the mainmast until the First Officer reappeared with two men and a coil of rope. He levered himself erect and turned his back to the quivering trunk. He held his arms above his head so as not to impede them and noticed that, at some point, it had started to rain. It made no difference. His detachment had held. He waited until the men had worked their way out of sight and then he launched into the prologue of the Storm Slayer.

He foraged out, but the deck beneath his feet plunged and bucked at his concentration, testing his control. The gale attacked him malevolently, drenching him anew, fishwifing in his ears and denying him the sound of his own voice. He squeezed his eyelids together in denial, but the storm would not be gainsaid. It ripped the words from his lips and tore them to pieces. It jammed his mouth open and probed for his heart. It shattered his concentration and told him that he would die; that he was too puny for this task. It was no mere collection of conjured thunderheads and he was no more than a classroom braggart who had the hubris to think that he could face down Nature. There were gods in the sea and they were angry at his arrogance.

He clung grimly to the core of himself, fighting off the threatened violation. A wave broke over the rail and wrenched at his body. He gasped and choked on the brine and his skin tremored. The words of the incantation resumed as his head went up in defiance and the sonorities of the trochees carried him on and back into control. He stilled his skin and chanted lower to preserve his voice. No point in trying to outshout the wind. He looked up into the clouds and perceived the roiling patterns behind them. He generated spirals of heat at the weak points in the pathway of the tempest and the deck receded from his consciousness. He was caught in the swirl of vapors and the ragged banners of clouds that whipped past his inner eye.

All that he was able to do at first was to deflect the gusts and shield the *Steady Wench*'s stern. An unnatural stillness descended on the vessel and, alone in all that wavering space, she was sacrosanct and no wind touched her. She had momentum still and the marching waters kept her reeling Westward as Jarrod strained at his bonds, chest heaving, hands reaching and splayed out. The words were a torrent now and they helped to enlarge his comprehension.

He went looking for the center of the turmoil and passed through a region of sky-supporting water spouts. He knocked them down, one by one, and watched the heaps of water ripple out as they subsided. His aroused capabilities ranged on and found the area where the sun beat the surface into gold leaf and sucked the moisture up. He pushed back clouds to cut off that flow and looked on as the still center collapsed. Moving swiftly then, a dervish in full transport, he broke the vast circle of the storm.

There was one last verse to go and he felt himself spinning out too finely, tiring too fast. The hands stopped clutching at the sky, their task accomplished, and he felt the onset of euphoria. He threw a desperate thought toward the immeasurably distant Place of Power, but it was deaf to him. He struggled to begin that last verse and, slowly, the first line came. The essence of him went into the words and he tried to slow down the waves, to smooth their crests and valleys. The sea would not be contained and mocked him as it continued to play ever-shifting, angry games. It gave and then swelled again a moment later, spreading him like scud on inclines without number.

He had no voice left for combat and his throat was too sore to swallow. The ropes had been tightened by the water and bit cruelly into his sides in a sadistic embrace, but he croaked against pain to the incantation's end. Waves of rapture replaced the wet and cold as they curled over him and sustained him in an oblivion of whispered babbling. His body sagged against the ropes.

The sea calmed itself in its own good time, but Jarrod was not aware of it, nor of the ship's turning. His face came back from the middle age that the Magic had imposed on it as the *Steady Wench* limped painfully toward home. It was Jarrod who lay in the bottom bunk now and Martin who tended him. The bunglebird went back on deck, but it was a sennight before Jarrod followed it.

He felt like paper as he gingerly paced the deck and examined the jury-rigged mast and the patchwork repair of canvas that passed for sails. Deckhands stopped and watched him and murmured together after he had gone by. He did not stay out long the first day, but his strength built as they neared their destination and his airings became longer. Martin would contrive to be on deck at the same time, though she was careful not to intrude unless he asked to be accompanied. He was grateful for her concern and touched by it.

The First Officer felt no such reticence and walked with Jarrod any time that he was not in command of the poop deck. By tacit agreement, there was no discussion of the storm nor of Jarrod's part in quieting it. Finally, Alsond backed into the subject the day before they were due to reach port.

"Where'll the two of you be stayin', may I ask?"

"Well," Jarrod answered companionably, "we're supposed to meet a guide at an inn called The Golden Knave, but I don't know whether he'll have stayed around."

"Doan 'ee worry. If 'e isn't there I'll find you someone good. Where you bound, then?"

"We, er, we want to do some climbing in the Saradondas, on the Songuard side."

"And what 'ud a Magician of your powers be doin' in the Saradondas or oughtn't I to ask?" Alsond cocked an enquiring eyebrow in Jarrod's direction as they reached the rail and turned.

"Look, forget I'm a Magician, will you? I told you that I wasn't supposed to do any Magic on this trip. Besides, all I did was a little weather control." He moved off again, awkwardness in his gait. Alsond was at his side on the instant and reached out and swung him around. He looked up at the younger man with intensity.

"My friend, I know the sea and I know the difference 'tween a 'urricane and a bad blow. You doan 'ave to be modest around me. Say what you like, that was one Mother of a job and if t'weren't for you, I'd not be 'ere.'' His eyes bore in as if to underline his sincerity.

Jarrod smiled down at him. "Thank you for that. I appreciate it." They resumed their pacing and, as if liberated by the broaching, a sailor rubbed his fingers lightly on Jarrod's sleeve as he passed.

"I don't think I'll ever get used to that," he said nervously. "Did I flinch?"

Alsond laughed at the question. "No. You were good, but t'weren't gratitude, you know. We sailors are a superstitious lot and you're the best bit of luck we've 'ad. You can't blame us for 'opin' some of it might rub off.''

"You know it doesn't work like that." Jarrod was stern in his surprise.

" 'Course we do. But strange things happen, like your bein' on board when we needed you." He grinned wickedly to seal off the argument.

Jarrod chuckled and, nodding toward the wheel, said, "Well, anyway, there's one sailor who doesn't want to touch me."

"Oh, you mustn't mind the Captain. It's not that 'e's not grateful, it's just that 'e's a bloody good seaman and it goes 'ard for 'im to thank another for savin' 'is ship. Especially, you'll forgive me, one that's only just begun to shave."

"There's nothing that he could have done about the storm. It wasn't his fault," Jarrod expostulated through Alsond's smile.

" 'Course not, but logic and pride are only distantly related. You'd best remember that alongside your spells." Jarrod shook his head ruefully in reply. He hadn't stayed on his pedestal for long.

CHAPTER VIII

BELENGAR THE BEAUTIFUL, THE WORLD'S MARKETPLACE, THE
Great Whore of the South, Queen of the Nightwinds and City of
the Gods. She had many names in every tongue. Belengar was
very old and all the songs that have survived say that she was
founded by Errathuel when first he came from the Far Side. It
was a place of tall buildings, built high, still, against the fear that
one day the enemy atmosphere might seep back down to the
Inland Sea. The crooked streets were bracketed in balconies,
some stone, some iron, all intricate, that were hung with pots of
ferns and baskets of bright flowers.

There were sudden parks and there were cloistered plazas
surrounding old, plumey, fronded trees, all made green by water. There was water everywhere. It flowed in fountains at the
center of squares and at the corners of streets. It gurgled under
narrow bridges and into ornamental lake gardens. It fell down
courtyard waterfalls and chuckled down the gutters of the streets.
It swept the refuse toward the barges that would bear it out into
the quick pull of the tides.

That shops and markets should abound in a city given, soul
deep, to the making of money was not surprising, but for reli-
gion to thrive as richly was. The population was a mixture of all
lands and all cultures whose ancestors had accumulated there over
the centuries. Men came there still in search of fortune and they
had a wonderous variety of customs, cuisines and deities to

100

choose from. There was not a tongue or dialect that someone did not speak, and printed books in many languages were freely sold from stalls.

Whole quarters were given over to particular enterprises, the most beautiful of which was the Exotic Bird Mart, but the best known throughout Strand was undoubtedly the Old Quarter. It was bounded on one side by the wall of Errathuel's Estate, a ribbon fifteen cubits high with but one, resplendent gateway. In the small streets that scurried from it, a legion of ladies of negotiable virtue, their eyes made hot by concupiscence and kohl, paraded. The cramped buildings, ancient as the trade they housed, were combs of single rooms, each preoccupied with a bed.

Jarrod stood by the taffrail, isolated amid the hurly of the deck, and stared at the approaching city. He had been fascinated by the sights and sounds of the earlier maritime center, but now it seemed limited and provincial. There were more masts here than there were trees in the royal forest. It seemed to him, as they were warped to anchorage past ship after ship, that there was a whole city afloat. It was a world of slim, wooden spires, with flying buttresses of hemp, connected to the shore by the plying of sharp-prowed barges bearing a myriad of cargoes.

Martin and he bade farewell to the still taciturn Travert and were ferried toward the busy quays that fringed the city like a dust ruffle protecting a creation of robust allure. Behind them, Belengar lay waiting to welcome them as it welcomed all who came to her. If you had a need, she would fill it, providing you had the price and harmed no one. The metropolis appealed to and assaulted all the senses simultaneously. The eye was dazzled by the profusion of peoples and things and by the endlessly changing light. It dripped off the blades of the oars, dappled the approaching cobblestones and fractured from window panes. It was as bold and fickle as a prostitute.

Jarrod's sense of smell struggled to identify the wind-borne scents, to catalog and remember before they diminished into a catch-all aroma of spices and excitement. His ears gave up well before they reached land. Seabirds cried, orders floated in from everywhere in incoherent snatches, wavelets slapped at everything they could reach and Martin kept talking about standing on something that did not move.

The two of them were the first up the iron ladder to the wharf and took two strides away from it before they turned and clung to each other. Martin's face was a study in mute incomprehension, but Jarrod was too busy trying to get his balance to notice. The First Officer and the shore detail had followed yarely with their baggage and were roaring with laughter at the swaying couple and their staggering dance.

"Welcome to Belengar," Alsond said, wiping his eyes. "If it's any consolation, we all take a while to get our land legs back. Try walkin' around a bit while we scare up some chairs to get this stuff to the inn." He walked with them until they had regained a precarious measure of control.

"Tell you what, my brave young friends, the men and I, we've bin thinkin'. 'Bout how we could best say thank you. And we reckon the least we could do is give you a proper introduction to our favorite port; the only place on land a body could abide. Right men?" The crew chorussed assent, but further revelation was postponed by the arrival of the first of the sedans.

They took a room and the host told them that a man had been coming by every day looking for them.

"D'you know 'is name?" Alsond asked.

"Sandroz," said Martin.

"Sandroz? Short feller? Songean?"

"We don't know what he looks like," she replied, "but he's supposed to be Songean."

"Am Songean," said a deep voice from behind them. The figure by the door nodded to Alsond as they turned. "Afternoon Thession." He looked up at the taller of the two young men. "Am Sandroz. You are much late." The tone was impartial.

"Thank you for waiting for us. We just got in. I'm Martin Gwyndryth and this is Jarrod Courtak. I gather you already know Mr. Alsond." Sandroz scanned her methodically and Martin withstood the scrutiny in even silence.

"Practiced," was all that he said.

"I might 'a known it'ud be you they were goin' to meet. Makes sense I suppose." Alsond turned to the pair and said, "This stunted specimen is married to our Captain's sister. They've a special word for it in Songean. They always do when it comes to relationships. As you can tell, she has to do the talkin' for all three of 'em.'' He smiled at the newcomer good-naturedly. ''We're gonna take the boys out on the town tonight, starting with dinner at Katie's. You wanna come along?''

Sandroz regarded him solemnly. ''You will make them drunk. We have much to do. Far to go. I must come.''

''Good. That's settled then. Why doan you bring 'em over and we'll meet you there. Round nine, say?'' Sandroz nodded and looked over his new charges.

''I show you room. You sleep. It will be long night. Tomorrow we buy horses.'' He stooped and picked up the bunglebird cage. ''We take this?''

''No,'' Martin replied before Jarrod had a chance to open his mouth, ''we'll take him to the roof and send him off. They must be worried about us back home. They expected to hear from us well before this.''

''Good.'' Sandroz marched to the stairway with the unprotesting bird and waited while they made their goodbyes and gathered their belongings. They were still wavering on their feet as they followed him and the sturdy back seemed a silent reproach for their tardiness and their weakness.

Jarrod's mind was racing, but he waited until Sandroz had left them alone before he blurted, ''We can't go out on the town like that.''

''Whyever not?''

''We just can't, that's all.''

''I don't think that's much of an answer.'' Martin was puzzled and then enlightenment spread across her face with an accompanying smile. ''You think they're going to take us to the Old Quarter, don't you? Well, of course they're going to take us to the Old Quarter.''

''But you can't go in there.'' Jarrod's eyes had widened.

''And why, pray tell, can I not go in there?'' There was malice in the question and it flustered him.

''Well, because it wouldn't be right,'' he said uncomfortably. ''It just wouldn't be, er, wouldn't be right.''

''Because I'm a girl?'' she asked, enjoying his discomfort.

''Well, er, well yes.''

"You simple-minded ninny, can't you see that's precisely why I have to go tonight?" She was mockingly impatient with him. "I mean, whenever am I going to get the chance to see whatever it is that gets you men into such a fever, again? Besides, I thought you were supposed to be thinking of me as a boy?" She caught him off guard and he was furious with himself for blushing.

"I do, most of the time. You're certainly bossy enough to be one. What are you going to do if we end up in a brothel?"

"If?" She snorted derisively. "When." She gave him an evil little grin. "I shall let them all think I'm too young. After all," and she broke into a high trill, "my voice hasn't broken yet, has it? And you, you great big man you, you're going to have to control yourself."

Jarrod felt himself blushing again and tried, unsuccessfully, to think of something clever to say while Martin laughed. I bet she'd just love it if I did go. It would give her a better shot at the unicorn, he thought ungenerously as they unpacked. He simmered with resentment and, to get out of the room more than anything else, he took the bunglebird to the roof. He coached it, launched it and watched as it made untidy circles in the hot sunshine before lumbering away inland. He wondered what he was going to say to Alsond when the time came. He felt disparagingly toward Martin, mostly because he knew she was right, but he didn't have to wait long to get his own back.

When it was time to get ready, she went off down the hall in search of a hot bath and returned in ill-concealed dudgeon.

"What's the matter?" Jarrod looked up as the door slammed. "No bath?"

"Oh yes. Two, as a matter of fact. One for men and one for women. And d'you know what?"

"What?" Jarrod asked, as guilelessly as he could.

"I can't go into the women's with these clothes on and I can't go into the men's without them."

"Yes, I see. You've got a problem, haven't you? What are you going to do about it?"

"Do? Do? Nothing, you flea-bitten oaf. What can I do? And I'll thank you to stop snickering. It isn't funny. There are times," Martin said witheringly, "when you behave like a juvenile brat. And speaking of that, go and shave off that revolting fuzz. It looks absurd on you."

Jarrod said nothing, but he was still smiling broadly as he dug out his shaving gear and slung a towel over his shoulder. He turned at the door and said, "Don't worry, I'll fix it about your bath."

"And just how do you propose to do that?"

"Simple. I'll just tell the host to send up a tub of hot water. I'll tell him you're still too young and shy to take your clothes off around grown-up, naked men." He ducked out as a hairbrush came clattering and strolled down the corridor whistling.

They were both clean, though rumpled, and restored to good spirits by the time Sandroz came to get them. They showed their palms in greeting and took stock of him as they accompanied him down. He was a light brown man, both in hair and skin, although his round eyes were black. They both knew instinctively that he would be able to make himself invisible against a dry hillside. His face came down to a sharp chin and the tanned skin was weathered. There were lines around the eyes and a delta of tiny, broken blood vessels that dressed the cheeks.

The neck was short, thick and corded and the shoulders wide and knotted. He wore a sleeveless jerkin that revealed arms that seemed too thin for those shoulders. The veins and the muscles were clearly drawn. He was deep of chest, which contrasted with the small waist. The admixture of delicacy and mass was repeated in the well developed legs, arched by years in the saddle, that tapered to a small pair of feet. He, in turn, had looked them over. "You'll be hot," was all he said.

The daymoon was still up as they emerged onto the crowded street and the ancient patina of the buildings was washed with a rosy light that made the blemishes of age less visible. They were fading courtesans enhanced by evening, but to Jarrod, as his eyes strained upward toward unexpected steeples and the grace notes that adorned the cramped buildings, they were beautiful. The city was, for him, every bit as magical a place as Celador.

The entire population seemed to have taken to the streets and was strolling easily along in the soft air. There were no chairs, no carts, neither carriages nor horses to be seen. There was nothing but hundreds of carefree people, seemingly without even a hurried purpose, whiling away the dusky hour. Music drifted out of doorways, children sat or stood on balconies and looked down on all the heads, taller for once than all the rest. Women leaned from windows, their silk headshawls glowing in the warm light. Though neither of the visitors entirely trusted their balance, they were both in fine humor as they reached their destination and ducked inside, leaving the linklighter to his daily task.

If the street outside had been filled to the jostle, Katie's was an overcrowded uproar. One wall was a pocketed glitter of spit fires and ovens, veiled now and then like the local ladies in gossamer smoke. Birds of every size were being turned with mesmerizing regularity. Sweating girls, in long skirts that discouraged pinching, moved between the long tables carrying jugs and platters, loaves of bread and pitchers of wine. As the trio wove their way down the room in search of the complement from the *Steady Wench*, the noise seized their ears and blanketed their minds. The task seemed impossible until a sailor appeared at Sandroz' elbow and towed him into a comparative backwater, an unexpected rectangle in the right-hand wall.

"Best table in the house, courtesy of Katie and thanks to our good friend, Ratlines Chief Escordy Jassen." Alsond gestured with formality and a winking pewter flagon toward a towheaded young man. "Doan let 'im fool you," he continued, "Essy's looked the same for the sixteen year I've bin servin' on the Wench and 'e wasn't no cabin boy then, neither." There was a touch of unexpected spite that accompanied the words. "I knew I could count on you to be punctual, so I ordered for us all. You know 'ow long it can take 'ere," this to Sandroz, "but the Mother knows the food's worth the wait. Come on," he said, gesturing with his free hand, "sit you down."

"Your order will be good," Sandroz acknowledged as he wedged himself in.

Jarrod eased himself down onto the backless bench on one side of the First Officer while Martin sat on the other. He found that he could look out into the main room as if a players' frame had been set up to draw the eye to the entertainment.

There was little time for observation, as wenches, no less sturdy than the figurehead they had but so lately quitted, served a cool, spiced wine, whose dark red hue looked black in the light of the candlelamps. Jarrod sipped cautiously and found that he liked it. He was embarking on a decent draught when Alsond rose into the growing conviviality, forcing his benchmates to shuffle back.

"Men," his voice was in fine quarterdeck form and carried easily over the din, "afore we gets distracted by the first good food we've seen in a long time," he bowed in the direction of a squinny-eyed redhead who had tended the galley and the rest laughed. "And afore we get too drunk to remember . . ." He paused to let the comments die. "I'd like to propose a toast. I'd always thought of Magic as bein' kinda quaint. It works o'course, but it's a bit old fashioned, not too efficient. Hey, I'm sorry Jarrod, no disrespect, but that's what the rest of the world thinks. Well, there's those of us 'ere tonight as can swear that it works just fine when it's in the right 'ands." He waited for agreement and applause. "The *Steady Wench* got lucky when it took an old fashioned Magician aboard, even if 'e doesn't 'ave to shave but once a month." The laughter came easily. "If it weren't for 'im, we'd none of us be 'ere. So, gents, I give you Jarrod Courtak, the most masterful Apprentice Magician there ever was." He reached down and hoisted his cup and, to Jarrod's embarrassment, they all stood and drank. He got up after a beat and raised his wine to them and was left standing when they all resumed their seats.

"Thank you, thank you all. I've never done anything quite like that before and, er, and I'm glad it worked." He was surprised by the laughter. "No really," he said, "I was, er, I was very scared at a couple of points. It was really difficult to submerge myself . . ." he was interrupted by laughter again and looked around grinning. "I'm just glad we all got out of it all right. And we wouldn't have, not without the lot of you. You did all the really hard work. But, er, but thank you very much." He sat down abruptly. The party cheered and raised their cups again and the evening was off.

Jarrod was not walking entirely straight when they regained the street, but he felt marvellous and he put it down to his sea legs. He stared voraciously around him, imprinting visions on his memory. It was all so wonderfully new and different. Night was well fallen and the flaring links cast hearth-like shadows over walls, wet gutters and cobblestones. If the nightmoon was out, he could not detect it and, as they passed the mouths of impenetrably dark alleyways, he was glad of the cheerful company. The streets had emptied while they ate, though there were passers-by enough abroad, and tales of footpads and lurking cutpurses flashed through his mind. They found no lasting purchase there.

Alsond linked an arm through his and wheeled him into another street with far fewer people and only intermittent linklight.

"Where are we going?" Jarrod asked, although he knew the answer.

"Thought we oughta end the evenin' in the Old Quarter," the other replied, looking back to see if the rest of the party had negotiated the turn. Some of them had started to sing a dirty chanty and Jarrod guessed that Martin would be straining to catch the words.

"Yes," Alsond continued, "I thought we oughta show you and young Martin some of the local sights and then we'll end up at Lucinda's. She runs a good, honest, clean house and we can get you taken care of properly, eh lad? Our treat."

Jarrod felt a determined nudge in the ribs and smiled inanely back. He did not want to lose face, now more than ever, in front of these friends of his and he couldn't think of a good reason for crying off. He fretted briefly and then, unable to sustain concentrated worry, decided to deal with the problem when it arose. He'd think of something.

The streets were narrow and dim and the tall houses rose up steeply to shut out the stars. To either side were tiny shops, their doors and windows barred and shuttered. There were ceramic plaques fastened to the walls at some of the street corners, each with a name and a small painting, none of them legible. Jarrod had lost all sense of direction and was content to let Alsond steer him.

They crossed a small square and plunged down yet another curving ravine. The gutters had no water running down them here and there was a feeling of decay and of a past that would never be a future. There were peeling handbills on the walls and refuse on the pavement. There were almost no shops, but, instead, the darkness was punctuated by the lamplit glow of cavelike drinking places. The singing of the men behind them was not the only music to push against the heaviness of the night. There were occasional drunks and dogs slunk from doorway to doorway.

Yet another corner was turned and there the young man stopped and gaped. The rest of the group, perforce, came to a crowded halt and the singing died away as they all looked into the very large plaza they had reached. They spread out under cloistered arches and stared up at the lighted building that dominated the area.

In style it was not unlike the Great Hall at Celador, save that it seemed to be made almost entirely of colored glass. The surrounding stone was a mere fretwork to encase the black-rimmed jewels. Down its entire length, the night sky was interrupted by a series of delicate pinnacles and it was blotted out entirely by the twin belfries that rose on either side of the massive doorway. Above the carved lintel of the monumental bronze doors, there bloomed a large, circular window, patterned strongly, yet exquisitely. The lights within set it glowing.

"It's the most beautiful thing I've ever seen. What is it?"

"Yeah, she's a beauty all right. That's the Church of the Mother. Biggest one in the world, outside of Umbria."

"It's quite extraordinary."

"That it is. Caused a lot of trouble when they built it. They tore down a great chunk of the Old Quarter and that didn't sit too well with a lot of folk. Nothin' they could do about it, though. The Church 'ad bought the land fair and square. Got some support from local people too, those that thought the Quarter was 'an unspeakable den of iniquity that should be swept into the sea.' Anyway, I think it was worth it. I'm no Maternite, mind, but I likes to come 'ere of a night and look at 'er."

"Only reason you come 'ere is 'cause it's on the way to the brothels and you knows it!" The interruption came from behind them and they moved on in laughter.

The good people who had hoped that the presence of the Church might reform the neighborhood would have been shocked to discover, had they overcome rectitude sufficiently to have penetrated this deep, that the shadows of that mighty edifice cloaked the infamous Porbel district. There, men and women satisfied a wide variety of needs, unhindered by the Church and unhampered by the law.

Almost immediately outside the square the women appeared, clothed in the nothingness of sheer silk, their eyes quizzical or demanding, but always decorated. They were stationed, like so many galleys riding at anchor, at intervals of twenty paces. They carried themselves with pride and eyed the passing men as candidly as they were scrutinized and, though the eyes promised much, not a word was spoken. They came in all shapes and shades. Some had elaborate hairdos, others the kind of simplicity that takes high art to achieve. Jarrod did his best not to goggle and Martin wore the nonchalant air of a connoisseur. She fooled no one.

"Ever seen anythin' like this, lads?"

"Never," Jarrod said fervently. Martin's expression was unreadable in the nocturnal gloom, but her eyes were wide. She shook her head, but whether in amazement or denial was impossible to determine.

"You can 'ave anyone you like," Alsond said, "but I'd recommend waitin' 'til we get to Lucinda's. You gotta be a mite careful with the girls on the street. You'd be surprised 'ow they look, some of 'em, when you get 'em near a lantern and you can't be certain they're not poxed. For meself, I've no wish to wake up at sea and find as I've a dose."

"Oh, don't worry, I'm quite happy to look," Jarrod replied. "Good heavens," and he pointed wordlessly to a lighted window up ahead. It had three clear, wide panes of glass that ran up almost eight feet, separated by thin slats of wood. Behind them sat a beautiful woman on an ivorywood chair. The deep mocha richness of her skin was enhanced by the wood as she sat like a burnt offering to the gods of lust. There was a row of small lamps across the window's front and all the rest was a deep, red velvet. It was as if the seated figure were an artifact brought out for inspection. She leaned forward slightly as they drew level, a small smile animated the lips, and she beckoned sinuously as Martin and Jarrod stopped to stare.

"Come on," Alsond said, tugging at Jarrod's arm. "There are more of those further on and you should see some of the settings the girls come up with. Very elaborate some of 'em; twisty too."

"And I thought the Exotic Bird Mart was the place to see," Martin said, finding her voice.

"Well, in a manner of speakin', that's just what you are doin'."

Eyes agape, they made their way through the inconsistent streets until the First Officer stopped at a doorway covered with iron grillwork and tugged at a bellpull.

"This, in case you 'aven't guessed it, is Lucinda's," he said as the muffled pealing died away. He draped a convivial arm about both their shoulders and, ignoring the comments around them, continued. "Really fine woman is Lucinda. Keeps the best 'ouse in the Quarter."

As if on cue, the door swung open, spilling a rectangle of light over them, and there stood a woman, aureoled.

"Why, Thess, what a pleasure to see you again." Jarrod couldn't make out her features because the light was behind her, but the rounded excellence of her figure was quite apparent. "And I'm delighted to see that you've brought paying customers with you. Come in, gentlemen, come in. Friends of Mr. Alsond's are friends of mine." She stood aside and made a sweeping gesture.

Once inside, and when his eyes had adjusted to the lamplight, Jarrod saw that she was an attractive, open-faced woman who looked to be in her thirties. Her gown was cut low and left her arms and shoulders bare. The blond hair was tricked into curling intricacies and the large, blue eyes had a knowing and mischievous directness.

"Lucinda, my lovely," Alsond said, putting a possessive arm around her waist, "time spent away from you is always too long."

"La, Sir," the black lashes fluttered briefly, "you are too kind, and if I know you, that means you want something." They smiled warmly at each other.

"Smart girl. You're quite right. I've a special favor to ask of you tonight."

"Not if it'll hurt my girls." The tone was firm.

"Come on, love. You know me better than that. No, it's just that I've a couple of lads with me who, 'ow shall I put this? Who've never 'ad a chance to perfect the social arts."

The immaculately coiffed head swung. "These two, I'll warrant." She smiled at them. "They're certainly a handsome enough pair. Two of my girls get lucky tonight. Gentlemen," she said to the rest of the group, "my parlor is just through that curtain and there are some very lonely young ladies waiting. Now, my dears," she said, turning her attention back to them, "the first time is always the most important one. You're lucky that Thess brought you here. There's nothing for you to be afraid about and I guarantee you'll like the girls. So come along with me, my dears, and tell me which one interests you the most."

"Excuse me, Madame," Martin broke in, "Mr. Alsond is very kind and, er, thoughtful, but I'm afraid he's being a little premature. I mean, he thinks I'm, er, more precocious than I am."

"Just as you like, my dear," Lucinda said with a pleasant smile. "There's no need to rush things. Just be sure to come back again and see us when you're ready. Why don't we all go into the parlor and you can wait for your friends there.

She took Alsond's arm and led the way through the curtain into an opulent room. It was thickly carpeted and there was silk on the walls and on the ceiling. There was a subdued brocade on the chairs and sofas on which the girls sat. Some talked softly among themselves and some had paired off with men from the *Steady Wench*. Martin took herself over to a sofa at the edge of the room and sat to watch, while Jarrod groped through the remnants of the evening's wine for a good excuse.

"Let's go and sit over there," Lucinda said to the two remaining men, indicating a group of chairs around a low table. "We'll have a glass of wine while our young friend—by the way, my dear, what's your name?"

"Jarrod Courtak, ma'am," he mumbled.

"Jarrod? Well, Jarrod, my dear, you take your time and have a good look round. If you see someone you like, I'll ask her to join us for a drink. Oh, and as usual, my sweet," she said, turning to Alsond, "if there's anyone you'd rather for tonight, the same applies." Alsond leaned over and caressed her cheek.

"If you say that once more," he said quietly and tenderly, "I'll get very angry with you. You know bloody well there's no one 'ere, or anywhere else for that matter, that I'd rather be with.'' They smiled into each other's eyes and she reached over and squeezed his hand.

Jarrod decided to pretend to get ill when his eye was caught by a girl who couldn't have been much more than his age and who looked completely out of place. She had long, flowing brown hair and shy, blue eyes whose entreaty was echoed by the hesitant smile.

"My dear," Lucinda's voice pulled him away, "I think you've got excellent taste. Samanthina's quite lovely and she's only just come to us." She beckoned to the girl and, before he was able to collect his wits, he found himself walking up the curving staircase with her.

"You did it, didn't you? You pig! You, you man!" It was morning and they were both back in their room at the inn. Martin was sputtering with anger. "How could you? You've got no more self-control than a three-year-old. Oh you men are all alike." She was pacing across the boards, impelled by outrage. "You realize that you've jeopardized the whole search, don't you? You ought to be ashamed of yourself! I just hope you had a really good time," she wheeled on him, "since you've thrown away so much for it."

Jarrod sat propped up on the pillows in amused detachment. He met her glower with equanimity.

"An excellent good time, I thank you, and, since you seem to be able to fool everybody else with your walk and the way you speak, perhaps you'll be able to fool the unicorn, too. Now, how was your evening? Did you have fun in the parlor with the rest of the girls?"

"No, I did not, you unspeakable creature. I had a perfectly miserable time. And you, you disgusting beast, stayed upstairs and stayed and stayed. The men started to make bets on how long you'd be. And if that wasn't bad enough, one of the girls said they had a customer who liked boys as well and I could make myself some good money." She threw herself at Jarrod, trying to get through his staving hand to hit him, but his arms were too long for her.

"What if I told you," he said, heaving her back and swinging his legs over the side of the bed, "that nothing happened up there?"

"Oh sure," Martin said sarcastically, "and I suppose that's why she gave you that long kiss goodbye." She drew herself into an attitude of mock demureness and the voice was an oversweet caricature. "Goodbye nice man. I'll never forget you."

"There's a reason for that. Ouch! Don't kick me; just let me explain."

"This better be very good."

"I told her that I was an Apprentice Magician and that we weren't allowed to before we passed our final exams. She said that that was the worst excuse for being afraid that she'd ever heard. So I had to prove myself."

"That's the problem, he man."

"No, stupid. That I was a Magician."

"And just how did you do that, pray tell?"

"Well, I took all her clothes off without touching her. She had a beautiful body." He shook his head in reminiscent appreciation. "Anyway, she said it wasn't fair for her to have no clothes on and for me to be fully dressed, so I took my clothes off."

"And then?" the voice was dangerous.

"And then nothing," Jarrod replied with a touch of smugness. "We sat on the bed, naked, and we talked. I asked her how she came to be a prostitute and she told me that . . ."

"Yes, yes, I'm sure it was all very sad and interesting, but do you honestly expect me to . . ." She was interrupted in her turn by a loud knocking.

"Are late. Much to do. I wait downstairs," said a deep voice. They looked at each other with startled guilt and then dove for their boots.

"I swear it's true," Jarrod said as he bent over and pulled. Martin looked up, with an eyebrow raised in disbelief. She walked to the door, wrapped in a meaningful silence, and Jarrod followed her. He was smiling.

CHAPTER IX

SANDROZ KEPT THEM CONTINUALLY BUSY FOR THE REST OF THE day. They bought ropes and stout boots, extra pitons, provisions and two stocky mounts and by nightfall they were almost too tired to eat. He rousted them early the next morning and by nine they were on a barge being towed upriver toward Lake Grad.

Martin was far from happy to have to commit herself to waterborne transport again, but survived the sennight-long trip without visible discomfort. Jarrod soon tired of watching the jungle on the Umbrian bank and the steady plod of the horses on the towpath. The locks that raised them to the level of the lake came as a welcome relief. Jarrod noted the men and the machinery needed to cope with the traffic and thought, somewhat smugly, that, at home, one Magician could have done it all.

They reclaimed their horses and rode around the lake, passed the bustling town of Grad, and pushed on Northward beside the Upper Illushkhardin. They crossed the river, grown younger and more turbulent, at Faringford, stopping briefly to buy more food, and headed into the foothills of the Saradondas. The road died out and the terrain grew rougher. Trees were sparser and from time to time they had to dismount and lead the horses around boulders or across scree. To make matters worse, High Summer arrived in a rush and patience frayed in the itchy heat. Hungry swarms of flies materialized with it and performed all the clichés of their kind except the one about dying. By day, Jarrod envied his horse its tail and by night, its hide.

It was a bad fortnight as they angled upward. They managed to keep ahead of the rains, but it was too hot, even in the dusty wind, to ride all covered up. The salt from their sweat drew the insects to any area of exposed skin. They ran short of bread and what little they had was so stale that it needed a good soaking before it was edible. They eked it out, knowing that it was the last that they would have until they made it back to civilization. Jarrod hunted from the saddle, but the rock rabbits eluded his arrows with ease and the crag leapers stayed well out of bowshot.

Sandroz' irreducible brevity made them feel that conversation was an imposition on him and soon they scarcely talked. Nobody commented on the beauty of the vistas that opened up before them or the view across the valley to the indistinct haze of the sister range. It made Jarrod miss Tokamo, with whom he had once been able to share such things.

The Saradondas had looked big from the first, but the further they penetrated, the higher the peaks became. There were no signs of habitation on the inhospitable slopes, though there were infrequent signs that the trail, such as it was, had been used. It came as a shock when, cresting a rise onto a brief plateau, they came upon an encampment. Sandroz gestured curtly for them to stay and rode forward to investigate. When he came back he was smiling and beckoned them forward toward the circle of hide tents.

They had met up, he explained, with a mountain village on its annual migration back to the high lands after a Winter of grazing in the valley. The men and the new wives herded the ronoronti that were central to their existence. They were everything to the village. They were wealth, food, clothing, shelter and beasts of portage. They were even providers of fiddle strings and fuel.

The villagers made them welcome and made of them an excuse for a feast. Their stomachs were nothing loath and after three hard sennights the idea of taking easement in excess was very welcome. They joined the men in hunting while the women brewed quantities of fermented milk and prepared the ronoronti. They pierced the ears of the yearlings and strung bright, plaited red and green threads through them. All of the older animals had the faded remnants of feasts gone by woven into manes and tails or fluttering from the tips of slim, upstanding ears.

That accomplished, the women fanned out in search of dead wood. Living trees were precious to them and no Songean would take an axe to one. It was held that they contained the spirits of the great raptors that wheeled effortlessly around the peaks. Once in every bird's lifetime, it was confined to a rooted existence so that, when it was reborn to the air, it would appreciate the divinity of flight.

Fires were lit in the long dusk and spits were turned. They drank the kvass the women had made and chewed on chica leaves as the sky turned to deeper shades of plum on its journey into indigo. Then they sat to eat. They ate with slippery fingers and slick mouths until their stomachs were distended. The bowls were taken away, a broad space was cleared and the drums began. The rhythms were an invitation to excitement, a growing insistence in the blood.

The visitors sat and watched as the young men spun and stamped and ululated in a dance of compelling, but incomprehensible ritual. The fire-thrown light licked across the hideous intricacies of demon masks, lending them an animation past the carvers' art. In and around them all were the reverberant pulsations that urged them to their feet. Warriors in paint and plumes appeared and the demons were put to rout. The drum beats pattered away into silence.

They came back with the accompaniment of fiddles and an altered tempo. There was no resisting them and the three guests found themselves dancing counterclockwise beneath the stately wheeling of the stars. The women circled the other way, leading the bedecked animals. They stayed on the outside as if to use the ronoronti as wards against the potent and erotic magic of the men.

The slow acceleration of the music had Jarrod firmly in its grip and a small, observant part of him was surprised at the ease and dexterity with which he was performing. Martin danced in front of him and it was obvious that she was having a much better time playing a man at this celebration than she had had at the last one. The dance became endless and took their bodies past tiredness. The drums' insistence drove them over the threshold to the place where the music and they became one. Around them, the glistening bodies grew indistinct as the fires died, but they danced on to the orgiastic climax.

They took their leave the next day when the sun was already high. They were not feeling at their best, but there was a greater sense of ease between them. Even Sandroz seemed less taciturn and conversation, which had withered in the face of his perennial concision, sputtered into life again.

"D'you know where he's taking us?" Jarrod asked of Martin during the noonday break.

"Not entirely. We did discuss it on the barge, though discuss isn't really the right word for it. I was trying to get to know him better and I asked him if there was an area where there were valleys hidden away. Somewhere that people seldom if ever went. He said, 'In middle. I take you.' Seems there's some sort of sacred mountain there. He called it the Anvil of Creation and it's supposed to be off-limits."

"Why?" Jarrod's voice was awake with interest.

"He didn't say. You really didn't expect him to, did you?"

"No, I suppose not. You got more out of him than I have. I asked the people back there about their legends, but my Songean is pretty rudimentary and I didn't understand half of what they said. They seem to have a lot of stories about cloudsteeds and someone whose name I can't pronounce who was the father of all crag leapers, but nothing that sounded remotely like a unicorn."

"From what I could see, when you weren't dancing and ogling the girls, you were lost chewing on those leaves. I'm surprised you remember anything at all." Jarrod looked at her sharply, suspecting criticism, but Martin grinned and winked and punched him lightly on the shoulder.

They kept climbing obliquely across densely wooded valleys that might have sheltered a dozen unicorns, but yielded only startled deer and shy foxes. The trio began to feel very remote from their fellow men, even though the track occasionally revealed their presence. It had been widened in spots and there were old blaze marks on some of the trees. It was far easier to follow than it had been at the outset and Jarrod took to riding ahead when he hunted. He liked the time to himself and, alone, he felt that he gave the game less warning. He seldom returned empty-handed.

The time that he liked best was after he had Made the Day, while the others still slept. The air was sharp and clean and the shadows long as he saddled up on the fifth morning after the feast. He was humming quietly to himself as he urged his horse into the chill of a rock-walled canyon and he held his notched bow comfortably in his left hand. His next sensation was one of shock as an abrasive weight enveloped his head and shoulders.

He dropped the reins and clawed at the cordage around him. His disconcerted mount reared and he was dumped, with bone-rattling pain, onto the hard ground. When breath returned in burning whoops, he started to thrash reflexively and was rewarded with a sharp explosion of blackness at the back of the head. It spread instantaneously.

Jarrod's eyes were hammered open by pain and immediately rejected the view. Dirt and pebbles were going by above him. His head was very hot and things drifted in and out of focus. Then he discovered that his hands were tied to a rope beneath the horse's belly and his mind righted the picture. Not much else made sense. He was being jounced around across his saddle and had no way to brace himself against the kidney-crushing sway. He strained his neck to try to see where they were going and if the others had been taken prisoner, but all he got were glimpses of ponies and trees. The effort made his head hurt. Red-hot needles pierced his temples and forced him to relax. He willed himself, unsuccessfully, to lose consciousness again.

After the spasms of nausea had subsided and time had become an immeasurable ache, the animal stopped moving. Sisal sheaths protecting legs in leather came into his upside-down view. A man bent down and cut the rope and then he was unceremoniously shoved off backwards. He landed heavily on his tailbone and whimpered. He was shocked more than hurt by the boot that immediately drove into his ribs.

From somewhere unconnected there came harshly spasmodic breathing that he recognized, belatedly, as his own. He was very frightened and that was doing uncomfortable things to the pit of his stomach. Underlying his fear was a sense of outrage and resentment. Things like this just didn't happen to people like him. Yet there he was, stunned, submissive and impotent. His body was numb with the promise of pain to come and his will was paralyzed.

He was hauled to his feet by a stocky, bearded man, over whom he towered precariously. He felt he should do something to assert himself, but his hands and his feet were still bound and his co-ordination was out of kilter. The cord around his ankles was cut and he was pushed into a shambling trot that brought him to a line of men who were chained together at the neck. He stood in an unprotesting daze as a wooden collar was hasped to and he was joined to the sullen column of Songeans who had been captured before him. He shook his head to rid it of the buzzing, but all that it did was to gall his neck.

He looked around and was relieved that he caught no sight of Martin or Sandroz. There was a possibility of rescue. Then it occurred to him that they had no idea of what had happened to him. Gloom set in and he turned his attention to his captors. They were dressed in the bright cloth of the tribesmen, but his ears confirmed his suspicion that this was some sort of Umbrian raiding party.

That was as far as he got before the line was prodded into action and whipped into a staggering lope. Jarrod's world narrowed down to the space between his feet and those of the man in front of him. It took a great deal of concentration to stay in line and not to lurch from side to side, but his pride was back at work. He would not allow himself to be a hindrance to the other prisoners. The moving chain seemed to have a life of its own and he was glad that he was the last and had enough room to pull up in when the inexplicable stoppages occurred.

About a mile up the path, the collar began to chafe as the sweat ran down his neck. The salt stung and blurred his already woofy sight and his side began to hurt. He changed his breathing and the length of his stride. Then he held his breath as he ran, but the stitch got worse. He tried to go into himself to put matters right and tripped. The man in front cursed automatically, but he did not stop or slow and Jarrod was tugged back to scrambling balance. He ground his teeth and got into stride again, but now he felt as if his mind had been jerked back into function along with his body. He took stock of his situation.

He had been taken prisoner by a well-armed and organized group of Umbrians posing as Songean clansmen. It was, he admitted, a well-chosen disguise. The Songeans were always fighting among themselves and the casual observer would simply assume that the chained men were prisoners of war. No one was likely to interfere with a war party. Sandroz was an excellent tracker, but Martin and he would have lost irreplaceable time waiting for him and then in looking for him. The Umbrians were clearly doing something illegal and would probably have taken pains to cover their traces. They were just as unlikely to advertise their passage. With his hands tied, there was no way that he could shed something that might serve his friends as a clue.

It was going to have to be Magic then, despite Greylock and his rules. The thought went through his mind that the Umbrians might have found out about his mission and the rest of the prisoners were merely camouflage for his capture. Too far fetched, and if that was the case they would have waited and taken Martin, too. No, it had just been bad luck. Back to Magic. What to do? Shapechanging was risky and he certainly couldn't do it while running along an uneven path. He could distort the area immediately around him, but if he couldn't get out of the collar it wouldn't do him any good. Anything more major would have to wait until he could concentrate properly and his aching head gave no promise that it would be anytime soon. One thing he did know. When he got free, he would continue with the quest, even if he had to do it alone. In the meantime, there was nothing he could do except keep up this brain-jarring jog and wait.

They were fed and watered in the early afternoon. The only difference between what the prisoners and the ponies got was that the prisoners' oats had been baked into a flat, dry cake. The ponies also got to eat and drink their fill. They stopped again after sunset and were herded into a rough circle, facing outward. Jarrod was hooked onto the man who had been the leader of the column. The man looked at him incuriously as they were being linked, but Jarrod was filled with pity by the sores on his neck. They bespoke long bondage. He wanted to say something but didn't know what to say. The other said nothing, then or later.

Water was poured into their mouths and they got to suck thin porridge out of a bowl. When it was gone, they were led away,

one by one, to a nearby stream and then they were yoked up
again. The Umbrians' cooking fires were doused and the prisoners scrunched backward until they could lean against each other
for a little meager warmth and mutual support. Jarrod felt very
alone in the huddle as the nightmoon rose.

He was awake in time to Make the Day and was relieved to
find that sleep had dispelled the fogginess of the previous day,
although it seemed to have done nothing for his bruised flesh. He
longed for the comfort of the ritual, but knew that he couldn't
move without waking the men on either side of him. They were
too much in need of rest for him to be able to do that and he
resigned himself to wakefulness and the contemplation of methods of escape.

The fact that he was already awake did not spare him the kicks
that got the others up. He was taken off to the stream again, but
he wasn't fed or reaffixed. Instead, he was pulled along by the
neckchain to the Umbrian side of the clearing. He waited quietly
and apprehensively while a man who was obviously the leader of
the raiders finished his breakfast. The aromas made Jarrod's
stomach twinge and talk. The man took his time. Finally, he
pushed his plate away, looked up and looked the young man
over.

"Well, what have we here?" He spoke in colloquial Umbrian
and Jarrod cocked his head in an effort to understand. "Doesn't
look like a Songean to me, wrong build altogether, but no
matter. He looks strong enough. On the tall side for work in the
shafts, but he's young enough to last for a while."

"Pretty one, too," someone in the group said slyly.

"Just the Superintendent's type," another chimed in, and the
ensuing laughter held a snigger.

"We could always break him in for the Super. 'Course you'd
have to climb him to get to him."

Jarrod's lack of fluency was no protection against the meaning
and he stood mutely as the coarse laughter swirled around him.
He felt unclean.

"We lost the last one you tried that on. We haven't taken
enough men to risk losing any more." The leader reasserted his
authority in a flat, matter-of-fact voice. He looked around at his
men. "Get the rest of them ready to travel and break camp.

We're going to have to catch another migration or raid a village that has already got its men back. I want to be out of here before the bad weather sets in. They die off on you when it's wet." His left hand dismissed them and he turned his attention back to Jarrod.

"Arundel or Paladine, boy?" He had switched to Common.

"Paladine."

"Speak up, boy, I can't hear you." The voice was level, but Jarrod felt a tingling of disquiet.

"I said Paladine."

"Paladine, Sir." Jarrod dutifully echoed him.

"You're a long way from home. What are you doing here?"

"I'm on a climbing holiday."

"Sir!"

"Sir."

"I've seen your equipment," the Umbrian acknowledged. "Now, where are the others?"

"There are no others, Sir, I'm by myself." The lie came out easily.

"D'you take me for a fool?" The tone was impatient. "Nobody goes climbing in mountains like these alone. Where are they?"

"I'm good enough to climb alone," Jarrod replied sullenly.

"Don't try my patience, boy. There's no point in being stupider than you have to be. You'll tell me everything I want to know soon enough. They all do." He smiled with cold satisfaction. "How many more of you are there?"

"I'm on my own, Sir."

Jarrod sounded convincing in his own ears, but it did him no good. His inquisitor turned to one of the other Umbrians and said, "Take him back and give him ten lashes in front of the rest of them. It'll be a good object lesson and it'll make him less stubborn. We'll speak again, young man." His voice was emotionless and his attention already elsewhere.

Jarrod had only been wearing a shirt, trousers and boots when he was knocked over the head and now he lost the shirt. The knout had six strings and by the time they had been applied ten times, the cloth was shredded and the flesh looked like a field of red clay after ploughing. He felt the impact of each knot with absolute exactness, but he experienced no pain. He had gone within before the first stripes seamed him and taken control of the nerves and the blood supply. The action was completely instinctive and the body, devoid of resistance, was flailed from side to side. He allowed a little more blood than was necessary to escape through the slicings so as not to alert the Umbrians. There were atavistic fears at work and he in no way wanted them to find out that he was a Magician.

He was reattached to the end of the line and set off in a red and trudging haze. The sun beat down and the breeze was not strong enough to discourage the insects that gathered to feast on his exposed back. Jarrod was lost in a universe of pain absorbed and counteracted. Every time the column came to one of its abrupt and unfathomable stops, he shambled blindly into the unprotesting mass of the man ahead. Only after the sun had passed behind them were they pushed into a patch of shadow that had been gouged out of the rock face by the ice of long ago.

They were given water, but nothing to eat. They sprawled where they had stopped and the rest cursed feebly at Jarrod for attracting the flies. Their throats were too dry, even after the water, to keep it up for long and the grumbling fell into a stupified silence broken only by the sound of slapping.

Jarrod was oblivious to men and insects alike. Now that he did not have to control his legs, he could permit his mind more freedom and he discovered that he was angry. He felt a sustaining wash of hatred. He must get his strength back and when he did, he would kill them all. Not a single Umbrian would escape. His fellow prisoners would be too self-absorbed to notice what went on and no one else would be left alive to carry the tale that Magic had passed this way. The raging mind began to go through spells, selecting destructions of ever-increasing nastiness. The act brought calmness to him. He went back into himself and examined his wounds from the inside. He decided that he was going to carry the marks for a very long time, but that it looked worse than it was.

Kicking brought him out again and his back flinched reflexively. The afternoon promised to be as uncomfortable as the morning had been, but the advent of a heavily wooded valley proved an unexpected balm. After a while a rushing noise made itself heard, rising until it drowned out the jingle of the harnesses. The path widened and the line of captives clotted up. Over the heads Jarrod could see the far bank of a swiftly moving river and guessed that they had reached the headwaters of the Illushkhardin. They did not look in the least inviting.

They waited until a rope had been stretched across and the pack animals had been taken over. Two of the heavily laden ponies were swept away. Then they were hauled into reluctant motion. The hands of the man at the head of the chain were retied around the rope and they were urged into the ice-cold tug of the water. The men turned their backs to the current, hooked their hobbled arms over the rope and edged out. The water quenched the flames in Jarrod's back with stabbing icicles, staining itself with his blood as it cleansed the striations. His feet were unfeeling on the slimy rocks as he hitched along and he was acutely aware of the thrust and suck that rose slowly to his armpits.

He was more than halfway over and beginning to feel safe when a cry signalled someone's loss of footing. The quick river pounced the man away and used his accelerated weight to peel those on either side of him from their holds. Jarrod's collar slammed up under his chin and dizzied him. His shoulders were hauled over the rope, but he curled his knees up and held onto them with numb fingers. His neck was racked and the greedy water foamed around him as it fought to dislodge him.

The collar forced his head up and he was unaware of the guards who had waded out until he felt them behind him. Slowly the human flotsam was hauled back and he was re-established on his feet. Progress was infinitely slow and Jarrod had to be half carried up the bank. There he lay in hoarse agony as the feeling returned to nerveless limbs. They crawled eventually into the shelter of the trees and lay wet and moaning as the soaked bonds tightened. That night they were well fed.

The next day they were on the march again, but the pace was slow and the afternoon halt stretched on toward evening. Jarrod at first put it down to the undoubted exhaustion that all of them, Umbrians included, were feeling after the battle with the river, but the continued comings and goings among the captors made him reconsider. He began to watch them more closely and it

soon became evident that some sort of plan was coming into
being. From what he had gathered during his questioning, it
seemed evident to him that some village or encampment was
going to be attacked. It was confirmed when he saw the Umbrians
muffling bits and braces with strips of sacking.

Decision crystallized within him. It was obvious that the only
prisoners taken were male and healthy. It was equally obvious
that the Umbrians would leave no witnesses behind. He remembered, almost as if it were a scene from another lifetime, the
hospitality the three of them had received from the villagers and
he determined that, this time, the Umbrians would not succeed. It
was also the chance that he had been waiting for to effect his
own escape.

His miseries were forgotten as he called on his weather lore
and sent himself in search of a thermal that would mark the
position of the Songeans. It did not take him long. At the head of
the valley, scarcely a league away, there was a rising mass of air
that was too constant to be accidental. It was still too early for
herders to have called a halt for the night. A village then. He
conjured up the memory of one of the demon masks he had seen
during the dance and reassembled it, face down, over the place
where he judged the center of the village to be.

He threw all the energy he could muster into making the
image as solid and realistic as he could. The natives were, by and
large, superstitious and the apparition should frighten them sufficiently to make the young warriors arm themselves in defiance.
If anyone looked up and saw it. He concentrated further and
made the image swoop from side to side. He felt his energy
waning and let the image fall toward the ground before it winked
out. There was nothing more he could do for the moment.

The Umbrians inadvertently aided him by serving the prisoners both porridge and oatcakes. He assumed that they wanted to
build up their strength for a long march on the following day, but
he had no intention of being there. He obeyed passively when
they were bedded down for the night as the light turned to ashes
of roses and died. He sat quietly, feigning sleep, as the woods
settled down into the nightly rituals of roosting and hunting and
the clouds came up and put out the rising moon.

He dozed in the dark until the quiet sounds of the Umbrians

mustering brought him wide awake. The moon was still veiled, which suited his purposes and, above him, the leaves rustled under the wind and masked the noises of small predators astalk in the night. He watched them ride out and sat up, causing the men who flanked him to sag together behind his back. He muttered a litany of concentration under his breath and felt himself drawn in.

He pushed his awareness upward and hurried up the wind. He brought in more clouds to make the early hours more profound and slow the Umbrians' approach. He needed all the time he could get to muster as much force as he could. It should take them an hour to reach the village and he could put the time to good use. What he needed was thunder and lightning followed by a clear sky, and that wasn't going to be easy. He went deeper inside and set himself to summon a storm and position it with pinpoint accuracy.

An hour later, he pulled a thunderclap out of the stacked clouds. If the villagers had missed his earlier warning or retired to bed anyway, they would not be caught asleep. He lit the night with bolts for good measure and then spat the wind out to shear away the cover he had created. The clouds scattered and the moon shone down. That was all he could do from this remove, and he set himself to conjure up a spell to loose his bonds. He had overestimated his strength and, try as he would, he lacked the residue of power to free himself.

He left off then and returned to the black and silver clearing. Movement caught his eye and he heard a horse neigh. He looked over toward the picket line in time to see the sentry who had been left to guard the animals sit down suddenly and hunch over into sleep. His ears caught a series of rapid sounds and then a thud. His name was hissed out.

"Over here," he croaked, sudden hope weakening him further. A slim figure blocked out the light as it bent.

"How do I get this bloody thing off?" it asked.

"There's a latch at the back of the collar."

"Hold still. Got it. Now put your hands up and stretch them as far apart as you can. Steady. One more strand. There, there you are." He grasped the outstretched hand and hauled himself to unsteady feet. He rubbed his wrists as they and his hands began to burn. A stocky figure materialized beside them.

"We go now," it said.

"Both of you help me." Jarrod ignored him. "We've got to get them loose." He turned to the nearest shoulder and shook it.

"Undo first two. They do the rest." Sandroz stooped and deftly cut several bindings. He straightened up and pushed Jarrod toward the trees, causing a gasp of pain as hand met back. "You fetch horse. I take him," he said to Martin as he helped the staggering figure into the woods. The Songean supported him through the latticed gloom until they reached the two mounts. Martin appeared moments later leading Jarrod's horse.

"They seem to have kept all your stuff together," she whispered. "All except your bow. I couldn't find that."

"I can't thank . . . I didn't expect . . . I never thought . . ." Jarrod was too far gone to complete a sentence and they lifted him into the saddle. Martin caught sight of his back and swore bitterly as she tied his cloak around his neck. They rode off on either side of him to keep him from falling. Within minutes of being freed, Jarrod was confined again, but, had he been aware of it, he would have been grateful.

CHAPTER X

MARTIN WAS PICKING BERRIES AND GETTING SCRATCHED AS SHE pressed deeper into the patch. The corners of her mouth were stained a dark blue and the phrases that came out of it were entirely unladylike. A fair number of them were centered on Jarrod, who had mended in the five days that had passed since his rescue, but not to the point that he could resume his share of the foraging.

Her views on the stamina of Magicians in general, and this one in particular, were both unkind and untrue. There was no real malice in her muttered invective, but it was a symptom of the strain that had developed. Most of the blame for it could be laid to Jarrod. He resented his lapses into helplessness and assumed that others felt the same way. He also had a nagging suspicion that either of them could have contrived to escape without assistance and, detecting silent criticism where none existed, he had become moody and defensive.

The crystals of his self-doubt precipitated out around the loss of his bow. If he had his bow, he could pull his weight by hunting from the saddle. Whenever they stopped, he spent his time looking for a usable stave. He settled, finally, on a straight bough with a tense spring to it. He took care to break it off the tree when Sandroz was off hunting, but felt guilty about it anyhow. He set out to tame it with adversarial intensity and spent his evenings soaking and stretching it. His companions watched his nightly rituals with tolerant, but unexpressed, amusement.

The weather was no help either. The upland nights were cold and damp and the days were plagued by uncontrolled storms that blew up to drench them. The slopes ran with unexpected streams and water flowed out of solid-seeming rock faces. They were so far North now that they could no longer see the Illushkhardin. When they looked directly across the valley to the West, they found that the Central Mountains blocked out all but the tallest peaks of the Gorodontious. Everything seemed remote and desolate.

They seldom saw traces of the native clans and had put them from their minds until, one blustery morning, they came upon a small, squalling bundle lying in a sodden nest of grasses. Sandroz, who now took the lead position all the time, urged his pony past, but Jarrod's horse, spooked by the noise, shied and pranced. Jarrod brought it quickly under hand and, in order to cover his loss of mastery, dismounted and looped the reins around a fir root.

"Wait up!" he yelled over his shoulder at Sandroz and bent to investigate. Martin pulled up beside him and leaned out of the saddle for a better view. Jarrod pushed back the top flap of the swaddling and peered.

"It's a baby and it looks very young," he said. "Sandroz. What in the world is this baby doing all alone out here?"

"Balagoshna." The Songean was his usual laconic self.

"What does that mean?" Martin chimed in.

"Abandonment. Only for the weakest."

"You just leave them here to die?" She was incredulous. The two youngsters exchanged a puzzled look, unwilling to grasp what had been said. Sandroz, unmoving and unmoved, sat and watched them.

"But that's inhuman." Understanding brought anger to Jarrod. "You can't just expose children like that. That's barbaric."

"It dies anyway. Songuard has little food. It is our custom for long time." He looked at them for a beat. "We go now." The words were flat and absolute. They brooked no denial, but outrage gave Jarrod the strength to oppose him.

"We can't just leave it here." As if in response, the child

began to cry again. Sandroz ignored them all and kneed his mount around.

"Jarrod, what are we going to do? We can't just leave it here to starve to death, or be . . . or be . . ."

"I know how you feel," Jarrod cut in quickly to stop the thought before a picture of it formed in his mind. "We'll take it with us." He scooped the foundling up and stood rocking it in his arms.

"I don't know the first thing about looking after babies," Martin confessed and Jarrod thought he detected nervousness in her voice.

"Neither do I," he replied, more brusquely than he had intended, "but I can't leave it to be eaten." He was deliberately callous. Martin looked over her shoulder at Sandroz and Jarrod followed her gaze. His arms tightened instinctively around the child.

"We must go. Am much late because of you." The Songean's deep voice fell on them. "You interfere," he continued with a nod at the little shape nestled against Jarrod's chest. "You anger our gods."

"I didn't know you had gods," Martin retorted.

"All men have gods. Some are clever enough to know it. Now we go." He kicked his heels gently at his pony's flanks.

"I'm bringing it," Jarrod said hotly at the retreating back. "I don't care if you like it or not." If Sandroz heard him, he gave no sign of having done so.

They ate apart from him that evening. They tended to the infant with fumbling gingerliness and fed it broth. They slept on either side of it and woke together when she cried in the night. When they rode on in the morning, the baby lay hammocked in the hood of Jarrod's cloak. After a while, he found it easier to wear the cloak backwards so that the baby bounced gently against his chest. He tucked his chin in and watched the impossibly small and perfect thumb climb toward the warmth of the expectant mouth and found that he possessed emotions he had not known about.

They entered shadow and he looked up again as the timbre of the hoofbeats changed. The mountain overhung the path and formed a three-sided tunnel around them. It was water-shined or lichen-green for the most part, except where the left-hand wall should have been. There was nothing there but a hazy view and an unnerving drop. Around them, the hooves clicked and multiplied until it sounded as if they were part of a caravan. When they rounded a curve and came face to face with another mounted party, it seemed as if they had approached in stealth.

The two groups halted and sat staring at each other. The riders that Jarrod could see were robed and cowled in grey, giving them an unquiet appearance in that place. The silence was interrupted by the drip of water and the scrape of a hoof. Then Sandroz grunted and held his right hand up, palm forward and fingers spread. Jarrod knew that the cloak would prevent him from getting to a weapon, but he was determined not to be taken again, even if it meant using Magic.

Sandroz pulled his pony up before the leader and bowed from the waist. Jarrod didn't catch what he said, but the skin between his shoulder blades twitched as he recognized the language. They were beckoned forward and Jarrod rode up warily. Even if there were no more of them out of sight, he reckoned the odds at two to one and the Umbrians had the reputation of being good fighters. He held the reins loosely in his left hand and his right arm girdled the baby protectively. Sandroz looked at them and permitted himself one of his rare smiles before turning back to the newcomers.

"Lady of the Mother," he said and the voice echoed in the enclosed space, "these my travelling companions." He had switched back to Common. "Like me, they come in peace."

"Where is the child you spoke of?" The Umbrian's face remained unreachable within the shadow of the cowl, but the voice was musical and resonant. There was no detectable accent. Jarrod made no move, but Martin's voice answered from behind him.

"In the Mother's name we offer peace and openness." The traditional Maternite greeting sounded easy on her tongue and Jarrod was suddenly reminded that she had been brought up to rule a large Holding.

"May the peace of the Mother be with us all and may Her world be fruitful," the priestess returned. The hood dipped fractionally in acknowledgement.

"We had not bethought ourselves so fortunate as to encounter Her representatives so far within the wilderness. Are you all upon some mission?" The formal mode sounded strange to Jarrod's ears after all this time, but he could detect no guile in the voice.

"We are upon Her errand, but this is no place to discuss it." The Maternite was businesslike. "It is easier for you to turn than for us. We have pack animals with us. Do you go back until there is an open place and then we must see to the child. It needs proper food and care."

They retreated back the way they had come until there was space enough for them all to dismount. Jarrod surrendered his burden reluctantly, handing her down to one of the women. It was taken off to where her sisters were unpacking saddlebags. Two young boys came into view leading a string of panniered mules and drew them up alongside the path. The Lady Mother threw back her hood to check on her group and revealed a pleasant, weathered face and short-cropped grey hair. She motioned to the women and two of them detached themselves and went and lifted three small bundles from the lead mule's baskets. The air was suddenly filled with infantile raucousness.

"Behold," the bareheaded woman said, sweeping the group with an inclusive hand, "the chief recruiters for the Maternite clergy. In answer to your question, young man, we make two expeditions a year." She paused and moved her shoulders wearily around to dispel their tightness. She put both hands in the small of her back and arched against her stiffness. "We come ten months after the Midwinter Festival and ten months after Greening Day." She gave a short bark of laughter. "Men are so predictable."

"But I thought," Martin said hesitantly, "that only women could become . . . I mean, there are no Maternite priests, are there?"

"Quite right, laddie." She looked at Martin questioningly, then understanding came. "Oh, I see. You don't really suppose that the Songeans would expose a boy, do you? Not unless they were certain that it wouldn't live. Oh dear me, no. It's a very rare boychild that survives Balagoshna."

"But what if one does?" Martin persisted, her head tilting to a disputatious angle.

"There are many ways to serve the Mother, child, and room within Her embrace for all." Her voice was placid and confident as she watched her companions tend to their charges.

"What will happen to, to . . ." and Jarrod pointed to where the new recruit was being fed.

"To the baby you found? We shall take her back with us. She will be looked after and raised in the faith. One day she will take her place among the ranks of Her servants, according to her talents and the Mother's needs." The priestess smiled reassuringly at him. "We shall take good care of her, I promise you. I commend you on your concern." She turned in the saddle and asked a question in Umbrian. "My sister says that she seems healthy. It was fortunate that you came upon her when you did. The Songeans always think that the girls are the weaker. They are wrong, of course. It is surprising how long some of these little mites can wait for the Mother, but we cannot reach them all in time." She nodded to herself, preoccupied by some train of thought. "We must press on," she said, coming to herself again. She issued crisp commands in her native tongue and the other priestesses began to pack up. She returned her attention to the three travellers.

"May the Mother guard and guide you," she said formally. "You have served Her well this day." Her cloak and robes swung as she bowed to them and then she turned to supervise the departure.

"What do you make of all that?" Martin asked when they were out of earshot.

"Seems to me that, one way or the other, the Umbrians end up with both the girls and the boys. They just collect them different ways, that's all." Jarrod was short with her, obscurely upset with the loss of the little one. He kicked his horse into a canter and caught up with Sandroz just as he reentered the overhang. The clattering din made further conversation impossible.

The Songean was silent for the rest of the day, but the two Westerners thought little of it. They were used to his self-containment and they had preoccupations of their own. The scene with the priestesses replayed itself in Jarrod's head and he tried to sort out the ambivalent feelings that it produced. His treatment at the hands of the press gang had soured him on the subject of Umbrians and he could not help but be suspicious of the Maternite child collectors. Part of him knew that he was being unfair and rejoiced at the fact that the child had been rescued.

He knew that he and Martin weren't equipped to look after an infant, especially not on the kind of expedition that they had undertaken. The priestesses had clearly been on a mission of mercy and had already saved three small lives, but, as a Magician, he was prejudiced against the church. He wasn't sure exactly why, but it was so. He tried to parse his feelings as he rode.

Martin had different concerns. The plight of the baby had moved her, but she had found that she was affected by the child itself in quite different ways. Women were supposed to find all babies beautiful, but to her it had been merely red and creased and ugly. She had resented its helplessness and found the cleaning and feeding of it repugnant to her. It had made her feel clumsy and awkward.

She had never been around really young children. The servants had babies, of course, but they had been kept out of the way until they were old enough to perform useful tasks. Nevertheless, she had always assumed that she would marry, have children and be a good mother. Her reactions during the past two days, she admitted to herself, cast doubt on the last assumption and that worried her.

When the sun began to slip down behind the Gorodontious they stopped and pitched camp. There was no need for instructions. Everyone knew what they had to do and performed their tasks with the automatic efficiency born of long practice. There seemed nothing unusual about the single-minded quiet with which they devoured the meal, so when the explosion came, neither youngster was prepared for it.

Sandroz set his plate aside and said, without preamble, "You should go back." There was anger in his voice.

"Go back? Why?" Martin asked, startled out of her reverie.

"You not belong in Songuard. You blaspheme. You unbelieve." The emotionless mask he always wore was gone.

"We can't do that," Jarrod expostulated. "We haven't reached where we're going yet."

"You go home. Go back." He was vehement and his voice had risen.

"Are you still upset about the baby?" Martin asked.

"You interfere. You mock our customs. Have no respect for our ways."

"But the Maternites would have saved her. She was left right on the trail. The mother must have wanted her to be found," Jarrod intervened, his puzzlement plain.

"They serve Goddess. You Magician—believe in nothing. Think you have powers. Powers belong to gods, not to men." His eyes blazed in the firelight.

"I didn't realize you felt that way," Jarrod said slowly, feeling hurt at the wholesale rejection of his kind. "You never said anything."

"You not speak my language, not speak Umbrian. Your tongue not easy for me."

"But you agreed to act as our guide."

"They not say you Magician, but I know when I see you. Too tall for ordinary man."

"Why didn't you say something at Belengar if you felt that way?" Martin asked.

"I make agreement," he replied. "I keep my word." His head went up in pride and defiance.

"Look," Martin said placatingly, "Jarrod and I meant no harm, we didn't mean to offend. We didn't know your customs."

"I tell you. You say you do if I like or not." He was not prepared to be mollified.

"Try to understand how we felt," Martin continued. "That little baby hadn't done anything to deserve death and in our countries we try to protect the helpless. Leaving it to die would have been like murder to us. Can't you understand that?"

"You come from rich places. If all babies live, everyone here suffers."

"I can see that now, but it is still a difficult thing for us to actually experience."

"It's wrong, that's what it is," Jarrod muttered under his breath.

"I tell you. You have no respect," Sandroz said, ignoring him.

"We can't go back now," Martin said quickly to forestall Jarrod. "Our mission is vitally important. You must believe me when I say that. We aren't allowed to tell anyone what it is, but, if we are successful, it may mean an end to the war. If we fail, all of Strand, Songuard included, will go under. You've got to help us."

"We can't fail. We mustn't," Jarrod added fiercely.

"We promise to do everything you tell us to. Besides," Martin said shrewdly, "you did give your word." Sandroz grunted disgustedly and stared at the fire. The others waited apprehensively.

"I not like," he said finally, "but I give my word and I take money." He glared at them, challenging them to argue with him. Jarrod held his breath and his tongue. "You wash plates, pot. Then we sleep." They both scrambled to obey.

For the next three days they rode North accompanied by an unshakable sense of strain. Sandroz held himself aloof and ate by himself. When he communicated, which was rarely, it was with a nod, a pointing finger or a monosyllable. His charges were constrained to similar silence by the weight of his displeasure, but, beneath it, both were goaded by a rising feeling that they had been unfairly judged. They took care, however, to anticipate his wishes and give him no further cause for complaint.

On the fourth morning, Jarrod returned from Making the Day to find the Songean perched high on a rock, his hand shading his eyes against the reflection of the dawn in the far-off snow. He was scanning the dark mists of the valley. It would be at least an hour before the sunlight crawled down and dispersed them, but they seemed to have provided him with the information he sought. He chivvied them into an early start and set an unusually crisp pace. He kept it up.

They rode through the noontide hours without any sign of pause or explanation. They kept the pace up until early afternoon, when they rounded a tricky spur and headed East along the side of a valley that fell in easy folds to a watercourse. The current ran strongly between banks grouted out in the snowmelt month of Greeningale. Runnels, broadened by game going down to drink, cut their way to it. It was close to one of these that Sandroz finally halted. He swung down from the saddle and watched the other two ride up.

"Make camp," he announced. "Find flat place down there," and he indicated the slope with a flick of the thumb.

"This is as far as we go today?" The surprise was evident in Martin's voice.

"Yes. I leave you here. Rejoin garrison in Fort Bandor. Am late." The tone was as flat as ever. It was a plain statement of fact without the slightest tinge of apology or the heat that had surfaced so unexpectedly a few nights before.

The visitors sat in their saddles and digested the news. He's still angry, Jarrod thought, and mostly with me. I'm a Magician and I'm the one who slowed us down.

"You're going to leave us? Already?" The words came out of Martin's mouth with the stilted politeness reserved by hostesses for guests committing a social gaffe.

In reply, Sandroz turned the other way and pointed to the valley. Strung across it, well below them, was a dark flock of birds weaving its way South in a drunken ribbon. It broke apart and reformed itself into a wavering arrow as they watched.

"They are always first," he said. "New snow in high passes in six sennights."

"But that's before harvest time," Jarrod objected.

"Maybe in your country. No harvest in mountains." There was disdain underlying the utterance.

"But you haven't taken us anywhere," Martin complained.

"You no tell me what you look for. Just 'high valley with no people.' "

"Well, aren't there any that we can reach in time. We can't go back without trying at least one." Jarrod was distressed to hear his voice going higher.

"One. Maybe two. We make camp. I make map." He clicked his tongue at his pony and it moved obediently.

The two looked at each other in frustration and doubt and then Martin shrugged and dismounted. Jarrod did likewise and followed the rump of her horse over the rim of the path. They took the animals down to a slow rill that sank back into the ground within a hundred paces. They let the creatures drink and looked

around. Sandroz was squatting on his haunches, methodically
going through a saddlebag. Jarrod found that he did not like this
place where the earth seemed to suck the moisture in. It did not
seem like a good spot, nor a good time, to be losing the man
who had shepherded them for so long.

"It's difficult to keep track of the days, but I was sure that we
had longer than this," he said as he unbuckled the girthstrap to
accommodate the horse's swelling stomach. "I know he doesn't
like us, but I could have sworn he'd stick with us, at least until
he'd shown us the place he's been aiming for."

"I know. So did I, but it's obviously not going to do us any
good to argue with him. He's as stony as these bloody mountains. We'd better pray that this unicorn lives near here." She
sighed. "I suppose we get to prepare the campsite and do the fire
again." Jarrod wasn't sure if the sigh meant that she was as
down in the mouth as he, or if she was objecting to having to
do the work.

"With Sandroz in the mood he's been in, we don't have a
choice. I can't see enough big stones there for a hearth ring. I
reckon we'll have to lug some in from somewhere. You want to
get those first or clear first?" He tried to keep his tone light to
mask the turmoil he felt.

"Let's get some of the big ones first. We're bound to need
some of the smaller ones to fill in the chinks. At least he's taught
us how to build a proper fire, even though it is a pain in the
neck." She, too, was masking her emotions. "Two bloody
stories high and fifteen bloody great rocks for each. Come on
then, let's get unpacked and get going."

It didn't take long for them to locate and drag back what they
needed, but their arms ached as they tamped the last pebbles into
place.

"Wood?" Jarrod asked as he stretched.

"Let's get rid of the loose stuff first. Then why don't we get
the wood together?" Jarrod was surprised and pleased: they
usually separated. He nodded and smiled and busied himself
flinging away small stones.

Sandroz sat and ignored them. He drew patterns in the dirt.
Sometimes, when Jarrod looked over at him, he would rub away
a line that had been a river or a track made by crag leapers, it

was too far to tell which. The stick in his right hand wrote and the heel of his left smoothed away. He marked and remarked as the other two untied a rod and hung a pot over the unlaid fire. Then they got out cloaks to carry the faggots in.

The outlook was not promising. There was a line of osiers that looked invitingly dessicated, but Jarrod knew from bitter experience that their roots would burrow through rock to get to water and that the apparent dryness was caused by sticky bark that caught the dust to shield itself from the Summer sun.

"Let's push along the trail a bit," Martin suggested, her disquiet partially dispelled by the work, "and see if we can find something a little further on. There wasn't anything the way we came, was there?"

"Not that I saw. Mind you, I wasn't really looking. I didn't think we'd stop this soon."

"All right, let's go up and try then. By the way," she added with a sideways look, "how fit are you, really?"

"You mean, can I go on without Sandroz?" There was irritation at the edges of the words. " 'Course I can. My back's all healed up and my neck doesn't hurt any more. I don't know if I'm up to a major climb yet, but it shouldn't take too much longer."

She looked at him and grinned unexpectedly. "I certainly hope you're better company without him. You groan wonderfully, especially in your sleep, but it's a very limited repertoire. Between the two of you, I feel as if I'm turning into a mute."

"You haven't exactly been a purling fount of conversation yourself, you know."

"I know. I'm sorry, I shouldn't have said that. The truth is that I'd rather come to depend on him and this animosity of his has upset me. I didn't mean to be so sarky."

"That's all right. I know just how you feel. There must be something more to it than the baby, but, unless he just hates Magic, I don't know what it is."

"Well," she said judiciously, "not everybody's that comfortable around Magicians."

"What are we going to do if this valley of his turns out to be a dud?" Jarrod asked to change the subject.

"I don't really know." Martin shifted her cloak from one

shoulder to another. "I hadn't thought about it. I just assumed we'd find it—what with that verse and everything."

"Well, I'm not going back until we've had a thorough look." He paused and scanned the mountains around them. "There's got to be more than one valley."

"Let's see what the weather does and, in the meantime, let's hope we can find enough wood for tonight's fire. Anyway," she added aggressively, "how am I supposed to know what's going to happen? You're the one who's supposed to be under the hand of prophecy." But the next instant the caustic tone was gone. "Maybe it means that we're fated to be lucky and the bloody thing will be sitting and waiting for us." She glanced at him and gave him a tight little smile, moved to the side of the path and scooped up some dead needles to use as kindling.

The rest of the afternoon passed in a whirl of sunlight and stooping. Gradually their mood lightened and they turned to laughter and good-natured competition. It was impossible for them to believe that they were in the fag end of Summer. The skies were clear and the air was too soft, the sun too hot, for that. In spite of the Songean, time seemed elastic and the season without end. They foraged companionably and Jarrod covertly watched the light imprisoned in Martin's hair. Sandroz' defection made him feel very close to her.

Waking well before dawn, as usual, Jarrod was surprised to find that Martin was already awake and puffing at the glowing embers. He nodded to her. The pallid light cast no shadows, it merely failed to penetrate past things, but years of habit had made him comfortable in the dregs of night. He looked up into the mountainside, hidden in the blackness of its own devising. Somewhere under it, he knew, was the sun he sought.

He reemerged into morning and looked at the thin, high clouds that had materialized with disfavor. He rose with a litheness that pleased him and made his way back to the fire. Martin ladled out a steaming mug of chai and handed it to him. Sandroz too was up and sat on his haunches on the far side of the fire stirring something in the cooking pot.

"Is that what I think it is?" Jarrod asked softly.

"I expect so. It's a special farewell treat. It's not every day that we get a chance to eat Songuard's famous oat pudding."

Martin's voice was even, but her eyes gave her away. Jarrod
kept his sigh inside.

"Not again," he said in Arunic. "He really must detest us.
There ought to be some way that stuff could be used against the
enemy; it's lethal."

"It would probably turn the tide," Martin answered in the
same tongue. "It looks and smells just like the glop they live in,
so they wouldn't know what hit them until it was too late."
Jarrod chuckled and switched a little guiltily into Common to ask
if there was anything he could do.

"No need. Ready soon. Oat pudding. Last time you have
chance for it in maybe long time." Jarrod smiled at him and
thought that the prospect of leaving them had certainly put the
man into a good humor.

"That's probably true," Martin said, deadpan.

"What time are you going to have to leave?" Jarrod asked
politely.

"We eat. I go after I show you map I make." He pointed to a
pile of provisions he had stacked off to one side. "You take
those. I not need." He looked back and his teeth gleamed
suddenly. "You not worry," he said, "I not leave oats," making Jarrod wonder just how much Arunic the man understood.

Martin got up, went over to the animals and took off their
feedbags. Sandroz went on stirring the pot placidly. Finally, as
much to break the silence as anything else, Jarrod said, "I know
it's my fault that you're late and I'm sorry. If I hadn't let myself
get captured, we'd probably be at your valley by now. Will it get
you into trouble?"

The Songean looked at him and made a small shrugging
movement. "Maybe. Not important. Umbrians not your fault.
Being sick their fault, not your fault." He nodded. "Call Martin," he said, rising effortlessly. "I show you map now. Pudding can wait."

Jarrod halooed downslope and Sandroz went and got a thin
roll of parchment out of his saddlebag.

"Breakfast ready?" Martin asked with a conspiratorial wink
as she came up.

"Not yet," Jarrod replied, "but Sandroz is going to show us
the map he's made. Don't worry, the pudding won't spoil."

He pulled his lips in to stop from smiling as Sandroz joined them. Martin shot him a venomous look and settled herself on the other side of their soon-to-be-former guide. The little man unrolled his map and weighted it down with a couple of large pebbles. Then he jabbed a blunt, broken-nailed forefinger down.

"You here. This trail go on ten, maybe fifteen leagues. Then it go down." The finger squiggled back in the direction of the Central Mountains. "You not go down. You cross that." The finger flicked over the Northern spur. He glanced from side to side and they nodded to show their comprehension. "No big trail there. You walk horses. Trail again on other side. Go this way, then North, four five days." The finger moved smoothly upward, stopped and flicked to the right. "Above here. On mountain. Not see from below. High. Almost at top."

"That's the valley you mentioned?" Martin asked, craning over his shoulder.

"Yes, but not real valley."

"I'm afraid I don't quite understand," Jarrod said from the other side.

"You will see. Not have proper words," and with that they had to be content.

"Are there any others?"

"I mark them," he replied, his finger touching down at three more points, all further North.

"I see," said Jarrod, "and what's this Anvil of . . . I can't read the rest of it."

"Gods. Anvil of Gods. Sometimes Anvil of Creation. Sacred mountain to us. Very special place. Not for you." He gave them a meaningful look.

"Why not?" Martin asked ingenuously. Sandroz pushed the pebbles off and the map rolled up on itself.

"Only for dead. Not for you," was all he said as he handed it to Martin. "We eat now. Then I go."

"We do thank you for this," Jarrod said as Martin rose and went to put the document away in her pack, "and for all the other help you've given us. We couldn't possibly have made it this far without you." Sandroz merely grunted and attended to his pudding. He ladled out three large bowls full and handed one to Jarrod.

"Remember, you not stay long. If you come again, you come earlier. You have map now." He gave the young man a long, level stare and then started in on his breakfast.

The oat pudding remained a taste unacquired, but the two foreigners made a special effort to put on a show of appreciation. If it registered on Sandroz, it was not apparent. They cleaned off the utensils in the rill while Sandroz packed up his pot and saddled up his compact little mount. He strapped on his saddle-bags and turned to shake each one solemnly by the hand, bowing slightly as he did so.

"If gods wish it, we meet again. If gods wish it, you find." He forestalled any further thanks or farewells by mounting immediately and riding off down the valley. The other two called out their goodbyes and waved until he was hidden by a fold. He never turned around or lifted a hand.

"Strange wee man," Martin remarked as they made their way back to the fireplace. "Oddly enough, I think I'm going to miss him; him and his bloody oat pudding." She blew out her breath and rubbed her stomach. "I feel as if someone had poured lead into me."

"Me too. I suppose we'd better divide up the food he left."

"Right," Martin said, authority returning to her voice. "Then we'll push off. We can't afford to dawdle any more."

She picked up her bags and went over to the pile of supplies. Jarrod followed her over amid stirrings of resentment at the way that she was taking over again. He had a contrary feeling that he was going to miss Sandroz more than she would.

CHAPTER XI

MARTIN SET A CRACKING PACE THAT WAS MUCH HARDER ON HER
horse than it was on Jarrod's longer-legged one. As a result,
evening found them in sight of the rocky divider that Sandroz
had indicated, although it was still a good half day away. They
pushed right on through the red-lit hour and had to make do with
sleeping ground that was neither level nor sheltered. They were
too tired to hunt for wood in the uninviting dark and contented
themselves with gnawing at the last, bone hard pieces of cheese
that had materialized from Sandroz' pack. It rained on them a
couple of times in the night and they rose, stiff, damp and
cranky, well before dawn. Martin waited while Jarrod completed
his ritual and then they set off in the drear early morning
greyness.

The ridge proved further off than the eye had promised and
they had to settle for a night at its base. Their long-suffering
mounts slipped and slid at the ends of their lead reins and the
humans fared no better. It was hard and disagreeable work and
they crested it sweating and short of breath. They rested for a
little while and then sidestepped down to a well-travelled game
path that, mercifully, appeared where Sandroz had said it would.
Martin led the way North, keeping the map resolutely in her
possession.

Thereafter their choice of trails was, for the most part, made
obvious, but there were stretches where the track had been

washed away or blocked by rockslide since Sandroz had last
passed that way. They were forced to dismount and detour
several times and Martin fretted at the delays. Jarrod, however,
found himself in an inexplicably good mood. He completed his
new bow and hunted happily whenever Martin allowed a halt.
For the first time since his capture by the Umbrians, he hummed
and whistled to himself as he rode along.

The pair were warier than they had been under Sandroz' shielding tutelage, especially when they came across a trail that looked
as if it might lead to one of the high villages. While they talked
very little to each other, neither of them felt the desire for
outside company. The silences between them were companionable and remained so. The riding and the hunting kept them
pleasantly weary, but it was the satisfying tiredness that comes
when people feel that they are accomplishing something.

The weather was cooperative for a full sennight and there were
days and nights of unsurpassed splendor. The Central Mountains
were often hidden by haze, but there were always closer sights to
catch the eye and the imagination. Herds of tiny pop-up deer
bounced away from their approach on stiff legs and there were
birds everywhere, flocking in preparation for the migration. Here
and there, fireblanket trees stood in splendid isolation, their
scarlet fans, starting well above the riders' heads, attested to the
depths of the snows to come. Jarrod found that, since he didn't
know precisely what he was looking for, nor where he should
look, he looked at everything as keenly as he could.

There were times when he wanted to pull over and savor some
unknown animal, or a panorama studded with snow-capped peaks,
but he didn't feel like trying Martin's patience. The nights had
their rewards too. They were cool but spectacular, and on a
couple of them Jarrod forced himself to stay awake to see the
nightmoon rise. He sat with his back against a tree trunk,
stroking his lengthening beard and drinking in the stillness. He
watched as it grew from crescent to orb above the screen of the
Gorodontious. The mountains seemed to be holding the moon
back, but, once it had broken free, it sailed up the sky and
outlined the sleeping Martin and her tumble of tawny hair. Jarrod
was aware that Greylock's specific prohibition was making the

girl more desirable to him, but the knowledge did nothing to restrain the emotion.

On the morning of the eighth day after the crossing of the trackless ridge, they rode into an evergreen belt at the foot of what they thought was the mountain that Sandroz had shown them. The trail petered out among the trees, leaving them to pick their way up a sharply canted slope. They heard the rain above them long before they felt it and it added to the sense of foreboding the forest had imposed on them. The lack of sun added to their feeling of being lost. Martin kept consulting the map, to no purpose. She pressed on, nevertheless, and they finally dismounted when the going got too steep. The wet leaves were slippery under the soles of their boots and the trees dripped on them as they plodded on.

"Are you sure this is the right mountain?" Jarrod asked.

"I certainly hope so. My legs seem to have lost the habit of walking," she replied as she kneaded a calf muscle. She looked up and gave a little shrug. "If the map's right, and as far as I can tell it is, then this should be the right mountain."

"Then Sandroz' place should be up there somewhere, shouldn't it?" He pointed up to his right.

"That would seem to follow. Trouble is, I can't even see the mountain."

"What if I climbed one of the trees?"

"It couldn't do any harm."

Jarrod tossed his reins to her, crossed over to a likely tree and worked his way up and out of view. He was back again in fifteen minutes, hair plastered down against his scalp, hands black and face smudged. The front of his clothes was a bark-besmirched mess. Martin grinned at him as he came up.

"You look just awful."

"Thank's a lot, Martin. Remind me to pay you a compliment one of these days."

"A compliment from you?" she said in mock amazement. "Pigs'll fly first. Did you see anything from up there?"

"Not too much: the ceiling's very low. These trees go on for at least another mile and then it gets bare and rocky. At least, that's what it looked like through the rain."

"Anything that looked like a usable path?"

"Not that I could see."

"Did you spot a waterfall?"

"No. Why?"

"Because, according to the map, the valley's supposed to be above a waterfall. At least, I think that's what it means."

"Want me to have a look?" Her icy stare was all the reply he needed. "There is a stream though."

Martin gave him an enigmatic smile. "Then I suppose we better have a bite to eat and then go on up there and find out."

"The sooner the better," Jarrod replied, gesturing to his dirty clothes with hands of like condition.

His personal estimation of distance proved to be a little off and they spent the rest of the afternoon among trees that continued to drip on them long after the sun was out. They toiled on doggedly until the daymoon dyed their surroundings. They bivouacked just inside the tree line and rolled up for sleep earlier than usual.

When Jarrod woke he spent a bemused while watching the nightmoonlight make patterns across his cloak and listening to the trees talk with the nightwind. He roused himself and hoisted himself to his feet. He circumnavigated the sleeping shape of his companion and went out beyond the trammeling of the tree-cast shadows. He made his way along an outcropping of rock and leaned against its wind-scoured point to stare out across the landscape. The moon was bright enough to read by and it sparkled off a ribbon of water far above.

The sight brought no inner tremors, just a sense of certainty and excitement. He sat himself down under the impersonal benison of the stars and sank happily into his diurnal rite.

Now it was Jarrod who was eager to be on the move, but, after a brief argument with Martin, he was persuaded of the wisdom of spending half a day in hunting and the search for dry wood. They gathered all that they could, tying the brittle sticks into two equal bundles, and roasted the game that they had snared in the remnants of the previous night's fire. They stashed their saddles, changed into their heavier clothes and hid the rest of their gear. The last thing they did was to secure the horses on long tethers, close to the stream. There was grass enough on the banks and they would not lack for water. That done, they set out up the lone streak of watered green in a grey land splotched with browns.

There was very little of Jarrod's lightness of heart left after two hours. The climbing boots he had bought in Belengar chafed him above the heel and across the instep. The bundle of firewood strapped across his shoulders jounced awkwardly and threw his balance off. The sky was clear and the sun had finally roused itself and was taking its revenge. Jarrod felt the sweat trickling into his beard and down his ribs. When they finally took a break, he emptied his water flask over his head and then refilled it from the gurgling rush. He sat down and eased his boots off.

"Can you believe this view?" Martin said, as she sat composedly, breathing easily.

"What?" Jarrod looked up from the inspection of his feet. "Oh yes. The trouble is that I'm beginning to think that I'm taking all of this for granted. I didn't think it could happen, but we've seen so much that it takes something really special to catch my attention now."

"When you live in the country, instead of at court all the time, you get into the habit of watching Nature. You'll find that, if you look closely enough, it keeps on changing. By the way, you should put on another pair of socks. You did bring a spare pair with you, didn't you? If you don't, you'll get blisters."

"My feet are hot enough as it is, thank you. They're burning up."

"Suit yourself. When you can't walk any more, I'll just have to go on without you. We don't have enough time left to sit around waiting for you to get fit again." Jarrod bit back a retort, but he rummaged around in his pack for his extra pair.

"And speaking of time," Martin said, "I think we should push on, don't you? I must say, we don't look any closer to that waterfall. I thought the mountain air was supposed to make things look as if they were nearer." She slipped into her pack straps, adjusted her faggots and helped Jarrod to strap his on. They set off again in silence and, for Jarrod, the pleasure in the day was quite gone. His interior comments on Martin were far from kind and, for a while, conversations ran through his head in which he said witty and unpleasant things.

They reached the bottom of the waterfall by sunset and pitched camp. The part that took the longest was finding a place out of the wind where they could lay a fire against the coming drop in temperature. Jarrod was grateful now for the thicker clothing and he had to admit that Martin had been right about the socks. He struggled with a recalcitrant tinder while the thoughts passed through his mind.

"I do not understand," Martin interrupted the wandering reverie, "why you don't just Magic the fire alight. You can do that, can't you? I mean there's no one up here except me to see you and I already know that you're a Magician."

"Because," replied Jarrod with gleeful patience, happy to be getting the last word in for once, "Magic changes things. It changes the patterns that things are made up of. Those changes can be felt, if you know how. The hardest thing to do is to change just one thing without affecting lots of other things. The differences are tiny: you can't see them, but they're there all the same. Now," he continued, sounding like an echo of Dean Sumner, "I think we can safely assume that a unicorn is a Magical creature and hence quite likely to detect the workings of Sorcery, even the simplest of tricks. If he's up there, I don't want to alert him."

"I suppose that makes sense," she conceded. "Unless, of course, it's expecting us." She continued to cut strips off the meat. Jarrod ignored that and decided to press his momentary advantage.

"Do you think I can have a look at the map?"

"Certainly. It's in my pack and my hands are all . . ." she broke off and waved them briefly. "It's right on top."

"Thanks," Jarrod said and went over and got it. He had no real need to see it, since it had remained firmly imprinted from Sandroz' demonstration, but he felt the need to assert himself.

They ate in silence and slept back to back to conserve heat and their supply of wood. It made for an uneasy night for Jarrod.

They tackled the fall in the morning and found it surprisingly easy. The rope that linked them served more as a reassurance than as a practical aid. There was a pool at the top of the falls that proved to be the source of the stream, but of a valley there was no sign. They scoured the mountain from their new viewpoint, but, apart from a raggedness at the top that had not been apparent the day before, saw no hint of a significant indentation.

"I suppose we better keep going up," Martin said. The voice was cheerful but the mouth drew in with disappointment. "That bloody man said something about not being able to see it from below, but I thought we'd be able to see it from here, didn't you?"

"Somewhere around here," Jarrod agreed. "There was a sideways 'v' and 'valley' written right over the waterfall."

"Well, he was certainly right about this being away from any major trails. I wonder how he came to find it in the first place?"

"I can't imagine, but I suppose we ought to be glad that it's so remote and well hidden. It makes it a more likely place somehow."

"First we've got to find it," Martin replied discouragingly.

"Oh, I'm sure we will. I've got a sort of feeling about it."

"I just hope you're right. You ready? I think we should head for the middle one of those." She pointed toward three irregular, black patches below the summit. "Unless you've got any better ideas?"

"No. It'll probably be easier to spot from above," Jarrod replied with an optimism he no longer altogether felt.

They checked the knots and set off into the swirling wind. The clouds had come suddenly close and it grew colder as they climbed. White plumes came and went more frequently from their mouths and their pace began to slow. Two difficult faces were negotiated with the help of pitons and Jarrod thought back gratefully to their earlier experiences in Paladine. Despite that training and the protection of the leather that they were wearing, they bruised and scraped themselves. 'It better be up here,' Jarrod said to himself after a particularly painful encounter, but he kept his counsel.

"Are we going all the way to the top?" he yelled into the wind when they took a rest.

For answer Martin said, "Take a good look at those dark patches. Do they suggest anything to you? I'm feeling a little woozy, so I can't be sure." She saw the look on his face and hastened to reassure him. "No, I'm all right, really. It's just the altitude."

"What do you think you see?" Jarrod asked cautiously.

"Do they seem to have depth to you?"

"Depth? You mean you think there's something growing up there?"

"No, I don't think it's . . . I'm not sure what I mean, except that they don't look flat to me. I don't see anything up there that would be big enough to throw those kinds of shadows. I don't know. This may sound peculiar, but d'you think that sign could mean through the mountain rather than on the mountain?" She sounded dubious.

"Through?" Jarrod asked musingly. "You mean it's on the other side?"

"I don't know about that. No, I was thinking more in terms of caves."

"You could be right, you know," Jarrod said, excitement beginning to well again. "That might be it. It would explain those cryptic things that Sandroz said." The aches were forgotten. "What are we waiting for?" he asked. "Let's go and find out."

The stiffness of the morning was dispelled, the thinness of the air was transformed into a tonic and all traces of friction vanished as they tackled the steep scarp. If Jarrod had been carrying as much wood as he had the day before, he would not have felt it. His mood of anticipation was back and it was stronger than ever. He could not be sure, of course, that it was a unicorn that awaited them, but it was something important, of that much he was certain. The only conversations he held with himself as he spread-eagled upward were attempts to keep his expectations under control.

The technical difficulties of the climb did that for him. There were plenty of holds for toes and fingers, but the going was very rough and a gentle overhang made them lose sight of their objective. It took most of the afternoon to work their way up to the ledge that ran below the vertical face containing the three openings, for openings they proved to be. They scanned the mountainside below them as they rested. They looked for any trace of a valley or an opening that they might have missed on the way up, but there were none.

Jarrod stood up and began to prowl carefully along the ledge. He looked up and studied the three, toothless mouths. The rightmost was the lowest, but the rock beneath it was worn and smooth and gave no hint of crevices or bosses. The lefthand hole was more approachable, but it was the smallest of the three. The one in the middle was both larger and higher up. He craned his neck back and stared at it, half expecting a horned, white head to pop out and look back down at him. When Martin spoke at his elbow, it startled him.

"I'm sorry, what did you say?"

"I said we'd better get up there. The sun's going down and I don't want to spend another night in the open if I can help it." She smiled at him. "Come on," she chivvied good-naturedly, "check your knots and let's get going."

With Martin in the lead once more, they spidered their way up. It proved easier than Jarrod had feared it would be and, twenty minutes later, he was hauled onto the bumpy floor.

"It's just a cave," he said, looking around, and the disappointment was clear in his voice and face.

"Yes, it looks that way, doesn't it? Oh well, it's a good place to spend the night. It'll be warmer than it is out there." Jarrod knew that she was trying to make the best of things and willed himself to emulate her.

"Good thing we brought the wood," he said feebly.

"Come on, cheer up. Let's look around and see if we're alone in here." Her voice echoed off the ceiling.

"All right, but if we're not it must have flown in or been born here. Let me get the tallow out." Sparks jumped in the gloom and jumped again before the wick caught and the yellow light bloomed. Shielding it with one curved hand, he moved away from the roseate glow of the cavemouth.

"Looks like it goes back quite a ways," he said. "Oh no," he added as the light was reflected by the stone just ahead of him, "this seems to be the extent of it." Then the candle went out.

"Hey, Martin, what did you go and do that for?"

"I didn't do anything. Hang on, I think I've got a flint in my pocket. Where are you? Oh, there you are. All right, hold still." Sparks flew twice and then the candle came alive again.

"There," said Martin. "Hello. Wait a minute. There's an opening over there. At least I think that's what it is. Bring the

tallow over here, will you?'' Jarrod advanced, guarding the
flame carefully as it guttered.

"You're right, there's a bend.'' He edged around in front of
her. "And look, isn't that light? It is, Martin. It is. It is.''

"All right, all right. Careful with that candle.'' They moved
forward and turned to the right, walking single file between the
narrowing walls. The tallow winked out again, but they could
see their way now in the pink spill from the back entrance. Jarrod
had to hold himself back from running to it. When they reached
it, the heavy richness of the air was the first thing that struck
them. Martin swayed and gripped Jarrod's arm.

They found themselves looking down into a bowl. It was deep
and the upper third was a ring of cliffs that fell straight down
toward the dense foliage that was dimly perceivable below. The
mountain rose another two or three hundred feet above their
heads, but the far rim had been broken off at some point in its
history and the ledge they stood on was level with its top. Lush,
moist scents drifted up in a heady commingling.

The cliffs that faced them were divided into horizontal bands
of color. They were clearly defined even in the waning light.
They were earth tones all; rings of umber and burnt sienna, a
marl red over ochre and a broad stripe of sulpherous yellow
edged about with bassaltine black. Here and there an exposed
vein gleamed as it marbled the stratum that held it. In places, the
mountain had shouldered the order aside and buckled the level
run, but, for the most part, they looked as if they had been
painted on a long time ago. The picture had deteriorated since
and pockets had been eaten into the yellow layer, but it had lost
none of its ability to surprise and overawe.

CHAPTER XII

THE TWO STOOD THERE TRANSFIXED. MARTIN'S BREATH WAS COMING and going, short and shallow, through her open mouth and Jarrod found that he wasn't breathing at all for long stretches. His knees felt insecure. The place was so fitting, so primal and apart, that the fantastic was easy to accept. It was the perfect place to find a unicorn, replete with the atmosphere of timeless seclusion. He let his breath out slowly and eased himself to the edge of their aerie, looked down and then quickly up again as he felt the pull of vertigo. He stepped back and stared ahead to still the whirl. His eye was caught by what seemed to be movement at the back of one of the cavities in the sulphur stratum. His heart bumped and he screwed his eyes up in an effort to see better, but the ebbing light defeated him. He was about to enlist Martin's help and then thought better of it.

They stood in silence until the light had faded entirely, unable to tear themselves away. They had come so far for this and been so close to disappointment. When they could see no more, they turned reluctantly back to their cave, relit the tallow and made their way to its other opening.

"D'you think it's down there? I do," Jarrod volunteered as he laid a stingy fire.

"I didn't see anything, but it's certainly impressive enough. You really think this is where the unicorn lives?"

Jarrod weighed his words. "I certainly want there to be one," he replied, "and I'm very glad, all of a sudden, that I didn't bring my bow."

"What's that supposed to mean?"

"It's just a feeling, but I'm glad I didn't bring it."

"You and your feelings," Martin said with a mischievous smile that convinced Jarrod that he had been right to keep quiet earlier. "You can't see anything through the tree tops. The only things I spotted were some birds."

"More than I did, but then I wasn't too good about looking down. It doesn't affect me usually, but that was just too far straight down for comfort."

"Doesn't bother me, luckily." Martin passed over a piece of cold, cooked meat. They sat and chewed for a while, each lost in their own thoughts, and then Martin looked across the dying flames and said, "By the way, what are we going to do with the unicorn once we've found it? Have you come up with anything yet?

"Not really," Jarrod admitted, feeling relaxed and content. "You remember what Greylock said. We'll just have to wait for inspiration when and if it turns up."

"Well, that may be good enough for you, but I always like to have a plan. As it is, I don't know how we're going to get down there, let alone get a unicorn back up again." She reached for her flask and took a pull.

"We'll just have to wait for morning and see, but there's got to be a way down. I can't believe that we'd be allowed to get all this way and then not be able to get down there."

"What do you mean 'allowed'?" Martin asked as she moved closer to the tiny fire.

"This isn't an ordinary mission, you know," Jarrod replied severely, irked by her lack of understanding. "It's not like hunting for my lady's slipper on Greening Day. I'm meant to find that unicorn." His tone was fierce.

"All right, all right. Don't get carried away. There's no reason to get so indignant. Anyway, there's nothing we can do about it tonight, so we might as well turn in and try to get some rest. I don't know about you, but my arms and legs feel as if they're about to fall off."

"I'm sorry I got excited," Jarrod said, mollified. "It's just that, well, you're going to inherit a fortune and a Holding and a title and the whole thing and this is the one thing that I'll ever get to do. So you see, it's rather important to me. I didn't mean to go off the deep end. I suppose I'm just keyed up at being this close.''

"All the more reason to get some sleep. Come on, let's turn in.''

"In a minute.'' Jarrod got up and put his cloak around his shoulders to ward off the creeping chill. "I'll just go and take another look.'' He stooped and lit the candle from a glowing end of wood.

"Well, goodnight then, and be careful with that tallow. We'll probably need it later.''

"I shan't be long. Sleep well.''

Jarrod walked along the lefthand wall, looking for rocks that might trip him on the return journey, and blew the taper out when he reached the ledge. There was no nightmoon and the air below him was inky. Above him, the stars burned with unaccustomed clarity, or so it seemed to him. Random sounds drifted up from the depths and he strained to identify them. There must be creatures living down there, he thought, and if there really is anything out there controlling all of this, please show me how I get to them.

The night vouchsafed no answer and he sighed and turned back. He knew that he was too excited for sleep, but it stole him away anyhow. It was a night for dreams, but none troubled him or remained with him when he woke.

For once in his life, Jarrod was impatient with his need to Make the Day and when he finally reached the ledge he found Martin there before him. Hearing his approach, she turned and then pointed wordlessly. He peered across the valley in the dim, dawn light.

"Where? What is it?'' he whispered.

"Right over there. In the yellow,'' she whispered back.

He followed her finger and sucked his breath in. There was movement. He was almost sure that there was movement within some of the indentations. Tendrils of mist rose and made him doubtful.

"I can't be sure," he said, still in the same hushed tones. "The light isn't good enough for me to see clearly."

"We'll just have to wait for the sun then."

"And that's the last place in the valley it'll reach."

"Well, we might as well get a bite to eat and then see if we can find a way down. Whatever's over there isn't going to run away," Martin said gently, responding to the bleakness in his voice.

The light was stronger when they returned, but the far side of the bowl was still in shadow.

"Which way do you want to go?" Martin broke in on Jarrod's thoughts.

"Hm? Oh yes. I must admit that neither side looks too promising."

"Had you noticed that only one of the other passages comes through?" She pointed to a second dark maw off to their left.

"No I hadn't. The other one must just be a cave then."

"I suppose so. Got any premonitions this morning?" Jarrod glanced at her sharply, trying to detect sarcasm, but her face was passive.

"No. No premonitions, no preferences. We might as well try this side first." He was longing for action of some kind to break the tension that was building up in him and started off.

"Wait a minute," Martin said. "I think we ought to rope up. We don't know how solid this thing is."

"You're quite right." He felt sheepish. "What a nasty thought. I want to get to the bottom, but not that fast." He was trying for humor, but it sounded flat in his ears.

He proceeded cautiously, the rope tied firmly around his waist. He concentrated on the uneven stone in front of him, looking out to his left as little as possible. The going was slippery in places and, in others, water had collected against the mountain, pushing him uncomfortably close to the edge. He checked the rock wall above him from time to time, but nowhere did he see a feasible way of climbing upward had they had a mind to. Once he heard Martin slip and fall and braced himself to anchor them, but there was no jerk on the rope, only vivid swearing.

"I'm all right. I'm all right," she said. "Let's get on with it." He moved off again, but it was several minutes before his heart was back to normal.

He had become accustomed to the smell of the air and no longer noticed the verdant aroma, but he couldn't get used to the winds. They arrived with varying force and from different directions. They kept him on his guard and off balance. The feeling was especially acute when they came to a section where the majority of the ledge had been carried away. He fought off the unease that spun through him when he contemplated the two-foot wide ribbon that was left. He swallowed hard and then resolutely turned his face to the wall and started to shuffle sideways. The gust caught them when they were about halfway across the shallow arc and they clung to the surface as it shook them.

"Bloody, stupid wind," Jarrod screamed into the buffeting, his composure dissolving.

"Easy, boy. Easy there. We're going to be all right. It's gone now. We're all right." Martin talked to him as she would to a nervously prancing horse and Jarrod, stung by his lapse, summoned up fortitude. He recited his litany of concentration silently and then resumed his crab-like progress. By the time they reached broader footing, he had himself well in hand, though he did not tempt fate by looking down.

His pace was faster now and he kept it going until he reached a spot where the ledge widened out. There he was stopped by a jumble of rocks. They tried to clear a way through for half an hour before they admitted defeat. They retreated the way they had come and Jarrod found the going much less nerve-wracking than before. This time he knew it could be done and this time he was following.

It was difficult to tell the passage of time, since the sun had yet to put in an appearance, but they reckoned that the trip had taken them a good hour. They retrieved their flasks and sipped as they waited. It was obvious now that there were living things at the backs of the caves opposite, but what they were remained a mystery. They watched the continuing and incomprehensible activity and shielded their eyes when the sun finally crested the rim. Gradually the light rose up the far side, illuminating the bands, one by one, and bringing them to vivid life.

The movements opposite ceased, as if by accord, and nothing moved until the whole expanse was bathed in sunlight. Then the creatures began to stir. One after the other they emerged from their shelters and threw themselves out into the empty air. Jarrod's body stiffened and he cried out in horror and denial as the shapes fell. Then wings began to spread, with a series of snaps that echoed and overlapped, and the beasts began to glide on a downward curve across the valley. As each reached its appointed spot, it arced into a slow, upward spiral. They acted independently, and yet there was order in the powerful stroking. Cloudsteed after cloudsteed left the ledges and soared out into the morning sun to cavort in stately fashion and to graze on the treetops below. They were beautiful, majestic and riveting, but they were not unicorns.

The visitors sat staring at the graceful beasts as they went about their morning's feeding. Neither had ever seen a wild cloudsteed before, nor so many of the breed together in one place. The bowl was so thick with them that it was hard to tell how many there were. There was such a coming and going that Jarrod couldn't be certain whether the same animals were involved or whether the various waves were completely different aerial herds. Every time he tried to concentrate on a particular animal he lost it in the complex flying pattern.

"They're very beautiful and very graceful. I don't for the life of me understand how they avoid crashing into each other. I could watch them for hours, but I think we ought to get back to looking for that way down of yours." Martin broke a silence that had lasted a good forty minutes. "The unicorn obviously isn't over there, so we don't have to bother trying to get round."

"Might just as well." Jarrod got awkwardly to his feet, using Martin's shoulder as a way station. "I've never seen anything like this before." He shook his head wonderingly.

"I don't suppose anyone has, outside of Sandroz perhaps. And speaking of him, why do you suppose he never said anything about them."

"Who knows? Maybe they weren't here when he found the place. Except with him you never can tell."

"Let's go and get the rope. D'you want to lead, or shall I?"

"I'll go first. It's my turn again."

Jarrod led off five minutes later and, when they reached the other tunnel, found that it emerged from the mountain at a level with his waist.

"It must bend round like ours does," he said, leaning into it. "I can't see any light from the other side."

"It might not be the same one. Ours may be the only one that goes all the way through."

"Hadn't thought of that; and we picked it first time. See, I told you we were meant to find this place."

"I don't know about that, but I think we're about to be discovered ourselves. If I were you Jarrod, I'd turn around very slowly and then keep absolutely still." He heard the tension in her voice and obeyed instantly. "I've got an idea," she added, "that we're about to be inspected by the local inhabitants. Look over there," and she nodded an indication.

One of the cloudsteeds was climbing through the air toward them. The wings paused momentarily and it spiralled skyward on an updraft before resuming its effortless stroking. The steed approached, looming larger, and then angled up sharply. For a moment Jarrod thought that it meant to fly out of the valley entirely, but it circled and hovered about twenty feet above their ledge.

Both humans shrank back against the mountainside and continued to gaze upward, their hair whipped about by the wind generated by the wings. The young Magician reflexively tried to discern the living pattern while his hands followed older instincts and gripped the lip of the cavemouth. He stared up at the cloudstallion, for at that distance, and from that angle, there could be no mistaking the gender.

It was white and, in the full morning light, the coat gleamed in ways that hurt the eye. The sun flashed from the great hooves and shone down legs held stiffly out as the animal stayed aloft. Great, blue veins ran across the underside of the wing membrane up to the massy, jointed forebones. The skin on the hairless belly was smoothly distended and pink. The hair on chest and legs was bright and whorled in places. The mane and tail were full and streaming and half a shade darker than the body. The enormously muscled shoulders made both croup and hindquarters look slight by comparison. Large, bulging, blue eyes, with bloodshot whites, stared back. It did not convey a sense of friendliness.

Jarrod let go of the rock and held his arms up, palms out and fingers spread. If the cloudstallion understood the gesture it gave no sign of it. The tableau held for several minutes and then the huge beast snorted loudly and wheeled away, banking steeply. It flew swiftly toward the far side, diminishing as it went. Martin exhaled slowly and straightened up.

"Oof. I can't say I liked that at all. What on earth possessed you to put your hands up?"

"I felt disapproval very strongly, a sort of sense of outrage. It just seemed natural at the time."

"Who knows?" said Martin, not taking her eyes from the dwindling cloudsteed, "it may have done some good. Would you look at him move. No loops or swoops; he's going straight home. I think he's landed on that sort of balcony in the middle, but I can't be sure. The sun's in my eyes. Anyway, if that was him, he's gone inside."

"D'you get the feeling that he's gone to report?" Jarrod asked.

"Could be. I don't know enough about cloudsteeds. What I do know is that we ought to get back to work. D'you want to explore this passageway first?"

"We can always do this on our way back, so why don't we find what else this ledge has to offer?"

They went over rope and bootlaces and set off along the projection again. Jarrod gradually picked up speed as the footing remained firm, but he noticed that he tended to keep his left arm close to the wall and smiled ruefully at himself.

"Jarrod. I think we should stop." The voice was low and urgent. Jarrod froze.

"What's wrong? Are you all right?"

"Oh, there's nothing wrong with me. It's just that our company's coming back and he's bringing friends with him." Jarrod slowed and saw four approaching shapes on a slow climb toward them.

"What are we going to do?" asked Martin. "I don't much like the look of this. And I don't much fancy facing the turbulence generated by all those wings."

"You're right. Let's see if we can get back to the other cave. They've a ways to go yet."

The sun was a dazzling hindrance now and made the oncoming steeds difficult to see and distances hard to gauge. They pelted along with their eyes glued to the footing, not quite knowing why they felt compelled to flee, but commanded by the pricklings that ran up and down their spines.

They reached the first opening without mishap and stopped to peer out at the winged shapes. They were much closer now and any hope that they might not be headed for the intruders became unrealistic. Jarrod looked at Martin and his eyebrows rose in question. Martin nodded quickly and turned to run for their home base. Jarrod raced after her, holding the rope clear, his fear of the height overridden by more pressing anxieties. The cloudsteeds caught them before they had attained their goal.

Winds propelled by their wings hurled themselves at the pair as they clung to the side of the mountain. They tore at clothes and blinded them with their own hair. Breathing became haphazard and they felt themselves being pried loose.

"Keep going!" Jarrod yelled. "They'll get us if we stay here." He pushed at Martin's shoulder and she moved at once. One of the cloudsteeds dropped toward them and lashed out with a sharp, horny hoof, causing them to flinch, even though the blow was remote. They flung themselves on in a stooped, shuffling run and were only aware of the second attack when the force of the creature's wings slammed them into the wall.

"On, on, on, on, on!" Jarrod found himself screaming as he surged for the hole that meant survival. He caught Martin with one arm and hustled her forward. Martin was screaming too, but he couldn't make out the words. He flinched again as a shadow cut across them. He risked a look upward and saw that the creatures were circling. He lowered his head for the last dash.

The winged wardens continued to monitor them after they lay sprawled on the cave floor, chests heaving and bowels churning. Slowly, the sobbing breath subsided into evenness and they pushed themselves up.

"I thought," Martin said tiredly, "that cloudsteeds were supposed to be man's noblest allies."

"Whoever said that had never met a wild cloudsteed. I don't think they liked us at all. We bloody nearly got killed."

"Why did they do that? We did nothing to provoke them."

"Except come here," Jarrod said wearily.

"They must be very touchy." Martin's spirit was returning.

"Perhaps they're protecting the unicorn?" Jarrod suggested, sounding unconvincing. He got up and dusted himself off, checking for cuts and bruises.

"It's more likely that we've stumbled on their private breeding ground and they resent the intrusion. After all, this is their territory."

"Well, territory or no territory, we've got to get past them. I wonder what they're up to?" He moved toward the pool of sunlight inside the mouth of the passage.

"Wait a minute. You don't mean that you still want to get down there?"

"Of course."

"You're out of your mind," Martin said, staring at his back. "Touched. Gone." She threw an arm out toward the opening. "They're never going to let us out of here. We can't hunt for the blasted unicorn if we're dead. They don't want us here, they've made that perfectly plain. They're still out there waiting, aren't they? Well, go ahead and see. See if they aren't still out there waiting?" Her voice had risen to shrillness.

"One of them's up there patrolling," Jarrod reported with as much calmness as he could muster.

"There you are. What did I tell you? There's no way we're going to get off that ledge." Both hands were gesturing broadly.

"There has to be a way. I told you that I felt it was the right place." He tried for coldness, but the strain showed clear in his voice.

"Well I don't care what you feel. It's not as if we'd seen the Motherless thing. This place belongs to the cloudsteeds and they don't want us here. Can't you get that through your stupid head?"

"Shut up!" The aftermath of fright and the beginnings of disappointment proved too strong for Jarrod. He took a deep breath and fought for patience. "Look," he said slowly, "if there was a unicorn here, it would make sense for them to guard it. Don't you see? This might be a test. You don't deserve a unicorn if you're frightened off at the first try." His words fell into a strained silence. Martin's eyes were blazing.

"It is not because I am afraid," she said glacially, each word separate and precise. "If you want to go out there and try it again, I'll go with you, even though I think you're a damned fool. But I warn you, if they don't let us through, I'm going back down the other side. Is that fair enough for you?"

"Fair enough. I can't do it without you and you know it. Listen," he added tiredly, "it doesn't do any good for us to fight like this. I'm sorry I yelled at you." There was appeal in his eyes as he tried to repair the breach.

"Oh, forget it," she said ungraciously. "This is supposed to be a joint venture. Mind you, if I think it's hopeless, we come straight back and tomorrow morning we head for our kind of horses again. Is that clear?"

"Quite clear, thank you. Let me go and see what's doing out there." He felt keyed up and confused and his sense of certainty had deserted him, but he knew that he couldn't leave without trying again. He turned back and peeked out of the entrance. The sentinel still flew, gliding around in tight circles, but it did not react when he stepped out. Jarrod stood for a while and waited and then began to walk carefully back and forth in front of the opening. When the only change was an intensification of interest, he returned to Martin and the two of them knotted the rope around their waists.

Jarrod was first out and moved immediately along the ledge to his left. He kept an eye on the cloudstallion and when it continued to content itself with observation, he tugged on the line. Martin followed him out onto the ledge and almost at once the attitude of the cloudsteed changed. It began to fly back and forth in an agitated manner and flung its head back to bugle a challenge. Jarrod refused to be intimidated and moved on.

The note of the creature's warning modulated and it flew down at the girl, its forehooves striking out at the air before it. Martin screamed and ducked. The animal pulled back and circled away. The rope was stretched tautly between them now and Jarrod waited impatiently for Martin to move again. He was about to yell encouragement to her when the guardian dived again, aiming for him this time. He backed hurriedly against the rock and raised a forearm to block out the sun. Suddenly the huge, winged horse was above him and turning swiftly. Pieces of stone began to fall around his ears and the wall behind him shuddered. The back legs lashed out again and rock bucked. He felt the tugging on the rope and turned as Martin waved frantically. He glanced over his left shoulder and saw the animal swinging around and readying itself for another pass. He gathered up the rope as he ran for the tunnel.

Once he had regained his breath, he undid the knots, stumped heavily and wordlessly to the other end of the passage and began repacking. Martin followed him, recoiling the line. She was on the verge of saying something several times, but she drew back.

"Look," she said at last, "even if there is a unicorn down there, you know we're not equipped for the job. We'll go and look at one of the other valleys and, if we don't find anything there, at least you know where this place is. We can come back next year with the right equipment, or extra help, or whatever it takes. All right?" Jarrod nodded mutely and continued to stow things away. He was drenched in sweat and it stung his eyes. He was also miserable and dejected.

CHAPTER XIII

IT TOOK THEM FAR LESS TIME TO DESCEND THAN IT HAD TO GET up, since their sliding feet were hastened both by the sense that time was running out on them and by a nagging feeling between the shoulder blades. It was only the uncertainty of the footing that prevented them from glancing up every few minutes to see if the cloudsteeds had flown out of their sanctuary in pursuit. The exertion had lifted Jarrod's mood somewhat and he was in the process of convincing himself that they had ventured where they had no right to go, that they had stumbled on some ancient spot forbidden to mankind. It reminded him of the way that he had felt when he had approached the Place of Power on that fateful night. That seemed such a long time ago. If there were already two such places on Strand, he argued to himself, then surely there would be more and one of them would be home to his unicorn.

The two scarcely spoke, except out of practical necessity, and Jarrod was deliberately withdrawn. Part of him wanted to punish Martin for being right, but it seemed to make no difference to her and she showed not the slightest trace of guilt. It added to his feeling of being out of sorts. The feeling was intensified by a storm that blew up without warning just as they reached the tree line and the discovery that both horses had slipped their tethers.

Martin found hers quickly enough, but hoofprints on either

bank proved that Jarrod's had forded the stream. He waded off in
search as the downpour drummed above him. By the time he had
caught and haltered the creature, he was soaking wet and smol-
dering with a resentment that the horse's evident pleasure in
seeing him again could not alleviate. By the time he got back,
tears were pricking at the edges of his eyes. Only his refusal to
embarrass himself in front of Martin enabled him to hold them
back. He took refuge in a hunting trip that gave him no solace
save that of solitude. He was tired and hungry and his bow was
no good in the rain.

He caught nothing, but he did find some bone comfey to add
to his stock of herbs and gathered some mushrooms so as not to
return entirely empty-handed. His mood was not improved by
the discovery that Martin had been able to bring down a rock
rabbit with an improvised sling.

Jarrod woke in the last of the deep black that prefigured dawn
and found that a strong wind had driven the clouds North. He
rose to Make the Day and when he returned the world was
new-washed and sparkling. The woods were alive with birds,
singing and rustling about in the undergrowth in search of their
morning meal. The privacy afforded by the trees allowed them
both to take their time washing in the stream and, as he scrubbed
down with the last of the soapwort, he determined to make it a
day of new beginnings. His skin tingled in the early chill and the
parts of him under the water were warmer than those above it.
He was moving quickly when he came back to the hearth and he
was whistling. Martin looked up from the fire in surprise.

"I'm boiling water for chai," she said guardedly. "Want
some? It may be our last. We're almost out of it."

"I've got a better idea," he replied and went over to his pack
and extracted a small bundle of dried leaves. "Calamint," he
said, holding it up. "I found some about a fortnight ago. I'll
make us an infusion."

"What does it taste like?" There was little enthusiasm in
Martin's voice.

"Very pleasant, as a matter of fact. Fresh tasting. It's very
good against ailments brought on by damp: very good for loosen-
ing chest colds. After yesterday we could probably do with it.
The best thing about it though is the way it makes you feel. You

have a sort of warm glow for about four hours. You may feel a little giddy right at the beginning, but that soon goes. I don't know about you, but I think we need to feel good before starting out again.''

''You already seem a lot more cheerful than you were yesterday. Those rainclouds had nothing on you. You sure about this stuff?''

''Oh yes. You needn't worry, I'm very good with simples. You need lots of herbs for Magic and the Collegium has a fantastic garden. I spent quite a lot of time there. The other boys used to tease me and say that I was training to be a Wisewoman, but it comes in useful and the gardeners liked me.'' He broke the leaves down and then rubbed them to powder between his palms. He poured the boiling water on and then set the pan on the fire to bubble gently.

They drank in a silence that was comfortable for the first time in a while, enjoying the warmth of the brew as it went down. They finished the remnants of the previous night's meal and while they saddled up, a mild and pleasant glow stole over them. When they set off they kept close to the tree line, unaware of the nip in the air. They struck North along the flank of the mountain toward its smaller, but craggier neighbor. There was mist in the valley below and the range beyond was blanketed in cloud. It seemed to them that they were alone in a timeless world, caught in the unrealities of mist and cloud.

''It's almost enough to make you believe in Magic, all this.'' Martin gestured across the view.

''What do you mean, 'almost?' '' Jarrod said, rising to the bait instantly. ''You know Magic works. You've seen me do it.''

''Well, I didn't actually see you,'' Martin replied with a straight face. ''Whoa, whoa. All right, I believe you. No, I know that Magic works, but that's just intellectually. It doesn't make it altogether real to me. I mean, I can see those cloud castles, but they aren't real. Maybe Magic was the wrong word. Maybe what I ought to have said was that it almost makes me believe in those gods of Sandroz', though I hope they don't get as angry as he did. Just look at it, Jarrod, with the sun beginning to spill all over it like that. Doesn't it summon up feelings of worship in you?"

"Not worship, exactly," he replied thoughtfully. "That's difficult when you're trained to look for the patterns underlying everything, but I get prickly bumps and a funny feeling in my throat when I see something like this. I don't believe in gods, but I can understand why people do."

"Don't Magicians believe in gods or spirits at all?"

"Oh, there are quite definitely Powers that some of us can tap, but they don't direct things. Look," he broke off and pointed. "See that green bird over there? When I see something like that, I really wish I had a god to thank for it, but, unfortunately, I haven't found any evidence to support even one."

"I'd have thought all of this would be evidence enough."

"It really is beautiful, but I can't believe that something deliberately arranges it."

"Well, I think there's got to be something or somebody behind it. Didn't you feel anything when you were fighting the sea? No great big god with a net and wavy hair lashing out at you for daring to challenge him?"

"No," Jarrod replied, warming to the argument. "It was just too big for me to hold in my mind. I couldn't penetrate the structure. I was able to alter some of the surface, but I couldn't even hold that for too long. No, I didn't find any gods, just disorder too deep to fathom." Martin groaned at the pun and Jarrod smiled in spite of the fact that it had been unintentional.

They rode on under the trees in easy quiet, unwilling to hurry on such a day. It was an assuagement after so much discomfort and disappointment.

"I'll tell you what I did do," Jarrod said, picking up the conversation as if there had been no lapse. "I decided what sex the sea is."

"What sex the sea is? When did you do that, when you were putting down the storm?"

"No," he replied with a grin, "while you were doing your wonderful imitation of a man dying."

"I see," she said, with a sidelong glance. "Let's hear what you decided and how."

"You know how everyone talks about 'Mother Strand'? I

think that's probably where the Maternites got their Great Mother from. Anyway, when I first started watching the sea, it seemed very female to me."

"Really, this is going to be interesting. Let's hear what you think 'very female' is." Martin's voice was gently mocking.

"Well, you know, it was very unpredictable, kept changing all the time. It was sort of moody. And when we were at Seaport it struck me as being very flirtatious, playing with the ships and the jetties." They started into a sun-dappled clearing and he watched her reaction through the filtered light.

"Oh, thanks a lot, Jarrod. Unpredictable, moody and flirtatious. You certainly have a wonderful view of the opposite sex."

"That's not all of it, of course, but you know what I mean."

"I'm not so sure that I do, but I'll try to think like a man. Do go on: this is fascinating." The sarcasm was wasted on Jarrod.

"Even before it got rough I decided I was wrong. The sea was male. Mother Strand was right, too. I mean, the sea gets all puffed up and angry and it storms about: it can be very frightening. The land just ignores it and lets it lash about until it calms down again. If the worst comes to the worst and the sea pushes her too hard, she just opens up and swallows it." He looked across as they ducked under low branches and smiled bashfully. "I even started thinking of it as Father Sea."

"You did, did you? If I didn't know you were an orphan, I'd have said that you came from a terrible home. So, what did it feel like fighting Father?"

"Very, very tiring," Jarrod answered with a laugh. "I never did feel that I'd got a good grip on him. Hey," he added, changing the subject, "the trees are thinning out. Can we canter for a bit?" He kicked his horse into action without waiting for an answer.

It took them two days to cross the slope of the smaller mountain and, while the days remained fair, some of their sparkle was lost in leading the mounts over treacherous scree and around sharp thrusts of rock. This mountain supported less vegetation than the others that they had traversed. The feeling that it gave off was one of enduring age. It was like an old man, with dryly flaking skin, who had sunk in on himself until the bone showed clear. Its valleys held no villages, the birds avoided it and the only animals that showed themselves were the supercilious crag leapers.

They rounded the last arid abutment in midafternoon and the taller mountain it had shielded came into view, but it was a while before Martin lifted her head up and caught sight of it.

"Hey, look at that. It must be the Anvil of the Gods that Sandroz talked about." Jarrod didn't answer her. He sat transfixed, staring at the mountain as if he were committing it to memory.

The mountain warranted his respect, towering in its unconventional beauty, sublime and sure of itself. It was as indifferent to his admiration as a king's mistress. He let his eyes travel up the green folds of its skirts to the black, straight collar of its peak. Only there was no peak. If it had ever existed, it had been shorn off cleanly, like the head of a fallen favorite, or hammered flat by some unimaginable force. It was so geometric in its precision that he felt that it could not have been formed by accident. Logic told him that Nature had been the only mover, but his mind conjured up the race that had built the Giants' Causeway. He found the mountain calling to him in ways that had nothing to do with logic. His skin crawled and the nape of his neck bristled. He shivered convulsively.

"That's it," he muttered hoarsely. "Martin, that's it. I know it is. It's got to be." Martin glanced back at his intensity and shook her head.

"There you go again. It's pretty impressive, I must admit. Doesn't look natural at all, does it? Well, let's go get us a closer look, but don't go overboard on me again, all right?"

"It's got to be the place, Martin. It's making me feel very peculiar and we're still quite a ways away."

"Oh, you and your feelings," she said in mock exasperation. "You were so sure before and now you're sure again. What happened to the place with the cloudsteeds? Didn't that make you feel peculiar? It certainly made you act peculiar. Besides, remember what Sandroz said. It's not for us. It's only for the dead."

"I don't give a damn what he said. I'm not so sure that he really wanted to help us. If anything, it makes me feel even more strongly that this is the right place. You don't understand," he explained, "this is different; quite different. I was probably too anxious before. We've been gone a long time and anyway, I wasn't prepared to admit that we hadn't found him. This is something else altogether. I suppose it's like they say at the Collegium, 'when you're really in love, you'll know it.' "

"Oh, they say that at the Collegium, do they? How deep." Her eyes gleamed mischievously. "I never realized that boys were such romantics."

Jarrod felt himself blushing and said, petulantly, "I wish you wouldn't tease me like that. I'm serious."

"Well I suggest you wait until we get there before you go all mystic on me. Next thing you know, you'll be believing in gods." She laughed at her own sally. "If the unicorn does live there, I hope he has the sense to live on the lower slopes." She tugged at her reins and went plodding on toward the Anvil of Creation. Jarrod followed her unwillingly, not wanting to take his eyes from the mountain's top.

That's the place for a unicorn, he thought. On top of the biggest pedestal in the world. It looked close, but he knew it was not. The heavily wooded slopes looked smooth, but he knew they would not be. It was hiding things from him, distracting him with its obvious attributes.

Morning showed them a different wonder. The mountaintop was covered by cloud and they could see rain falling, like a grey veil, over the shoulders. From their vantage point they could see breaks in the trees and what seemed like well-defined paths. As they stood and scanned, Martin grabbed Jarrod's arm and pointed silently. He squinted down the extended finger and saw flashes of white moving through the trees.

A twinge of apprehension fibrillated through him. Let it not be people, he pleaded inwardly. Not here of all places. He wanted no other human beings violating this sanctuary. The press gang again? Villagers? It made no difference. If there were people, there would be less of a chance for a unicorn. He looked up at the truncated mountain and it loomed reassuringly over him. He took a deep breath and admonished himself. This mountain could obviously shelter an army and still have room for a unicorn to dwell unperceived in peace. He looked hastily back for the interlopers, but Martin was no longer pointing and he couldn't find them.

"Were they people? Did they look like people to you?"

"It was a bit far to tell, but they looked like people when they crossed that clearing."

"Which clearing?"

"The one over there with the cinder trees. Incidentally, isn't this a bit far North for cinder trees?"

"How many were there," Jarrod pressed, ignoring her question.

"Don't know. Not too many, I don't think, but it's difficult to tell from down here. Whatever they were, they seemed to be going fairly slowly."

"I don't like it." Jarrod shook his head. "Villagers probably. I don't think it could be the press gang. Still," he said with a wan smile, "I promise to be more careful this time. I wonder if they're the reason Sandroz warned us off?"

"Who knows. There's nothing we can do about it anyway, and if I don't get some food in my stomach fairly soon, I shan't have the strength to go and find out. Come on, get that bow of yours out and let's go and see if we can find breakfast. Lunch and dinner, too, for that matter."

The day became hot and sticky as they hunted, but they had no difficulty finding game. The creatures, to their cost, seemed unafraid of man. The rest of the morning passed in skinning and cooking.

"They must get much less snow here," Martin remarked as they saddled up the horses. "Did you notice how low the branches of the fireblanket trees were?"

"Well, if that means that we can stay here longer, so much the better. I really wasn't expecting to be back in Summer clothes again. The only trouble is that these damned flies bite straight through them. Let's hope it gets better once we're moving." He slapped fretfully as they guided the animals up the overgrown trail.

"You still sure this is the place?" Martin asked as they rode.

"This is the place," Jarrod said firmly, refusing to allow himself any doubts. The mountain was important, of that he was quite certain, but there was something potent and daunting about it. "Come on," he said, "let's try and go straight up."

The following day dawned windily clear and when they glimpsed the summit from a glade it was headless and improbable once more. It was all gold and green under the talkative trees. Butterflies lurched through the air in search of nectar, fledglings clung to branches in unsteady fear of flight and somewhere a hammerhead drummed insistently. The world seemed peacefully fecund. Even the insects appeared to have declared a moratorium. Only the thickets proved intractable and when they came to a clearly defined pathway they did not hesitate to take it. Nature was busy reclaiming it, but it made for easy riding as it wound back and forth seeking the gentlest gradient.

After half an hour, Martin turned in the saddle and, looking back at Jarrod, said, "It's lovely to be able to ride like this again, but we don't seem to be getting anywhere. Has this new sense of yours got any sense of direction to it?" Jarrod was surprised that she was taking his intuition seriously. Still, he hesitated before he replied.

"Yes, as a matter of fact it does, but I'm not sure that I trust it."

"Well I don't feel anything at all, so I'll let you choose."

"All right, but I don't think you'll like it. It's all the way up to the top again." Martin groaned in exaggerated anguish.

"I might have known it. Oh well, up we go then." They turned the horses' heads and struck out between the trees again.

They cut across the trail they had abandoned several times and then rode out onto another, narrower pathway. The bed was too firm for footprints, but the sight of fresh saw marks chilled the sweat on Jarrod's skin. They hurried across it and dismounted when they were sure that they were hidden from view. They tethered the animals and sat on an outcropping of black rock, their heads close together, and talked things over very quietly.

A quick and cautious reconnaissance was decided on and, keeping well within the trees, they followed the little road. They moved with the automatic skill and stealth that they had acquired, leaving no tracks and making few sounds. The tended path led to an open space where a part of the mountain had fallen away or folded in upon itself. There was grass, kept short by a tethered shegoat, and a fenced patch of garden where herbs and vegetables grew. At the back of the level semicircle, nestled up against the rockface, was a small stone cottage with a roof of woven boughs. The crude door stood ajar. They crouched and watched for movement from within. They saw nothing save the browsing of the insatiable goat and the comings and goings of birds.

"I'm going to take a quick look," Martin whispered and, without waiting for a reply, she slipped through the ferns and ran rapidly across the tiny sward. She looked carefully around the doorway and then signalled for Jarrod to join her. He sprinted across the clearing and looked over her head into the ordered little dwelling. He saw a simple and spotless room that was clearly still inhabited. He stepped back feeling that he had read a message intended for someone else, turned and froze. He reached behind him and tapped Martin.

"Whoever lives," she started to say as she swung round. Her eyes widened as her voice died away.

An old man stood watching them, leaning on a businesslike staff. He was thin and alert and though his hair and beard were white and his face lined, he looked fully capable of laying about him to good effect. He shifted easily and hefted the staff over his right shoulder, his feet apart, ready to swing at the first sign of ill intent. He spoke rapidly and menacingly.

"What did he say?" Jarrod asked.

"I couldn't catch it."

The old man switched to Common. "What I said was, do you dare the wrath of the gods and my own anger by disturbing the rest of the ancients and the last days of those you should venerate? I took you for youths from one of the clans, but you are foreigners. Do you not know that this is a sacred place, this mountain? Why do you violate the sanctuary of the old?"

He spoke carefully and with a strong accent, but his authority needed no translation. He was elderly and alone, but there was no fear in him. The voice was low and compelling, accustomed to being harkened to and obeyed. Though the thickness of the accent betokened a lack of formal education, there could be no doubt that they were in the presence of a rare and important man.

Jarrod was the first to recover and said, placatingly, "We meant no offense, Sir. We have not seen a human dwelling in a very long while and we were drawn to it. My brother and I are truly sorry. It's just that we, oh by the way, my name is Jarrod

Courtak and this is my brother, Martin.'' They both made short bobs with their heads. ''All we knew was that this mountain was called the Anvil of the Gods and we were curious. I mean, it looks so improbable from down there,'' and he gestured to the panorama that opened up at the end of the little lawn, ''so we thought we'd take a closer look. Oh, not at your house, of course,'' he added quickly. ''Er, no, we wanted to get a closer look at that extraordinary summit.''

He was rattling, as he always did when he was nervous. He knew it, but was powerless to stop it. ''We didn't mean to pry, really we didn't. It's just that that's the first . . .'' and he finally ran out of words.

''You know nothing about the mountain?'' The deep voice was sceptical. ''Where be you from? You boy, silent one, where do you come from?'' He lowered the stave and leaned comfortably on it, in complete control of the situation.

''Arundel, and it please you, Sir.''

''That's a mortal long way, boy. You better be telling me the truth, for you're breaking the law, as you probably very well know.'' He shot them a shrewd look and stroked his beard with his free hand.

''We didn't know anything about a law, Sir. We meant no offense. Perhaps we should just go back the way we came,'' and Jarrod mustered the best smile he could. It wasn't good enough.

''Not so fast, you little cub. I gave you no leave to go.'' The staff was in both hands now and the stance was forward. Then he relaxed and smiled and the whole face was lit by it. ''Forgive me, boy,'' he said easily. ''There are times that I forget that I no longer rule, or rather that my subjects now are all dead or dying.'' He gave a short and mirthless laugh. ''And you do not know where you are. Well then, my young friends, know that you are in the realm of the dead and that I am their king.''

CHAPTER XIV

THE TRAVELLERS LOOKED AT EACH OTHER DUBIOUSLY AND THEN back to the imposing old man. He didn't look mad, but one never knew. Perhaps age and loneliness had turned his wits.

He, in turn, watched them watching him and, as if in answer to their unspoken question said, his voice level and matter-of-fact, "I was an important ruler once, you know. Oh, yes indeed. I held sway over more villages than anyone had ever done before. I was a very big man." He did not say it boastfully, but rather as if he were stating a fact and underplaying it. He smiled again. "Why don't we go into my palace?" He gestured to the house behind them. "I was very lucky. The previous owner expired not long before I found it. He's over there," and he turned and pointed with the staff to a mound of black rocks between two mountain maidens, then shepherded them into the cottage.

"The goat was his, too. I brought seeds with me, but it never occurred to me to bring a goat. But enough of me. I wish to know what you two children are doing on the mountain of death at your age. And I'll thank you to speak slowly to me, since my Common has rusted and your accents are atrocious. That I could speak it at all was considered an affectation by most of my former subjects." He propped his staff in a corner and turned back to his visitors.

"Here, take a gourd and dip it in that cistern over there.

Water's all I have to offer, alas, until I've milked the goat and I no longer dine from ceremonial dishes. It's not the custom for those who go to die to take much of this world with them. We are a poor people and life is most oft hard. It wouldn't be fair to deprive the living of what they need. But I wander. I ask questions and then I do not let you answer, but, if the truth were known, I am finding it a wonderous release to be talking to someone other than myself.'' He stopped and watched them drink.

"If it please you, your Majesty," Martin said, putting her gourd back on the shelf, "we meant no disrespect. We were exploring and, seeing the fantastical shape of the mountain, we were drawn to see it more nearly. We did not know that we would be forbidden, we only knew that the mountain was named the Anvil of the Gods by some.''

Jarrod looked appreciatively at his companion. She did not seem to be overawed by the man's force and presence. That he had been a ruler was easy to believe, for his manner and carriage bespoke it. Her use of the formal mode to him seemed quite natural.

"You know nothing more of this place?" The question was sharply put.

"And it please your Majesty, nought save the name and the preeminence it holds among its brother peaks." The old man relaxed again as she spoke.

"Listen, lad, don't call me Majesty. I take no title here. I am plain Attarus now, and you will indulge me by not using the formal mode—it makes it a lot easier on me. Neither of you speaks Songean?" They both shook their heads. "Oh well, no matter. I'll do the best I can and if I make mistakes, don't correct me. I'm old enough to know that I haven't the slightest desire to perfect anything any more." He looked them over once more. "Hm, so you're exploring, are you? Well, I believe you're not Umbrians, you're both too tall for that and the accent's wrong. Good thing, too, for I'd be tempted to set on you, for all my years, if I thought you were. They speak fair of friendship and of treaty and of common heritage, but they bleed us. They think I do not know why they go about the hills and mountains tapping at the rocks, but I am wise. I am not beguiled

by them. I know that it is the very earth itself that they covet.''
The voice had risen in volume and the timbre darkened. The
eyes flashed as he spoke and his whole bearing had changed. He
seemed more solid as the emotion rang in his words. It was
obviously a speech that he had made before and it was almost as
if he were not addressing them at all.

"First they take our strong young men for their accursed
mines and now they seek to take the stuff of our very land. Oh
yes, they spoke to me in honeyed tones and thought me all the
while a stupid and an ignorant barbarian, but I'd have none of
their 'improvements.' '' There was scorn in the word. "I pray the
gods that my son, now that he rules in my place, will send them
packing too." He paused and the fire in him waned. "But no
matter," he said more quietly, "I cannot control things now. My
time has passed." He stopped again and shook his head, sending
the long, white hair moving across his shoulders. He looked at
them speculatively.

"You are 'exploring' a very long way from home."

"Aye, Sir," said Jarrod. "This is about as far as we can
come. We'll have to start back soon, since Winter comes so
much earlier in the Saradondas than it does at home."

"Don't remind me, boy. This'll be my first, and possibly my
last, Winter here and I can't say as how I'm looking forward to
the cold. You can help me gather some wood before we part
company." He gave them the calculating look of a man accustomed to having things done for him. "I'm hale enough, but
these two arms can only carry so much and the Winter nights are
mortal long and have sharp teeth."

"Of course we shall, shan't we Jarrod?"

"Oh yes. We'd be glad to, Sir. We shan't be able to stay too
long," and he shot her a meaningful glance, "but we'll do what
we can."

"Good, lads. I'm grateful to you. I can't offer much in the
way of hospitality, but what I have is yours and, truly, I shall
enjoy some lively human company for a change."

"We've a few things back with the horses," Martin said.
"My brother and I are good at hunting, aren't we, Jarrod?"

"You would have to be if you managed to get this far and I
confess that I am relieved to hear that you have horses. To have

come so far on foot, unless you had come from the Umbrian stronghold at Bandor, would have frayed my credulity beyond the snapping point. Any addition to the pot is always welcome. Now, if you, Jarrod? Jarrod, if you would care to help me lay a fire, Martin could go and fetch your animals.''

I'm being kept here as a sort of hostage, Jarrod thought as Martin set off obediently.

They passed the afternoon hunting and gathering wood. The old man chatted at them between trips, told them that once he had been known as Sigeitander, High Thrall of all the Thralians, and directed their labors. When it finally came time to wash and prepare the dinner, they were both filled with the tired contentment that follows productive labor.

It was cold once the sun had gone down behind the distant mountains and there was nothing to cover the windows with but skins. The three of them crowded unceremoniously around the central hearth. They ate voraciously with their hands while the smoke curled up over them on its way to the hole in the ceiling. By the time they were done they were greasy and sated. Jarrod, knowing himself to be the youngest, automatically rose and filled a bowl from the cistern. They dried their hands at the fire and replenished it from the now ample stack of wood outside. Then they settled back to talk.

"When was the last time we ate under a roof, Jarrod?" Martin asked.

"Belengar, I reckon. Unless you count the barge."

"It seems so long ago. I feel as if I have been riding and clambering for years. I know it can't be much more than three months, but it certainly seems longer. Do you know what the date is, by any chance, Sir?"

"No I don't. I started to keep a tally stick when I left Cariathal, but I threw it away before I got here. Things go slow at your age, but at mine time's as fast as a wild warcat going for a kill. Still, it's a great relief not to have to live by the calendar. When you're the Thrall there are innumerable rites to be attended. It was bad enough when I was just a village chieftain, but when you rule over more than forty villages it's impossible. Most of the things that people celebrate are the same, so you'd think we'd pick more or less the same days. Not a bit of it. Do you know that there are no less than seven separate Midwinter days in the confederacy? I tried to standardize some of them, and not just by picking the ones my home village celebrated. I tried to be very fair, but it didn't work. You can conquer folks, or they come to you and swear allegiance because they think you can protect them, but move a holiday? Never. I ended up having to observe different days in different places every year. It meant that I saw and was seen more, so I suppose it turned out for the best. No matter, we all end up here anyway.'' He shifted his weight to his other hip.

"When you get to be my age you lose the natural padding you young ones have. It may be that old bones get sensitive the way old flesh does. You'd think they would get dulled with habitude, but they don't. They feel the cold more and the joints develop an ability to foretell the weather. Fascinating, but rather depressing to live with.

"So," Sigeitander said, changing the subject abruptly, "you know nothing about our sacred mountain? You are ignorant of the legends? Splendid. That gives me the excuse to lecture, and I dearly love to lecture.'' He threw back his head and laughed delightedly at himself. ''Oh dear me, you'll just have to put up with me. This may be the last chance I ever get to indulge myself and I couldn't bear to miss it.''

"We'd like to hear about the mountain and most especially about the legends," Martin said politely as they squirmed around and made themselves comfortable. Jarrod drew his cloak around him because his back, away from the fire, was cold.

"Would you indeed?" Sigeitander was patently pleased. "Well now, one of the advantages of being declared Thrall is that you have a ballad maker assigned to you. Mine made up perfectly dreadful epic songs about me. That was the bad side, having to listen to them at formal feasts. By the gods, that man did go on.'' The eyes drifted away into memory and then their host came back with a, by now, characteristic shake of the head.

"The good thing was that he knew all the legends, part of his stock in trade. I made him tell them to me instead of singing as often as I could get away with it. Hm,'' He grunted softly to himself and smiled at them through the smoke. ''I always did think that I could do a better job of storytelling than he did.'' His eyes were merry in the jumping light. "Have no fear, I'll give you the short version and I promise not to sing. You boy, Jarrod, be a good lad and get us a few more logs so you don't have to get up in the middle of a dramatic passage." He chuckled and Jarrod did as he was bidden. He built the fire up until it blazed and made the roofboughs rustle with the heat. Old Attarus Sigeitander sat up.

"Martin, could a man borrow your saddle to lean against? It makes the storytelling easier. And Jarrod, a little of that goat's milk would be good for the throat." He smiled at them as they brought their respective gifts. "Ah. That's better." He snuggled back and stared at the spiralling smoke for a while. Then he commenced in a quiet, unemotional voice.

"In the earliest of days, there were no moons, there were no stars and the sun slept beneath the world. All was darkness and in that darkness none lived, save the gods. Around them was naught but earth and air and water. Though they saw through the darkness as others see in the day, they were bored. 'Of a surety,' they said among themselves, 'there must be more things here below, or there above, than we can perceive. Let us therefore make light that we may see down into the depths and up aloft into the roofless firmament and thereby shall we discover their wonders. Thus shall all things be made plain to us.'

The ageless voice had taken on a lilting resonance and his hands moved before him, amplifying his words. The eyes were dilated and the gaze elsewhere.

"So they took earth and they took water and they made all manner of marvels. They labored mightily and they wrought subtle splendors, but they could create no light. Then one of them, Lonzago, Lord of all that lies within the ground, found fire in his domain. Though he knew full well that he had by chance discovered what they had all striven to bring forth, he sought to conceal it so that he might use it for his pleasure and for purposes that were his alone.

"But the fire from the heart of the world, once unbound, would not be hid. The light and the heat of it crept up the tiny fissures that the delvings of the gods had made and it glimmered, even as it does today, in marshes and in places where the land grows thin. The others saw these wondrous and elusive visions

and were amazed. They pursued the glowings across waters and
through the primal ooze, but in no wise could they tame or
capture it.

"One among them, the goddess Saradonda, for whom these
very mountains have been named, guessed that the living light
came from Lord Lonzago's realm beneath the ground. She ar-
rayed herself in comeliness and she paid visit to him at his palace
beneath the Central Range. She was bewitching in her beauty
and the Lord Lonzago was not proof against her loveliness. He
sought to have her as his own, but she laughed her silver laugh
and she refused him.

"Each time she said him nay his desire for her grew and he
looked the harder for ways to win her favor. So besotted did he
become that, at last, in desperation and deep want, he offered
to share with her the miracle he had found. 'You are happy here
beneath the tall mountains,' she said, 'but I am a creature of the
air and must needs return. How then can I enjoy this wonder that
you show me? If I am to be yours, you must bring me flame to a
place where the breezes can caress my cheeks and the winds can
make my tresses flow.' Then, for love of her, Lord Lonzago rent
the roof of his domain and let the fire forth." Sigeitander paused
and took a sip of his milk as his visitors, caught by the spell he
wove, sat silent.

"Then all the gods and goddesses rejoiced. First, they lit the
moons to show them what lay hid among the foldings of the
earth, but they were not enough. Then they conjured up the sun
that it might show them something to sate their senses. Many
new things were revealed to them and, for long days, they did
disport themselves on land and in the seas. Soon they had seen
all that there was to see and time hung heavy for them once
again. Then they fared forth into the heavens to see what new
delights they held and, one by one, they lit the stars. They
travelled far across the celestial canopy, but nowhere did they
find aught to make them tarry. At length, they returned hither to
make report on all that they had seen and done.

"First one and then the other confessed that they had found no
wonders to engage the mind and, when the last was done, they
did resolve to create what they had failed to find. This mountain
is the anvil on which the glories of the earth and sky were made.

Trees they fashioned and all manner of green things. The glittering dust their labors left were swept off into the firmament and there it lingers still.

"For many of their years they were content among the wonders they had wrought, but, once again, after time unimaginable had gone by, they tired of them. Their days became too long and their nights mere repetition. In their dissatisfaction they returned to Strand and lit the forge anew. On the Anvil of Creation they hammered out new forms, which they annealed, and into them they blew the breath of life. They set the creatures to browse among the green things they had made and marvelled at them for a while. But they were not enough to keep them occupied, and so they formed a man and a woman to provide constant and changing entertainment for all the years that time can span. They watch us still and we amuse them mightily."

Martin and Jarrod lay by the fire transfixed. Their host looked happily from one face to the other and beamed.

"I can see," he said, "that you doubt me." Sap hissed and popped in a burning log as his hand flew out to cut off protest, though he knew that there would be none. "I tell you that everything there is was made by them and it was made up there." His finger jabbed toward the ceiling. "They labor up there still, when they've a mind to. Mere mortals may not see them, so they drape the Anvil in cloud when they wish to work, but you can hear them rumbling and banging and see the sparks when the hammers strike.

"From time to time, they repair the fabric of the heavens and the earth. Molten rock and metal fly. You can see it everywhere on the sides of the mountain. Have you not noticed strange black rocks that have no business here? Of course you have—my predecessor's grave is marked with them. There are places where the mountainside has fused and run with their forging. This, then," and the arm swept round, "is the base of the Anvil of Creation whereon everything that should have been made has been made." The closing words were clearly ritualistic and they were delivered ringingly.

This time the fire burned down uninterruptedly and Attarus Sigeitander sat back against the saddle and relished the silence that was his best applause. The other two roused themselves slowly and reluctantly. Martin sighed contentedly.

"What a marvellous story," she said, her voice still fogged in wonder. "You do that so well. There must be more; something more recent? Great heros of the mountain? Incredible beasts?" Jarrod smiled gratefully across at her.

"Ah, the young," Attarus said, the white hair swinging. "Insatiable. Like the gods, always hungry for new things. Yes, of course there is more, but you will have to wait until tomorrow for that. Now it's time to sleep. The pair of you can sleep here, by the fire, as I intend to. If these old joints of mine will work, I'll go and ready myself for bed. You already know where everything is. I must say," he added appreciatively, "you two are a wonderful audience. Not a single cough."

"It was too interesting for that, Sir," Jarrod said truthfully. "You've made tomorrow worth waiting for."

"Thank you, lad. I'm glad you'll be staying. You give me something to look forward to as well. Will one of you see to the fire? This place gets a little chilly if it goes out." He climbed slowly to his feet. "I can't tell you what a pleasure it is to have you both here."

The next day passed in another round of hunting and gathering and in the cutting and trimming of boards to be made into shutters. The old man bustled about the house doing domestic chores. He was lavish with his praise, spurring them on to further tasks, generating a feeling of cheerful and useful endeavor with his words. It was only when Jarrod was washing off his aching body in the chill waters of a spring-fed pool that he realized that the wily old man had got them to do the bulk of the work that would enable him to face the coming Winter without once having issued an order. He had even made Jarrod feel grateful for the opportunity. It was easy to see, he thought, why he had held sway over all those villages. They had probably thought it a rare privilege to be ruled by him. He smiled to himself in rueful admiration as he splashed.

The former High Thrall may have stayed home while they went out and toiled, but they could not fault the meal he produced. They were pleasantly overfull when they leaned back to listen to the tale of the night.

"When you first saw us, you were angry with us. I mean for more than just looking into the house while you were gone, and you never really explained why," Martin said to start him off.

"Yes, I was. I took you for a couple of local louts come to play pranks and disturb the peace of those who have come here to die. But you don't know anything about that, do you?" They both shook their heads. The fire sputtered as it consumed the grease that had fallen from the birds Jarrod had brought down that morning. The shadows danced around the walls. Outside, the trees moved constantly and the skins at the windows bellied. Once again Sigeitander watched the patterns of the swirling smoke.

"We of the mountains are poor folk. We are a proud people, clan upon clan, but pride has never fed us, though it has often made hunger bearable. Our main wealth is in the herds. The soil is too thin and unprofitable for farming, and so we must take the beasts down to the valley during the Winters. Those too old, or too infirm, to follow the ronoronti stay behind in the high villages and, if there is no one who can still hunt, or if the gods have taken away the game, a whole villageful of elders may well perish before their clan returns.

"Thus it is, by tradition unbreakable and without exception, that a man or woman, should the gods favor them and permit them to live for three score years and ten, must, upon completion of that year, go forth from their village and make final pilgrimage to Aharatouroun, the Sacred Mountain, the Anvil of the Gods, whereon all the futures of the earth are made. It is a journey from which there can be no return." He stopped and cleared his throat. His voice had risen and become oratorical, but when he resumed it was in a quieter vein.

"That is the law and that is our custom. It is, of course, forbidden for anyone else to come here. No grieving relatives. There is nothing to steal here and, if there are grudges still held against the aged ones, it matters not. All scores are soon settled here without the need of man's intervention. There is nothing else to bring anyone here, except grief or curiosity. To tell the truth," he said with his illuminating smile, "I was shocked and a little fearful when I came upon you."

"You certainly didn't sound it," Jarrod said as he got up to put more logs on.

"Looking as if one is in control at all times is one of the arts that a ruler has to learn if he is to survive, and it's not that easy, believe you me."

"But why do you have to be here, Sir? I mean you're perfectly healthy and vigorous and you obviously weren't a burden. Besides, you were the High Thrall. Surely you didn't want to give it all up?"

"Of course I didn't. I enjoyed being Thrall. I enjoyed it a great deal and I had a lot of things that I still wanted to get done. It always takes longer than you think it will, you know. But being a ruler has its disadvantages and one of them is that you keep on having to set an example if you expect other people to obey you. It's a responsibility that comes with the job and it never stops. I might possibly consider giving an extraordinary dispensation to an individual who was desperately needed, although I can't really think of a circumstance offhand, but the one person I could never make an exception for was myself. Oh, I hated to go and, confidentially, I don't think my son is bright enough to hold down the position for very long. The confederation will break up into warring clans again and most of my work will be undone, but there are some parts of the system that you can't change, not if it takes the bread out of the mouths of children. No, if you're going to try to set uniform standards and measures, you can't start making exceptions. There'd be no end to it."

"But I bet you'd make a wonderful king for lots longer," Martin objected.

"Thankee, son, so do I. But I'm not going to sit here resignedly and wither away. I intend to be around for a few years yet and there's always work to keep me busy. There are my fellow exiles. I don't bury them any more—my back's not up to it and the only tools I've got are a couple that I've made, but I make them tidy and save them from scavengers if I can find them in time."

There was a long silence and the night crept back among them. They sat or lay around and watched a fat log fall in on

the perfect place to find a unicorn. On the top of a sacred mountain. No one's ever been up there, unless you believe in Sig's gods, so he'd feel quite safe. Anyway, there's something about this place. Don't you feel anything?''

"Damp and uncomfortable.'' She shrugged under the heavy folds of the cloak. "I stopped you the last time and I don't have any better ideas this time. Maybe it's best to have some kind of goal instead of just wandering around aimlessly in the woods. Who knows, maybe we'll get lucky and bump into it on the way up. Well, I suppose we ought to get off the path and strike upward if we're going to get there. Come on, Jarrod. Since this is your show you better lead the way.''

"And get all the wet branches. I know,'' Jarrod said as he pulled on the reins and urged his horse forward.

Morning fog hung around past any polite hour of departure and the long rains persisted. The trees protected them from the wind, but their wet clothes were chill against the skin and chafed in unexpected places. By the end of the second day it became difficult to find enough dry wood for the fire. Though the game remained plentiful, cooking became an unpleasant chore whose chief reward was the infusions that Jarrod made. In spite of the pleasant feelings they induced, Martin became wary and waspish and Jarrod alternately argumentative and sullen. When the rains stopped the mutual edginess continued.

Once again, they cached their saddles and hobbled their animals by a stream. They argued about what provisions to take, they argued about the best route to take to the top and they agreed on nothing. They shouted at each other and Martin boxed Jarrod's ears. When they set off up the scarp of porous grey stone it was in stiff silence. The first bare, mountain night revealed that neither had brought wood, but mutual culpability formed no bond and they slept, coldly, at a distance.

Now that they were committed to the flat, planed-off peak, Jarrod's inner doubts grew. His certainties faded and his intuitions did nothing but irritate him. He kept scanning the edge, so far above them, whenever he wasn't watching where his hands and feet were going to go. It was not perfectly regular, but then he hadn't really expected it to be. He could not distinguish any openings in its side, but it was difficult to tell if the black

patches were rock, or shadow, or the mouths of caves. The
going was difficult and both terrain and necessity kept the two
close. Privacy became a matter of co-operation. Then the clouds
came back and they were immobilized for a day and a half.
When they finally withdrew to the summit, the clouds sat there
like a mourning garland.

They reached the bottom of the collar five days after they had
ridden out of the little enclave of order. They stared up the
vertical sides and found that, at close quarters, they did have a
slope to them, albeit a very steep one. There was no obvious
way up, no ascending ledges, no helpful fold in the weathered
surface. There were plenty of handholds, but the wind was fierce
and erratic and neither of them really felt like tackling the face.

Jarrod tapped Martin on the shoulder to attract her attention
and pointed left. He didn't wait for a response, but went crawling off along the bottom of this final obstacle. The wind fretted
at his pack. Since they were roped up, Martin had no choice but
to follow. Jarrod had reached a point where logic was not
playing any great part in his deliberations. He no longer really
cared if there was a unicorn up there. He was possessed by a
need to prove to Martin that there was another valley up there. It
was less important that there be a unicorn than that there could
have been one.

He peered up as often as he could, but it took an hour before
he yelled and pointed. Two hundred feet above was a cleft and
sky was visible through it.

"There's another valley up there. I told you there was!"

"Doesn't look like much of anything to me, and anyway we
can't get up to it." Martin had come up to him and was shouting
over the wind.

"Let's go on a bit." He turned and resumed his laborious
progress. It was another fifteen minutes before he yelled again.
A wall of rock fifteen feet wide stuck out from the side of the
mountain and blocked their path. Its top looked lower than the
lip they had been scanning.

"This must be what makes it look square," Martin said.

"I'll bet there's one just like it on the other side. It's as if two
halves of different mountains have been put together. We could
get up there, couldn't we?" His eyes were shining when he

turned to her. "We can climb this corner, can't we? The one in the Assaras was worse."

"I can if you can, but I don't think it'll do any good. D'you want to climb with full packs?" The question was intended to be ironic, but Jarrod took it seriously.

"Might as well," he said, with a sudden access of cheerfulness. "Never know how long we'll be in there." He smiled at her and the long, black curls and soft whiskers gave him the look of a woodland creature. "Come on," he said, coaxingly, "let's get going before I remember how hungry I am."

"Have you run out, too?"

"Some dried venison, that's about it." He checked his knots. "I'll go first, so if you've got any extra pitons, hand them over." He held out his hand. "Thanks. All right, here I go," and he started to spider his way up the angle.

Martin waited until the line was almost tight and then started up after him. She levered her way for five minutes before she came to the first piton. She was forced to duck her head away as a shower of dust and chips fell about her. She wanted to rub her eyes, but did not care to spare a hand. She pushed on up and cursed herself as she scraped her knuckles. She was trying so hard not to let the burning bother her concentration that it took her a moment to realize that the rope was slack. She squinted up at the feet not far above.

"Are you all right?"

"Just fine. You will be too when you get here." Jarrod's voice drifted down. "There is a valley. There are two bowls joined together, just like I said. We're at the join. It slopes down inside so the going should be easier. I'm going on over."

"Don't go too fast before I'm over the top," she called.

Back pressed resolutely to the jut of the chimney, she negotiated the last few feet. She had no time to pause and appreciate the view because the line was already tightening. She swung her legs through and began the descent down the inside. If there was a slope, she wasn't aware of it. She dug her fingers into the crannies and was careful with her toe placements. She was so preoccupied that Jarrod's hand on her ankle made her gasp. He guided her down and then she turned and gasped again.

They stood at the bottom of a circle of cliffs and the valley curved on down below them to a lake. It was nacrous with the reflection of the daymoon. The rest of the valley looked as if the gods had repaired two broken mixing bowls and put the wrong halves back together. The Songean bowl, up whose side they had climbed, was smaller and shallower than the Umbrian one, and the join left a second line of small cliffs to form the Western boundary of the lake.

There was green everywhere. It hung like an arras across the plunge of stone that distinguished the Eastern end of the valley and merged lushly with silken heads of the phragmites that fringed the lake. There were trees aplenty, but not in the clustered disorder of the other hidden valley. Instead, the effect was of a wild parkland, cunningly varied with groves of quircus and agitated copses of widow's veil. It was dotted with fruit trees, either in bloom or fruiting. Lush grass was splashed with the yellow of jothoniums and enlivened by the piercing blue of squill. Insects hummed and bright birds flew. Down on the mountain's side Old King Sig might be preparing for Winter, but here the seasons had stood still.

"Oh Jarrod, it's beautiful and there's fruit on those trees, I can smell it."

"I told you there'd be another valley here," Jarrod said smugly

"Yes you did, and you were right. Mind you, there have been times during the past few days when I could have cheerfully strangled both you and your bloody feeling. D'you think we can get down to the lake before it gets dark?"

"Doubt it, not if you want to eat first. And if you don't, I do." He untied the rope and began to coil it. Martin clamped a hand on his shoulder.

"Look," she whispered.

"Where? I don't see anything."

"On the other side of the lake, by that stand of quircus. There. See? Oh, now they've gone into the trees."

"What's gone?" Jarrod asked, screwing his eyes up, unwilling to grant first sight of the unicorn to anyone else, even Martin.

"I thought I saw some animals . . . white animals," she said tentatively.

"Probably a couple of crag leapers," Jarrod said. "Let's go down and find some fresh water and something to eat. My stomach's been talking to me." He settled his shoulder straps and set off downslope, but some of the elation he had felt at finding this secret place had evaporated.

They slept beneath a cinder tree close to the water and in the morning the Making of the Day was an ecstatic act for Jarrod, performed in the balm of new-found privacy. In spite of his efforts, the sun seemed to take forever to come up. He was aware that he was stretched out thin by anticipation, but self-knowledge had not stopped him from slipping away as soon as he had finished the rite, nor from doing it so quietly that Martin stayed asleep. He felt as though he were in a heightened state, keenly aware of details he did not usually notice. He drank in the myriad variations in form and color that surrounded him. The touch of the wind was familiar to him and he could both smell and hear the grasses. His senses ranged out to the encircling green-clad slopes. He probed with everything he could bring to bear. He called silently with every nerve ending in his body, but nothing vouchsafed an answer.

The tall, thin frame approached a grove of copper osiers with diffident hunger. The eyes catalogued and sought for signs of the unusual, noted several plants not encountered before and moved on. The trees fluttered pleasingly, as was their wont, and insects busied themselves. There were paw prints in the damp earth of a gully bottom and there were some shallow holes of recent date, but they were remarkable only in that they existed in a place as remote as this. The loneliness of it reached out to him and brought tears to the eyes. Jarrod tried to open himself further, to be aware of as much as he could grasp and more than he could see.

There was nothing there for him. There were whole worlds to observe, dramas of life and growth for the witnessing, and there was much beauty in unsuspected corners. There was no unicorn. If there was one around, it was obviously impervious to the yearnings of men, even one blessed with the Talent and deemed acceptable by the forces of the Place of Power. Jarrod realized with a small, guilty start that he had not given them a thought in sennights and he sent a prayer in their direction, just in case it could do some good. Then, disappointed that the grove was still no more than a grove, he turned abruptly in his tracks and retraced his steps to the sleeping place and to Martin.

Martin had also been out exploring and was in a cheerful and playful mood. It was quite light, though the sun hadn't reached into the bowl yet, and there was a bouyant feeling of imminence abroad. Martin's attitude was infectious and Jarrod's optimism was restored. Quite how it turned into a laughing chase, he never could remember, but he vividly remembered the moment when they stopped trying to topple each other into the lake, looked at one another and suddenly stopped laughing. He remembered kissing Martin on the mouth and there was no way that he would forget the slap that followed. She had flowed against him in total surrender and then pushed him back and hit him so hard that his head snapped to the right.

"Oh, I'm sorry," she said, her eyes wide and her hand now to her mouth. "I really didn't, er I, I didn't mean to do that. I was just taken by surprise." She was plainly at a loss and shocked at herself more than at Jarrod, but he was too busy feeling hurt to notice.

"It's all right," he mumbled, rubbing his cheek. "I got carried away. I'm sorry. I won't do it again." His face was crimson except for the white splay of fingers across the left side. He turned away and she watched the pattern reverse itself as the fingermarks turned red.

Martin tried to get a conversation going on a neutral topic, but Jarrod wouldn't be drawn. He wouldn't even look at her. He barely heard a word that was said to him. He was angry at her, but he was furious with himself. That he should have lost control and made an idiot of himself was intolerable, but what really mortified him was the knowledge that, for a moment, he would have given up everything he believed in, the work, the hopes, the pride, the patriotism, the ambition that burned in him, the search itself, if Martin hadn't put him sharply in his place. It was a bitter discovery.

"Would you prefer it if we went off looking in different directions today?" Martin's words caught his awareness. He nodded.

Martin watched in helpless exasperation as the boy extracted what he needed from his pack in silence. She was out of her depth and she felt uncomfortable. She wasn't used to being either. She was almost as anxious as Jarrod to be off on her own. She had been startled both by the kiss and by her instinctive reaction to it. She wanted time to sort through her feelings. She found herself thinking, if only he'd shave off that ridiculous attempt at a beard . . . and shook her head at herself. She went over and started to get something together for a midday meal and when she looked up she saw Jarrod hovering over her. He looked so young and defenseless, standing there awkwardly with all his emotions chasing themselves across his face, that she felt a surge of solicitude, a desire to comfort and cradle him.

"Which way do you want to go?" she asked as noncommitally as she could.

"West?" He cracked on the word like a boy whose voice is changing and she felt his embarrassment physically.

"Surely. I'll see you back here around sunset then," she said as she got to her feet. Jarrod nodded and turned mutely away.

"Jarrod?" He faced her again. "I take it as a great compliment," and she smiled. He blushed and ducked his head. He almost spoke, but decided against it. His eyes slid away and he bobbed his head again, then he turned on his way. She watched him with a taste of sadness before she shouldered her pack and set off in the opposite direction.

The object of her concern strode along through the long grasses in a flux of emotions, of which relief was the foremost. He had got away with it. He was going to be given another chance. He followed the path his body had created earlier in the day filled with a righteous determination to keep himself true to his mission. Besides, came the unbidden thought, there's always time for that later, and she had kissed him back. His mood lightened and his happiness returned.

The going beyond the osiers was enough to test anyone's elation, but Jarrod was humming as he highstepped through bushes and vines. Stiff-twigged branches clawed at his jerkin and kitbriars snagged at the leather of his trousers. Insects hummed along with him and small things, screened by the waist-high vegetation, went crashing from the intrusion of his boots. He pushed his way through, keeping the lake on his left, detouring away from it when the thickets grew too close. There was still no sun to be seen, but it was getting steadily hotter.

He glanced longingly at the slopes on his right where there were meadows and stands of tall trees. Beyond them rose the steep green sides of the mountain, capped by the naked ring of black rock and, as Jarrod looked, the laggard sun emerged behind him to light the black lip and the foliage beneath it. As the light slid downward, a ripple of purple shook itself into being and flowed down as if in pursuit. Reds and blues erupted gently and filled in patches that had escaped transformation. The trumpet liandras were opening to the sun and they looked like a rainbow melting.

As the colors continued to spread downward and sideways, a cloud formed around him and rose in winged multiplicity to greet the blossoms and the sun. Those that flew across the lake caused the surface to boil as the fish threw themselves out of the water after them. It seemed to Jarrod that the whole world was in motion. It was a moment of magic as potent as anything he could perform and it reinforced his feeling that this was the place for a myth to come to life, here in the gods' hollow anvil.

The flowers on the Western vines were all open now and the cliff looked like a massive tapestry glowing in the sun. Breezes caused by the warm air rising from the surface of the lake made it shift and billow. Its beckonings drew him and he started to push his way through the brakes. But they were too cunningly interlaced and he had nothing with which to cut his way through.

The sun was climbing toward the thirteenth hour and the temperature in the center rose with it. Jarrod made his way toward the lake in a welter of discomfort. He came to the wooded edge of a ravine and swung himself down by branch and root into the cool gloom of the dormant watercourse. He followed it stooping until he could stand comfortably beneath the brown and green barrel vaulting. A herd of unicorn, he thought, could have hidden down here and, if I was tramping around above, I'd be none the wiser. It was a discomforting idea.

His secret tunnel, for his mind had already played that game, ended abruptly in a brief fan of fine gravel and a dazzle of light. It played in spotted patterns on the tracery above his head. It made it difficult for his eyes to adjust and it took a while for the view to come into focus. He was at the lowest point in the valley and, from the waterside, it looked immense. The distant curve of mountain seemed unreachably far away, but he scrutinized it nonetheless. He badly wanted to see a cave, or a cleft, or a defile that might form an entryway. He saw nothing suitable.

He watched the cliff opposite grow bright and luminescent. He toyed with the idea of taking a swim, but his conscience drove him back up the ravine. He followed it as far as he could and then fought his way up to the meadows and spent the rest of the day in an unrewarding search among the different groups of trees. It occurred to him that the valley was a nursery where every kind of tree was kept and flourished according to its own cycle.

He found time difficult to keep track of once the sun and the daymoon had gone down below the Western rim. All the sides were still and uniform once more and the footing seemed to get worse as the light began to die. Upheld by his newly formed resolutions, he tramped on doggedly, but there was no sign of what he was after. He turned back at last and trailed into the firelight.

"You look all in," Martin said, looking up from the pot that she was stirring. "Dinner's ready, so why don't you go and splash your face in the spring and come and sit down. I put the pot back on when I heard you blundering around out there." Jarrod groaned and massaged the small of his back with both hands.

"I feel as if I've been in battle. I've been tripped by roots, ripped by thorns and bitten by every insect up here."

"Only half of them. The other half was having the meal of their lives off me." Jarrod ignored her suggestion about the spring and slumped down beside the fire.

"Whatever that is smells very good. I suppose you had about as much luck as I did?"

"What you smell is a lapin that was so tame that it walked right up to me and no, there wasn't a single unicorn to be seen." The exigencies of the day had rendered them slow and easygoing and there was no feeling of constraint between them. Jarrod was relieved.

They woke to thunder out of a darkness so intense that it was

palpable. The peals rolled round the valley in earsplitting pursuit
of one another. It sounded and felt as if all the mill stones in the
world were grinding down toward them. They crouched, staring
into the nothingness, their hands pressed over their suffering
ears. Their skins and nostrils were burdened by moisture and it
fell in droplets from their hair. There was a stabbing blaze of
light, diffused and magnified by the thick mist it revealed and
took away in competing afterimages of red and white. The
patterns repeated themselves and died with infinite slowness.
The air around them rumbled them toward deafness. They clung
to each other, shaking in the malevolent night, as the universe
faded slowly back to black. The thunder gave them no such
respite.

Light hissed alive again, but this time it was behind them so
that the world was suddenly radiant. The air pearlesced around
them. Martin threw herself, face down, on the ground with a
whimper that was drowned out by the bass music of the clouds.
Jarrod hesitated for a beat and then made a shield of himself over
her. They pressed themselves into the stable and resistant earth
as the universe went berserk around them.

Lightning struck randomly, thither and yon, as the air crackled and fluoresced in pools of incandescent grey gossamer. They
trembled and the ground, as if in sympathy, trembled with them.
They were suffused by an abject need for survival as the sky
exploded around their shoulders. There was so much energy
concentrated in that cloud-bound cup that their hair stood on end
as they lay prostrate beneath the assault. The thunderclaps bounced
them and rubbed them shudderingly across one another.

It seemed to Jarrod, as he lay there in fear, that he had spent
his whole life waiting for death. There was nothing before this
storm and nothing existed outside it. It buffeted and abused him
until a rage at the ridiculousness of his position built up in him.
He forgot all about Martin and his instincts of protection. What
was innate and strong in him fought back against the annihilation
of self that was being imposed by the elements. He pushed
himself to his knees and found that there were winds swirling
about. They were severe and irrational, but an equally irrational
drive within him forced him upright. They swooped down on
him, making him stumble over Martin and stagger in puppet

dance. He stood, finally, arms spread like the wings of a raptor's chick, screaming defiance at unacknowledged deities.

When the rain struck, it did so in a solid mass that deprived him of air to scream with and knocked him back to his knees. He curled his head beneath his chest and gulped for air in the pocket that his body created. The rain slashed at him and made the grass, in which his fingers had automatically twisted themselves, slick and yielding. He coughed and fought for breath in a world that had turned to water. He was battered and foundering.

Jarrod felt as if a cooper was doing a demonstration on his chest and he knew that he would die. Then the rain stopped as suddenly as it had started. It was a shock to the heaving lungs and the arching back and he collapsed over Martin's inert body. Around them was a constant, low-level grumbling, but the sounds of water on the move grew. It began as a dripping and escalated to a malicious gurgle.

Light blazed again and his hair became a sparkling corona. The arms spasmed independently, giving Jarrod the aspect of an obscene marionette, before they settled into a jerky stroking of Martin's cloaked back. The stare was mindless, couched in deep, skin-stretched pockets, and the mouth smiled aimlessly, belying the fierce crooning that came from the throat. A small spark inside him grappled for control, but it was not until the thunder had growled off in search of other peaks that sanity slowly drifted down on him. Around him the waters raged at the constriction of their channels.

Trees that clung to the banks were undermined and leaned with fatal fascination over the destructive torrents. The clouds thinned down to streamers of fog, made beautiful by the unjudging nightmoon, but the night was filled by the moaning and rending of a world in the painful process of disintegration. Jarrod could no longer absorb it and, with something close to gratitude, surrendered to unconsciousness.

He came back slowly from a dream that was imprecise and threatening and was not sure if he had crossed the border between sleep and waking. Everything was moist and the world was filled with glowing opacity. It was day, though clouds were back to cloak the sky, and Martin was shaking him gently. The world that enclosed them turned to gold and the invisible mountain chuckled and gushed.

"Come on, Jarrod, wake up. Please."

"It's all right. I'm awake. What's happening? What time is it?"

"I'm not sure, but it must be pretty close to thirteen. It's been light for a long time, but it doesn't seem to get any clearer." She looked down at him and smiled and then sat back on her heels. "Are you really all right?" she asked. "I was afraid you were never going to wake up. Did you Magic the storm away?"

Jarrod hesitated, tempted to boost himself in her standing, but then he looked up shyly and said. "No. Not this time. I was too petrified to be able to do anything. I really don't remember too much about it." He sought back in his infallible memory and found only partial answers. It was as if part of the fog had become lodged in his brain and it made him feel very precarious. His mind shied away from the blank area. An ability he had come to take for granted had been impaired for the second time and, cocooned though he was in woofy gold, he felt disturbed and adrift.

"It sounds as if we're sitting in the middle of a waterfall," he said to cover his confusion, "and everything's still sopping wet."

"I know. I hope the sun burns through soon. It's ridiculous, because we're out in the open, but this is starting to make me feel shut in." She glanced around anxiously and, as if in answer to her desire, the fog became dazzling and then unravelled away.

The valley sparkled in the brightness of the newly revealed sun and everything stood out with great clarity. The far side of the lake looked close and everything had a specific vividness, an almost personal shade and hue. The air came to their nostrils all green and wet and fresh, with an underlying tang from the lake's waters. Jarrod inhaled it gratefully as his eyes became yare again. They watched as the ground smoked and the drop-hung twigs and leaves glittered as they slowly and silently wept. The too sharp outlines became bearable again, but the winesap smell of the day lingered.

"Shall we go off looking?" Martin asked, a smile hovering.

"Just as soon as I've dried off. I really don't fancy pushing through wet thickets just now."

"Well then, come with me and have a look at my meadows. We've only half a day left anyway." He looked up quickly, but her face was unrevealing.

"I think I'll take you up on that," he said carefully.

"All right then. Let's spread our stuff out to dry in the sun and then we can get going." The eagerness in her voice matched his feeling of beginnings that went with a newly washed world.

The only trouble, in this case, was that the washers had been overgenerous. Their boots squelched as their feet came down. The ground seemed to suck at their soles and each toe felt individually wet. They slogged on around the shoreline with exaggerated gait, arms half out for balance, until they came to a foaming culvert. It was bush-clogged and abrim with boiling water. Martin pulled up and looked at it, fists on hips.

"We'll never get across that. We'd better go up until we find a convenient tree trunk." There wasn't a hint of a question in the way that she said it, nor in the way she automatically took her own advice and strode off uphill. Jarrod kept pace and said nothing.

They found a fallen tree and crawled across on all fours while the water chattered angrily beneath them. The going on the other side was no better. The footing was tussocked with bearded grasses that leaned drunkenly after the binge of rain and they zigzagged across it in search of higher ground. The breeze riffled the sheets of standing water and made the mountain maidens dance. Jarrod pulled up by a cinder tree and leaned against it as he caught his breath.

"I thought the going was easier on this side."

"That's the trouble with you Stronta folk," Martin said teasingly, "you're nice, but you haven't got any stamina."

"I'd argue with you," Jarrod replied with a grin, "but I'm too tired. Besides, my calf muscles wouldn't agree. Would you look at these boots," he added, lifting one leg and regarding its end with dismay. "They'll never make it back home." He pushed himself away from the tree trunk. "Well, I suppose we ought to keep on looking. If we spot any dry wood we ought to collect it or there'll be no way to light a fire tonight."

"As I remember it, this stand's quite broad. By the way, have you noticed how mixed all these groves of trees are? It's weird."

"Yes, I know what you mean. I even thought of this place as the Nursery of the Gods. It's almost as if there's one of everything here. I caught myself feeling that these were the originals and everything out there is a copy."

"You're getting stranger, Jarrod. I swear you are. I just hope it's a good sign. We can't stay here too much longer, you know."

"Right," Jarrod said with a half sigh. "Lead on then. They are your meadows, after all."

They threaded their way between the trees and admired the fall of light through the branches. Somewhere at the bottom of their awareness there was the sound of running water, but it was overborne by the conversation the trees were holding with the wind. The garrulous vegetation thinned out and beyond it, in a gently curving meadow, there gambolled a grown unicorn and three colts.

CHAPTER XVI

JARROD CAME AWAKE IN BROAD DAYLIGHT AND STARTED TO STRETCH. Nothing happened. He told himself that he was still asleep, but decided to try to move his fingers anyway. The message never reached his left hand and an edge of uneasiness crept into him. He tried for the fingers of the right hand and felt a flash of relief when they moved. As they did, his sense of place returned and the inertia that held him prisoner in his own body resolved itself into Martin, asleep on top of him. That in itself was unlikely enough for a dream, but he knew that he was awake, even though the inside of his head was misty. Recollection returned. There had been a storm and they had huddled together for protection while the world turned to water. He ought to be soaking wet, but his exploring fingers encountered nothing worse than damp. Had they slept a whole night and a day away while the world returned to normal?

He inched his way out from under Martin. His left arm flamed as he drew it clear. Pain flooded back down it as it came to life. He rolled Martin gently off trying, successfully, not to wake her. He rubbed his burning shoulder as he sat up and peered about. The campsite was completely changed. He struggled to his feet and drew his breath in with a gasp as his muscles reacted. He must have overdone it to be this sore. It felt as if he had been bruised all over and his head ached.

He looked around him with self-imposed slowness and care,

but he knew before he had completed a quarter turn that he was nowhere near the campsite. He made himself complete the circle. He had no recollection of this place. None of the grassy, open spaces he had come across that day was this large. The partial memory of a nightmare bathed in moonlight flitted through his brain, but he did not remember fleeing from the storm. He pushed his mind to bring the nightmare back so that he could examine it for clues, but all he retrieved were inchoate snatches: a patch of light, fog and a thread of terror too insubstantial to contain an answer. There was something else down there as well, but it refused his summoning.

The lake at the bottom of the slope was lapping high and the flotsam brought by the storm disfigured its surface. A swirling wind was crosshatching it, white froth stark against the unyielding blackness of it. It looked sinister to him under the pale and impotent aqua of the early morning sky.

The air smelled wet and the battered foliage along the bank looked clean. Vines, torn from their rock-bound moorings, washed forlornly back and forth, while uprooted trees spread their branches to the inconsistent breezes and sailed along with as much dignity as they could contrive. On this morning, the valley did not look so likely a spot for a unicorn to choose, but Jarrod's needs would not be denied. Resolution flared in savage intensity. Somewhere along the shores of this misbegotten, bitter-tasting lake there was a unicorn and he was going to find it.

The desire felt subtly wrong to him, but he couldn't imagine why. The hunt for the unicorn had become his destiny. He had been chosen for it. It couldn't be wrong. Not wrong; no longer necessary. The thought was suddenly there, naked and unsupported. It stopped him in his tracks. He stood, inhaling the odors of the morning and worrying at the idea. Nothing came of it and he moved on, turning his attention to the brightening world around him.

Slowly the picture of a unicorn formed in his mind. She, and he knew instinctively that it was a female, was bigger than any image he had conjured up before. She gleamed in a mixture of health and sunlight.

"I thought they had beards," he said aloud, and a piece of the recent past came back in a rush.

They had found the unicorn—a whole family of unicorns—and he had been able to talk with the young ones. He viewed the idea with suspicion. Fantasizing, he cautioned himself. You want it so badly that you imagine you've already done it. But the image was too real for that and he probed at the murk that surrounded the vision like a boy with a loose tooth. It produced the required twinge. Something bad had happened. Something that he didn't want to remember.

His name cut across his thoughts dimly and then repeated itself. He realized that someone was calling him. He turned to see Martin running down the field toward him. She skidded to a halt beside him and he put out a hand to steady her.

"Jarrod, are you all right?" Her eyes were wide with concern and inquiry.

"I'm a little sore, but not too bad. Yesterday's clambering took more out of me than I expected." He took his hand off her shoulder and let it drop by his side. Should he ask her?

Before he could make his mind up she said, "We didn't do any clambering yesterday." She cocked her head and now her eyes were wary.

"You may not have done," he temporized. "You got a lot of meadows, you said, but I didn't." Jarrod felt that his accompanying smile was unconvincing. "Er, I've got a question to ask you and I, er, I know it's going to sound rather silly . . ." She waited for him. "Well, what happened to the campsite?" It wasn't the question he had intended to ask, but it would do for a start.

"The campsite? The one by the rock? You don't remember leaving that one?"

"No. No, I don't." There was caution in his voice. "Ought I to?" A hollow feeling was developing under his breastbone.

"What was the last thing you remember?" she asked guardedly.

"Last night's storm?"

"Nothing since that?"

"Nothing that I'm sure of." Without Jarrod being aware of it, his body assumed a defensive posture. Martin noted the hunched shoulders and the hands that rose up the torso. Her emotions tangled. Did he suspect? Would it be better not to tell him that they had found the unicorns and lost them again? He would blame her—blame her for bringing meat along, even though there was no way that she could have known that the unicorns would react so strongly to the sight of dried venison.

"I see," she said slowly, trying to gain a little time. "Well, you seem to be suffering from a mild form of amnesia. How's your memory otherwise?"

"There's a day missing." It was a flat statement that covered his hopes and his uncertainties. Here it comes, she thought.

"Nothing much to be worried about, then," she said with the brisk cheerfulness of a Wisewoman. "It'll probably come back slowly, like after a bad spill on a horse."

"What happened?" Jarrod was not going to be gracious and drop the conversation. Martin looked up at him steadily. She held his eyes for two long beats.

"We found the unicorns."

"That's a relief," he said with a lopsided smile, confounding her entirely. "And?"

"And?" she repeated and knew that she sounded stupid the moment the word was out of her mouth.

"And then what? Where are they? What happened? How many were there?"

"Slow down. Slow down. They were at the top of this field and we sort of walked up on them. Oh, Jarrod, she was beautiful. She was so beautiful." She had abandoned her caution. "And you, you were talking with, well, communicating with, the young ones . . ." His smile grew in answer.

"You knew."

"Not really. I just had this picture in my head and a sort of conviction. How many were there?"

"Four. One female and three colts."

"Four?" There was wonderment in his voice. "What happened to them?" There the question was: inescapable.

"I don't know, Jarrod, I really don't know."

"What do you mean, you don't know?"

"They disappeared," she replied with partial truth.

"What happened to me?" he demanded. "I feel like I did when the Umbrians caught me."

"That's a little hard for me to explain. You could think directly to the little ones and I think they were too much for you to handle all at one time. I thought you were going to die,'' she added defensively.

"They did this to me?" He gestured at his chest with his hands. "Did they mean to?"

"I don't think so, Jarrod. I really don't think so. They got frightened, that's all."

"I think," he said with a quiet control that surprised her, "that you had better start from the beginning."

"Let's see if we can find something halfway dry to sit on, or I could tell you over breakfast if you're hungry. It'll have to be fruit though. I'll explain about that later on: it's part of the story." They turned and retraced their steps and she told him everything she could remember, including her offering him a strip of dried venison when they were both hungry. She told him of the unicorns' taking flight at the sight of it. She expected recriminations, but there were none.

"They'll be back," she concluded soothingly, seeing the stricken look in his eyes. "Just you wait and see."

Wait they did, for there was nothing else they could do. Jarrod was pensive for the rest of the day. He found himself cast into lethargy and could scarcely get up the energy to help Martin gather more fruit and berries from the surrounding coppices. The loss of the unicorns, combined with the loss of his memory, sapped him of will and, for the most part, he sat listlessly in the sun. By the end of the second day, Martin's guilt and sympathy were beginning to fray and the change in diet was upsetting her system. It was that, more than anything else, that started to bring Jarrod back.

He was all solicitude when he found out and insisted on brewing suspicious tasting tisanes from his stock of herbs. These Martin endured and found that they did what Jarrod claimed they would. They did nothing, however, to erase her personal sense of loss. It was even keener than Jarrod's since she had a very clear memory of what had gone from them.

Thereafter, they both did their best to keep each other's spirits up, but by the end of the third day the smiles were wearing thin and the bright words of mutual reassurance were beginning to sound cheap and unconvincing. The weather stayed bright and warm and the sense of peace and beauty it engendered served to

underline the sense of hollowness that they both tried to hide. On
the fourth morning Jarrod could no longer remain inactive and
set out immediately after the Making of the Day to work on his
frustrations. He didn't quite know whether to believe Martin's
explanation, but every time he probed the blankness that was that
day he found nothing. Thus it was that Martin was alone when
the unicorns came back.

She was sitting in the meadow, close to where she had last
seen the family, waiting and watching, while Jarrod was off
hiding his desperation behind tree trunks. The grass by the lake
had dried out and the streambeds were reduced to damp trickles
once more. There were butterflies wafting erratically from flower
to flower, though it should have been far too late for butterflies.
She lay on her stomach watching their progress and felt bored.

One minute the lea was a realm of small things that hopped
and hummed and flew and the next there were four unicorns
standing fetlock deep in grass and wildflowers. They shook their
manes out in the gilding sun. Amarine, the dam, gave a soft
whinny of pleasure, trotted over to her and mumbled at the hair
over her ears. Martin giggled and rolled over and then sat up to
rub the velvet hide that covered the bony nose.

The three colts stood around them for a while, quite still and
seeming to concentrate, and then ambled off to crop. Their
mother turned her head to watch them before settling down with
what sounded like a histrionic sigh. Back legs first and then
forelegs, she maneuvered until she could comfortably lay her
head in Martin's lap. That was how Jarrod found them.

He was astounded by the sight of them and elation poured
through him like a decanting of rare wine. He stared ravenously
as he came down the slope. He kept tripping because he could
not bear to take his eyes off them. The colts saw him coming,
but they made no move. They kept their distance and, if they
made any effort to communicate with him, he could not feel it.
Perhaps, he thought with a pang, he had lost the ability to hear
them. He walked as nonchalantly as possible to the two females,
taking care not to come too close. Envy gnawed at his composure.

"How long have they been back?" he asked softly and was
embarrassed by the catch he heard in his voice.

"Oh, there you are," Martin said, looking up. "Not very long at all. They suddenly appeared. It was weird, Jarrod. One moment there was nothing in the field but butterflies and then, there they were. It was as if they had suddenly decided to stop being invisible."

"Can you talk to them?" He tried to make the question sound disinterested, but his own ears told him that he had failed. Martin seemed not to notice.

"No. I've tried really hard with her, but nothing happens. I didn't think to try with the colts." She looked back down and stroked Amarine's head again. Jarrod was not proud of the relief that washed over him. "Isn't she just beautiful? Isn't she everything I said she was?" When Martin looked up, her face was transfigured.

"So you don't know why they came back? Were you doing anything special? Like praying?"

"No, not that I know of. Have you tried reaching the colts yet?"

"Not yet. To tell you the truth, I'm a little afraid to," he said, with his eyes fixed on the tableau. "She really is beautiful," he added, unable to help himself. Martin smiled proudly, as if she were somehow responsible.

"The most beautiful animal in the world," she said sentimentally. "And your colts are, too. Here they come. Coming to see what's going on, no doubt." Jarrod turned and saw the three young creatures approaching on precise feet. He wondered how he had managed to get through to them before.

You really don't remember us at all, do you? The thought popped unbidden into his mind. He froze, all his senses hyperalert in an instant. There was a brief feeling of overfullness within him and then he heard Beldun, and knew instantly that it was he.

You aren't angry with us, but there is fear of us deep down. I'm afraid we hurt you rather badly.

You have a weak mind, came with disdainful reproach from Nastrus. There was a snort from behind Jarrod and Nastrus was back. *Mam's angry with us. She says that we don't know our own strength and that we ought to apologize. Eating flesh is still absolutely disgusting.* There was rebellion in the tone.

I, for one, don't need prompting. Pellia's presence was gentle and there was contrition evident in it. *I had no idea that I had*

*done any harm and I certainly didn't intend to. I was just so
shocked that I had to get away. Mam's already told us that we
need to learn control and I, for my part, intend to try.* Jarrod
stood there overwhelmed. The actuality of contact was so much
more intimate than he had imagined. He tried projecting tentatively.

*After all those years of doing exercises to develop concentra-
tion and control for performing Magic, I rather thought that my
mind was stronger than most, but it obviously isn't. At least, not
when compared to yours. Did you use your minds to get away?*
he asked shrewdly.

'Course we did. The tone was obviously Nastrus'. It was a
little condescending. Jarrod was abruptly aware of Pellia's amusement in a corner of his mind.

Yes we can, Nastrus said, answering a question before he had
really formulated it. *Everything you think and feel and I don't
think that was a very nice description.*

I can see, Jarrod replied, trying for a wry twist to the thought,
*that this is going to be a lot more complicated than I ever
dreamed.*

That's what you thought the last time, Beldun chimed in.

I can also see, Jarrod replied silently, *that we are going to
have to develop some rules about privacy. If you're going to
stay, that is?* They all caught his underlying anxiety and the
pressure eased fractionally before Beldun was back.

*You need not worry. Mam says we have a mission with you
that we can't avoid. A destiny is the way she put it, so it seems
we've got to stay.* Jarrod just stood and stared at them while a
beam of triumphant happiness lit up his face.

"I imagine you're back in contact," Martin's voice broke in
on him like a splash of cold water. "You've got an idiot grin
plastered all over your face. I forgot to tell you that one of my
complaints before was that I had no idea what was going on. I
still don't."

"Yes, I'm back in contact all right, though it's a bit scary, but
that isn't the important part. Guess what? They've decided to
stay with us. The mother said it was their destiny."

"Her name's Amarine, by the way. You told me that last
time. Do they know how?"

"They just said no." Jarrod's face was flushed and his eyes were dancing. He was so excited that he could barely hold still.

"Well, that completes the circle. Nobody knows." She looked at him and thought how much like a little boy he was at moments like this.

"We shall," he said with happy confidence. "We have to."

"You men," Martin said teasingly, "you always wait for something to turn up."

"I'll see if I can find out where they went when they disappeared," Jarrod replied, refusing to be drawn. He turned back to the colts and saw that they were grazing contentedly. He sent out tentative thoughts that elicited no response, so he resorted to the time-honored method of clearing his throat. He had to do it several times before he felt a questioning. He couldn't identify the touch, but, since the one he thought of as Beldun was looking in his direction, he concentrated on him.

Back a little bit I asked where you went when you disappeared and nobody answered me. Where do you go? The imagegram that materialized in his mind meant nothing to him.

I'm sorry, I don't understand. Can you try to explain it in words? Beldun withdrew for a moment and Jarrod knew, without knowing how, that he was consulting the family's communal memory and it heartened him because it might mean that his own memory was coming back. When the colt returned to him, thoughts formed inside the young Magician's head.

We go into Interim, where all the lines travel side by side, and we travel down the lines of force to a where we want to find again, or to a when.

Oh dear. I'm not sure that I'm doing any better with the words. What was the humming grey nothing that filled my mind before?

That's what Interim feels like to me.

Well, thank you for showing me, Beldun, but it doesn't seem like a place I'd like to spend much time in.

We don't spend time there. It's just the way across.

You don't get lost in all that? Humor reached Jarrod before he had completed the query.

You might come out at the wrong place if you were careless, especially a creature like you, but you can always get straight

*back to where you came from. Once a trip's been made, it's in
The Memory. If any one of us has made the trip, it's in there. Of
course, we're still too young to have made any on our own, but I
expect Mam will allow us to soon.* Hope bloomed suddenly in
Jarrod.

Have you been anywhere else on Strand? he thought.

Mam and the Sire have.

Is it your father's memory as well?

*Oh no. Sires never stay around long enough, unless something
happens to the dam, that is. If that happens, it's his memory that
forms the basis of the family one. Does that make sense?*

Almost.

Beldun disengaged to return to his grazing and Jarrod tried to
explain what he had learned to Martin, but without conspicuous
success. He turned back to try to clarify a point and found the
three youngsters facing the other way. They looked round briefly
at him and he was suffused with a feeling of happiness. He
thought for a moment that he was the cause, but Nastrus quickly
disabused him. He turned to follow the direction of their interest
and found himself watching the unfolding of the vines as the sun
spilled into their charmed circle.

A ceremony of spontaneous richness cascaded down the mountainside, pouring downward with increasing slowness after the
first burst. He was gripped by a sense of wonder. He felt that the
time and the place were hallowed and that he had been sent a
sign. He stood behind the unicorns as the glowing curtain was
shaken out and joy and certainty descended on him.

He turned his attention to the colts and caught the fringes of
their contentment with a familiar miracle. He noticed details that
distinguished them, one from another, and wondered why he had
not seen them before. Pellia was clearly smaller and more fine-
boned than her brothers. She was also darker than the males. The
other two had lighter patches which caused the illusion of a
slight dappling.

All three had longer coats than their mother and they looked
fuzzy and a little uneven. Beldun had the shaggiest and the more
spotted and was a little more heavily muscled than his brother.
His lines were also somewhat better. Like Pellia, he had the
dam's aquiline nose. Nastrus' rounder muzzle and smaller ears

gave him the appearance of being less sculpted and hence more individual. Like a hound pup with a patch over one eye, Jarrod thought, and immediately felt a shaft of disapproval from the subject. He grinned at the indignation being projected.

He'll be wanting to look at our teeth next. He could almost hear Pellia's mental snort as she kicked up her hooves and took off up the meadow at a gallop, pursued immediately by the males.

Jarrod continued to watch as they pranced and reared, a lilt in his heart at their evident enjoyment of life. They possessed in full measure the awkward grace of the very young of all species, so that to watch them was to smile. He turned back reluctantly to Martin and to Amarine, whose head was still in the girl's lap.

"Were you talking to them all this time?" she asked.

"Most of it, yes. Why?"

"Well, it's just that it's very strange watching you stand there staring first at one and then at another without making a sound. It's even weirder when your body reacts the way it would if you were talking out loud. Your hands move and your head goes up when you're surprised. At least that's what it looked like. It's as if I'd suddenly gone deaf. I'm glad," she added with a short laugh, "you don't move your lips when you do whatever it is that you do. Then I'd really think that the altitude had affected me." There was an undercurrent to her voice that bothered Jarrod for a beat until he realized that she envied him.

"I must look pretty odd," he said placatingly. "I'd no idea I was doing that. Have you had any luck getting through to the big one?"

"No." The monosyllable was flat. "Perhaps, since you're so good at these things, you should have another go. You might be able to do it this time."

"I tried before?"

"Yes. You didn't get anywhere, though."

"I couldn't hear her when she talked to the colts a little while ago. I know what she said because Nastrus relayed it to me."

"What's the matter? You afraid to try again?" Jarrod's eyebrows rose at her tone.

"No," he said blandly, turning aside the tension by ignoring it, "I'll try it again if you like. It's just that she's so obviously attached to you that it doesn't seem very likely that she would want to talk to anyone else if she could get through to you.''

"You smooth talker you," Martin said in mild astonishment. Then, with a wry half smile, "I keep forgetting that you were born at court. Go on then, have another try."

Jarrod walked slowly across to the pair and around to the far side so that he could look at Amarine directly. He hitched up his trousers and squatted down on his haunches in front of her. He closed his eyes and tried to make himself open and receptive. He strove for inner silence and sensitivity, stretching his awareness like a drumskin that waited to amplify the lightest tap, the merest whisper of a ruffle. It was in vain: there was not even the shadow of a presence.

He opened his eyes and looked at the indifferent unicorn.

"Amarine," he called softly, but she did not move. He spoke again and then more loudly still. She looked up then, but only to satisfy her curiosity. He seized on the opportunity to try to contact her while he had her attention. He tried to send a message of friendship and reassurance. He concentrated so hard that he felt as if he were squeezing himself down a tube at her. His eyes shut tight again with the effort. He opened them again after what seemed like a long time and was disappointed to see the unicorn's head back in Martin's lap.

"It's no good. I can't get through at all," he said sadly. "We'll just have to talk to her through the colts—if we can get them to stay still long enough." As if to illustrate his words, the three cantered round the group, manes atoss and tails switching, before they frisked off up the meadow. Jarrod gazed after them hungrily.

Martin watched him follow them as she continued to stroke the tumble of white and gold along Amarine's neck. Her fingers were no longer surprised by the coarseness of it. She saw the intensity of his gaze and knew that she would never be able to provoke its like. She was very well aware of the effect that she had on Jarrod and, though she had told herself that he was too juvenile even for sport, she was surprised to discover that the emotion she now experienced was jealousy. She resented his overweening adoration of the young unicorns.

"Do you think," she called, "you could persuade our young

friends to join us? We really ought to put our heads together and think of a way to get out of here. There's a war going on back home. and, when we left, it wasn't going very well." She was taking control again and felt the better for it.

"There's one thing I want to try first, if Amarine will let me."

"What's that?"

"I want to see if anything happens when I touch her horn."

"Her horn? You think it'll do any good? I've touched it and I didn't feel anything."

"I don't know, but I think I ought to try. It's up to her, of course. She may not let me get that close."

"If you're going to upset her, I think I'd better stand up."

"No, don't," Jarrod said quickly, "I think that might make her nervous. I promise I'll go very slowly and I'll stop the moment she seems not to like it."

"Well, it's her decision," Martin said somewhat ungraciously.

Jarrod walked quietly over and squatted down again. Gradually, almost stealthily, his hand crept out and inched toward the slim wand with the deadly point. The unicorn rolled her deep blue eyes back once so that Jarrod knew that she was aware of him. Then she shut them and lay still.

The hand hovered over the base where the spiral started and the forefinger descended to rest lightly on the ivory. There was a mild tingling, so faint that Jarrod thought that it was wishful thinking. He took his finger off the cool surface, carefully reached a little further, and curled his hand around the shaft. The shock was immediate, like touching iron in Winter, and energy pulsed out into him. It whirled up through his body as it had in the Place of Power. He plucked his hand away and shook it to dispel the stinging. The muscles in his arm ticked randomly.

"What's the matter? You're so pale. What happened?" Jarrod took his time before answering, waiting for the pains to subside.

"There are tremendous forces inside her, great energies. She can transmit them through the horn. Have you ever jumped into a pond when there's a little ice on it?"

"The river. When I was a little girl. My father said that it built character."

"Then you've got an idea what it felt like."

"She hasn't even moved," Martin said wonderingly. "I don't suppose she sent along any messages with it?"

"If she did, I couldn't catch them. It's a little difficult to listen when you're being flayed alive from the inside out." He knew that he was being defensive and it annoyed him. Martin was no help.

"Oh, come on now," she said, "let's not exaggerate. It can't have been that bad."

"Now I'm sure that you didn't feel anything when you touched her horn," Jarrod retorted.

"That's why it's so nice to have a Magician along," she said sarcastically. Jarrod was spared the need for an answer by Amarine, who pushed up and articulated her way to her feet. She moved off and turned to look at them and shook her head vigorously before she started to graze.

"Now look what you've done," Martin said.

"I'll see if I can call the colts." Jarrod felt that he was somehow in the wrong, but he didn't know why. "I'm not very good at attracting their attention unless they're looking at me and I've never tried it this far away." He paced slowly up the lea and sent summons after summons. The colts paid not a blind bit of notice.

He gave vent to the frustration that Martin had built up in him in a mental bellow. The effect was almost comical. The colts stopped short, stumbled and froze. Slowly, the heads swung around and then the bodies followed rapidly as they broke into a trot toward him. Beldun took the point. Jarrod looked back at Martin and smiled with such unfettered happiness that Martin felt it dissolve the tensions in her.

He faced front again and tried, unsuccessfully, to quiet the barrage of questions that pressed in on him. It hurt, that rushing pressure of concern, but he was overjoyed to find that they cared. He tried to send soothing thoughts out of his buffeted brain and his body held out his arms in a broad gesture of embrace.

We need your help, he said to them.

You said that before. From Nastrus. *He doesn't remember, stupid.* Beldun. *Males.* An admonition from Pellia that bore the hallmarks of the oft repeated. *We said that we were going to help you and that was after you started remembering things again,* arrived, accompanied by a note of triumph, from Nastrus. *Let him finish,* from Pellia. All these came and went in his head with bewildering speed.

I don't know how much I've already told you, but the first thing we have to do is get out of this valley and back to one of the Magical Kingdoms. We don't have too much time. Winter's coming on and the two of us can't survive it in the open. He felt them withdraw before he had finished the thought and was afraid that they had changed their minds. Then he realized that they had gone to consult their memory. Nastrus was the first one back, and then Pellia. They engaged in an exchange that was both too fast and too alien for him to follow. He felt like a child whose parents have suddenly stopped speaking slowly and clearly and have gone off into a conversation of their own, composed of words that he had never heard before, interspersed with ones that were tantalizingly familiar.

He understood that he would have to change his emotional assumptions about these extraordinary creatures. He had been thinking of them as a kind of cross between a very bright child and an adorable young animal and neither attribution was really applicable. His realization was accompanied by amusement and encouragement. The amusement was Nastrus' and it was tinged with the sardonic. Jarrod sighed inwardly at the futility of trying to have private thoughts while the colts were around.

Well, he thought out somewhat grumpily, *have you come up with any answers yet?*

Several, Pellia replied. Behind her thought was the kindly laughter of the other two. Jarrod was aware that his head was lifted in surprise and, remembering Martin's words, felt uncomfortable. He looked over to where she was standing.

"Would it help if I said my part of the conversation aloud?"

"It would probably be better than this mime show. At least I'd know what the subject was."

"I asked them if they had any ideas as to how we could get out of here and how we could get home."

"Good thinking. Sorry, no pun intended." Jarrod shook his head slightly in acknowledgement.

"They said they had several."

"Like what?"

"Don't know yet." He looked at Pellia. "Like what?" he said aloud.

There are recollections of a number of visits to places on this planet, but none of them were inhabited by man. Several of the loci, however, are located in what you call the Magical Kingdoms. It would not be difficult for us to get to any of them.

"Well, that's a start. At least there won't be any trouble for you. It'll take us quite a while to get back and then, of course, we'll have to find you again."

Given your physical shortcomings, it was Nastrus, *it's going to take you a very long time to travel that far on foot. I'm not totally convinced that you'd be able to reach us if you got there. All the places that Mam and Sire visited were what you would call remote.*

They found us here, didn't they? Pellia remonstrated.

Luck, from Beldun.

"What if we went with you?" Jarrod asked hastily.

You said you didn't know anything about Interim, Beldun reminded him.

"Oh, I don't mean by ourselves, we don't know how. I mean, could we ride you through this Interim?" There was the silence of withdrawal and this time it was a long one.

"You're doing it again, Jarrod," Martin's voice interrupted. "You're talking in your head again."

"No, I'm not. They have a sort of communal memory and they've gone off to consult it. At least I assume that's what they're doing."

"Oh, sorry. It just got so quiet for such a long time . . ." she let the sentence trail off. "I don't quite know how we'd manage it. You're too heavy for Amarine."

"I don't know either. It seemed like a good idea. I can't think of any other way of getting there together. We could never get them through unnoticed with us. The first Isphardi merchant we met would have them in cages in a jiffy and exhibit them all over."

"Oh Jarrod! That's obscene!"

"You know it's true. They'd be worth a fortune."

"That's degenerate." Her tone was genuinely offended and

Jarrod shrugged his shoulders and turned back to the unicorns. They were waiting for him and he wondered if they had overheard him.

You we understood. We do not understand your speech with the mouth. We can't make contact with her at all. The thoughts came in a braid.

"She was angry at me for being able to think such thoughts. She thinks too highly of you all to be able to entertain such notions."

Then she can't be too clever.

You always jump to the worst conclusions, Nastrus.

I think Mam's wrong, Nastrus answered his sister, *I don't think that age has anything to do with the instinct to protect unmounted females of this species. I think sex has. You do it. So does Mam and it's because all three of you are females.*

What has this to do with getting to wherever it is they're going? Beldun intervened.

It's not a question of whether you could ride on us, Nastrus said directly to Jarrod, *but of whether you could survive in Interim. There's nothing in The Memory about humanoids travelling the lines of force and I'm not at all sure that Mam would agree to let your female try.*

"Her name is Martin, by the way. Well, it's really Marianna, but I call her Martin. At least for now."

You really are the most peculiar animals.

Nastrus!

"We don't think of ourselves as being animals," Jarrod said uncomfortably.

Well, you are. You ought to. Nastrus was enormously pleased to be having the last word and Jarrod left it to him.

"If Martin rode your mother, could the rest of you carry me?"

Course we could. I certainly couldn't. The latter from Pellia.

"What if I was tied across all three of you?"

Possible, said Beldun.

"Could one of you please ask your mother if she'll help us? If she'll allow Martin into Interim?" There was a hesitation. "What's the matter?"

We do not have a strong enough argument. Pellia's reply was reasonable and tinged with sympathy, but quite sure of itself.

"But why not? You know how much we need you."

"What's the matter, Jarrod?" Martin asked anxiously, while Pellia replied regretfully, *The risk is too great. She would never permit it.* Jarrod turned away dejectedly and kicked at the turf.

"What's going on? What's wrong?" Martin was insistent.

"They say that Amarine won't let you travel with them through Interim."

"What's the problem with it?"

"They think it could be fatal to us if we tried." Jarrod's temples were beginning to throb.

"Just to me?"

"No, but Amarine is determined to keep you from harm and the colts say that they haven't got a strong enough argument to convince her to let you risk your life."

"It doesn't matter if it's dangerous, just so long as we can get them to somewhere where they can be of help. It doesn't matter if we arrive dead. After all, there isn't anything else about us in the poem, is there?" she demanded with chilling logic.

"The only places they know how to get to are places like this, places where people don't go."

Martin looked at him speculatively while she thought. "There's one way round that, but you're going to have to set the scene for it," she said slowly.

"You're going to appeal directly to her for support?"

"No. You're going to convince her that our need is so great that I am prepared, no eager, to try. I don't think she'll be able to refuse me my last request."

"That's your last request?" Jarrod was trying to follow her.

"No. My last request is that she take me home for burial. That, at least, will get them to Gwyndryth. Unless you want to tell her that I live in Celador."

"I don't think I should care to lie to that lady. You really don't think she'll go along with it, do you?"

"I told you that you were going to have to be good." She smiled at him complacently and added, "You'll have to find out where these remote places are so that we can pick the best one to die on the way to." The smile continued and Jarrod looked at her askance. She opened her eyes wider and nodded emphatically. He looked over at the colts, clustered now around their mother.

He walked toward them and then stopped and detoured for a short walk around the field. He found himself curiously unwilling to begin the dialogue. He told himself that he needed time to marshall his arguments, but he knew that he had an inescapable one. It was better than Martin's, but he was loath to use it.

The unicorns were so different, so beautiful, so unworldly, that he balked at involving them in the affairs of men, even though he knew that that was what he had been sent out to do. Underneath those feelings was his reluctance to disinter precariously buried horrors. Was he leading them into harm? Could anybody say that they were less important than human beings? We don't think of ourselves as animals. You are. You ought to. The thoughts stalked each other around his mind and indecision ate at him like rust.

He knew what he had to do, though it was risky and would be painful. There would be no amnesia to prevent recall and his spirit procrastinated. His feet, however, took him back to the unicorns. He faced the colts. He peeled the layers back logically for them as he presented the beleaguerment of mankind by the Others and, when he knew that he had them hooked, he forced himself to open the breeding ground of nightmares that were his memories of the Archmage's vision.

The scenes oozed out into the light of recognition, a world incarnadine, battered and despairing amid the bleak desolation of defeat. His eyes were shut tight and tears seeped out from under gummy lids. He was silent, but his body talked for him and finally he felt them flee from him. He sagged, uncertain and afraid.

The colts tore up to the top of the slope, followed, a little more sedately, by the dam. Their manes and tails streamed out behind them as they raced around and, every now and then, they bucked as if trying to dislodge the images they could not outrun. They slowed finally and came to a spittle-flecked, flank-heaving stop. They wandered off to drink from a stream. From time to time, Amarine would turn her long neck and look down toward the humans.

Martin and Jarrod stood close together and Martin had put an arm of comfort around him. Jarrod couldn't see the dam clearly through his blurred eyes, but knew, nevertheless, that they were being weighed, as well they might be. What he had shown the colts, and through them their mother, was enough to curdle any soul. The memories, once they had been brought near the surface, had swarmed up into consciousness in unruly and uncontrollable riot. They were stoppered up again for a while, but he realized how thin the membrane of enforced forgetfulness was.

The silent colloquy at the top of the meadow, if that was what it was, drew out interminably. The humans sat down and waited until hunger drove them in search of fruit trees. Martin said nothing, but she stayed with Jarrod and watched him with surreptitious concern. She hadn't asked what reasons he had put forth, but she could guess from the look of him. She understood why the unicorns were taking their time. They might not be overly concerned with the slaughter of people, but they were kin with the horses and the cloudsteeds and their agony was every bit as intense as the pain felt by men.

Movement at the top of his vision brought Jarrod back and he saw that the family group was breaking up. Amarine was cropping and the colts were ambling about and shaking themselves. He waited for them to approach, but after a few minutes it was obvious that they had no intention of coming down. A pang shook him. He had been given a second chance and he had failed again. His stomach turned over and distracted him from the self-pity that was sure to follow.

He mastered his stomach and then the rest of himself by falling back on exercises he had neglected since he had travelled beyond Greylock's reach. When he looked up again, he noticed that the grass was touched with a dusty rose light. It clung to stalk and blade and gave a brownish cast to the squill. It was late and he felt that he needed to do something to rectify the situation.

They sensed his movement immediately and Amarine moved out to position herself between him and her offspring. All four were pink in the long twilight and her horn was an eye-compelling whirl of nacre. Her stance was far from reassuring and the human approached her with great care and trepidation.

He halted a fair distance from her and thought out timidly, but encountered nothing. He called on everything that Greylock had taught him about the use of his voice and then he began to talk, to explain, to try to convince the dam that he was no threat and had meant no harm. He knew that the menacing figure, her head lowered in anticipation of danger, could not understand his words, but he hoped that his tone would convey the earnestness of his intent. He stopped and waited for some kind of reaction, but there was none.

He pleaded then in eerie silence composed of the sound of the wind among leaves and grasses, the gentle movement of the lake against its shores, the premature song of a night bird and the crepitations of the insect world. His anguish spoke to the youth of those who listened and, at last, they responded, startling him with their simultaneous arrival in his mind.

You have learned to modulate, Pellia remarked. *You're more complex and interesting than I had imagined,* came from Nastrus. Mild indignation and *we told you that we were going to help,* from Beldun. Jarrod felt the tears well up and turned away hastily to collect himself and to spare them. Relief made him weak and he staggered slightly as he walked a few paces to regain his composure. He stopped and looked at them with a long, fond regard.

"Thank you," he whispered. He left them and walked back down to the lake on cautious legs. He availed himself of the stream and the coldness of the water seemed to refresh his spirit as much as it invigorated his flesh.

"I think it worked," he said. "I don't know about Amarine and Interim yet, but I'm too tired to do any more."

With that he wrapped himself up in his cloak and lay down. He curled himself into a tight ball and slept.

He woke to see four silver shapes in the starshine and felt a wild lurch of joy. His body told him that it was time to Make the Day, but he felt a reluctance to disturb them. It wasn't strong enough, however, to overcome the crescent pressure within and he rolled carefully to his feet. He avoided the dark mound that was Martin, skirted the unmoving animals as quietly as he could, and set off up the gentle gradient. A solid shadow resolved itself into a thicket and he looked up at the almost unmoving dance of the constellations to orient himself.

The Shield blazed down at him, but the Battleaxe had lost half its handle, chopped off by the sharp rim of the mountain. They shone up at him too from the calm surface of the inky lake, but neither image could conceal the vast emptiness that lay behind them. It was like looking into a Mage's cowl and encountering the infinite. He felt compelled to bring up the sun so that none might see that there was no back to the cowl.

Thoughts and awareness flickered in and out of his head as he climbed and he realized that he was being followed. There was no sense of unease with the knowledge, just the certainty that the three young unicorns were behind him. He did not turn his head to verify his feeling, nor did he reach out with his mind to touch them. They accompanied him to his chosen position and waited while he settled himself.

They listened with respect to the cadences of the litany and followed him effortlessly inside himself as he took hold of the pattern of his own being. They glided toward the dormant orb with him and were around him as he eased the bright bulk of it upward. They did not interfere at all; they were a presence of comfort and curiosity, no more. That did not prevent it from being the most intimate thing that Jarrod had ever done. He was sharing himself and his art in a way that he had never imagined to be possible. He emerged into what his heightened senses knew to be the infinitesimal paling that preceded the false dawn.

He was elated as he had never been before. His body vibrated with happiness and he felt light and clear. He rose to his feet with an elastic ease and turned to his companions with a dancing smile. He opened his arms wide in a gesture that enfolded them all.

What a wonderful morning, he greeted.

It certainly was a pleasure to be in your mind today, Pellia returned. *Really most unusual. It would be good to do that again.*

Not until tomorrow, Nastrus. I only do that ritual once a day, but it would be a privilege to have you with me. I must confess it's never felt that good before.

Can we go back now? Beldun inquired and they turned and began the long descent as the contrast bled from behind the stars. Martin and Amarine awaited them.

"Good morning," Martin said, "I take it you've seen to it that we shall have another day?"

"It's going to be a wonderful one."

"Well done, Jarrod." Her voice was warm and her eyes sparkled. Martin had suddenly vanished and Marianna looked out at him with approval. Nastrus intruded.

We don't have any labels for what is going on underneath your direct thought processes, he said, throwing Jarrod into confusion. *Some of the things that move you are meaningless to us and others have very little weight, so it's difficult to understand you. Often the things you say directly to the female are quite different from the eddyings going on beneath. I do not think we have such a beneath. Do you detect one in us?*

"No, I don't," Jarrod said, blushing, "but that's probably because I'm not skillful enough."

"You're not skillful enough for what?" Martin inquired.

"It's a bit difficult," Jarrod was clearly flustered. "I'm not quite sure I know how to explain."

"You could try," she said patiently.

"The colts noticed that sometimes, when we talk, the words and feelings are different. Nastrus wanted to know if I had come across the same thing in them. I don't think they quite understand our emotions yet."

"I see. I think. Could you ask them about getting out of here now? I don't really fancy facing another of those storms. Have you all decided where we're going to come out? Is that what one does? Come out?" Jarrod turned obediently away and when he looked back at her he was smiling.

"Oh, you're just going to love this. They know exactly where they can go. To wonderful, inaccessible places called Where the Mountains Jump into the Sea, Rift in the Desert, the Sky Bowl, which I presume is here, and a couple more." Martin groaned.

"It's too early to cope with that. I'll tell you what I'd like to do. I'd like to go back to the campsite and change into something that smells less strong. We can bring our gear back here and tackle the problem then. It's a shame we don't have a map of the world with us."

"All right. Let me tell them."

No need, Beldun commented, *It's already in your mind. We'll wait.*

"They'll wait," Jarrod relayed.

As they walked back under the apricot clouds of the real dawn, Martin linked an arm through Jarrod's and asked, "I've been thinking. How good are you at drawing maps?"

"Don't know. I haven't done it since Dameschool."

"Have you ever seen a really good map of the world?"

"Greylock's got one and there was a big map of the Magical Lands on the library wall at the Collegium."

"That would probably be better. We don't want to end up in the Empire by mistake."

"I don't quite see what you're driving at."

"You're supposed to remember everything you've seen, aren't you? So why don't you draw the map for them and see if they can recognize anything that would help?"

It took about an hour after their return to reproduce the Collegium's map on a patch of white clay that fanned from the mouth of a once and future stream. The colts kept away until he indicated that he was finished. They looked long and hard and then retreated into The Memory. When they emerged, their minds were going too fast for him to follow and he was surprised when they turned and scrambled back up the bank without making direct contact. He was relieved when Amarine returned with them. A consultation then. A submission of differences to an arbiter.

She remained at the top of the clifflet as the three came sliding back, obliterating a border. The presence that was Nastrus announced that the map was of little use since they always arrived at a place and not above it.

The only possibility, according to Mam, is here, and he kicked daintily with a sharp-pointed hoof, *where these mountains come down to the water. There is one place where we can look down on such a view. If there are other such places that are not represented here, we could be wrong, but if these are the only mountains that crowd the sea, then I'm sure we're right.* Martin leaned round Jarrod and studied the drawing.

"That the place?" she asked and Jarrod caught the excitement in her voice.

"They think so, yes. Why? Anything wrong?"

"Far from it. That's the Barrier Reach and, better yet, it's not too far from Gwyndryth. Best of all, we have a hunting lodge there, right above Glorion Bay. That's where we went for Summers when I was a girl. I know every gamepath and cave."

"It sounds too good to be true. Is there anybody still at the lodge? Wait a minute," he held up a hand to forestall her and turned to the colts.

Martin said, he thought at them, *that this place is near where she spent her Summers as a child. I thought you said you stayed well away from places where there were people?* Nastrus' amused condescension flooded his mind.

The Memory, he said with complacent pride, *goes much further back than people. We haven't been anywhere near there, but we have an ancestor who has.* Jarrod acknowledged the answer ruefully and faced Martin again.

"I'm sorry. Is there anybody at the lodge?"

"Just a skeleton staff at this time of the year and there are lots of empty stables . . ." She broke off, her eyes bright. "Oh Jarrod, when can we start?" He checked with the colts and, through them, with Amarine.

"Whenever we're ready."

"Well, what are we waiting for? We're already packed." She didn't wait for a reply, but tackled the bank on all fours.

They followed the colts' instructions and used the climbing rope to lash their possessions onto Amarine and then to tie Jarrod across the backs of the three young ones. Memories of his capture by the Umbrians went through his head as Martin secured the knots.

"What are we going to do about the horses?" he demanded suddenly.

"Mother! I'd forgotten them. Oh well, I expect they've chewed through their tethers by now and are grazing themselves into an obese old age. There's nothing we can do about it now."

"Perhaps Old Sig will find them," Jarrod said wistfully. "Do these knots have to be quite this tight?"

"Can't have you falling off en route," she said, with irritating cheerfulness. "Let's just hope it doesn't take too long." She gave the rope a final tweak and then went and jumped up on

Amarine's back. She landed on her stomach and wriggled herself up into a sitting position. She grabbed two substantial handfuls of mane and called over.

"Tell them I'm ready whenever they are. Oh Jarrod, just think," her voice went on breathlessly, "nobody has ever . . ."

There was grey and cold, marrow-numbing cold that made the backs of the eyeballs ache. Brutal and unanticipated, it cut off all movement of breath, of lungs, of blood. An impression of an endless web hurt Jarrod's retinas, but there was nothing with which to scream. There was nothing but awareness in an implacable void, frozen without hope and beyond time. There was one sensation, but it was that of knowing that he was going so fast that motion was meaningless.

CHAPTER XVII

THE BARRIER REACH SHOULDERED ITS CRAGGY WAY INTO THE SEA, its knobby old bones poorly clad in sparse green. Trees foolhardy enough to cling to its inhospitality were tortured into shapes of pain and beauty, but there were enough of them, when added to the salt-sculptured bushes, to soften the scoured-down rock. Two-thirds of the way down the peninsula, under the wheeling arguments of gulls, was a shallow green cup with a rainwater pond at its center. The pond had shrunk once the rainy month was over, but the bottlebrush reeds that surrounded it showed where the water had stayed long enough to let roots take hold.

To one side of it, the air began to shimmy and the dust motes began a contradance up the slanting rays. Waves of heat rose from the short, stiff grass as if it were sand and the day hot. The motes began to simmer. There were brief smacking sounds and four unicorns stood beside the water shaking their heads. Had the two humans tied to them been conscious, they too would have been trying to get their ears to pop. The one slumped over the neck of the largest unicorn was the first to stir, but time ran on awhile before it sat up and looked around.

Marianna felt as if she was in the early stages of a cold where nothing makes too much sense and the world is coated in cotton wool. There was a three-headed animal saddled up beside her. The moment that she recognized the saddle as Jarrod, the enormity of what they had accomplished broke through and triumph

and relief shot through her. She laughed weakly and patted
Amarine's neck. The unicorn whinnied softly and lowered herself so that Marianna could get off. She slid down untidily and
turned and grabbed for the animal as her ankles turned to junket
and betrayed her.

She pushed herself upright and stood wobbling. Pain pricked
up her legs and her stomach felt odd. She fought for breath and
control, waited until her swaying had stopped and moved carefully forward. She unlooped the rope that linked her wrists from
around Amarine's neck. She walked, wincingly, over to the
other animals.

"Jarrod?" Her voice sounded thin and squeaky. She reached
out a fearful hand and joggled the inert form. "Jarrod, wake up.
We made it. We made it through. We're on Barrier Reach, I
swear we are." She shook him more firmly, but was rewarded
by nothing other than the lassitude of unresponsive flesh. "C'mon
Jarrod, wake up. Please wake up. Jarrod?" Her voice skittered
and went up sharply on the last syllable. Fear plucked at her. She
scrabbled under the unicorns' bellies for the knots that she had
tied somewhen ago. It would be so stupid to come through all of
this and lose him now.

It was as if her fingers had been blanched in boiling water.
They mumbled uselessly against the rope until she heard herself
sobbing in frustration. she stopped then and lay back, taking in
deep draughts of brine-spiced air. The colts moved restlessly
above her and she renewed her efforts, but to no avail. Teeth
were of no help to her either. Heels and elbows worked her out
from under and she stood up slowly and dusted herself off. She
spoke soothingly to the animals and reached out with a hand that
shook only a little. She turned the slack head while the fingers of
the other hand probed for a pulse at the throat. It took her a
fright-laden eternity to convince herself that she had found one
and then she broke away into a shuffling run to Amarine and her
pack.

She got out her knife, returned to the patient animals, crawled
under and severed the rope. She backed out and then grasped
Jarrod under the armpits and began to haul him off. Once the
midpoint was passed, the dead weight of him took over and
tumbled them both onto the grass. She was winded and fought

for air. She lay there until she felt strong enough to maneuver and then she wriggled her way from under him.

She doffed her cloak. The moist wind felt welcomingly cool as the sweat began to dry on her body. She turned the unresisting Jarrod over and dragged him by the heels to the margin of the pond. Let him be all right, she thought, just let him live. The colts watched her progress and then moved to the far side to crop. Their mother joined them.

Marianna turned her attention back to her companion and undid his cloak and collar. His face was a greyish yellow and his thick, black hair was as dull and lifeless as he. The hands, when she held them, were bone cold. She felt his forehead, but it told her nothing. She shifted round and unbuttoned the jacket. She put her ear to his chest and tried to hear his heart. Her own was making too much noise.

She sat back on her heels and looked despairingly at him, taking up one of the hands and stroking it. For the first time she really felt that he might die and experienced a premature wave of loss. The thought that she might get sole control of the unicorns lanced into her and was banished by the disgust she felt at herself for entertaining it. The body by her side tremored as if the idea had passed through her and galvanized him. She was too self-absorbed to notice, but the groan brought her sharply back.

She swam out at him from a haze, all damp, dark red hair and shiny skin. She was upside down, but the protestations of Jarrod's body deflected him from the problem. He felt as if he had been kneaded and rolled out by a heavy-handed baker. His eyes were the only things that he felt like moving and they went back to the apparition.

"Are you all right, Jarrod?" it said. His mouth worked, but nothing else did and no sound came out. He swallowed and waited and tried again.

". . . are we?" Marianna leaned forward too late to catch the croak.

"Don't strain yourself: it takes a while. Going through Interim may not bother the unicorns, but it made me feel as if I'd been held underwater too long. But I'm feeling much better now. Just take it easy. You'll be all right in a while." She looked down on him fondly and brushed stray curls off his forehead. He seemed so helpless lying there.

"Hungry."

"You're what? You're hungry? Come to think of it, so am I. I'm starving, but there's nothing around here. We'll have to wait until we get to the lodge."

Jarrod tried sitting up and made it the second time. He prodded and patted himself gingerly and then smiled weakly at her.

"I seem to be all in one piece." His voice was husky, but recognizable as his own.

"You look as if you had been ridden hard and put away wet," she said after a judicious appraisal.

"Thanks a lot." He looked around with a sudden wave of panic as the absence of the unicorns came home to him. He struggled to unstable feet and looked wildly about him and then his shoulders sagged as he caught sight of the quartet. They all had their heads down, blunt teeth tearing at the sparse turf, and were unaware of, or uninterested in, his return to consciousness. Their lack of concern upset him and he turned away to look at their surroundings. Hunger came at him again as he took in the windswept rocks that were visible beyond the rim of the saucer they stood in.

"How far away is this place of yours?" he inquired.

"About half a league. Think you can make it?"

"If that's where the food is."

"Try walking around a bit first. Here, put your arm over my shoulders. There we go." They took three lurching paces. "How does it feel?"

"I feel like a toddler. I expect to sit down suddenly at any moment."

"Let's try a few more. I had to stagger around for a while before my legs started behaving. All right, here we go again."

They took a few turns up and down before Jarrod said, "Let me try it by myself. My legs seem to be working again. I just seem to feel so hollow." He disengaged and walked away with care, his arms half raised on either side. "I'm going to go and check on the colts," he said over his shoulder. "There's nothing the matter with Amarine, is there?"

"Not as far as I could tell, but I didn't go over her or

anything.'' She stood and watched as Jarrod made his slow way around the pond. All four animals had continued to graze single-mindedly and Beldun did not even raise his head when Jarrod patted him on the shoulder.

Jarrod sent out messages of greeting and thanks and congratulations, but he knew that he was broadcasting in a void. A wrenching doubt intruded. Had going through Interim destroyed whatever it was that had enabled him to share thoughts with them? He would not believe it and tried again. He still could not rouse their attention and methodically set himself to hear instead. He received no acknowledgments, but he became aware of what was blocking the contact. Hunger as fierce as his own echoed and excluded him.

He abandoned his attempt and waded through rushes to the water. He doused his face and then drank from cupped hands.

''Everything all right with them?'' Marianna asked as he returned. ''You weren't too heavy for them?''

''I don't really know. They looked fine, but they were too busy eating to hear me. They didn't even look up.'' She caught the disappointment behind the words.

''I suppose we'll just have to wait until they're ready,'' she said evenly. ''After all, they have just saved us a good couple of months of travel.''

''That's very true. I just hope they hurry. My stomach's about to declare war on the rest of my body.''

''It might help if you stopped talking about how hungry you are,'' Marianna remarked tartly. Relenting, she added, ''How's the rest of you feeling?''

''Not too bad. A bit hot, though. I think I'm going to stow my cloak. I don't suppose the unicorns will mind. They probably won't even feel it. Want me to take yours while I'm going?''

''If you would.'' She rolled her own into a neat bundle. ''You know where it goes, don't you?'' She was rewarded by a ghost of his old grin.

''I ought to by this time.'' He set off slowly round the pond again and when he returned he was trailed by the unicorns.

''They want us to know that they're very glad that we made it through unharmed,'' he said as he came up. ''They weren't at all sure that we would.''

"Charming. Well, I'm glad they're not disappointed. Are they ready to head for Treponthyd?"

"For where?"

"Treponthyd. The lodge."

"Aha. I should have guessed." His tone was enigmatic. "Will there be people there?"

"Shouldn't be. Not at this time of the year. Except for the caretaker and his family, of course. Daddy brings servants and cooks with him when we come and stay." They set off up the easy slope and along a narrow, rock-avoiding path in the direction of the distant mainland. The colts followed and Amarine brought up the rear.

"Can we trust them? This family?"

"They've served us for generations. There's been a Merieth at Treponthyd since my great-grandfather built it." There was pride in the voice. "Besides, the coastal folk are a close-mouthed lot and anyway, we don't have much choice."

"Just as long as they have the larder stocked."

She did not set a very rapid pace, but he was stumbling well before she motioned him into stillness.

"The house is the other side of the razorback. It drops quite steeply, but there are trees for holds, then there's a sort of plateau and the house and the outbuildings are built on it. Then it drops away, sheer, to the sea. The unicorns will never make it down this way. We'll have to take them further on. I'll nip down and see if there's anybody at home. We don't want to come marching in through the front gates to find the place full. It shouldn't take me long and they'll never know I've been and gone. I know ways to get in and out of that house that even the builder never imagined." Her eyes glinted with childhood remembered.

"How far to the road?" Jarrod asked anxiously.

" 'Bout a mile. Why?"

"I can't make it there and back without something in my stomach. I can barely walk as it is. The colts say that they're always ravenous after going through Interim. It probably does different things to them than to us, but at least that's the same. I don't know about you, but I'm completely drained. It's as if it took the energy out of me."

"I'm tired, but I don't feel that bad. Look, why don't you sit down and wait here with our friends while I go down and steal something for us. Tsk," she clicked her tongue and shook her head. "It's become a very strange world. Here I am about to break into my own house and steal food. You're right. The fewer people who know about this the better."

Jarrod watched her disappear over the crest and then settled down on a flat rock to question the colts about Interim and its effects. He found it hard to concentrate, so compelling were the gnawings of the legion of hunger's rats. He envied the unicorns their ability to digest grass. He watched as both his shadows stretched up the slope and took off his tunic. It was not much of an effort, but it made his head waver. The colts gathered close around him in concern as his head tilted forward.

"Fine watchman you make. Sleeping on the job. You ought to be ashamed of yourself." Jarrod surfaced at the sound of Marianna's voice and his nose drank in the odor of warm bread. His head was light and buoyant and he felt great good will toward her. His smile widened and his eyes filled in gratitude.

"Food?" he said, like an expectant four year old. She didn't catch the word, but there was no mistaking the message of the head as it dropped slowly to the side. The eyes went dim.

Taste was the first sense that came back to him, followed by the warm trickling of liquid down his chin He ignored the trickling and, eyes still closed, swallowed the soup.

"Easy, easy young 'un. Go slowly or you'll choke. There's plenty 'ere. C'mon love, sit up a bit if you can. There's a boy. That's better." The woman's voice was a comforting croon as she hoisted him firmly up. He opened his eyes and found himself in a big, old-fashioned kitchen. Pots and strange instruments hung from the blackened beams. They were blotted out by a soft, round face surmounted by a muslin cap from which strands of grey hair escaped at will. The support behind his shoulder blades became her arm and her other hand swabbed his chin. Then it advanced the spoon again. He ignored everything until the saucepan was empty and his stomach felt tight.

"That's enough now," she said. "You'll make yourself sick. You can have some more later." Jarrod nodded and pushed himself up on the settle. He looked around the room. The plump

woman beside him got up, shook out her skirt and took the
spoon and pan away to the sink.

"You'd best sit there for a bit and get your strength back. The
rest aren't due back from their break for another hour and the
young mistress will be back by then." Jarrod sat docilely as the
energy began to flow into him and watched her bustle about.
Behind her, the kitchen door opened unexpectedly to reveal a
tall, statuesque woman in a rich dress and pearl-studded snood.
A lady, and a forbidding one from the look of her.

"Mrs. Merieth, what is that disgusting ragamuffin doing in
the kitchen?" The voice was contralto, but devoid of the mellow
qualities of the range. The cook straightened up in surprise,
turned and dropped a perfunctory bob.

"Afternoon, your Ladyship. The young man's a climber as
got lost. 'E's in a bad way. 'Adn't 'ad anything to eat in I don't
know 'ow long."

"I must say, Mrs. Merieth, you never cease to amaze me."
The voice was hard and uncharitable. "And where, pray, did
you find it?"

"Outside the back door, an it please your Ladyship."

"I don't think it pleases me at all. It sounds like a clear case
of trespassing to me. I think my husband better settle this.
We're not running a guest house for waifs and strays. What's
your name, boy?" Jarrod sat silent.

"I don't know as 'e can talk, your Ladyship," the cook
intervened quickly. "Leastwise 'e asn't said anything yet. I told
you 'e was in a bad way. 'E fainted on me in the corridor and
I 'ad to carry 'im in 'ere."

"Revolting looking specimen. I hope he doesn't have anything catching." Her throat tightened and her nose wrinkled as if
she had just discovered a bad drain. "You keep him here and I'll
send one of the men to take him up to the study. My husband
will deal with him there. If anything happens to him, I'll hold
you responsible, d'you hear?"

"Oh yes, my Lady, I hear." Mrs. Merieth curtsied perfunctorily again as the door was closed firmly. "Never could abide that
woman. Carrying on as if she owned the place." She turned
toward Jarrod and her expression softened. "You're not to worry,"

she said reassuringly, "Sir Ombras is a proper gentleman. 'E'll do the right thing, never you fear."

"Thank you for the food and for sticking up for me," Jarrod said, trying to make his gratitude and sincerity obvious.

"Don't 'e think anything about it, m'dear. It'll all get straightened out when the young mistress gets back."

"D'you know where she went?"

"I don't know, m'dear. All she said was, 'look after him, Merry, and feed him if he comes round. That's what he needs most.' "

"Well, you certainly did that. By the way, d'you think I might have some more?" Jarrod felt embarrassed to ask, but the pangs were coming back.

" 'Course you can. You look as if you 'aven't 'ad a proper meal since the nightmoon was full." She waddled over and retrieved the pot from the hob.

"I hope Mart . . . the Lady Marianna gets back before they come for me," Jarrod said as she handed him a bowl and a spoon, but, when the door opened, it admitted two men.

"This what we got to take up to Sir Amyas? This scarecrow?"

"You go careful with 'im, you 'ear me? 'E's not well. 'Sides, 'e's a friend of . . ."

"Thank you very much, Mrs. Merieth," Jarrod said, rising and cutting her off. He handed back the hastily emptied bowl and took a couple of trial steps. His knees started to give and he grabbed the back of the settle for support. "I'm afraid," he said with a pallid smile, "that one of you gentlemen will have to give me a hand. I don't think I can make it otherwise."

"By rights, you ought to be in bed, young man," Mrs. Merieth said, sounding like the mother Jarrod had never had. "Well, don't just stand there, you great lummoxes, 'elp 'im."

The two went over to Jarrod and grabbed him under the elbows, took him through the door and into the passageway. They were followed by the admonishing voice of Mrs. Merieth. He walked between them on legs of string until they came to the stairs and it was no longer possible to walk abreast. One guard went first and the other shoved Jarrod roughly after him. Jarrod fell forward over disobedient feet, saved himself by taking the

stairs on all fours and set off up the infinity of coiled stone steps.
By midpoint, he was back on his feet again, but he gained the
top in ignominious exhaustion, head hanging, panting like a dog.
He was hauled ungently along and frogmarched into a panelled
room dominated by a table desk and a lustrous Isphardi carpet.

Jarrod fought to stay upright and the man who stood in front
of the desk wove in and out of focus. Jarrod forced himself to
catalogue him during the clear moments: tall and thin; beard—
pointed, trim, pepper and salt; long, straight, grey hair. There
was a prolonged period of wavering and then—sharp-edged nose
and large eyes, brown with grey eyebrows, tufty grey eyebrows.
Lines around the eyes, lots of them. Sharp lines around the
mouth, too—strange mouth; wrong, too fleshy, too sensual;
austere face, wrong mouth.

"Get him a chair. Can't you see that he's ill?" The voice was
even-tempered, but it brooked no denial. Jarrod was still trying
to piece the words together when a chair was thrust under him
and he sat. The room spun.

There was an explosion of sound behind Jarrod's slumped
head as the doors burst open. Martin stood just inside the threshold in the grip of two housecarls. Her leather jerkin and trews
were ripped and stained, the hair a rough-hacked thicket in
Autumn. The angry flesh beneath the cheekbone presaged a
vivid bruise. Her body quivered with intensity.

"What have you done to him?" she shouted, and the room
rang with the afterecho of her question. Prisoner or no, Martin
dominated the place and the situation. The silence held, as did
the eyes of the Seneschal and the intruder. Then there was a
subtle shift. Lord Obray's taut body relaxed and he performed a
deep, theatrical bow.

"Welcome home, my Lady. You must forgive the dimming of
these old eyes, but no amount of dirt, even when coupled with
somewhat outre clothing, could long disguise a Gwyndryth." He
looked at the two guards and noted that both had suffered
damage.

"All right, you men, you can let her go." He watched the
indecision and disbelief play across their faces. "It's all right. I
assure you that the Lady Marianna won't hold her treatment

against you." He smiled genially. "You may report back to your unit," he said dismissively. He looked back at the rigid figure in the doorway and smiled at her quizzically.

"The only thing I have done with regard to this young man is to order a chair for him. As far as I'm aware, he arrived like this. If he has been subjected to abuse, it was not inflicted here." She ignored him and strode over to the chair.

"Ring for someone and have him put to bed," she ordered.

"Since you are both of, er, of a condition, might one surmise that this is the young man who accompanied you on your travels?"

"One might. He's been through some rough times and he's not that old." Obray smiled. He walked over to the fireplace and pulled the bellrope.

"You both look as if you could do with a bath and a good sleep. Do you know what ails him? There's no Wisewoman here and I've no means of getting one, short of sending to the Hold."

"No, Sir Amyas, I do not, at least not exactly. He's a Magician and that complicates things. I do know that I've got to get him on his feet as fast as possible, but there's nothing any Wisewoman could do for him." She shot him an inquiring look. "How much do you know about our mission?"

"Nothing, except that you were going to be gone a long time, and you have been, and that you were going with a young Paladinian that your father hadn't met. He was not happy about that, as you can imagine."

"How is he? Have you heard?"

The last word that I received was that the Emperor himself had asked him to retrain the Imperial Cavalry and that he had his hands full. The war's been going badly, if you haven't heard." She ignored the last sentence.

"That's wonderful. They never let foreigners near their army. He really must have impressed old Varodias." Her eyes were alight and her voice alive. Lord Obray smiled again. There was a knock on the door.

"Enter," he called. "Ah, Merieth, this young man is suffering from exhaustion. Have him put in the green guest room and set one of the girls to watch him."

"Very good, my Lord. Will there be anything else?"

"Is the Lady Marianna's room ready?"

"Happen it'll need airing out. Why? Is she coming then?"

"Oh, Mr. Merieth. Don't tell me you don't recognize me?" The countryman looked at the dishevelled young man who stood by the chair. He peered through compressed eyes and took in the wild hair and the shabby clothes.

"It can't be," he said slowly as her smile answered him. "You can't be the young mistress."

"Oh yes I can. It's good to see you."

"Well, I can't say as it's a pleasure to see you looking like that, but it's good to have you back for all that."

He crossed rapidly and gave her an engulfing hug. He held her at arm's length and looked at her. "I'll not ask what you've been up to," he said. "I used to tell the missus you'd grow out of the tomboy. Happen I was wrong." He smiled fondly at her. "This a friend of yours?" he asked, jerking a thumb in the direction of Jarrod.

"Yes, he is, and I need him taken good care of."

"Oh aye? Well, we'll do our best." He bent and swung the unprotesting Jarrod up across a broad shoulder. He turned at the door and looked back at her. "I'm thinking I'd better tell the wife to start heating water." She caught the friendly and familiar taunt and laughed.

"Don't bother. I'll do it myself. If I don't get something inside me, I'll end up like him."

"That'll be the day," Merieth said and moved easily through the door with Jarrod bumping at his back.

This time the collapse was absolute and he spent days floating in illusion. Sometimes he found the unicorns and sometimes he did not. Gradually the lucid periods grew longer and Jarrod determined to use the time his body was giving him to do something about his susceptibility. He sank within the patterns of himself and was appalled at the changes the trip through Interim had made. The parts of him that Nature had commanded to defend his body had done battle with the leaching grey cold and had been routed. He set about the frustrating task of repair.

The damage was too severe for some cells to come alive again and he had to make some unorthodox alterations that would otherwise never have occurred to him. He appeared unconscious for long hours and sometimes could not be roused to eat. The servants who took turns sitting by the bed simply knew that he ailed and that there were times when, frighteningly, there was no sign that he was alive. The aftermath of Interim was an affliction for him, but he emerged annealed. Those who had known him before would say that the search for the unicorn had changed him. Others would say that success had made him arrogant. Only Jarrod knew that he had been forced to remake himself.

He was sitting up in bed when Marianna came in. The serving girl tucked behind the curtain of the four-poster got off her chair and curtsied.

"I'll take over for half an hour, Galyne. Go and get yourself a cup of chai."

"Yessum." The girl curtsied and scuttled out. Marianna closed the door and approached the bed. The new Jarrod found her just as riveting as the old one had. He took in the dark brown leather doublet and trousers, the high boots, the yellow, open-necked, silk blouse and the glossy hair. She had put on a little weight and it suited her, softened her. The body beneath the encasing leather was hard and supple and it was obvious, as she walked toward him, that she knew it.

"I heard rumors that the mysterious stranger was awake at last, so I came to see for myself."

"Rumor, for once, has the underpinning of truth." She stopped at the bed and smiled down to him and held out a hand which he took and squeezed.

"How are you, Jarrod?" she asked as she sat herself on the edge of the bed.

"I think I shall probably be better than I ever have been." She frowned slightly at that, trying to run the sentence through her head again, but gave it up and settled for the simple positive.

"I'm glad you're feeling better," she said, disengaging her hand primly. "You seemed to be a very long way off every time I dropped by."

"I had some internal Magic to do," Jarrod explained, pleased by what she had said. "And speaking of Magic, how are the unicorns?"

"They look wonderful. The Merieths are the only ones who

know that they are here and the three ofus have been taking care
of them. Now," she broke off and looked him over critically,
"have you any idea of when you'll be fit to leave?"

"Leave? Where to?"

"Gwyndryth, silly. I imagine that there are some very important people who need to meet with the unicorns and we certainly
can't put them up here. The Obrays have already gone back,
you can't expect a fief as big as ours to run itself for very long
and Daddy isn't back from Umbria yet. I was surprised to find
them here as it was," she added. "I had to let Sir Amyas in on
the secret. Gwyndryth will be properly guarded and we'll need
someone to open the postern gate for us."

"How far is this Gwyndryth of yours?"

"About fifty leagues. I can usually do it in three days if I
really push the horse, but we'll have to go much slower. First of
all, I have no idea how far the unicorns can go in a day.
Secondly, once we get to where our road joins the one that runs
by Oracle Lake we'll have to travel by night. There's always
someone on that road during the daytime. It doesn't matter what
the weather's like, there are always people who want to consult
the oracle."

"I'd forgotten how close you were to it, relatively speaking."

"Daddy took me there when I was little, but I can't remember
very much about it. He's never told me what he went to ask. But
you haven't answered my question. When do you think you'll be
fit to ride?"

"Right now, if you'd like." His confidence was absolute.

"You sure?" So was her scepticism.

"I told you I'd made some changes."

"Good, then let's plan to set off first thing tomorrow morning. I know, I know," she added as she got off the bed, leaving
Jarrod to wallow in the waves her move started in the feathers of
the quilt, "clothes." She looked him over again. "I think I'd
better see if I can find a larger size this time. I'd swear you've
grown. You look older, too. Is that the Magic?"

"What's the matter, don't you like me looking older?"

"Oh, I don't know," she replied pertly, "you might even
grow up to be handsome. Mind you," she added teasingly, "I

shall be far too old by then to appreciate it.'' She strode out. He wondered how he had ever been able to think of her as a boy. He had skirted a death with no valor in it and he would never, or so he felt at that moment, be able to see things quite the same way again.

CHAPTER XVIII

SEEN FROM HORSEBACK BY A RIDER WHO HAD GALLOPED DOWN THE
post road from the capital, or from the top of a laden oxcart,
Gwyndryth smiled in the mellow sunshine, all warm stone,
swept courtyards and enclosed gardens where flowers still bloomed
despite the lateness of the season. It seemed to dream in peace,
serenity girdled by walls whose thick functionalism was softened
by the honeyed light. The old fashioned ravelins, however,
concealed a fury of activity, whipped on rather than presided
over, by Myrgan, Lady Obray. Furniture clogged the corridors
as every room and hall was scrubbed. New girls were being
hastily trained. Others scoured the outlying woods and fields for
wildflowers and grasses for the floors and tables and for faggots
for the kitchen fires. Larders were being stocked with game and
the tantalizing odors of baking were omnipresent.

There was no secret about the reason for the uproar. The entire
Holding knew that the High Council of Magic had been con-
vened at the castle and rumors were rife. Why Gwyndryth?
Knowledgeable old men put forefingers to the sides of their noses
and said that the war was going so badly that it was the only
place safe enough to risk having all of them together in one
place. When the boys had come back for the harvest, the elders
recalled, they'd talked about some terrible new weapon the
enemy had invented. And hadn't they all had to go back to the
front again as soon as the harvest was in?

For the Seneschal's wife, the only effect the young mens' going back to the war had had was to deprive her of pages and serving men at the one time that they were needed most. Unaccountably, the notables would not be bringing their servants and their cooks and, while that meant that there would be fewer mouths to feed, it compounded her anxieties and the need to improvise. She hated to improvise.

There were spare girls aplenty, but this raw collection of country bumpkins they had wished on her was not her idea of suitable material from which to fashion an instrument for the entertainment of royalty. There were no cloths of state for these illustrious guests and no time to run them up. Then there was the problem of a proper seating order. Lady Myrgan fretted and fussed and wrung her hands. There was no end to the disruptions. Special stalls had to be built for the influx of cloudsteeds and, if all that weren't enough, the Holdmaster had picked this time to return home.

He, too, arrived by cloudsteed, looking terrible. He was thin as a pike staff and the long flight had clearly taxed him. The one good thing about it, from Lady Obray's point of view, was that he had gone straight to his bedchamber and stayed there. Marianna, shocked to the heart by the sight of her father, would let no one but the Wisewoman near him, but she stirred the household to a new fever pitch of fetching and carrying. She insisted on special foods and sent the butler to the cellar for a favorite wine newly come to mind. Lady Myrgan found it all most inconsiderate, but at least it got the Gwyndryth girl out from under her feet.

Speculation and stories grew and flourished as the great ones began to arrive. Flight after flight of cloudsteeds circled over the castle and came in to land on the platform in the main court. There was so much to talk about and so little time to do it in. The younger girls would gather in the corridors where the royal ladies had been allotted apartments, their arms still full of the flowers and sweet rushes they were supposed to be strewing in other parts. They clustered and giggled softly together until scattered into a shame-faced scramble by the Seneschal's wife, but, as if drawn against their wills by a force they could in no wise resist, they drifted back again as soon as their chores were completed.

Nothing, though, could rival the great Mages as a source of interest. Even though he arrived by cloudsteed and not in a thunderclap, no one who saw it would ever forget the advent of the Archmage. Ragnor was far from being the subdued man who had presided over the High Council of Magic in the aftermath of the Conclave. His long, thin arms flailed about as the leather bindings that had strapped him down to his mount were undone. From his lips fell a torrent of imaginative abuse that caused women to cover the ears of the goggling children. The caustic cadences were interspersed with moving, if unbelievable, laments on the indignities visited upon his person by the indecencies of winged transportation. It was an entrance that gradually assumed hallowed proportions as the years passed and the tale became a tradition to be retold around the fire of a Winter's night.

Greylock, Mage of Paladine, by contrast, provoked talk precisely because he did nothing out of the ordinary. He didn't even look like a proper Mage, not that any of the locals had ever seen a Mage before. He wasn't that tall and he wore plain robes. His face was stern and square and his eyes seemed to see straight through a man. It was an ordinary face for all that: a good, solid, yeoman's face topped by grey curls. He was as quiet and polite as the Archmage had been vocal and outrageous.

The members of the household, whether old-timers or newly pressed into service, toiled and chatted and drank and cursed their way through the historic occasion. There was so much to tell that it was difficult for them to listen to one another as they dwelt on the doings, real and imagined, of their own Princess and of the black-haired one from Paladine. Then there were the quiddities of the male necromancers and the possibilities of a romance between the young mistress and the strange stripling who had turned up with her.

Darius, their own Holdmaster, newly returned from who knew what adventures in the unimaginably distant Empire of Umbria, added fresh kindling when he finally made his appearance in the Hall. His white hair and pointed beard, cut, said those who wished to be thought worldly, in the Umbrian style, excited comment, as did the amount of weight that he had lost.

More interesting still was the attachment that those who sat below the salt insisted was developing between their lord and the Princess Naxania. Opinion was sharply divided on her. As a public personage she travelled with an invisible baggage cart of reputation, rumor and preconceptions. In Naxania's case, her rank, both as royalty and as a Member of the High Council of Magic, were known. Tales of her beauty had been heard by some and gossip had it that she was very demanding of those who served her.

These hot centers of interest and activity gave rise to the swirling currents of guesswork and embroidery that poured up through the Hold like the aromas from the kitchen fires. Before those same fires, the cooks chattered and sweated to keep the two ladies of the Hold satisfied and the growing horde fed. There were few broken meats to be distributed at the gates at sundown.

The cookfires had built up so much hot ash that the hearths shimmered all night long and stayed so hot that the slagboys couldn't clear them in the morning. Women worked in their shifts and the bakers in nothing but slippers and their long aprons. Neither had much energy left for talking, but the heat filtered upward through the stones and the rumors rose with it. No one thought to write them down, but everyone knew that, at last, they had stories to tell to equal those brought back from battle. Minstrels would sing songs, in the Great Hall of Gwyndryth if nowhere else, about these days going by in a last burst of Second Summer.

The most unusual inhabitants of the castle had entered unobserved and stayed on unsuspected. The unicorns had been smuggled in through the postern gate and housed in the caverns that had been hollowed out of the foothills on which the castle stood. In the years when it had been abuilding, there was need for a place to which the defenders could flee should the antagonists' air surge back over the Hold. They had never been used and the memory of them faded as the enemy was driven further and further inland until only the Holdmasters knew of them.

The secret was imparted to the heir when he attained his majority. Marianna knew and Darius had told Sir Amyas many years before and together they had shepherded their extraordinary visitors down to the cellars and through the tunnel to the caves. There was sweet air and running water for them there and, when the links were lit, light enough to see by. There was no sign of their presence and although the stablehands commented on the shortage of hay and straw, they put it down to the invasion of cloudsteeds.

The High Council, on the other hand, was unaware of the turmoil below stairs and Lady Myrgan was ever careful to disguise the strain under which she was functioning. When in the presence of her guests she was cheerful and obsequious to a fault. They took it for granted that their needs would be attended to, but, with one exception, their automatic graciousness to those of lesser rank made pleasure out of the performance of duty. The notables themselves were, in any case, too caught up with the creatures in the caverns to have noticed a lapse, except, perhaps, for Naxania. That lady had satisfied everybody by living up to her reputation. Nothing escaped her eye and no shortcoming the caustic edge of her tongue.

Each of them visited the unicorns, alone and in groups. They had tried, in vain, to contact them. They used every language that they knew. They tried it aloud and they tried it silently, but they all left baffled and awed by the beauty of the four myths made flesh.

Jarrod had taken over the care of the unicorns to free Marianna for her duties as hostess and to give her time to tend to her father. She knew that she should feel grateful, but she had very mixed reactions. It was nice to have the extra time to cope with the problems that sprang up every day, but she resented her separation from Amarine. She, just as much as Jarrod, had discovered the unicorns, but she had been relegated to domestic duties.

They were duties that, ordinarily, would have delighted her. She was acting as her father's official hostess at the most important time in the Hold's history. Her father, furthermore, was dependent on her ministrations for the first time in his life. It would have been all that she could have dreamed of before the quest. Now she had Amarine. She had grown beyond the Hold and it no longer satisfied her.

Jarrod, too, had his mixed emotions. He was happy when he was with the unicorns and pleased at the way he had been able to get bedding and feed down to them without being seen. He was unaware of the fact that he was the butt of a great deal of humor based on ribald speculations as to why a young man should be sneaking straw into the cellars.

He had also misjudged the reaction among the Council members to his ability to converse with the colts. He had expected to be congratulated, but the failure of his superiors to reach them provoked very different responses. Greylock was clearly proud of him, but he was greatly disappointed when Jarrod admitted that he had no idea how he did it and launched into his familiar lecture about the science of Magic. The Princess Arabella and the Archmage seemed to ignore him, but Naxania was the one who truly startled him.

His door was flung open one afternoon and a single glance was sufficient to bring him, round-eyed, to his feet and into a bow. The Princess of Paladine was in mourning purple for her uncle, but even so her shoulders were bare. The long, black hair was tousled and her color was high. She stood there, breathing heavily from the climb. Her eyes were so narrow and intense that they seemed to flicker at him like the leaves of a cinder tree. With the hair tumbling around her white shoulders, her bosom heaving, spots of red on her cheeks and those snapping eyes, she looked magnificent and dangerous. Her right foot tapped with ominous regularity on the stone-flagged floor. He stood and looked at her, nonplussed.

"You are our subject and we demand to know how you talk to those stupid animals. Why should you be able to get through to them when we cannot?" She paused and speared him with an angry look. "Well, what have you to say for yourself?" Jarrod bowed again to cover the resentment that flared up in him.

"I talk with the unicorns, your Royal Highness," he replied carefully, keeping his voice as neutral as he could, "because it is my destiny to do so and because Magic requires it of me. It isn't anything I sought, ma'am, you were the one who started it all. You were the one who prophesied. You said that I would lead them and you were right. I should have thought, Highness, that that would have made you happy." It was a speech that he would never have been able to make before the passage through Interim.

She looked at him then with a long, calculating stare, surprised at his firmness.

"Yes," she said judiciously, changing tack with the ease born of long practice at getting her own way, "you are quite right young man. I did prophesy this and you are quite obviously the one the verse referred to." She had dropped the formal mode. "We should not be at odds, you and I." The voice had become warm and seductive. She came over and linked an arm through his and turned him to walk with her to the window.

"We should be friends, you and I." She looked up at him with wide, dark eyes and a smile that made him suddenly nervous. "Partners," she added. "After all, there are only three of us from Paladine here and we should be allies. Would you not agree?"

"Yes, your Royal Highness," Jarrod said indistinctly. He kept his eyes on the floor as they paced side by side, burningly aware of the pressure of her arm against his side.

"So why don't you tell me how you do it? Friends should not keep secrets from one another." She smiled at him coaxingly, but Jarrod's annoyance returned.

"I'm afraid I can't do that, ma'am. Not because I don't want to," he added hastily. "It's just that I don't know how it happens."

She measured him again with her eyes and then said peevishly, "Oh, very well. If you won't, you won't. I don't know what sort of game you think you are playing, but I would advise you against crossing me." She had dropped his arm along with her coquetry. She turned to him and said, "Try to remember that you are a Paladinian," and then picked up her skirts and moved to the door. "Remember that," she said as she left. She did not bother to close the door.

The only person who seemed to appreciate his achievement was the Archmage. Once he had recovered from the imagined rigors of the flight, he had spent many fruitless hours in the caverns before he admitted defeat. Even then he continued to spend time there. Jarrod knew of his failure from the colts and he had expected the Archmage to throw a monumental temper tantrum, but when he was summoned to the Archmage's apartment, Ragnor was all smiles.

The Apprentice Magician was properly nervous, but the Archmage was at pains to put him at his ease. He was motioned to a hard, upright chair, and he noticed that the room was spartanly furnished, in contrast to the heavy, antique furniture that filled the other suites that Jarrod had seen. For the next hour he answered questions about the quest. Ragnor was even more thorough than Greylock had been, and far more unstinting in his praise.

"Now then," the Archmage said at last, "here comes the key question. Do you, or the unicorns, have any idea what they are doing here, or what they are going to do now that they have reached what might be laughingly called civilization?"

"I'm afraid not, Excellency," Jarrod admitted and waited for a reprimand. Instead the Archmage rubbed his hands together in satisfaction.

"Capital," he said, "absolutely capital. Just what I thought. Now that we've got 'em, no one has the slightest clue about what to do with 'em." He chuckled. "Well, I suppose I'll have to call a meeting of the High Council and hope that that minx from Stronta can get her mind off our host long enough to have another stroke of prescience.

"You and the Gwyndryth girl had better attend," he continued briskly. "You're the closest thing we've got to unicorn experts. Better make it ten o'clock tomorrow morning. I'll let you know where as soon as I find out what room is available." He smiled across at the young man. "Oh, by the way, I almost forgot. When you get back to your room you ought to find some blue robes there. I brought them with me. I hope they're the right size, Sumner wasn't very helpful about it. Know what it means, son?"

"No, Excellency. I mean, I know that's what Magicians wear once they've graduated from the Collegium, but that's all."

"And quite enough it is, too. I've decided to promote you to Magician proper. Greylock's told me about the tutoring he gave you before you left. Probably a damned sight better than anything Sumner can dish out," and the face was illuminated by a wicked little smile. "Besides, you've more than earned it.

"Congratulations Magician Courtak. You know what's expected of the rank and I'm sure you'll be a credit to the profession and all that." He smiled and nodded at the round-eyed young man and then the thin fingers waved in dismissal. "Run along now and close the door tightly behind you. The drafts in these old piles have a habit of making straight for poor old bones like mine. Well, don't just sit there gaping, be off with you."

"Yes, Excellency. Thank you, Excellency." Out in the corridor he leaned against the wall, giddy with excitement and relief. He pushed himself upright and went off down the long passage whistling jauntily. His brown gown swung above his ankles for the last time.

The next day he rose in the dark and decided to Make the Day outdoors. He had still not entirely adjusted to buildings again and the air seemed stale to him. He hugged his sleeping robe around him as he hurried to the jaques. His night-sensitive nose picked up the smell of mildew from old hangings and it seemed to him as if the thick walls soaked up all the castle's warmth and exhaled a dank chill. The floor was cold against his unslippered feet.

Once back in his room, he donned his new robe with considerable pride, fondling the fabric lovingly. It was made, as tradition decreed, from the finest of the year's shearing of Hirondel sheep and woven by the women of Eldermere. Best of all, it reached clear down to the ground. He thought a taper alight and examined his barbered image in the flecked looking glass with less censure than usual. He mocked himself for his vanity as he scurried downstairs. The need to raise the sun pressed in on him.

When he emerged into the shank of the night, his ears told him that, despite the darkness, bunglebirds were leaving. The creaking of their wings gave them away. It underlined the fact that, with Arabella of Arundel here, the center of the kingdom had shifted to Gwyndryth. The business of the kingdom had been brought here by the unicorns, and Marianna and he had brought the unicorns. He dwelt on the changes in his life during the course of the year and he was smiling to himself when he went within to start the ritual.

Returning to the front door under the opening glow of dawn, he was surprised to see the Archmage approaching from an angle.

"Morning, Courtak," he said as he drew level. "Think we've

given them another good one, don't you? Mind you, it won't be
too long before it gets too cold for an old man to do this outside.
Celador was freezing when I left. Incidentally, the meeting's
going to be held in the Holdmaster's study. Tell the Gwyndryth
girl for me, will you? I don't doubt she'd rather get the news
from you. Got her eye on you, that girl has, but I expect you
know that already. Young people these days seem to grow up so
much faster than they did when I was one of them." Jarrod's
head swung round in amazement.

"Now," Ragnor continued, waving a vague hand in front of
him, "I realize that you have been cautioned to, er, to suppress
any carnal feelings for the sake of the unicorns, and their con-
nection with you is certainly testimony to your devotion to duty.
It does you honor, lad, it really does. I admire your sacrifice and
your fortitude. Believe me, at your age, I might not have thought
the enterprise worth the candle, but, just remember, you're doing
the world a great service—and it won't go on for ever. Just keep
telling yourself that."

"Er, yes, Excellency; thank you, Excellency," Jarrod said,
embarrassed by the conversation. Ragnor sighed and smiled. He
seemed, to Jarrod, to be tempering his admiration with unstated
questions as to the reasons that made the self-denial possible.

Before he could sort it out, the Archmage added, "I wouldn't
want to be your age again for all the wealth in Isphardel."

Jarrod said nothing as they mounted the steps. He did notice,
however, that Ragnor's easy gait gave the lie to his assumptions
of antiquity. A guard opened the smaller door set in the massive
wood of the main one and let them back into the castle.

"Try to think of anything you've noticed about the unicorns
that might give us a clue, would you?" Ragnor asked before he
strode away, his white hair wild from the morning breeze.

Jarrod thought hard as he walked through the corridors. He
stopped a servant and sent her off with a message for Marianna.
Then he went back in his mind and called up all the details of the
first encounter that he had salvaged and everything that had
happened since. Interim was a possibility, but it was dangerous
and limited. He was still trying to come up with something when
he arrived at the Holdmaster's study. He found that he was the

first there and distracted himself from nervousness by examining the room.

It was smaller than he had expected it to be, and gloomier. Since it was on the ground floor, the windows were narrow and deeply recessed in ways that reminded him of Greylock's Outpost. Here, though, the war had been so far away for so long that they were no longer flanked by buckets of damp clay. Both the sun and the daymoon were up, but little light penetrated. The room was chiefly lit by candles. They polished the linenfold panelling and made the surface of the dark, slab-solid table wink, but they could do nothing for the twelve square carved chairs. Account books leaned against each other along two shelves and manuscript books filled the others. Jarrod was about to inspect the titles in his host's collection when Greylock entered.

"Hello, Jarrod. Punctual as always, I see. Oh, and congratulations on your promotion."

"Thank you, Sir. I owe it to your tutoring. The Archmage said it was better than anything I could get at the Collegium." A thought struck him. "Does this mean that I don't have to go back?" Greylock smiled roundly.

"Not unless you want to. Besides, I expect the Council will have other, more important work for you to do. Ah," he said, swinging round at the sound of footsteps, "here come the rest now." He walked forward, nodding to each. "Give you good morrow, Highnesses. Good morning to you, Ragnor, and here comes the lovely Lady Marianna. Most becoming, my dear, most becoming." Marianna dropped him a curtsey.

When they were all settled, the Archmage looked around at the other five and said, "You all know why we're here. The war's going shockingly. As I hear it, Lady Marianna, had it not been for your father, the Imperial army would have suffered a nasty defeat. The enemy have made some very rapid strides in weaponry and I'm not sure that even the Umbrians can catch up to them. We certainly can't. Which brings me to the unicorns." He paused and sniffed.

"Any of you, Courtak excepted, had any luck getting through to them?" The Archmage's eyebrows rose in inquiry. "Thought not. If it makes you feel any better, neither have I. That leaves us with Courtak, but that doesn't help if we don't know what to ask them. That's the nub of it. Now we've got 'em, what are we going to do with 'em? Anybody got any bright ideas?'' There was a glum silence.

"That's what I was afraid of.'' Ragnor swivelled in his chair and looked at Naxania. "I know I've asked you this before, my dear, but has any hint come to your mind? In a dream perhaps? Any clue as to who might have chosen this roundabout way of assisting us?''

"Nothing, Archmage. I have tried everything I know. I was very methodical about it,'' she said with a smile at Greylock that found a faint echo on Jarrod's face, "but I could come up with nothing.'' Ragnor sighed.

"Then we are in completely uncharted lands,'' he said.

"How so, my Ragnor?'' Arabella asked. "Have you not parted the veils that guard the future and mapped out what is to come? It does not seem to me that we have yet reached the limit of your vision.''

"Oh, I'm sure you're right about that, but there is a wonderful saving grace. I saw absolutely none of this.'' There was glee in him and his eyes twinkled in the candlelight. "Not one single bit of it.'' He leaned back triumphantly and was surrounded by silence. "Well,'' Ragnor said impatiently, "don't you see what that means?''

"That the vision was wrong.'' Greylock was matter of fact.

"No, no, my friend. At least I don't think so. No, I called the special Conclave precisely because I hadn't seen one. Naxania's verse was as much of a surprise to me as to anyone else in the room. Better yet, while the battles have come out as predicted, the details have been subtly different. Take that Prince of yours . . .'' He broke off.

"I'm sorry, Highness, I wasn't thinking. I am truly sorry that your Uncle could not outwit my prophecy, but what he did may turn out to be as important. He changed the threadwork of the dream and now, because of you, we may have changed the very woof of it. What it means is that the future can be changed, is changing. Whatever the unicorns do, it's bound to accelerate that change and maybe, just maybe, we shall be able to avoid the fate that I foresaw.

"In any case, I find myself unable to repress intimations of hope.'' The old man sat back again and beamed, his face like crumpled parchment that has been smoothed out again.

There was an expectant pause and Jarrod found himself looking at the Princess Naxania, half hoping for, half fearing another revelation. Instead, a notion popped into his head and he found himself blurting, ''I've just thought of something. Oh, I'm sorry your Excellency. I didn't mean . . .''

''That's all right, son,'' Ragnor said easily. ''What did you think of?''

''Well, I don't know if it means anything, but when I was examining Amarine—I was trying to see if I could talk to her the same way that I do to the colts. I can't. Anyway, she let me touch her horn.'' He turned to Greylock. ''It felt just like it did that night at the Place of Power. I couldn't stand very much of it, it was shaking me apart. This time, though, I was able to let go.''

''The same, lad? The very same?'' The question was sharp.

''I have no other samples for comparison, Sir, so I can't be certain, but my instinct says it's the same.'' Greylock smiled unexpectedly and the square, unyielding face flowered.

''Same old instinct that has always got you into trouble with me?''

''Yes, Sir,'' Jarrod said, abashed and wishing that he had never let the words out.

''I've kept count, you know,'' the Mage remarked. ''Habit. That instinct of yours has only been wrong three times in ten years, which, considering your age and inexperience, I find significant.''

''But you've always said,'' Jarrod started to protest and then realized where he was.

''Yes, I know what I've always said, but, as our Archmage has pointed out, we are chartless on the high seas.''

''That's not what I said. I rather wish I had and, at some future date, I probably shall,'' Ragnor interjected. ''Now, will one of you please tell me what the blazes you're talking about.''

''Yes,'' Greylock said. ''I find this strangely difficult, but,'' and the Mage took a breath and eased his shoulders, ''ever since this boy was brought to me, I have had the feeling that he would succeed me. I regret to say that I had no rational basis for that feeling. It persisted nevertheless." There was a hiss of indrawn breath from Naxania and the look that she shot Jarrod was far from friendly.

"I watched him and taught him and the feeling grew. Other than his memory, he had no extra special gift. He was quite obviously a strong, raw Talent, but so are lots of youngsters. True, the Talent showed itself unusually early, but I have encountered other prodigies. So why this one?

"I would peer at his face, when he didn't know that I could see him, to try to detect some resemblance to someone I had known, something that might account for this bond, but he has never reminded me of anyone else. I am told that he is growing to look like his father, but I never paid much attention to the King's hunting companions." Jarrod had been increasingly uncomfortable throughout the Mage's recital, but he was unprepared for the thrill that went through him at those words.

"Be that as it may," Greylock continued, "Before we sent the boy off on a fool's errand I thought I'd try an experiment. I took a risk, I own it. I knew the power of the forces that reside in that ring and I thought he was probably too young to cope with them, but I took him to the Place of Power and presented him anyway." There was a bated silence. "They accepted him," he said simply. There was another swift intake of breath from Naxania and then silence again. Jarrod felt the scrutiny through it and tried to look impassive.

"That so?" The Archmage's head was cocked to one side as he looked down the table. One bushy eyebrow was raised in what could either have been query or disbelief. "Tell me, my young friend, what did it feel like?"

"Ragnor!"

"Oh, come off it, Greylock," the Archmage said with a touch of testiness, "it's an experience that I've never had and you won't ever talk about. I'll bet you didn't even ask him the question." Greylock smiled resignedly.

"You're always making bets and you usually win. Oh, very well then. Jarrod, tell the Archmage what you felt that night."

"It was like blazing pokers," Jarrod said quietly.

"Speak up, boy, I can't hear you. You mustn't let us overawe you. Except, of course," and Ragnor broke off to include the women with a wave of his hand, "for the great beauty of the ladies."

"I said it felt like red hot pokers blazing away inside. And it shakes you until you think you're going to fly apart into dust. I was terrified," he admitted. "I fainted."

"Courtak didn't faint," Greylock interjected flatly. "Oh, I know you think you did, lad, but you didn't." He waited a beat. "Those that dwell in the Place of Power have enormous energies at their command. When they send me power, it is of a sort that can shake a man apart from deep within. It is necessary to prepare with great care. The body, though, has wisdom of its own and when it has absorbed all the energy that it can take without doing itself true harm, it cuts one off from the source. I own," he said with a soft look at Jarrod, "that I do not know exactly how, but it is as if a lock gate had been slammed down across a current. The boy didn't faint, his body just protected itself. No, Courtak did remarkably well for the first time. It takes practice to gain stamina and learn control, as it always does, but, considering his youth, he did as well, or better, than I would have done had I tried it at his age."

"And you kept this to yourself?" Arabella asked the question lightly, but the censure was audible.

"Aye, your Royal Highness, I did. I was sending him away on a venture that I believed in, but knew to be difficult and dangerous. I accepted Naxania's verse totally, but which of us could say that he was the right 'young man'? And if he was not, what guarantee had I that he would survive? The Place of Power had accepted him, but he has no knowledge yet of how to invoke their aid, he does not yet wear the Ring of the Keepers. Better then, I thought, to keep my own counsel. Well, now he's back and he has proved to be the one to whom the prophecy referred."

"The Gods of the Odds have certainly been kind lately." Ragnor interposed drily. "They've granted us success on our first throws. And you got the same kind of feeling from the unicorn's horn? That right, son?"

"Yes, Sir."

"Ever feel anything like it before? Doing exercises or conjuring?"

"No, Excellency. Just those two times."

"What about you, young lady?" Ragnor had swung away and was addressing the other end of the table.

"Me, your Excellency?" She tried to sound meek and surprised, but inside she was rebellious. If it hadn't been for her, the mission would have collapsed in the early stages. Jarrod was getting all the credit now, but who had kept things going when he was too weak to be of any use? She couldn't have done it without Sandroz, but who had babied that brat through the wilderness?

"Yes, you m'dear. You're very close to the big female." Well, she thought, they're finally realizing it, but all she did was smile. "Have you ever touched her horn?"

"Several times," she said firmly. She was aware of the pressure induced by the presence of so many powerful people, but, she thought as she squared her shoulders, this is my home.

"Well?" the Archmage encouraged.

"She doesn't particularly like it," she conceded, "but she lets me do it."

"It didn't affect you physically?"

"Well, of course it was thrilling," she said, half on the defensive, "but no, I didn't feel anything physical." She made the last word sound distasteful.

There was a muted hum of conversation. Here it was again. She was being edged out just because she didn't have the Talent. It was unfair. No one else had the kind of relationship that she had with Amarine. They had all tried and they had failed and yet, here they were, discussing Amarine and her horn and ignoring her. Just because she hadn't had a physical reaction, they had dismissed her. Resentment flared, was suppressed as being unworthy of so great an undertaking, and flared again anyway.

"Anyone else get to touch the dam's horn?"

"I tried to," Naxania admitted. "She was very friendly to me and allowed me to stroke her and talk to her, but when I tried to touch the horn, she turned her head away, just as the Lady Marianna described."

"Same thing happened to me," the Archmage said, " 'cept she wasn't that all-fired friendly. Kept walking away." He snorted. "It takes a unicorn to tell me that I have become an old bore," and he chuckled to himself. "Did you have any trouble touching the horn, son?"

"No, Sir, but that's the only time I ever tried. Mar . . . the Lady Marianna has this special tie with her and I can already talk to the colts, so that's how I thought it was supposed to be."

"It seems to me," the Archmage said pensively, "that while you may not be able to speak to her, she spoke quite clearly to you."

"She did?"

"I should say so, wouldn't you, Greylock?"

"I might, if I knew what you were talking about."

"Well, she doesn't like to have her horn touched. Won't even let that fetching Gwyndryth girl at it, except for special treats. When she does touch it, nothing happens. None of us can get anywhere near it. Yet when this Courtak fellow reaches for it she lets him. And what happens? Magic. That's what happens."

"A portable source of power. Like my ring," Greylock exclaimed.

"Precisely, but with perhaps one difference. Am I not right in thinking that the power from your ring isn't as strong as the energy you command when you're actually in the Place of Power?" Greylock nodded. "Well then, it may just be that that unicorn is as strong as all your sources combined. They both felt the same, that's what Courtak said. Can he work your ring?"

"We've never tried. Why?"

"Just curious, that's all. 'Course we don't really know what the upward limits of her powers are. We don't really know how much Courtak can contain."

"There is one way to find out, of course." Naxania's cool voice dropped into the discussion.

"What's that, my dear?"

"If the Mage of Paladine would consent to try, and always supposing that the creature will consent to cooperate, he could hold the horn and find out just how much power she can generate. He is the only one with the kind of prior experience needed to make the experiment valid."

"Very good, your Highness, very good," Greylock said approvingly. "I should be happy to try it. I think it would be best if I prepared myself in exactly the same way as I do at home. We should try to make conditions as nearly similar as we can. Besides," he added candidly, "there are always risks when dealing with great forces and here we are also dealing in the realm of the unicorn."

"Quite right, good brother, quite right. We can't afford to take chances at this moment. The war doesn't permit it. Those terrifying stories that our host told at dinner last night point that up only too well. How long do these preparations usually take you?"

"It's been a while, but I should be able to do all that's necessary by tomorrow morning. If I can find the necessary herbs, that is."

"Good. Can we all watch tomorrow, or does this have to be a private experiment?"

"By all means, come and watch. In fact, I may need some of you to hold her for me. Unless Jarrod can convince her through the colts."

"Capital. I think we're getting somewhere, Ragnor said before Jarrod could object to the idea that Amarine could be coerced. "Mind you," the Archmage continued admonishingly, "we still have to think of what it is that we want to do with all this power. For myself, I should dearly like to know more about our enemies. It burns me that we've been fighting them for hundreds of years and we still know no more about them than our great great-grandsires did. There's no way to penetrate that murk of theirs and every time we get hold of one of their suits, it inevitably has a puncture in it somewhere and the body inside has been reduced to sand." He stopped himself and looked around calculatingly.

"I'll let you in on a secret," he said. "I wasn't trying to see into the future. I was trying to find a way of seeing what goes on in that disgusting fog. I wanted to find out more about them and to be able to give the army advanced warning of their movements. Well, I did that all right, but not in the way I meant to." He sat back and appeared to enjoy their surprise.

"Unless anyone has any additional questions or thoughts," he resumed, "I'll see you all in Hall tonight and in the cellars tomorrow. Can we do it right after the Making of the Day? There won't be too many people about then."

"I don't see why not," Greylock replied.

"Right then." The Archmage rose stiffly and pushed back his chair. The others followed suit and began to drift out, talking with quiet animation.

"Jarrod," Greylock called and the young man hurried over. "I'm going to need your help. I'd appreciate it with the preparations and I think you should guide my hand when I try to hold the horn."

"Of course, Sir. I don't know what herbs you brought, but I've been collecting on the search and I could probably fill out what's missing."

"You're a good lad, Jarrod, and you've done very well. I'm proud of you." Greylock patted his shoulder. "If I've not said so before, I'm happy to have you back." He smiled up. "I'll see you in my apartments in a while, then," he said and followed the others out.

Jarrod was about to do likewise when a hand gripped his sleeve and halted him. He looked down at Marianna and saw anger and indecision in her face.

"What's wrong?" he asked.

"Oh, I don't know. A whole lot of things. We were both picked for this quest at the same time, weren't we?"

"You know we were. In fact, you knew about it before I did."

"Well," she paused and drew a breath. "Then why are you getting all the pats on the back and all I'm getting is condescension and a cold shoulder?" It was out and she felt relieved.

"That's not true. Everybody is being very deferential to you and Ragnor pays you compliments all the time."

"That's because I'm the Holdmaster's daughter, not because I have anything to say about unicorns. Oh no, you're the man, never mind your age, so you're the unicorn expert. Well, Amarine and I have something together that you'll never be able to match. She's my unicorn and she'll do whatever I tell her to do. She won't do it for you or anybody else."

"The unicorns don't belong to us," Jarrod expostulated. "They just agreed to help us."

"If I want something badly enough, she knows it and she'll do it." Marianna was defiant.

"And just what is it that you want to do?" he asked.

"I'm going to ride her into battle, that's what I'm going to do." She stopped, hands on hips, leaning forward, challenging him.

"That's ridiculous!"

"Listen," she said witheringly, "I've grown up around war-horses and you haven't. None of them had her strength and adaptability. I'm going to train her and I'm going to ride her into battle. You have your opportunities and I have mine and I'm not going to pass this one up." She glared at him, daring him to oppose her.

"Unicorns aren't supposed to fight," he said weakly, taken by surprise by the idea.

"You don't know that, nobody does. I say she will and I'm going to prove it and neither you nor any of your high-fallutin' friends can stop me." She turned, swirling her long skirts around her ankles and left him gaping, once again, in her wake.

CHAPTER XIX

JARROD'S MIND KEPT WANDERING OFF ON TANGENTS AS HE SWEPT the mixture of rushes, wilted wildflowers and grasses to one side. He prepared to pace out the hexagon in the center of the room, but the thought of Marianna kept on interrupting him. The burnished tresses, the wink of a white shoulder of an evening— these bothered him far more than the occasional glimpse of flesh had done while they were in Songuard. On the other hand, what he had taken for bossiness on the quest had shown itself as something even less appealing on her home ground. Now he found her stubborn and overbearing. There was an unexpected and, as far as he could see, an entirely unwarranted hostility toward him that bewildered and hurt him. Despite all of that, he admitted to himself, any accidental physical contact with her produced disturbances in both mind and body. He wondered if his hunger for her was based on the fact that she was the only girl he had ever spent a lot of time with: whether the firestorms she caused in him had been fueled by the special circumstances of their mission.

He forced himself back into the present and looked round the room slowly as a way of regaining his concentration for the job at hand. Greylock had been allocated the former Holdmistress' withdrawing room. He catalogued the furniture that Marianna's mother had chosen for herself. It was delicate and the quiet silks of its upholstery echoed the tapestry that dominated and warmed the West wall. He looked at Greylock, tucking in to a hearty meal at one end of a ball-and-claw-footed table, and thought that he looked out of place.

The rest of the table was covered with heaps of dried plants and roots, bowls, mortars and pestles of varying sizes. In the fireplace, wood flamed steadily in several small piles and trifooted, iron cooking rings squatted over them. On the hastily acquired hob, three of the Hold's kettles stood, copper gleaming in the wanton licking as they began the long climb to boiling. He made one last, flourishing sweep, propped the besom in a corner and wondered how such a fastidious man as the wizard stood the inevitable disarray of a Magician's workroom.

He fetched a nail and a length of twine, borrowed a pestle from the table, then hammered the one through the other in the center of the space he had cleared. He returned the pestle, fished a piece of chalk from his sleeve and began marking the six corners of the figure. In spite of, or perhaps because of the precision he knew he needed, he found himself pausing to watch the showers of small birds. Those harbingers of the coming cold darted toward the bright windows, larger here on the topmost floor than elsewhere in the Hold, and veered away at the last possible moment. They pelted for the South side of the mountains and the roosts of Winter.

Above and behind the avian invasion the clouds drifted in the direction of the distant Celador, propelled by the weatherwards stationed on the flanks of the Melnikons. Life, he thought, would be so much easier if he could join their ranks and leave all of this behind him. But he had a job to do and, right now, that job was to assist Greylock.

He began to draw in the lines with a straight ease born of many years spent shuffling backwards on his knees. If the weatherwards sent snow North early enough, his mind continued unabashed, Marianna wouldn't be able to carry out her crazy scheme of training Amarine for battle. He shook his head and continued to draw. Perhaps if he got Greylock to talk to her. She certainly didn't seem to be in any mood to listen to him.

He brought himself back with an effort and finished off the lines. He glanced guiltily over at Greylock, as if his thoughts had been audible, but the Mage was bent on his meal. Jarrod straightened up and flexed his back before opening the familiar travelling chest that he had helped to pack so many times. He carefully withdrew three vials of powder, one filled with blue, one with orange and one grey. He poured the grey powder along the defining lines. It required full concentration and a steady hand and there was no room for outside thoughts. That accomplished, he limned an inner circle with the orange salt and connected the two with the blue.

He stepped back and reviewed his handiwork critically. He made a tiny, and unnecessary, adjustment to one of the lines and went over to stoke the fires in the hearth. He turned the kettles.

"Can I open one of the windows?" he asked over his shoulder. "The fire's taking all of the air out."

"Have you bonded the lines of the hexagon yet? If you haven't, you'd better do that first or the whole thing will blow away."

"Yes, Sir," Jarrod said, furious with himself for having overlooked something so elementary. That would teach him to keep his mind on the job.

What he had to do was simple enough, but it took patience and control. He relaxed his shoulders and his breathing automatically deepened as, holding the pattern in his mind, he went within himself. He began to raise the temperature of the powders. It had to be done very slowly and absolutely evenly so that all the lines would burn at the same rate when the time came.

Something within him felt the heat in them rise as the grains began to fuse. He had the same kind of sense for this as a cook who waits for milk to come to the scald and knew, to the instant, when to desist. He reemerged sweating and turned gratefully to push one of the paned casements open. He let the moist air cool him on its way to the chimney. He followed it and found that he needed a cloth to turn the kettles this time.

He went to join Greylock, who was busy grinding down the ingredients for the three potions that were the only other sustenance that he would take over the next thirteen hours. Jarrod's eyes swiftly checked the water clock on the wall to see if it needed topping up. It didn't, but he dwelt with pleasure on its intricacies. It was obviously an old piece, decorated with enamels, with a finely chased and molded catch basin that reminded him of the fountains at Belengar.

Behind him the kettles began to sing and he went and drew water. He crossed to the table and began making a paste of the crushed roots and simples. He added to it slowly until the broth was complete, emptying first one kettle and then another. The basic stock would cleanse and reinforce the Keeper's body so that it would be able to withstand the great forces that they both knew would whirl through it. Greylock added the esters that would keep his head clear enough to direct that energy.

The old wizard named them off as he unstoppered and poured. Endragon, kitspur, jessamin and theony, a potent litany that continued to sound in Jarrod's head as he lugged the heavy basins back to the fire and placed them on the cooking rings to simmer and thicken. He returned with the last of the kettles and poured hot water for the rite of outward cleansing.

Greylock began to shuck himself out of his robe and his muffled voice fought its way out of the folds.

"You know, it feels very good having you back to assist me." That, at least, is what Jarrod thought he said and, since it made him feel good, he left it at that.

"Thank you, it's wonderful to be back at the old tasks," he said as the Mage's head came clear of the hem.

"Not too hot, I hope. Ah, no. Just right." The thorough laving commenced and, while his master was thus engaged, Jarrod kept the water in front of him hot and clean. He alternated bowls at need. The room filled with the musky scent of leaf and tuber as the basins in the hearth bubbled.

When the cleansing was completed, Greylock donned a fresh robe and sandals and slipped the Ring of the Keepers back over a thick knuckle. Jarrod stirred the cooking basins and carefully measured out a brew. He took the cup and set it beside the Mage to cool and then took the vessels off the fire. He stirred them again, inhaling the heady vapors until he felt slightly muzzy. Then he divided the contents between two large, sheathed flasks which he set with exactitude inside the rim of the inner circle.

"Thank you, lad. You may watch with me if you've a mind to, but I don't think I'll really need you. I have to take the second draught in five hours and the last one four hours later. I'll position myself so the water clock's in plain sight, but you might check and see that I haven't drifted away. An old man like me isn't immune from napping and the timing ought to be fairly accurate. There's no need for you to hang around in between, though. I'm sure you have things of your own to do.''

"I'd be happy to keep an eye on the time for you," Jarrod replied with a small smile, "and I'd like to start the vigil with you, if it won't be too much of a distraction.''

"No, lad," Greylock said with an answering smile. "I think I shall probably be capable of concentrating. No, no," he waved a protest away before it had formed on Jarrod's lips, "I know you didn't mean it that way. Of course you can stay. Just one thing, though. I know I'm stating the obvious, but that never hurts. If I doze off and it's time for me to drink again, do whatever you have to do to attract my attention, but on no account cross that line." He pointed to the jointed grey band that outlined the whole. "Even if I seem in dire distress and I plead with you, you are not to enter the hexagon until the full time is up. No matter what. Is that clear?''

"Yes, Sir. Are you expecting something to happen?''

"One never knows. Nothing ever happened to my predecessor, Torthon, or at least if it did he never told me. Nothing's ever happened to me, either. There are always parts of the trance that are blank to me, but, on the other hand, I've yet to miss a potion. Still, there's always the first time, so I'd be grateful if you'd keep an eye on me.''

Jarrod was sensible of the honor being done him. He had never been asked to help with the rites that were connected with the dwellers of the Place of Power. He bowed his head in acknowledgement.

"Well," Greylock said with a sigh, "I suppose I'd better stop puttering and get down to it. He turned away. "You better close that window again. I don't care too much for the damp down here and sitting still for thirteen hours does strange enough things to the joints as it is.''

While Jarrod moved round the lines to the windows, the Mage lifted his robe clear of the floor, grabbed a cushion from one of the chairs and made his way carefully to the center of the figure. He placed the cushion on the floor and sank down to it yarely enough. Jarrod pulled the casement to and latched it. He turned to see his teacher sitting relaxedly, but erect, facing the water clock.

He was waiting for it, expected it, but he still jumped when the powder lines exploded simultaneously into flame. No matter what the color of the powder had been, the steady light that glowed up was a bluish white. He walked all the way around the incandescent area and scrutinized it. He was pleased to see that his handiwork had stood the test, despite his lack of recent practice. The hexagon and the circle glowed evenly around the Mage and harmed neither the Magician nor the planks beneath them. Satisfied, Jarrod folded himself down and began the breathing that led to meditation. Marianna, the unicorns and the war vanished as he plunged, with something close to relief, into his craft.

It had been long months since he had been able to run through so many spells and incantations. The familiar troches were told off in immemorial order, one following the other in silent succession. He experienced a growing sense of well-being and elation as the uncounted hours slid by. Reluctantly, he allowed himself to surface again half an hour before the next potion was due and gazed fondly at the figure in the middle of the room.

The Mage's eyes were open, but they saw only inward landscapes. The back was still straight, the hands gathered loosely in the lap, hidden, in part, by the folds of the robe. The whole man—eyelashes, chest, the hair peeping from the nostrils—was immobile. He looked like one of the carvings around the Temple of the Oracle and the thought made Jarrod wonder if anyone had sought to consult the High Priestess. Greylock would know, but the frozen body could give no answers now. He was as still as death, but Jarrod knew that, within the chrysalis, Greylock's body was in a fury of activity as the drugs did their work.

It was almost time. The young Magician's eyes flicked to the water clock. Night was far fallen and the fires had died to a warm glowing, but the hexagon gave off enough of its eerie light for him to see clearly. Raintime had come and gone without his being aware of its drumming and, looking at the old man, he wasn't sure that he could break into that iron concentration. Time trickled inexorably downward and the mark came and was passed. The Mage remained marmoreal and Jarrod's new won sense of well-being vanished. He rose to his feet and cleared his throat in preparation. Then, with relief, he saw Greylock's left hand rise up slowly and jerkily.

When it was clear of the knee, it moved to the left in short, smooth bursts. It pivoted on the elbow until it was over the neck of the flask. There it stopped, descended, picked the beaker up and moved at right angles toward Greylock's face. Jarrod shuddered involuntarily, for nothing about his master, save the unreal movement, had changed. The man had not blinked his empty eyes and still did not seem to breathe. It was as if the hand had acted on its own.

The gesture was an almost mechanical one and the idea upset Jarrod. He watched the Mage raise the flask to his lips, jut his lower jaw and drink the contents without otherwise moving his head. The vessel was returned by precisely the same route to precisely the same spot. Jarrod was used to the unnatural, but this particular process bothered him. He decided that it was time for him to take a turn outside. He replenished the fire and walked slowly to the door. He opened and closed it quietly, though he was aware that, even should he let it slam, it would make no impression on the man he was leaving behind.

He adventured out into the nighttime Hold, a Hold that he had been surreptitiously exploring during the times when he was awake and away from the unicorns. It was, after all, the place that she grew up in and the better he knew it, the more he should be able to understand her. He saw precious little of her these days.

She always seemed to be so busy, he thought as he negotiated the ill-lit passageways—supervising this, organizing that or trailing around after her father and scolding him into drinking hot possets. There never seemed to be a chance to be alone with her and find out why she had become so angry with him. He must have done or said something to offend her, but he couldn't think what it could have been. He wanted to apologize to her and yell at her all at the same time. Time was what he needed. Time to sort out his feelings. That and a chance to talk with her. Perhaps he would find her in the caves tending to Amarine. The unicorns were about due for feeding anyway.

The links on the stairway smoked and made grotesqueries out of his shadow as he made his way down. The Holding had been one of the first places to be settled after the foreigners had been driven North. It was older than anything he was used to and went a long way toward explaining Marianna's pride in her lineage. The centuries of continuity were all there in the thick walls and the stout cinderwood shutters, black from their years in place. In these quiet hours, it still had the air of a fortified outpost, though its men, these days, had a long way to go to find the enemy.

He detoured to the stables in search of fodder. He carried his bale through deserted passages to the cellars, went back for a second and then a third. When he let himself into the caverns, he was greeted by hunger, impatience and ribaldry. He did his best to ignore their speculations on the reasons for his tardiness. They were growing up very fast, he thought, aware that they could hear him. He concentrated briefly on the links in their sockets and when they kindled, busied himself spreading the fodder.

I've seen you do that a lot and I still don't know how you do it. Jarrod grinned in Nastrus' direction.

Nothing in The Memory? he teased.

Nothing at all, the colt thought, taking the question seriously. *It's come across Magic, but nobody has explained how it works.*

Tell us about the test we see in your head, Pellia interrupted and Jarrod thought an answer for them.

Speaking of horns, he added *the three of you are sprouting fast. They look longer than my handspan already. How long does the velvet stay on?*

Yes you may, the answer came into his mind before he was aware he had asked. He stepped up to Beldun and reached out his hand tentatively to touch the tapering hornlet, sheathed in what looked like grey velour. The tips of his fingers began their caress and then were pulled sharply back as Jarrod cursed under his breath. His mind was filled with questioning.

I got a shock, he replied. *I should have expected it. I got a much stronger reaction when I touched your mother's horn. Can I try again, now that I'm ready for it?*

He reached out again, his fingers hesitating, and then pressed gently into the down that surrounded the ivory. A surge hit up through the shoulder and into his body, but he kept his hand where it was. His system adjusted to the influx of energy. There was a slight tingling sensation all over his skin. He found it pleasant and began to feel stronger and more alert.

He curled his thumb and the rest of his fingers around the stem and held the horn lightly, ready to let go. The pleasant sensation intensified and he moved a pace to the left. He took the softness that was Pellia's horn in his other hand. He knew epiphany. In the high room under the leads Greylock stirred in his trance.

Jarrod opened his eyes and expelled his pent-up breath. Power bloomed in him, but the excess elation faded and left him feeling confident and in control. He felt much larger than he had been and, when he glanced down at his body, he half expected the hay-stuck seams of his robe to be gaping. There was no outward manifestation. The confidence mounted and he felt that, with these two, he could throw the enemy back single-handedly, could accomplish any spell, was invincible.

I think you should let go now. We know that it feels good, but I'm hungry and I'd like to get some of that hay before Mam finishes it all. Reluctantly, Jarrod obeyed and found, to his delight, that the sensations persisted. He walked around the caverns and pine brands sprang to life before him as he strode. The linklight created warmth and shadow on the brick vaulting above him. Their smoke eddied in his passage. As he moved, the feeling began to ebb and the faster he walked, the faster it dissipated. Finally, he remembered the waiting Mage and knew that he was back to normal. What should he tell Greylock?

Why not wait and see what happens tomorrow. Mother has agreed, even though you didn't ask her properly. The colts had arrived in a clattering echo of hooves.

Did you feel anything? Jarrod asked them. Their assent was very positive and heavily tinged with pleasure.

Never felt anything like that before. Can we do it again? I rather suspect that we shan't be able to do it again without you. That last, Jarrod knew instantly, was from Nastrus. There was silence as they absorbed his hopes and expectations.

I'm not sure that we can make Magic. I told you The Memory didn't know how.

Oh, Nastrus, Jarrod thought crossly, *just because your ancestors didn't understand Magic doesn't mean that the four of us can't make it now. My mother and father didn't have the Talent, but I'm a Magician.*

Only way to find out is to try, Beldun interposed with the finality of the obvious. *Not now, though. I'm still hungry. D'you think you could get us some more hay or some kind of oats?* The question became a chorus. As he doused the links before leaving, Nastrus said into his mind, *I tried to do that and I couldn't.* The thought was smug.

He knew that he would be late for the last flask if he did not hurry. He brushed rebellious black hair perfunctorily and recinched the rope over a stomach that was reminding him that he had missed Hall. No time for that either. He hurried on feeling vaguely guilty that he had left Greylock untended for so long.

He had no idea what it was that he was afraid he'd find when he let himself back into the withdrawing room. He glanced rapidly around and saw nothing amiss. It was very black outside, a foretaste of the Season of the Moons, and the fires had turned to grey ash around the legs of the cooking rings. A low gleam came from the lines on the floor.

He groped his way to the table and located three candles. He dared not light them by Magical means and fished around for a flint. Once found, he lit the candles and held one up to see the water clock. There was still a little time left and he turned to survey the still figure of the Mage. Nothing seemed to have changed and he was relaxing when the hand began to move with daunting independence.

Jarrod watched it while it sought out the final beaker. Greylock drank without distrubing his unyielding tranquility and Jarrod's stomach twinged. He ignored it and walked around the hexagon to see if any weaknesses had developed in the lines. He was pleased to find none. Reassured, he surrendered to the demands of his body and set off to try to find his way down to the kitchens and the promise of orts.

Despite the lateness of the hour, the kitchens were not only occupied but busy with preparations for the following day. The chief cook, however, was not disposed to feed him. She eyed his messy gown with disfavor and told him brusquely that the place for mendicants to get fed was outside the main gates and at the proper hour. It had been a long day for her and, as she sat perched on her stool with an egg muddler rotating between her palms, it was clear that she was not prone to sympathy.

Jarrod turned to go, his stomach rumbling at the aromas drifting in the chimney draft. He stopped as Marianna entered. She wore a brocaded gown and there were green ribbons in her hair, but the mouth was a straight line and the eyes were narrowed. She ignored him and her voice cut through the clatter as she heaped criticism on all and sundry. The kitchen staff stopped what they were doing and listened with weary resignation. She stood in the doorway, hands on hips, and was well into her harangue before she noticed him. She broke off and stared at him.

"So there you are. What's the matter, the food in Hall not good enough for you? Though the way things went tonight I can't blame you for skipping it. It might be nice, however, if you would deign to join us. I know your social conversation isn't up to much, but you could at least help me out by answering some of those questions about the," she caught herself, "about the technical side of things."

He drew back as if she had struck at him. Here was the animosity again and he hadn't said a word. He was dismayed, too, by the way she had spoken to the servants. This was in no way the girl he knew.

"I have been assisting the Mage of Paladine in the performance of important rites," he said with a steely pomposity, holding himself in check. If he let her reach him and touch him too nearly, he knew that he would say something that he would later regret.

"In that tattered old thing?" The sarcasm was patent.

"Perhaps if you screamed at the laundress the way you seem to be yelling at everybody else, I might be able to get some clean clothes," he replied icily. Her eyes registered the hit.

"I've too much to do to waste my time arguing with jumped-up Novices," she said nastily. "You can do your own washing and fetch your own meals as far as I'm concerned. Now," she turned her fierceness back onto the others, "the rest of you, tomorrow's performance had better be a great deal smarter than tonight's or, when our distinguished guests have left us, this Hold is going to see a lot of changes on the staff side. You've all become very sloppy with both my father and I away and I, for one, won't put up with it. See that you do better tomorrow.'' She looked around slowly in emphasis and then picked up her skirts and left with her head held high and her shoulders stiff.

The kitchens came back to life with a gust of laughter and the buzz of talk while Jarrod stood and stared at the empty doorway in disbelief. Nothing made sense. The people around him shouldn't be laughing and that wasn't the Marianna he knew. He might have expected that sort of outburst from Naxania, but not from Marianna.

"Don't take on so, young Sir," the cook said with a humorous tolerance she had not displayed earlier. "She's not angry with you, nor with us really. It's that father of hers."

Jarrod seized on the excuse. He had known that Martin could be willful and had a sharp tongue on occasions, but he had never made the transfer to the poised and sophisticated woman of the world that he had encountered in the Great Hall at Celador and refound here at Gwyndryth.

"The Holdmaster?" There was an eagerness in his voice. "Is there anything wrong? Has he had a relapse?"

"There's them as 'ud say that," the cook replied as she hoisted her bolster-shaped body off the stool. She smiled broadly and waddled over to a counter and added flour to her bowl. "Here, stir this for me until it's smooth, there's a good lad. No, bless you, the master has a wasting sickness, but he didn't catch it in Umbria." There was a wicked twinkle in her eye. "Oh no, he got it right here, and a bad case of it too, they say."

"What has he got? Is it serious?"

"I don't know how serious it is, though he's certainly not eating as much as he used to." The woman was enjoying herself. "Mind you, when a man's in love that usually happens."

Once it had been said it became obvious. That, of course, was what all the amused tension at Hall had been about. One by one, the sly references he had overheard fell into place. He had been so bound up with the colts and with Marianna that he had failed to notice what was going on under his nose.

"I'd be upset too if I was going to have the Princess Naxania as a stepmother," he said, matching her broad smile.

" 'Bout time, too, I say," the cook swept on, oblivious to the interruption, "but our little Miss High-handed just can't abide it. She's as riggish as a flyblown heifer." She chuckled. "Been the only woman in his life for a long time now and she can't take the competition." She paused and looked at him shrewdly as he stirred the mixture. "You've a Pallic accent by the sound of you. What do you think of your Princess and our Holdmaster?"

"I really don't know. I hadn't thought about it," he replied truthfully. What was uppermost in his mind, however, was the thought that Marianna would have to go to Stronta. She might even end up living in the palace and that would mean that . . . His train of thought was interrupted by the cook's snort of disbelief.

"You're the one as turned up with our young mistress, aren't you? Yes, I thought so. Well, you sit at the High Table, when you remember to eat, and you haven't noticed anything? Something the matter with your eyes, boy? Oh, wait a minute now, I'll wager they're all taken up by the Lady Marianna." She laughed at her own cleverness and her eyes were gleaming. "Look there now," she said roguishly, "the lad can blush. Well, she's a pretty enough little thing, I'll say that for her. Headstrong, but pretty." She cocked her head and looked at him out of one eye.

"Oh, don't take on, laddie, I'm just teasing you. You keep blending that for me and I'll fetch you a nice cut off the joint. It'll still be warm." She laughed delightedly and trundled off into the renewed confusion.

"No meat, please. I'm not allowed it," Jarrod called after her, not sure that she had heard. She bustled back, however, with a platter heaped with fish and vegetables. By that time the batter was smooth and so was Jarrod's outward composure.

"Thank you, laddie," she said as she retrieved her bowl. "Now, tell me, what's been going on down in the cellars?"

"In the cellars?" Jarrod repeated, caught off balance again.

"Oh, come on now. You can't fool me, I've been around too long. All that hay," and she winked and nudged him in the ribs. "There he goes, blushing again." She cackled gleefully, highly contented with her amorous logic, and repaired to her pots, sparing Jarrod the need for an answer. He finished his platter, thanked her and beat a hasty retreat. The cook's knowing laughter followed him.

He climbed back to the top floor, his mind less concerned with things Magical than ever. The Mage was still in trance and Jarrod sank down on the boards and tried, unavailingly, to concentrate. There was so much to consider. If Darius and Naxania married, Marianna would be the King's granddaughter and even further out of reach, socially, than she was now. If he could somehow win the war with the unicorns' help, he might be able to ask her to marry him. On the other hand, after the scene in the kitchen, he wasn't sure that he wanted to marry her. What he did want was nothing that he should be contemplating with Greylock present in the midst of making Magic. His remark to the cook about Naxania had been meant to be funny, but it was, he realized, entirely true.

He wondered why so few Magicians were married. Women were as likely to be born with the Talent as men, and both Naxania and Arabella were expected to marry for dynastic reasons. If the gossip was true, and he was fairly certain that it was, there was no prearrangement about this match. What would Strongsword do when word of it reached him? Forbid the attachment, as like as not. But if Naxania didn't marry the Holdmaster, Marianna would probably end up staying at Gwyndryth. It was all too complicated. If Martin had stayed Martin he wouldn't have to go through all this confusion. He forced his mind back to the litany and surrendered to it.

Time ran slowly down and, in the hour before the stars go pale with the fear of the coming sun, the Mage stirred in the dim, tall room. His eyelids drooped and then closed for the first time since he had seated himself on the cushion. He tilted his head back and rolled it around on the thick neck. He rocked himself to his feet and stretched. The lines of the hexagon shone quietly around him and the leaded panes caught and diffused the stars. He took in the shadowed form on the floor and smiled softly in the gloam, the affection he found so hard to express plain in his face. Then quietly, sonorously, the deep voice intoned a quatrain and the hexagon was no more. There was no trace that it had ever been.

Jarrod woke at the sound of the rich, familiar tones and

scrambled to his feet as his mentor approached. He bowed his head and Greylock nodded in return.

"Thank you for watching with me. My body tells me that it went well." Wordlessly, Jarrod opened the door and followed. Side by side they took the stairs in the not quite quiet of a castle at rest and went out into the morning.

Together they performed the Making of the Day beneath a sky that the wind had cleaned and polished while they were elsewhere. Onto it they thought the subtle bands of color that forced the stars into retreat. They diluted the dark blues and reds and superimposed rose and gold. Then, with a last effort, they heaved a dark red ball up over the edge of the world and lifted it into unwatchable white. As both of them emerged, they glanced over their shoulders and there sat the sun in the place they had thought it to. It was going to be a very good day.

"Too early for breakfast, d'you think? I'm famished," Greylock said mundanely as he strode briskly back.

"Soon I expect, Sir, but ought you to? I mean . . ."

"No point in taking a test if you faint before it starts. Besides, the potions burn it all up. I usually find myself eating twice as much as I normally would and it hasn't hurt me yet."

"Don't forget to stay away from meats. The unicorns can't abide them. We nearly lost them over a strip of dried venison."

"I remember. I've no intention of offending them. Certainly not today. Anyway, what I really like down here is the fish. Better than anything we get back home, or at Celador for that matter. Those tame carp can't compare to the stuff they get out of the river, and the cook certainly knows what to do with it." Jarrod's mind returned to the previous night's encounter and he kept his own counsel as they went up the steps and through the half door.

One by one, the members of the High Council of Magic made their way down the cellar stairs, stirring gossip and speculation in their wake, to the secret caverns. While curiosity burned behind them, there were none who dared to follow. They assembled in the main cavern where the unicorns, colts ranged behind their dam, waited for them. The women wore their scarlet and Ragnor had donned his official gown. Jewels glinted in the white hair and Errethon hung heavily from the gold chain of office.

Last to arrive was Greylock, accompanied by Jarrod in a clean blue gown that had materialized unexpectedly in his room. The Mage. wore one of his simple robes and his tiara. Amarine, her hide dappled black and orange by the links, stretched her left foreleg out and bent her right. The neck arched and the long horn dipped. Greylock bowed low in return, signalled Jarrod to a place on his left, bowed to his colleagues and then again to the now erect Amarine. He advanced slowly until he stood before her and then raised his arms, fingers straining for the bricks overhead.

Jarrod watched him intently and found himself wishing that Marianna could be there. It was a Magical occasion and, as one of the Talentless, she was automatically barred. If anything went wrong it would be kept within the Discipline. But Marianna was no tattletale and she did have a bond with Amarine that no Magician could equal. If finding the unicorns had been enough to make a fully fledged Magician out of him, she should at least be allowed to attend a ceremony that centered around the dam. The words that Jarrod had last heard in the Place of Power rumbled into his awareness and cut short his musings.

The torchlight gathered and flashed from the tiara and flickered over the fat, black ring. The stone itself gave off no light. The invocation continued, rising to a bass crescendo before it died. The Mage of Paladine lowered his arms and approached the serene creature before him. When he was almost at her head he stopped. He said nothing, but the dam, towering above him, dipped her head until her horn was parallel with the flagged floor. Somewhere in the cavern water ran and underlined the silence.

Greylock, without waiting for Jarrod's aid, extended his right arm with a slow grace. Jarrod put out his mind for the colts, but encountered nothing. He drew back, startled and a little upset with them, and concentrated on the Mage's hand. The fingers curled deliberately around the slender whorling and took a firm hold. The loose robe trembled as if the wind had struck, so violent was the shaking of the body beneath it. Greylock's jaw fell open in a silent scream, his eyes bulged and the hair on his head spiked outward as the energy poured through him and found no release. The blocky figure jerked spasmodically as the rest of them stood rooted.

Get him off her! Make him let go! Hurry, or he'll be killed. He isn't strong enough. The unicorns came back into Jarrod's mind in a shock and galvanized him into action. He ducked under the Mage's flailing arm and began to pry the fingers up one by one, wincing and gasping every time he touched the ivory. It felt like overheated metal to him. The process seemed endless, but, finally, the last finger fell away and Greylock with it. Amarine snorted and retreated several paces, shaking her head and making her mane fly. Greylock lay twitching on the floor as the circlet rolled to a wobbling halt. His right hand was twisted like a crippled claw.

Jarrod sank to his knees as the others rushed to the stricken Mage. This was when he could have used Marianna's help. Just her presence would have calmed Amarine. He loosened the throat of the robe and held Greylock as the spasms shook the solid body. Arabella cradled his head and let it thrash back and forth against the scarlet silk.

Is your mother all right? Jarrod thought out anxiously.

She is untouched, from Beldun. *He couldn't do anything to her,* from Nastrus. *She is worried about the man,* was Pellia. The jerking died down and the rictus that held the Mage's face relaxed. As Jarrod watched, the breathing deepened.

I think he'll be all right, but I can't be certain. If it's the same for him as it was for me at the Place of Power, he'll be knocked out for a while, but he's a lot stronger than I am and he's had a lot more practice with this sort of thing. He's a very great Magician. Jarrod caught the defensiveness and the undercurrents of worry in his own mind.

Mam says he'll recover, came Pellia reassuringly.

"You, son." Ragnor's voice brought Jarrod's head round sharply. "Go find Gwyndryth and tell him to lay on a couple of stout men and a stretcher. The girls and I will get him out into the cellars. No point in having half the Hold in here gawking. Hop to it now." Jarrod got to his feet and set out at a run as the royal ladies and the elderly Archmage prepared to lug the heavy body away.

CHAPTER XX

IN THE SENNIGHT THAT FOLLOWED THE TEST, JARROD TENDED GREYlock assiduously and fussed over him when he regained consciousness. He knew that all danger was passed when the Mage irritably demanded paper and quills and set about scribbling with his old intensity. He had to be very firm with the older man in order to get him to lay aside his equations and eat. He tried to fathom what was going on, but found the figures meaningless. When he asked, gently at first and then more insistently, what was going forward, he was waved away or dismissed with a 'Not yet: not 'til I'm sure.' On the ninth day Greylock sent him to fetch Ragnor, Marianna and the Princesses.

They gathered round the bed with murmurs of concern, which Greylock suffered gracefully. When the last of them was there, he looked around at them.

"Thank you for coming and thank you for worrying about me. It was foolish of me to think that I could control the kind of power that the unicorns represent, but one doesn't know until one tries and we know so little about these undoubtedly Magical creatures. It was quite an experience. I haven't felt anything like that since I was first taken to the Place of Power and tested there. Confronted with her, I was just as much of a novice as I was then.

"It was different, though, quite different. I know what it must have looked like, but I felt no pain. Great elation and great clarity of mind, but no pain. And yet I'm perfectly well aware that that rapture could have killed me . . . probably would have if Jarrod hadn't acted when he did.'' He turned to the youth and smiled. ''I should have said it before, lad, but I was too preoccupied. I'm very grateful for what you did.

''No,'' he resumed, ''no pain and no fear. All I could think of was a way to erect some kind of barrier to filter that force and, as I said, my mind was working more keenly than I can ever remember. I may have failed the test, but I have gained something that I think will be valuable. I don't think it's the reason that the unicorns were sent to us, I don't think we know what that is yet, but Magic works in unanticipated ways sometimes.'' He paused, savoring the drama.

''I think I have discovered the principle of a field that may well help us against the new weapons that your father, my dear, described so eloquently to us. I've done the preliminary paper work and now I must get back to Stronta as soon as possible so that I can begin the experiments.''

There was a brief silence while they digested the report and then Ragnor said, ''Will you need the unicorns for the experiment?''

''I don't know,'' said Greylock. ''I do know that I am not about to take hold of that horn again. There's no way to contain that sort of power.''

''I can, Sir.'' Jarrod felt almost guilty about the admission.

''You can?'' The Archmage's voice was careful.

''Oh, not with Amarine, your Excellency,'' Jarrod said apologetically. ''But I did it with the colts.''

''When?'' Greylock demanded.

''The night of the vigil.''

''What happened?''

''I held Beldun and Pellia's horns at the same time.''

''And?''

''It felt wonderful. I could feel the power in me growing and growing. It felt like I was bursting out of my robe, but I knew there was almost nothing that I couldn't do while I was linked with them.'' He fell silent, feeling that he had said too much.

''So,'' Greylock said slowly. ''Archmage, do you have the jewel?'' Ragnor nodded. ''Good. I'd like you to test the boy.''

''With Errethon?'' the Archmage inquired. ''Do you doubt him?''

"Doubt Jarrod? That he thinks what he says is true? Not for an instant. I just want to make sure that the feeling was a true one."

"Very well then. Come here, son, come and stand in front of me. That's it. Now, there's nothing to be afraid of: nothing's going to happen to you if you were wrong. The stone never makes judgements, it just reacts to the truth. The more complete the truth, the deeper the hue. That's all. You won't feel a thing. All you have to do is to recall how you felt, as best you can, that is. How's your memory?"

"Pretty good, your Excellency."

"Oh yes," Ragnor said as he followed a chain down inside his robe and withdrew the stone. "I remember now. You're being modest. Well, just you relax if you can with all of us breathing down your neck, and see what you can bring back."

The Archmage gazed down into his hand where the dormant stone lay. "Ah yes," he said as it began to glow. The color deepened steadily and yet the jewel grew brighter until it became difficult to look at.

"Remarkable, quite remarkable. Yes, that'll do, that'll do nicely, thank you, son. Well," he said, looking at the recumbent figure, "I don't think there can be any doubt about that. What your boy says is quite obviously true. I don't quite know what it means, but it's undoubtedly true." He stopped and an urchin grin stole over his face. "Oh, what a wonderful mess this is going to make of my vision. Anybody got any bright ideas?" He looked around, his face still alight. "No? Well I suppose I'm going to have to make all the decisions as usual.

"One thing we know, the war's heating up again. Continual skirmishes in front of Celador and Stronta. The enemy's been thrown back every time so far, but it's obvious that there's another major battle in the offing. There's nothing that I can do about that from this backwater—begging your pardon, Lady Marianna. It seems obvious to me that the unicorns will have to come with us. Trouble is, I don't see how. I can't see trying to strap them to cloudsteeds, and escorting them by land will take forever."

"We can take them through Interim, Excellency. The same way we brought them here," Marianna interposed cooly. This was her opportunity and she didn't intend to muff it. "I should be happy to accompany Amarine. Indeed, without me, I doubt she'll go anywhere." She looked around for opposition, but found none.

"From what I gather from young Courtak, they can only go to places that some other unicorn has been before. Have they ever been to the North?"

"The one time that they showed us places that they knew," Jarrod answered, "there was a spot that might have been the Place of Power. But, when it came to leaving the Anvil, they chose to come here."

"They had an ancestor that visited the Barrier Reach," Marianna cut in. "I imagine it was after the other side's air had dissipated and before we got here from the First Lands. Anyway, since my home was so close, it seemed the most practical thing to do." The Archmage nodded his head.

"The whole thing sounds risky to me," he said, "but I suppose we'll have to take the risk. After all, Greylock, you may need their help with your experiments. Anybody got any better ideas? No? That's that then." He sat back looking pleased with himself. "Tell me, old friend," he said, leaning forward again, "when are you going to be fit to travel?" Greylock smiled at his colleague's methods.

"You really can't stand to wait a second longer than you have to once your mind's made up, can you?" he said. "I can be ready by tomorrow if you like."

"Can't say as I relish the prospect of becoming aerial baggage again, but we're needed up North. I must say this, this Interim stuff sounds much more like it. Pop and you're there. None of this disgraceful trailing across the sky for days. Still, in wartime one must make sacrifices. Well now, unless anyone has any comments, I suggest we let out old friend get some rest. Marianna, my dear, would you tell your father that we shall be abandoning his hospitality, let's say the day after tomorrow." The Archmage was in full spate of organization.

"Thank you, Adran. I'm glad to see you on the mend. Come along now, the rest of you, come along, come along. Let's give the man a little peace and quiet before he returns to the fray of

Stronta.'' Ragnor rose and bustled everybody out, leaving Greylock and Jarrod to assess what had happened.

The Hold had already got enough to talk about to take it
through several Winters, but even the image of an inert Mage
being carried upstairs on a stretcher had been banished, that
same afternoon, by the appearance of the unicorns. They were
led out beyond the walls by the Lady Marianna and the young
man she had brought with her. They had galloped and rolled in
the grass with delighted abandon.

Anybody who could, and that included a fair number who
shouldn't have, trailed after them. Now there was really something to talk about for generations to come. Immortality achieved
by accident. Your great grandmother was one of the very first
people to see a real live unicorn. The tensions and difficulties of
the past sennights dissolved as the word spread and people came
flocking to see the marvel for themselves. The unicorns had
finally become public property.

The descent of the Talented on Gwyndryth was the best
theatre that any of the locals would ever see. It had everything
except tragedy. It was spiced by scandal when the foreign Princess elected to stay behind and relieved by comedy as a vitriolic
Archmage was strapped onto a cloudsteed again. He did not go
gracefully.

It had a strong element of mystery because nobody could ever
exactly pinpoint when or where the Lady Marianna and her
young man, as they now thought of him, and all the unicorns
vanished. There were plenty of folks there to witness the scene,
but no true eye could swear to the moment that they left. What
they did say was that the Autumn air lacked sparkle and that the
sun did not shine for a full sennight after they had disappeared.
In years to come they would say that the stars remained veiled in
discretion and the children did not laugh. It was a time of Magic
incarnate and it touched all who were present with glory and
made of humble lives an epic song.

This time it was Jarrod who had the easier trip. Interim seized
him and squeezed him into unconsciousness as before, but the
alterations that he had made to himself made him better able to
withstand the ghostly cold. He regained consciousness beside the

forward altar in the place of Power. Marianna came around almost as fast as he did, but found herself filled with a deep and shaking dread that paralyzed her. She knew that it was caused by the Place of Power, but that made no difference. She buried her face in Amarine's mane and would not, or could not, move.

Jarrod worked the knots at his ankles loose and went to see if she was all right, but she would not lift her head or speak to him. Once he had led Amarine beyond the menhir, the tension in her lessened, and by the time they reached The Outpost she was sitting up again.

They were expected, news of them having preceded them by bunglebird and via the Mage. Everyone who could find an excuse to come running did so. Magicians and Apprentices behaved no differently than scullions and sutlers and were every bit as susceptible to the beauty of the unicorn and the charm of the colts. Greylock was there to greet them and had Marianna whisked away and put to bed while Jarrod took the animals to the stables. Once they were settled, he hurried to rejoin the Mage, glad of the extra clothing he was wearing.

Jarrod took in the well-remembered room and felt a surge of affection for the old man in his habitual armchair. Though the building had not been erected that long ago, Greylock seemed to have inhabited this room, and the workroom above, for a lifetime.

"How's the work on the forcefield coming along, or haven't you had the time for it since you got back?" he asked.

"Oh, I've done all the calculations and somehow they all manage to be congruent," the Mage said with practiced diffidence. He bent over and took the pewter flagon from the chimney corner and topped up Jarrod's tankard. "Ah, lad," he resumed, abandoning his pretense of indifference, "you should see the equations. Such symmetry, such beauty of line and form. I know the screen is the answer, I feel it deep inside me. There is a certainty about it, so round and so whole, that one knows immediately that it is right." He smiled wryly. "I feel as if this is what I was destined to do. This is my contribution to this endless conflict and it will be remembered long after the dust of my bones has been absorbed." He shook his head. "Of course, it may be nothing but the longings of a man past his prime."

"Oh, come now, Sir, you know that can't be true."

"Don't be too sure. There's a problem—isn't there always?"

"Serious?"

"Well, I've managed to get a test model up, but there's no way a man can contain and project the amount of force that will be needed to bind all the particles over a large area."

"We'll be able to do it if we work together," Jarrod said with the sureness of his youth. "Just you wait and see."

"I hope you're right, lad, but we shan't get anything done if you don't go and get some rest. Leave us go and look in on Martin first though."

"She's not Martin anymore," Jarrod said wistfully as he got up.

Jarrod tried to visit her, but he was no match for Diadra and they both knew it. On the third day he was summoned to the Mage's chamber and found her there. She was wearing a dress once more. Her tan was fading, but the freckles were still there. Though he missed the companionship of Martin and found Marianna far harder to cope with, he had to admit that dresses became her a great deal more than trousers.

"Our guest is leaving us, alas," Greylock said. "The Palace insists that she be housed there as befits her rank." He turned toward her. "I am sure you will be more comfortable. Magicians live somewhat threadbare lives. We shall miss you however."

"I was sleeping in far less comfortable conditions not too long ago," she said with a smile. "Your Excellency has been most kind. I shall, of course, be back to ride Amarine. She needs the exercise and I'm the only one who can ride her." There was a proprietary note in her voice.

"I trust you will also come and visit us." The tone was avuncular and smacked of rote politeness. Marianna parsed it instantly and countered.

"Of course. I wouldn't deprive myself of the pleasure, but Amarine is my first care. There is still so much that the two of us have to learn." She smiled brightly at both of them and rose.

"I fear that it is time for you to go," Greylock said, picking up on the unavoidable cue. "It's a long way around the Maze."

"Oh, not again." Jarrod was surprised to see her actually pout. It was a word he knew, but he had never seen it demonstrated before. "Can't you two great Magicians arrange some

sort of pass or protection, or whatever, to get me through that
thing?''

Greylock's eyebrows rose at her tone and there was a moment
of silence before he said, ''There is one slight possibility. I can
detect no latent Talent in you, but your contact with the unicorn
may have made a difference of some kind. There are risks
involved. There are those who never emerge and those who are
driven mad. You must certainly not try it yourself, now or ever.
Still, it would be an interesting experiment.''

''It would certainly save a great deal of time, Excellency.''
Marianna's voice was clipped and self-assured, but the Mage's
mastery of vocal inflections made the new note of underlying
uncertainty clear to him.

''Jarrod will go with you,'' he said gently. ''Make sure that
you keep hold of him at all times. You are to turn back at the
first signs of trouble, is that clear? I want no stubbornness and no
attempts to be heroic. It is very old Magic that maintains the
Maze and it takes no account of human virtues or desires.''

''Yes, Sir.''

''Very well then. Jarrod, do you accompany the Lady Marianna and see that she comes to no harm. His Majesty sets great
store by the young lady and, now that the unicorns are here,
she'll become very famous. So, for that matter, will you.'' He
rose and the other two got to their feet.

''I entrust our charming guest to you,'' he said to Jarrod, ''in
the hopes that Errathuel's barrier will yield to beauty and accom-
plishment, with or without the Talent.'' He turned to the girl.
''You mustn't be disappointed, my dear, if it doesn't let you
through. It has never happened before.''

''Thank you, Excellency. I shall heed your words.'' Marianna
dropped a curtsey.

''Goodbye, my dear, and don't forget to come and visit us.
Send the duty boy up, will you, lad?'' He smiled at them and
nodded a couple of times in dismissal. Then he moved to the
window and watched the young couple leave, the girl tiny beside
the lanky height of his protégé.

''How long is it going to take, Jarrod?'' she asked as they
walked side by side through the afternoon's shifting patchwork
of light and shade.

"I don't know," Jarrod said, wondering if she was regretting her bravado. "It's different for everybody. It usually takes me about fifteen minutes from here, but it can vary. You can't see one another of course, but you can at least carry on a conversation."

"I'm not at all sure that I like the sound of this. What do you mean 'of course you can't see each other?' What can you see?"

"Depends on you. Here, let me get the gate for you. It takes images from your own mind and makes them real. Not the same ones every time, either."

"What sort of images?" She tilted her head and looked up to watch his reply.

"All sorts. For those who have the Talent there's always a path of sorts, some way through. Sometimes it seems to twist and turn and get absolutely nowhere and sometimes it's dead straight and boring. When you've had enough practice, you can get into the easy one any time you want to. Unless you're really upset, that is."

"You're not being much help, you know."

"I don't know how to put it any better," Jarrod replied. "Besides, you forget what you've been seeing as soon as you get out of it. I mean, you'll remember if you were scared, but you won't remember what it was that frightened you. I get dreams like that sometimes and I don't remember them when I wake up, just that I woke myself up because I was afraid." Then he smiled baitingly and added, "But don't worry, the Maze probably knows better than to let you in."

His everyday attitude helped to distract her from her growing nervousness. Despite the fact that she had spent so much time around Jarrod, there was something about Magic itself that invoked awe. She half wished that she hadn't made the request, but she wasn't about to admit it to him. She was not used to being afraid and her reaction to the Place of Power had shaken her more than the site itself.

There were two small knolls ahead and the path rose to pass between them. They were both crowned by trees whose leaves had long since fallen, but, despite their nakedness, their tatted twigs and branches screened the Great Maze effectively enough for Marianna to be surprised when they first came directly upon it. It seemed to her that the ground shimmered and, above it, the air twisted and rose as it does in a paved court of a Summer's afternoon. The moving mass had tints that spiralled through it so that one could not see what was beyond. The Palace was no-where visible, though she knew that it must be there. The veil was diaphanous but opaque and, for a split second, her mind jumped back to Belengar and some of the women she had seen. Then it was time to enter.

"Do we have to do anything special before we go in?" She inquired as levelly as she could.

"No. Just hold on to my hand and don't let go, whatever you see. If you start feeling lost, or if the Maze seems to be resisting you, say so right away and we'll turn back. Remember what Greylock said about not trying to be brave. There really have been people who never came out again, so please be sensible." She nodded silently.

"Right then, you all ready? Here we go." He took her right hand firmly in his left and stepped into the Great Maze. He felt her hand tighten and his whole body seemed to be concentrated in that one place of contact.

"Are you all right?"

"Yes. I'm fine," she lied as the tremors took over her legs. "I can't see anything, though. Nothing at all. It's like a fog." She was amazed that her voice sounded so calm.

"I'm fine, too," Jarrod said reassuringly. "I'm in the direct path and there's no trouble at all. I can't see you, naturally, but we're going through at the same pace."

"What do you mean, 'naturally?' There's nothing remotely natural about this place." Her voice sounded shrill to her this time.

"I suppose we ought to expect that a place created by Errathuel would be unlike anything else found on Strand. Mind you, anything we don't understand we generally attribute to him—if it's useful," he said, trying to fill the silence to give her confidence. He could feel the hand in his trembling.

Marianna stayed silent, battling her growing sense of unease. She didn't like walking blindly toward things that Jarrod couldn't, or wouldn't, describe. If there was something she could do, she knew she could deal with the situation, but there was nothing to hit out at, nothing she could tackle or bend to her will.

"Still nothing but fog?" His voice startled her.

"Yes. Nothing."

"Hang on. It ought not to be too far now."

She fought an urge to scream and forced her feet forward, one at a time. Then the angled walls of Stronta loomed up so suddenly that she gasped. One moment she had been scarfed up and the next instant the gate was in front of her, open wide in mockery.

"There we are, safe and sound. Now that wasn't too bad, was it?" Marianna turned and looked at him, relief enabling the tense lines around her mouth to soften.

"Thank you," she said as her chin came up and she brought her body back under control. "That was a very interesting experience. I'm not at all sure that I want to go through it again, but it is certainly gratifying to be the only 'Untalented' person the Maze has allowed through. This may be quicker, but I think I'll ride in future." She almost made it sound as if it was his fault that she had been nervous.

"It's odd that you didn't see anything," he said blandly. "It's as though the Maze simply withdrew from you." He paused to let her make what she would of that. "It must be the touch of the unicorns," he added.

"No doubt," she said drily. Then the acknowledgment of the danger she had faced hit her and, with it, an appreciation for what he had done.

Impulsively, she put her hands on his shoulders, raised up on her toes and kissed him quickly on the mouth. Then she turned swiftly and ran through the ever-open portals of the Maze Gate. The wardcorn's trumpet rang out and its brazen triumph matched Jarrod's feelings as he watched her disappear. He stood, staring, long after there was nothing to see. He was feeling almost as good as he had when he had held the furred horns.

Awareness of the cold finally seeped into him and he turned and entered the creator of chimeras. If his trip through had been easy, spiced with the awareness of the moist warmth enclosed in his suddenly massive-feeling hand, this passage was pure joy. The Maze took his happiness and sense of wonder and wove them into filigrees of gold and silver that opened and closed in ever changing intricacies. His head felt light and clear and his blood ran strong. He flung his arms wide in exultant gratitude and emerged into the anticlimax of the real world. Whistling and given to the occasional skip when he was sure there was no one to see him, he made his way to the stables to check on the unicorns before reporting to Greylock.

The colts were drowsy and well-fed. Greylock, by contrast, was unreachably into the realms of calculation, sheets of vellum in neat piles around him. Jarrod knew from long experience that it was useless to try to intrude at this stage and went down to his room to change for Hall.

He was slow to come out of sleep when the night duty boy shook him and he dressed groggily. He stumbled up the dark stairs, stubbing his toe on the risers and feeling clumsy and stupid. Greylock was pacing impatiently in front of the long table as the boy, looking even sleepier than Jarrod felt, made up the fire and restocked the log basket. The papers had been reduced to a single, compact stack.

"Oh, there you are. I thought I told you to report back to me after you had taken that girl home."

"I looked in on you, Sir, but you were very busy and I thought it best not to disturb you."

"Did you indeed? Well, no mind, come in and sit down." Jarrod did as he was told. Greylock poured himself a cup of wine, though he did not offer one to Jarrod, and sat himself opposite. "Things are moving too fast," he said. "There are some strange things going on at the interface. The foulness is advancing, but not all up and down the line the way that it normally does. No, this time it seems to be concentrating in front of the Place of Power. I can't say that I like the idea, but that's neither here nor there. I've got to get the screen finished in time. I've no wish for my epitaph to read, 'He did valuable preliminary work.' Did I show you the equations?"

"You told me about them, Sir."

"Beautiful. Absolutely beautiful." Greylock's face was ruddy in the light of the fire and of the beeswax candles. The eyes shone as their owner contemplated the abstractions of his construct. "Trouble is that the pattern's very difficult to hold in the mind," he went on, businesslike again. "It's the most complicated thing I've ever done. It takes all my concentration to reform the ether. Too much and no air or light gets through; too little and everything does. That's what we've got to get right. By the way,'' he said, changing direction suddenly, "how did the Gwyndryth girl fare with the Maze?''

"It let her through, and at my pace. It was odd, though, because she was scared. I could tell she was. She saw nothing; no paths, no barriers, no monsters, nothing. It didn't use her mind at all. It just blanked her out. She didn't like it one little bit, even though it was a very easy passage. She said she didn't want to do it again.''

"I can't say that I'm surprised and it's probably for the best. If word got out that an Untalented had gone through, there'd be a raft of foolhardy young men who'd get themselves into trouble.''

"It must be the unicorns.''

"Must it?''

"Well, I can't think of any other reason.'' Jarrod's heart was beating too loudly and the fire was throwing off too much heat. He squirmed uncomfortably in the chair. Greylock gave him a long, quizzical look.

"I may not be as young as I once was, but there's nothing wrong with my eyes. I've seen the way that you look at her and I saw the way her father looked at our Princess. Anything that affects the royal family is my concern.'' He paused and looked over again. "Oh, don't look so shocked, lad. You don't get to be a Mage if you're not a politician. Why d'you think Ragnor was appointed head of the Council of Regency when Arabella was growing up?''

"I thought it was because we were impartial, above politics. Because we have more important concerns,'' Jarrod replied stiffly, his voice putting the quotation marks of a rote response around the phrases.

"Of course. That's what we always say and that's what the people think, but a Mage who doesn't manage to become an indispensable counselor soon finds that the Crown begins to resent his authority and tries to undermine it. It always happens. That's what makes me so nervous about the situation here.

"I can control Robarth, more or less, but I have absolutely no influence with Justinex and neither does his sister. We must contrive a way, once this,'' and he gestured to the stack of papers and the night beyond the walls, ''is over, to make the two of you friends. He's not much older than you are and you come from a respectable family. I don't know if it'll work; he's pigheaded when it comes to Magic. Resents the fact that his sister had the Talent and not he. We'll have to do it, though, or it'll be very rough going for the Discipline in Paladine once he gets on the throne.'' He paused and took a sip of wine.

''But we've got to solve this one first,'' he said, tapping the papers, ''and I've a nasty feeling that time's running out on us. Our opponents' atmosphere looks darker and denser to me. I've asked the King to have a cloudsteed check made, but he tells me that I'm being an alarmist. Bah! When have I ever been an alarmist?'' He paused inquiringly, but Jarrod knew better than to answer him.

''That's not the worst of it, though,'' the Mage resumed. ''He's opposed to the forcefield.''

Jarrod sat up in surprise. ''Opposed to the forcefield? But that's absurd. Why would he be opposed to it?''

''He says that it'll turn the noble art of warfare into a pastime for cowards.'' The Mage's voice deepened as he imitated the King. ''Dammit man, where's the sport in shelterin' behind some unnatural shield like a green maiden behind a fan? Bad enough that these bloody creatures've taken to pickin' a man off at long distance. They're foreigners. Can't expect 'em to behave like gentlemen. But I'll not have my men sittin' all nice and pretty behind that sort of contraption.''

''But that doesn't make any sense. Hasn't he heard the news from Umbria?''

''Of course he has, but kings can be as stupid as anyone else. Stupider sometimes. One of the duties of a Mage is to know better and to protect the Crown from itself. We serve the realm, not the man.'' Greylock took another pull at his wine.

''Well, what are we going to do?'' Jarrod asked, getting up to poke the fire into a blaze and to feed it.

''Do? We're going to perfect that forcefield as fast as we can. I hear that everything is quiet in front of Angorn and that makes me nervous. I just hope the enemy used up all its new machines there, or decided that they couldn't do the job. Strongsword, for all his knowledge of war, still hasn't fully understood that things have changed. There simply isn't time to retrain the cavalry, even if we had someone like Gwyndryth around. Those Umbrian rotifer things, their flying machines, can't survive a shot from these new fire weapons, nor can cloudsteeds. If we go down, the blow to Magic may well be mortal. So you see, we've got to get the shield up, Robarth or no Robarth.''

"Yes, I see. You can count on me to do everything I can.''

"I know I can, lad, I know.'' The Mage smiled warmly through the firelight. "And that isn't the reason that I dragged you out of bed. I didn't mean to lecture, but I get carried away sometimes and you know how I feel about the forcefield. No, the real reason was this. Now where did I put the thing?'' He got up and went over to the table to search. "Ah yes. Here we are.'' He turned and brought a thick envelope with an imposing seal to the seated Jarrod and handed it to him. "After my, er, my discussion with his Majesty, he asked me to give you this.''

The parchment was so heavy that it was slick to the touch. Jarrod turned it over gingerly, noting the royal crest caught in the wax and his name in ink.

"Break the seal carefully, lad. You'll probably want to save it to show to your grandchildren.''

"What is it?''

"Open it and see.''

Jarrod got up and went to the table, laid the packet flat and found a thin-bladed knife. He broke the seal with great care, so that the top would stay intact, and slid the thick vellum out of the envelope. He read the contents through slowly and then started all over again while the Mage waited silently. There was a smile of anticipation on the lined face.

"But what's this for?'' Jarrod asked bewilderedly.

"For finding the unicorns, of course. You're a national hero and national heros get knighted, especially when things aren't going too well. Congratulations, Sir Jarrod.'' Greylock grinned with pride and delight and rocked back and forth on his heels. "I rather think this calls for a drink, don't you? I got a flagon of Assara up for the occasion.''

"I really don't know what to say, except thank you.''

"Don't thank me,'' Greylock said as he bustled about getting the wine and fetching a glass. "Here, open this for me, will you? No, no. You did it all yourself. Finding those unicorns was no mean feat and you deserve recognition. Now, here's to the new knight of the Order of the Great Maze." They raised their glasses and drank solemnly in the quiet depths of the night.

CHAPTER XXI

JARROD FELT NERVOUS AND BELLIGERENT. IT HAD BEEN A ROUGH ten days. It had cost the lives of two young Magicians, neither of them that much older than he was. They had been part of a group that had secured a sample of the enemy's atmosphere for the Mage to experiment with. The experiment itself had been a success, but the sight of the oleaginous globules rolling back and forth above the table while Greylock and he kept the air beneath them warped to their wills had sickened him. Every time he came across the tightly stoppered, thick, crystal vial that contained their remaining supply of the stuff, he remembered the fate of the two who had paid so dearly to obtain it.

There had been an atmosphere of forced jollity among the six volunteers who had gathered in Greylock's workchamber. They had joked as they had collected their bottles and the long, golden rods that they would clip them to. They had listened to the Mage's instructions and cautionings with youthful impatience. There had been danger in approaching the interface ever since the first spear had hurtled out of the murk and now, with these new weapons, the dangers had multiplied.

In this kind of operation the advantages were all on the other side. No one was entirely sure how well the enemy could see what was going on in Strand space. Earlier generations had assumed that, because Strandsmen could not see into the fog that surrounded the foe, their opponents were similarly handicapped. Recent events had made that unlikely.

The four who had returned were chastened and subdued. The party had reached the hated curtain without problem. In breath-bated silence they had attached the vials. Centuries of experiment had proved that gold and crystal were the only substances that would not dissolve in that denier of natural life. They had dipped the bottles into the fog and all seemed to be going well. Then two of the vessels had been grabbed by unseen hands and the wielders, too slow to let go, had been jerked into the foreign effluvium.

The other four had not panicked. One among them had been swift enough to grab the hem of a gown and, after a brief tugging match, the victim had been relinquished. Of his companion there was no sign. It might have been better, for the living at least, if both had been swallowed up. It was already too late for the rescued one. The lethal decomposition had set in.

The skin, where visible, was mottled and blisters were rising. As the survivors described it, the body seemed to collapse in on itself. The features flowed and dissolved, the limbs shrank and lost their discreteness. All that was left was a pathetic remnant of charred cloth and a black, sludgy pool of what, moments before, had been a human being. The oily residue steamed in the late sunlight and sank into the thirsty ground. A slick stain was the only mark of his passing. It was a heavy price to pay for an experiment.

The thought of the upcoming ceremony did nothing to make Jarrod feel more cheerful. He gazed at his image in the sheet of polished metal morosely and combed his rebellious hair into a semblance of order. The palace barber had done a poor job. He disliked what he saw. He shook his head in distaste at the sharp planes of the cheeks and the long jaw and dabbed forlornly at the indelible red marks. He had taken one of his sennightly shaves and the law that dictates that a man will cut himself when he wants to look his best had been in effect. He tugged at the gown and tried to make the cowl lie flat. He shrugged at himself and headed down the stairs.

He had felt pride when he had helped Greylock erect and hold the field across a broad area. He had been pleased that he had been able to master the intricacies of the pattern, especially since the Mage could not duplicate the feat alone. All that was gone now. He was filled with the certainty that he was going to make a fool of himself in front of the assembled nobility. It was, he admitted, nice to be made a knight and it was revenge of a kind for his abandonment by the rest of his family. But why did it have to be spoiled by a public display? His stomach hurt.

Greylock was waiting for him on the steps, the tiara in a box beneath his arm. He looked the young man over appraisingly.

"Not too bad," he said. "Here, carry this for me, will you? And stop scowling. It won't be that bad. Besides, you're going to have to get used to appearing in public." He smiled and nodded his head toward the Maze. "Let's get going, shall we?" He strode off with Jarrod trailing in his wake.

"No ceremonial robe?" Jarrod asked in a surly voice as they walked.

"I keep them at the palace. I've little reason to wear them over here and it's much easier. There are times when the weather stations have decided that it's time to let the clouds empty themselves, or when the winds get away from them. The robes are basically to impress the laymen and wet and muddy doesn't do it."

Jarrod unlatched the gate and stood aside to let the Mage pass through. He accompanied him along the familiar path and up the incline between the two knolls to the place where the Great Maze waited with implacable patience for fresh minds to feed on.

"Here we are," Greylock said cheerfully. "Tell me, when was the last time that we went through together?"

There was a brief silence before Jarrod said, "Two years, ten months and four days. You brought me to see the Tower right after your things had been moved in. It was just before I went back to the Collegium after my first Greening Day break. We went through together both ways." They were already in the area of uncertainty, but went on talking as if they could see one another, inured to the strangeness by habit. Greylock had caught Jarrod's continuing fears and uncertainties. He talked to put Jarrod at his ease.

"They'll probably put you next to Marianna at the banquet,

since you're both receiving orders and decorations, or whatever they call them.''

"Marianna's going to get the Order of the Great Maze too?'' Jarrod's voice was a mass of conflicting overtones. "I suppose that's only fair: I just hadn't thought of it.''

"Oh, she won't get the Maze. That's just for Paladinians,'' Greylock replied soothingly. "That confers nobility and that wouldn't do at all. She's a foreigner and a girl. No, no, she'll get something else. Order of the Fleece, I expect. The Chamberlain will know. Ah, here we come.''

Jarrod had no feeling that their trip through the Maze was coming to an end, but Greylock's senses proved more acute than his. They emerged suddenly in the clear space before the gate. It had taken, he realized, far less time than it usually did. Evidently the Maze had responded to the Mage's superior powers.

The Lord High Chamberlain's party was waiting for them, grouped before the open doors with their rusty, useless hinges. To either side of them the star points that characterized Stronta's defenses thrust forward. They endured a formal speech of welcome before being ushered through the soaring archway. The alert wardcorn blew warning of their arrival. From there to the Mage's official apartments, Jarrod was submerged in a running lecture on etiquette and procedure. The proto-knight's stomach began to ache again. His only pleasure came in the Chamberlain's evident surprise when he rattled off the instructions with precision and accuracy. They parted company in a flurry of elaborate bows.

"I can't abide that fellow,'' Greylock remarked as the doors closed behind him. "I suppose someone has to know about these kinds of things, but I just wish that I didn't get the feeling that he was made out of feathers. Well, I suppose we better get changed. It wouldn't do for you to be late to your own investiture. For once, we shan't be able to start without you.'' He smiled conspiratorially. "I sent word that you should have a set of suitable clothes waiting for you. I just hope the idiots got the sizes right. Mind you,'' he added, "since you insist on growing every day, I couldn't blame them if they got it wrong. They ought to be in the second bedchamber.''

They were and a quick attempt to wriggle into the hose

justified Greylock's pessimism. Nothing fitted. Jarrod looked down wistfully at the useless outfit of soft leather in butter yellow and brown. The shimmering cream silk shirt fitted, but there was nothing to wear with it. Even the mustard boots that would have completed the outfit were too small.

Jarrod regarded the unwearable collection with frustration and sat down heavily on the bed, oblivious to the fact that he was creasing leather and wrinkling silk. He sighed heavily and then got up and redonned his robe and retied the plain rope around his middle.

He repaired to the full length, polished metal mirror and tugged himself into the best shape he could. He ran his fingers through his hair to subdue it. There was nothing else he could do. It was going to be a fiasco, but the High Chamberlain had only given them half an hour to dress and there was nothing he could do about it. There was no time to get a new set of clothes and he would have to go through the whole thing, presentation to the King, ceremony, everything, in a plain blue robe. Everybody would be looking at him and they would be laughing at him. He wished he were back on the Anvil of the Gods. He wet his finger and rubbed again at the razor nicks.

He heard the Chamberlain knock at the outer door and went back into the anteroom. Greylock, in a dark green gown with runic signs stitched in black and silver, Staff in hand and tiara in place, stood ready and waiting. He raised one eyebrow at the sight of Jarrod, but was kind enough to remain silent. Jarrod went over and answered the door. The Chamberlain stood on the threshold in his official raiment, his wand in hand and a practiced smile on his face. The smile died.

"Why haven't you changed?" he demanded. "Or is this supposed to be a fashion statement? You really must hurry, young man. We don't have very much time and we can't keep his Majesty waiting, oh dear me, no. Off with you now and be quick about it."

"We shall not keep the King waiting, my good man," Greylock said, coming up behind Jarrod. He continued, pitching his speech in the formal mode.

"There are no subjects more loyal to the Crown than we of the Talent and we are pleased to show our humility before his august presence by our restraint in both manner and dress. Why else, think you, is the diadem of the Mage of Paladine set with common diamonds? We are quite ready and accoutered according to our stations, as is proper. Has my friend here been elevated to the peerage yet? Should he then attire himself above his manifest station? You do us an injustice, sirrah. Conduct us now, forthwith.''

The Chamberlain had drawn back at the rebuke and now bowed deeply before one of the chiefest men at court. He swung on his heel and paced his way down the corridor, his back a study in offended dignity and rectitude. Greylock gave Jarrod a wink and a quick smile and moved off. Jarrod followed.

Robarth Strongsword's reaction when Jarrod was presented was reassuringly jovial and his displeasure with Greylock seemed to have evaporated. He stood with one arm around the shoulder of his current mistress. He held a goblet of wine in his other hand.

''I see you are startin' a new tradition, young man,'' he said, ''and I must say I approve. The less a man spends on jewels and clothes, the more he'll spend on weapons.'' Jarrod was aware of the petulant look, quickly stifled, that appeared on the face of the King's paramour, but Robarth continued, sublimely unaware of undercurrents.

''I really should have looked into your circumstances before this. Your father was a good friend of mine, but runnin' a kingdom takes up all ones time. I'm glad, though, that you've turned out so well. Your father would have been proud of you, and so, for that matter, am I.'' Jarrod warmed to the words as the King continued with his self-justification.

''I was goin' to give you some sword trainin', but you ran out on me and tonight we're goin' to celebrate the results. Congratulations, young man. You've grown up to be a credit to the kingdom, and handsome to boot, wouldn't you say so, m'dear?'' He squeezed the woman's ample shoulder and smiled at her. She muttered something uncatchable.

''We need all the help we can get, you know,'' the King continued, turning to Greylock. ''The enemy keeps on testin' us. Sortie after sortie with these nasty new weapons and no hoses. Now they're buildin' up their atmosphere and pushin' it at us.

Can't you do anythin' about that, Mage? After all, what good is Magic doin' us if it can't hold back that revoltin' fug?''

"I do have a solution, Majesty," Greylock said, "but you have been opposed to its use."

"You're talkin' about that field of yours again, aren't you?"

"I am, Sire. I know you don't approve, but I think I can block the advance of their air and, without my field, you will have to give ground by default."

"Oh, very well, then. Deploy the bloody thing. There's no way I can fight that damned stuff. But that's not what we're here for now. We have an authentic, native hero to honor," he said, beaming at Jarrod. "Fascinatin' trip that must have been. We've heard somethin' about it from the Lady Marianna," Jarrod watched the woman on Robarth's arm react, "but you and I must sit down one of thse days and discuss it."

"Your Majesty is too kind," Jarrod replied.

"When are we goin' to see these animals of yours?" the King inquired, but, before Jarrod could answer, the monarch's attention had switched away. "Speakin' of the Lady Marianna, here she comes now." Jarrod had time before he turned round to notice the way the lines around the King's companion's mouth deepened. Then he turned and his own mouth opened.

Marianna had dressed relatively quietly while at Gwyndryth, but now she wore a green satin gown, cut disturbingly low at the bodice. It nipped in close at the waist before curving full over the hips and falling to the floor. There was a gold chain about her throat and a square emerald nestled between the upswell of her breasts. The red-gold hair was caught back and to one side, falling in long ringlets to bare shoulders. A black pearl, simply set, adorned her right hand. There was nothing of the tomboy in her demeanor.

"We were just talkin' about you, my dear," Robarth said, beaming ear to ear as he watched her rise from a deep curtsey. "I must say that you're lookin' excessively well, wouldn't you say so Courtak?" Jarrod heard himself mumble something unintelligent.

Greylock put an arm under the young man's elbow and drew him backward as the King bent over and said something quietly into Marianna's ear that made her throw her head back and laugh

delightedly. It caused emotions to churn in Jarrod, but, before
matters could develop further, the Chamberlain's voice cut across
them and announced the commencement of the ceremonies. The
King proffered his arm to Marianna and Jarrod, as he had been
instructed to, went over and bowed to the Princess Naxania and
escorted her down the stairs and into the Great Hall.

They walked slowly between the long trestle tables to the dais.
The benches were packed and heads turned as they passed.
Jarrod did his best to block them out. He took the Princess to her
seat and then took his place in the empty space at the front of the
platform. He knelt in front of his King. In spite of his practice in
concentration, he was unable to shake his awareness of all those
eyes upon his back, of the coughing and scuffling of feet and,
more intimately, of Marianna kneeling beside him.

The ceremony was mercifully brief. A sword that looked
ridiculously delicate in Robarth's big hand touched him lightly
on each shoulder and then he was rising to a roar of approbation.
He turned and faced the audience, reached out a hand for Marianna and bowed as she sank into a deep curtsey. The clapping
rose to a new crescendo and he stood smiling broadly, enjoying
the palpable rush of enthusiasm and affection that he felt coming
toward them from the assembled courtiers. They performed
their little rite of thanks four more times and then parted and
took their places at the High Table. The King sat and the rest of
the gathering followed suit.

Food, he discovered, was a far more potent magnet than a
newly created knight, and his fear of being stared at proved
needless. Naxania, to his added pleasure, was easy to talk to.
She was in a good mood and made most of the conversational
running as the tureens of soup were ladled and consumed. He
was about to try his luck with the King's mistress, whose name
he still did not know, when he was forestalled by a hush as loud
as the applause had been. He looked up and saw Amarine
coming down the Hall toward them. Pellia was rounding the
screen at the far end and her brothers emerged after her. His
mind flashed out and he found himself on his feet without
realizing that he had risen. His thoughts met smug pleasure at his
surprise.

Heads held high, the gold in mane and tail catching the gleam of candles lit against the early dark, the unicorns paced solemnly up the center aisle. Forelegs raised in unison so that their progress looked like a controlled and beautiful prance, they advanced upon the dais. The stunned silence was absolute and the sound of their hooves on the rushes was clear. Their precision was so exact that, had anyone had their eyes closed, they would have sworn that there was but one creature in the chamber. They ranged themselves, line abreast, in the cleared space before the dais and, with slow grace, dipped their horns and held their heads low for a long beat.

We came to add our congratulations. This is a big day for you. He really is surprised. We fooled him completely, from a gleeful Nastrus. The heads came up and Jarrod hastily bent low in return.

Thank you. Thank you, but how did you get here?

Mam put Lazla and his son to sleep, Pellia explained. *Don't worry, they'll be all right,* Beldun added. *They won't wake up until after we're back so there won't be any hue and cry. You mustn't have them punished. They've been very good to us, but they wouldn't have let us out and we can't get through to them the way we can with you,* Nastrus admonished.

Of course I won't, Jarrod expostulated mentally, *and I really am pleased that you thought of this. That was quite an entrance.*

Mam says we've got to go back. Besides, we can smell that dreadful cooked flesh. I don't know how you humans can do it. Bye, Jarrod, and congratulations again, came Pellia's warm thought. *Bye. Goodbye. See you tomorrow.* They turned with perfect accord and made their way back through the ranks of ogling, open-mouthed diners, with Amarine bringing up the rear in all her magnificence. Every eye followed them until the final froth of her tail disappeared behind the wooden screen.

There was a long pause before the babble of talk exploded. It was as if the assembly had been held in thrall and was now suddenly released from the spell. The unicorns might well have caused the stillness, Jarrod thought as he slowly took his seat again. After all, they had put the two grooms to sleep. There was no end to the surprises when it came to those beasts. The High Table reacted no differently from the rest of the crowd and awed remarks flew.

"What was that all about?" Greylock demanded calmly from beyond the royal paramour.

"They decided to come and congratulate me," Jarrod replied.

"What did they say?" Naxania asked.

"The unicorns thought it would be nice if they came and congratulated Marianna and me on the honor your father has bestowed on us, your Royal Highness." She looked at him with the detachment of a gem assessor and with new-found respect before turning to pass the word along.

Marianna leaned forward from the far side of the King when the news reached her and gave him a radiant smile that made him happier than he had thought possible. The meal resumed and Jarrod had no need to search for topics of conversation. Even Justinex had been impressed and questioned him closely in the withdrawing room after the feast was over. Jarrod was pleased to find himself being addressed as an equal and his good feelings were reinforced by Greylock's evident approval of the whole episode and the way that he had handled himself.

"That's the best thing that's happened for Magic in years," the Mage remarked as they made their way back through the Great Maze. "Our young Prince is going to find it hard to scoff from now on. Our friends have done us a signal service. Oh, yes indeed." They continued on in an easy silence that Jarrod found highly satisfying.

When he was on the point of leaving Greylock to seek his own bed, the Mage said, "You did well, lad, but I hope you won't let all this go to your head. Now, get a good night's sleep. Tomorrow I want to get that forcefield up again and you'll need to be at your best."

"I'd forgotten that Robarth had agreed."

"Well, he did and I've no intention of giving him time to change his mind again. Why d'you think we didn't sleep at the palace tonight?"

"Sleep's what I'll do. I'm exhausted."

He was quite sincere when he said it, but it was a long time before he managed to drop off.

CHAPTER XXII

THE NEXT DAY WAS COLD AND WINDY AND THE LEAVES OF THE bundle-up bushes were drooping as they rode past them on their way to the Causeway. The rawness gnawed at them as they stood atop it and surveyed the terrain. They conferred briefly and then sat side by side on the chariotway, their view obliterated by the parapet. Their memories served them for eyes as they brought a small area of the field into being.

Close up, the leading edge of the shield was shimmering as tiny motes of matter found release in light. It was not unlike looking at a candle flame when the eyes were wet or the irridescent bursting of a thousand tiny soap bubbles. They moved it forward toward the encroaching bulge a league and a half away. Those in the path of its passing would have felt a tingling that would have been put down, as likely as not, to a touch of liver or the result of the previous night's indulgence.

They broadened the shield and raised it until it was higher than the intruding substance and wider. Together, in a concerted rush, they heaved it at the foreign atmosphere, shoving it forward with every particle of energy they could summon. They were aware of the instant of contact and felt the foreign substance yield and retreat. Their triumph was short-lived. There was no knowing what was going on in that blank brown swirl, but it was as if the others had been taken by surprise. They were quick to rally.

The Magicians felt the opposition and their advance slowed

abruptly and then was halted. The pressure built against them. It increased and they sought and found new reserves of strength. The forcefield held its position, but they could not move it forward again. A silent and remote shoving match ensued. The Paladinian protagonists sat atop the wall, their bodies swaying back and forth. Their robes were pressed against their backs by the wind and the sweat poured down into their eyes. They both knew that they could not hold much longer and when Greylock shouted to him to let go, Jarrod dropped the shield with relief.

"We shan't be able to push them back," Jarrod said, panting.

"No, but we can hold them." The Mage took a deep breath and pushed himself upright. "I may have made a strategic error by alerting them to a new hazard, but, without field testing, there was no way of knowing exactly what we had. We can't do it alone, though. It's going to be a full time job and that means training some of the others. We'll have to do it fast, but the main thing is that the screen's a success."

He took a handkerchief from his sleeve and mopped his brow. Jarrod, less elegantly, used the skirt of his robe. The wind began to chill them.

"We've done everything we can today. No sense wearing ourselves out, so we might as well get back and try teaching a couple of men."

"I could do with a bath and a change of clothes," Jarrod agreed as he followed Greylock down the ramp to the waiting horses. Despite the unpleasantness of the day, they rode back slowly, gripped by the lassitude that follows great exertion and soothed by the feelings that accompanied it.

Hall that night was a stark contrast to the meal of the previous evening. With his star, ribbon and medallion safely packed away at the bottom of his clothes press, Jarrod was indistinguishable from his peers. Though they must have known about the previous day's ceremony and had probably heard about the appearance of the unicorns, no one thought to congratulate him and no one made the slightest move to include him in the conversation. He retired to the room at the top of the Tower feeling hard done by.

He refurbished the fire and waited for Greylock to come down from his workroom. When the Mage finally made his appearance, Jarrod noticed that he was moving stiffly and was pale.

He felt a stab of concern that must have been apparent, for Greylock said, "This morning took more out of me than I expected. I feel as if I could do with a nice long holiday. The enemy is usually quiet once harvesttime is passed, but not this year. A bunglebird came in from Ragnor this afternoon, sounded just like him, too, and reported that Celador is getting the same kind of probing attacks.

"I'm worried about the forcefield. We've gone as far as we can and it isn't really enough. It'll take six Magicians, and good ones, to duplicate what we did this morning. My body's telling me that I can't keep it up too long, not without help."

"You've got me."

"That's not the sort of aid I meant. I was talking about using my Staff and the ring. You'll have to use the unicorns, and that worries me."

"The unicorns worry you? What in the world for? You said just last night that they were the best thing that had happened to Magic in years."

"So they are, but we don't know how long they'll stay. And what's going to happen when the colts moult that protective covering? No, I think we're going to have to have something else to fall back on. I think it's time I taught you the words of summoning for the Powers.

"I don't understand them," Greylock admitted with a sudden burst of candor. "Torthon taught them to me syllable by syllable. It isn't the meaning that counts, it's the way you chant the words. You have to get the pitch absolutely right or nothing happens. It's also about time we made you a Staff." He made the last statement very casually, but Jarrod sat up and stared at him.

"But you can't do that," he said over the crackling of the logs. "Only Mages have Staffs."

"That's not entirely true. Only those capable of handling them have them. I admit that when a Magician reaches that sort of level, he's usually a Mage, but it's the man and not the office that does it."

"But I've only just been made a full Magician," Jarrod protested.

"You're very young for it, I grant you that, but, since you came back from the quest, you've shown that you can contain and control great force. That's what counts. The ability to withstand all that extra energy and still be able to direct it. That usually takes years to build up, but you just seem to be made that way." Remade that way, Jarrod thought to himself.

"Anyway," Greylock resumed, "we'll only find out by trying. We'd better take a couple of days off to rest and prepare. I can't say that I'd mind that." He smiled tiredly. "We'll need Naxania, too," he added. "No one does incantations as well as that girl. I don't suppose she'll be too pleased, though."

"Jealous?" Jarrod asked shrewdly.

"That and the fact that no one wants to look their worst when they're thinking of getting married. It's powerful Magic, you know."

"You really think she's going to marry Marianna's father?"

"If she gets her way she will, and she usually gets her way."

"I see," Jarrod said ruminatively.

"Well, never mind all that. Tomorrow we rest and eat and the following day we fast and prepare. I'll send a message to the Princess in the morning. As for you, lad, you're nodding off in your chair. You better take yourself off to bed." He paused and then asked, "Have you got enough blankets? The nights are getting really cold. I wish they could let down some snow. It always feels warmer after it has snowed."

"What are we . . ." Jarrod said as he rose and interrupted himself with a yawn. "Sorry. What are we keeping it up there for? To dump on the battlefield if things get rough?" Greylock grunted assent. Jarrod cocked his head and looked down at the Wizard.

"I wonder if snow gets through the field?" he said playfully. "We should probably test for that. I mean, we wouldn't want not to be thorough, now would we?"

"That's quite enough of that." There was humor in the voice. "Oh, one last thing. I'd like you to write out the steps for generating the forcefield for me. I'd like to send a copy to Ragnor, along with my equations. They're going to need it just as much as we are." He got up creakingly and fussed with the fireguard.

"I feel battle looming, lad, and I'm not at all sure that I'll make it through this one." His tone was leadenly serious now. "I also have to take precautions in case anything happens to you. So, you see," he added with an obvious attempt to lighten the atmosphere again, "I'd be obliged if you'd get it right for once."

"Yes, Sir. Yes, Sir. I feel as if I were back in Dameschool." He made the little, mock-military salute that he used to have to give his teacher and left with an impudent grin.

He wrote the stages out in the morning and sent them upstairs by the duty boy. Then he took himself off to the stables to take the colts out for some exercise. He half hoped to bump into Marianna, but she was nowhere around. The colts seized on his thoughts and teased him unmercifully. He took it in good part, having long since realized that he could keep nothing from them. He had been ashamed at the sexual fantasies that they had pried loose until he saw, with mixed emotions, that they found them hilarious. Seen through their eyes, however, he had to admit that the colts had a point.

In many ways he felt more comfortable in their company than with his own kind. When he was with them he lived in their heads and they in his and there was increasingly less need for questions. They constantly went beyond his comprehension, but it didn't matter. He accepted and was accepted. He stayed with them until it was time to go and get ready for Hall, aware that he would have no time to spare for them for the next few days. The thought saddened him.

The sun came up on the day of preparation, but it remained hidden behind lowering banks of clouds. They were tinged with an unhealthy yellow and swollen with undelivered snow. Jarrod felt a kind of kinship with them as he climbed the stairs. His throat tasted wry from the potions that the herbalist had given him and the previous night's larger-than-usual dinner still distended the stomach beneath the rope girdle. He had already emptied his sleeve pockets and once he reached the workroom he hitched his robe up clear of the floor and folded the sleeves back.

He had helped Greylock get ready so many times that there was a comfortable sense of familiarity attached to the ritual.

He checked on the clay in the buckets by the windows and, without waiting for Greylock, got out the cleaning gear. He went to work clearing the unruly surface of the table. He cleaned out the grate and lugged the ashes down the stairs. He climbed back up with kindling and relaid the fire. He was sweeping the floor when the Mage walked in. Greylock looked rested and seemed to be in a cheerful mood.

"Morning, lad. That as far as you've got?"

"Morning, Sir. It would have gone faster if I had had some help. Besides, I've always thought that the only reason we go through this is so you can have your workroom cleaned. If you can make a pentacle work in an open field, why do I have to scrub this floor?" Greylock chose to answer his teasing as if he had asked a serious question.

"You know as well as I do that we have to make sure that there is nothing to break our concentration. No bubbling from retorts, no dust or fumes to make one sneeze. I can't take any chances when you're around."

"Just because you can't concentrate," Jarrod began again, trying to cover his nervousness.

"Wait 'til you get to be my age, young man. In the meantime, I'll thank you to do more cleansing and less clacking. Did you charge the water?"

"Not yet, Sir."

"All right, I'll do that while you finish the floor."

They went to work in silence. The routine held its own satisfactions for Jarrod and the room gleamed when he was finished. Greylock had long since infused the water with the properties that he desired and now he went around dipping his blunt fingers into the embossed silver bowl that held it. He spattered drops across the floor and into the corners, around the door jamb and the window frames, chanting softly as he went.

When he had completed the preliminary rites, he turned to Jarrod and said with grave formality, "There is a Staff to be made. Shall it be yours?"

"Only if I prove fit."

"Will you use it well?"

"As well as I am able."

"Are the runes and responsibilities known to you?"

"They are known to me."

"Right then," Greylock said, dropping into normal tones and rubbing his hands briskly together, "there's a shepherd's crook in the cupboard. Be a good lad, would you?" He smiled encouragingly and took two vials of powder from the rack next to the parchment boxes. He sprinkled them unerringly in parallel straight lines until there were two squares, one within the other. Jarrod walked around the markings holding the long, plain, curve-headed crozier.

"Why so big, Sir?" he asked, nodding to the double square.

"The wood has a character of its own," the magister replied, "and there's no knowing how it will respond when the runes are branded into it. Now, put it in the middle and we'll activate the lines."

Jarrod did as he was told and the two men seated themselves on opposite sides of the Mage's design. They faced one another. With the impeccable timing born of long practice, they went within simultaneously and the powder lines began to give off light.

The air between the two pairs of sightless eyes crackled as the light crept along the sides of the figures; amber within, blue on the outside. Sparks began to play around the wood. The movements of the two chests slowed, but became larger as the breathing deepened. Both began to intone in unison, varying their pitch until the voices rang off each other like a wet finger running around the rim of a crystal goblet. As the harmony became more intense, the crook began to expand and writhe.

Both men were rocking backward and forward in perfect time as they chanted and, as the harmonies intensified, the wood lashed around its insubstantial enclosure like a caged warcat. Then it was transfixed by the first rune. The design pinioned it at the midpoint and the wood curved away from it as if trying to escape. It strained itself into a shallow arc as it thrashed like an unbroken yearling. The rune was implacable. It held fast and dug a smooth and spiralling trench around the captive wood. The crook shuddered to stillness and submitted.

The pitch of the voices modulated and counterpoint appeared

in the chant as the litany of the runes continued. As each strophe
was completed, the corresponding figure was etched upon the
stave, some crimson, some gold, some green, until the visible
surface of the now quiescent wood was covered. The voices rose
and fell and the Staff turned itself obediently, all defiance gone,
until there was almost nothing to be seen beneath the symbols of
summoning. Finally it lay at rest, spent and charged.

Jarrod was the first to emerge and was surprised that he felt as
fresh as he did. He glanced over his shoulder at the water clock
and confirmed his feeling that most of the day had passed. His
throat felt rough and his mouth was dry. He was suddenly aware
of the floorboards beneath his hip bones. He looked across at his
master in the dimness and noted the depth of the breathing and
the renewed pallor. The skin below his eyes had slackened and
the corners of his mouth drooped. By contrast, the top lip had
contracted and was striated by little vertical lines. What they had
done was more advanced than anything Jarrod had done before
and now the Mage was taking a very long time to come back.

There was nothing that Jarrod could do at this stage and
Greylock, he knew, wasn't the type to let himself be caught
within. He unwound himself to his feet and went in search of
water. There wasn't too much in the ewer and it was gone far too
fast. He eyed the basin of charged water doubtfully, but his thirst
was too demanding. He took a cautious mouthful. The liquid
made his throat tingle as it went down, but it helped. He took
another gulp and then went downstairs to replenish the ewer.
Greylock was bound to need some when he came round.

The Mage was still seated when he got back and Jarrod turned
his attention to the Staff. It looked fatter and heavier than it had.
There was no trace of the earlier hook and it seemed to pulse
gently. In the center, the twisting runes had graven both embell-
ishment and a place where the hand could grip strongly. It
looked for all the world like an enormous ceremonial bow waiting for a string. There was something immensely appealing in
the recumbent wood and he felt himself drawn to it, while
wishing that it was not quite so gaudy. He reproved himself for
the thought and then his attention was caught by the sounds of
stirring. He turned and saw Greylock climbing wearily to his
feet. The Mage winced and kneaded the small of his back before

coming over. He moved heavily. He stared down at the new Staff.

"That's interesting," he said. "I don't think I've ever seen one like that before." His voice rasped and creaked as if from long neglect rather than from overuse. Jarrod hurried to pour him a cup of water and Greylock drank greedily. He handed the cup back when it had been drained and wiped his mouth with his forearm. He looked at the Staff again.

"Maybe it'll straighten out when Naxania performs the incantations to bind it and make it permanent." His arms hung slackly by his sides and his shoulders sloped forward. "I don't know about you, lad," he said slowly, "but I'm going to lie down for a while before she gets here. There's a lot more to do, so I suggest you rest up as well. We can leave your Staff here. It'll be quite safe." He moved tiredly around the glowing squares and Jarrod came and took some of his weight on his arm as he guided him down the stairs to his rooms.

The Princess was punctual. Naxania was always on time. Greylock, to Jarrod's concerned eye, looked no more rested than he had two hours before. When the Princess doffed her cloak, Jarrod was obscurely pleased to see that she wore the plain blue gown of a common Magician. In it she paced about the square and scanned the Staff intently.

"They are strong, these runes of yours, Magister. They will need a deal of containing to bind them in. I do not think I have seen any that started off this bright."

"I know," Greylock replied. "There are very considerable forces pent up in there. Our young friend," and he smiled with rueful respect, "is getting rather difficult to keep up with, though I don't think he realizes it as yet. Do you think you will be able to handle it?" The Princess was silent for a long moment as she concentrated on the Staff.

"Not by myself. Not this time. There are so many of them crowded onto the wood. If I can draw energy from the two of you, I ought to be all right, but it is going to be a very long night."

Greylock sighed. "I was afraid of that. I shall of course support you. I do not know how much I have left to give, but I suspect Courtak has enough for both of us. Well, I suppose we had better get on with it. The sooner we start, the sooner we shall all be able to get some proper rest and recharge our energies. Come, lad, leave us get settled. Backs to the incanter remember.''

The two men sat themselves down on the bare floor, inches apart. Behind them, Naxania took several deep breaths, raised her arms, palms out and fingers spread, and launched into the first incantation of binding. It would weave in and out of her continuing threnody, a theme in the mounting motifs of control that she would impose upon the captive wood. It would culminate in the last, great incantation, the so-called Song of Permanence.

The air began to glow around her and it assumed a bluish tinge. The rich, contralto voice sang on, quiet and sweet for the moment, snaring and cajoling rather than demanding and controlling. Jarrod found it bewitching. He had never heard the Princess perform like this and had not anticipated the sheen on the voice. Since she was making no demands on him, he allowed the coils of melody to slide around him and add to the lightheadedness engendered by the day's fasting and exertions.

An hour and then another ran down the water clock and the thrilling voice rolled on, rising and falling, soaring in exhortation, dipping, low and resonant, to pin down the runic energies and force them into the very fabric of the wood. It filled the grain with compressed power. The room grew warm, though the fire lay unkindled in the grate. Perspiration began to trickle down their faces and there was a mounting awareness of strain in the air. Halfway through the third hour, Naxania's voice began to sound hard and roughness scraped its edges. Deep inside themselves, the two men were conscious of a reaching out and they began to direct a gentle flow of support toward her. The voice regained its purity and rose as joyfully as a cloudsteed that has been confined too long to earth.

The timbre of the incantations changed subtly and the unspoken demand for help grew. The harmonics became commandingly dissonant. The fingers of the incantress had curved, the arms were lower, the elbows bent, so that she looked as if she was pressing down on the air that separated her from the Staff. As each phrase was aimed at it, the wooden shaft bucked and clattered against the planks as if the assault were physical. The light above it and around the Princess had grown and was ruffed in orange. Sparks played intermittently along the periphery as the outlined figure swayed in time to the rhythms that drove her.

She was drawing heavily on the energies of the men behind her, unaware that she was doing so, lost in the exercise of her special talent. She had gone far beyond the point that she had thought of, secretly, as her limit. The occasion had swept her up and thrust her toward greatness. She was indifferent to the fact that the Mage was groaning.

Jarrod was wrapped deep in the Magic now and could hear nothing but the compulsive glory of Naxania's voice, oblivious to the sounds being torn from Greylock's throat. He felt the ebbing of force and stretched himself to reinforce his master. It was not enough. He opened his awareness to the Place of Power in the same way that he did to the unicorns and was rewarded by a surge of energy. It coursed straight through him and out into his companions. He was not conscious of it, but his body was shaking and the teeth chattered in his mouth.

The Princess' voice rose in volume in response to his sending and began to pour forth ecstatic sounds of jubilant command. Jarrod felt the pounding excitement of energy and an exquisite sense of physical pleasure wind up tight in him. They burst forth in a transcendental release as the final note belled out. The lights around Naxania and those that held the Staff confined died and the room was dark.

It was some time before Jarrod was able to rouse himself and grope for the tinderbox. That located, he crawled on hands and knees toward what he hoped was the corner where he had left the tapers. He detoured widely so as not to blunder into the extinguished squares. His arms and legs were trembling with the effort required and he felt weak and depleted. He was gripped by the inevitable let down that was one of the aftermaths of the making of Magic. His searching fingers found a length of beeswax and he got the wick to catch at the fifth attempt. He struggled to his feet and put it in a holder on the table and then retrieved and lit two more. He carried a fourth back with him.

The warm, yellow light showed him the Princess collapsed in an armchair by the wall. The long, black hair was hanging in wet

strands, the face shiny and sweat-streaked. Her eyes were shut
and her mouth hung open. He went to Greylock first. The old
man lay on the floor, toppled on his side. His robe concealed
whatever movement of chest there might have been and Jarrod
sought anxiously at the throat for a pulse. His fingers dug into
the slack and wrinkled skin.

The Mage looked ghastly in the candlelight and anxiety mounted
in Jarrod until he came upon a weak, but regular bumping. He
sat back on his heels, giddy with relief. After a while he got up
and hooked his hands under Greylock's arms and dragged him
over to the chair by the fireplace. It took several attempts to
heave the inert weight up into it and then he staggered to another
armchair and collapsed into it panting. He slid into sleep without
even glancing at the Staff lying in black-bordered state in the
middle of the floor.

He awoke with a start from a rest as deep as any made by
mandragore and looked around slowly. The tapers had burned
halfway down. Greylock's head was canted on his shoulder and
a rattling snore came and went from the slack mouth. Against the
wall, the Princess sat with her hands hanging and her head fallen
forward, her hair curtaining lankly down. He pushed himself up
and tested his legs. They were shaky, but they held him. He
walked gingerly to the center of the room and looked down at the
Staff in the burned-out boxes.

It was still curved, but the runes had darkened and there was a
shine to the whole as if it had been glazed and fired in a kiln.
Without stopping to think, he bent down and took hold of the
spiral design in the middle of the arcing nine foot length. He
held it, like a bowstave, with the points toward him. The Staff
twisted effortlessly in his grip and reversed itself so that the
horns faced away from him. He felt the wood flow beneath his
fingers until it conformed to his hand. His arm tingled as he
hefted it. The balance was perfect. It felt substantial, but it
moved with the ease of a quarterstaff.

"What do you think you are doing?" The Princess' voice was
weak and hoarse, but it startled him. "Do you not know that if
you cannot control it it will revert to mere wood? All that work,
my best work ever, gone in an instant?" She was angry and
indignant. "How could you think of testing it without us?"

Jarrod turned slowly to face her, the Staff topping him by a foot. He was exalted and her interruption an unneeded dent in his mood. He looked at her and saw a haggard, limp-haired woman. Understanding and compassion mingled in him pleasantly.

"Gently, gently, my Princess," he said in the tones reserved for beloved but fractious children and pets. "You have wrought exceeding well and the work will endure. There will be songs penned about this night and the name of Naxania of Paladine will go down in memory for as long as songs are sung. There will be many glories ahead of you, I am sure, but this night will be accounted one of them. As to the Staff, you see how it bends to my will. It is a wonder created not by you, nor by me, nor yet by the man who taught us both. It was made by the three of us with the support and participation of those that dwell within the circle of enchantment."

"Did you really feel them, or are you just saying that?" Naxania's eyes were wide. She was still challenging him, but she was subdued by his aura of control and authority.

"Oh yes," Jarrod replied, even as he felt the unnatural certainty slipping from him. "I felt them. Toward the end Greylock was faltering. Your song was growing ragged to my ear and I didn't think that I had enough energy left to support him and to keep you going, so I reached out to them and they answered me." Both heads turned to the chair by the fireplace where the Mage lolled in oblivion.

"Is he all right?" Naxania's senses, attuned by years of court intrigue, latched onto the change in tone. She may have been wearier than she had ever been in her life, but her training was so ingrained that it was instinctive.

"I think so. The heart's steady, not too strong, but steady and, as you can hear, there's not much wrong with his lungs." He, too, was aware of his loss of momentum and, to cover it, he went over and shook the Mage gently. Greylock grunted and the mouth made smacking sounds before it closed. He gave a small snort and returned to a deeper level of sleep. The Princess pushed herself up slowly. She joined Jarrod and they both looked down with fondness and respect.

"We'd best leave him here for the moment," she said, back to her usual habit of command.

"I'll rouse the night boy and send him to get some help," Jarrod countered. Under normal circumstances he would never have countermanded her, but, for the moment, the situation had changed and the rules of rank had shifted. He looked over at the Princess and was moved by her manifest tiredness. "Are you strong enough to return to the palace, Highness?" Half a day ago that kind of question would have been unthinkable from one of his station, but so much had changed in such a short time. "Shall I have them make up one of the rooms for you?"

He peered closely at her in the wavering taper light, taking in the splotched complexion and the circles under the eyes. It could have been the lighting, but she didn't look that much older, despite the magnitude of the Magic they had wrought. His eyes flicked to the Mage. His skin sagged and, even though his hair was damp, there were no traces of grey left in it.

"We had better get some rest," Naxania said, interrupting his train of thought, "and I think that I shall sleep better in my own bed. It would probably be more sensible to ride than to try to confront the Great Maze. I shall take it slowly."

CHAPTER XXIII

JARROD KNEW THAT IT WOULD BE A WHILE BEFORE GREYLOCK recovered so, after Making the Day, he went back to bed and indulged himself in dream-clogged sleep. He spent the next day riding and playing with the colts. He let them explore the corners of his mind and relived his experiences. Only Pellia reacted with the enthusiasm he had hoped for. It was the first prolonged period he had spent with them in quite a while and he noticed that, far more often than they used to, they went off into realms where he could not follow. There was a lurking fear in him that soon he would lose them altogether. If they caught his feelings, and he knew that they must have, they made no reply, gave no reassurance.

He exercised them on the third morning and had an unsatisfactory meeting with Marianna. She was waiting at the stables when they returned and was distant and perfunctory with him. All she wanted to do was to take Amarine out and practice with her. All Jarrod's recent feelings of happiness and of being in control were eroding.

He sought out Agar Thorden from whom all administrative orders flowed, and obtained permission to train four Magicians in the use of the forcefield. He spent two days in drilling them and then, accompanied by the three colts, took them off to the Upper Causeway for the practical application. He had sensed some reluctance on the part of his colleagues to being tutored by a younger man, but all that was banished by the presence of the unicorns.

They tried three times to think the shield into being, but failed to bind the necessary components. He built it for them and handed it over. It collapsed. They went over the formulae together and, once again, he brought the forcefield to life. The others joined him and it held. When he withdrew it wavered and dissolved. He kept them at it all that day and all the next day and, in the end, they achieved mastery and held it up without him.

On the ninth morning after the creation of the Staff, Diadra grudgingly allowed him to see his master. Jarrod, though prepared, was shocked by the evident frailty of the man propped up against the bolsters.

"Ah, you brought me the Staff," the recumbent figure said. "Didn't impress Diadra though, did it?" A phlegmy chuckle bubbled from the wattled throat. "That's the trouble with the motherly types. They won't let go of the image of you as a six-year-old with a runny nose and holes in the knees of your britches." The effort was costly and the breath whistled in and out uncomfortably. "Come over here," Greylock said after a long pause, "and let me see it."

Jarrod approached the bed and laid the Staff across the Mage's lap. He sat on the edge of the bed while the shaking hands caressed the long wood like hesitant butterflies.

"Splendid; just splendid." He looked up and his smile deepened the wrinkles. "It's stronger than mine, I'll wager," there was no trace of envy in him, "but then I didn't have the help of the Princess, nor of you. See you take good care of it, lad. Strand will have need of it." He reached out and patted Jarrod's hand. "Now, tell me," he resumed, "what's going on out there? Diadra tells me nothing. She doesn't want to worry me. The silly woman doesn't realize that not knowing worries me more. How are the unicorns?"

"The colts are fine and so is Amarine, as far as I can tell. Marianna has her out every day. The army is mustering behind the Upper Causeway and there are still skirmishes every now and then. That's about all I know. I've been trying to get the field going."

"You've been putting the forcefield up all by yourself?" The old eyes were bright and inquisitive.

"Well, yes and no. I've been teaching four of the men. We can contain their atmosphere now and keep it where it is, but we can't push it back. Of course, every night, when we're not there, it comes creeping forward."

"Talk to Thorden. Tell him I sent you and get him to organize a roster. He's first class at that sort of thing. Couldn't run the place without him." The wheezing was becoming more pronounced and the pauses between the phrases longer.

"I'll do that, Sir, and I should probably get on with it. If we are going to keep the shield up full time, I'll have to train a lot more men." He prepared to leave before he tired the Mage too much and brought Diadra's wrath down about his ears.

"Umph, it's obviously time I was up and about again and that means that I'll have to have a blazing great row with that tyrant in the morning. I don't think I'm up to it today," Greylock admitted.

"I don't think you should rush things," Jarrod said hastily. "We're going to need you very badly in a bit and it's best that you be as strong as possible."

"You're just as bad as she is. Oh well, thank you for bringing me the Staff." He stroked it again and seemed reluctant to give it up.

It was another sennight before Greylock was allowed to leave his quarters, a sennight that Jarrod spent instructing the new men and taking yet more lessons from the Mage. His new status made no difference there. A bunglebird arrived from Celador and Greylock used it as his excuse to get back into action. It reported success in duplicating the forcefield, though how many Magicians it took to do it was unclear. The bird gave a different number every time it repeated the message.

More ominously, it also brought word that sandcats had appeared on the Westerly borders. They had not been seen since the land had first been reclaimed and made fertile, driving the animals deep into the Unknown Lands and it was not pleasant to contemplate what might be pushing them back into the moist regions they abhorred.

Once he had escaped from Diadra's clutches, Greylock had

himself carried to the Causeway in a litter to visit the four
Magicians who were working the shield. He took Jarrod and the
other twelve on the roster with him. He studied the enemy's
position carefully and then gave them all a tongue lashing for
allowing the foreign atmosphere to advance so far. It was unfair
and they all knew it, but it stiffened their resolve nonetheless.

The Mage was no easier on the rest of the Outpost and men
and women were sent off to scour the woods South of the palace
for fresh stocks of herbs and roots. Others were set to weather
duties in an effort to blow back the encroaching, brown peninsula. It didn't work. It kept the cloudsteeds grounded and that
infuriated the King. They tried bombarding the area with lightning, but it was like being blindfolded and trying to fish in the
sea with a trident.

Greylock's preoccupation was broken by a summons from the
Palace and Jarrod was called back from the Causeway to join
him.

"You might as well find out what one of these audiences is
like. Besides, I suspect I shall need the moral support," was the
way that Greylock phrased his invitation.

Robarth was dictating to a scribe when they presented themselves. He looked up and broke off.

"Well, it's about time you showed up," was his opening
remark and his tone left Jarrod in no doubt that they were in for a
rough time.

"What are you fellers doin' about that disgustin' brown wen
out there? No one's been able to move through the gate for a
sennight now, what with the wind howlin' and the lightnin'
scarin' the life out of the horses. Doesn't seem to do any good
though, does it?"

"Alas no, Sire," Greylock replied with the patience born of
long practice. "We do not seem to be able to dislodge it, though
we have prevented it from coming any closer to the Causeways."

"Don't you fellers have any counter spells or anythin'?" the
monarch demanded, dismissing the scribe with a wave of his
hand. "What's the good of havin' Magicians if they can't deal
with a small cloud?" The scribe was backing out hastily and
Jarrod stood very still. Stories of the royal temper were legion,
but he hadn't been close to one of the eruptions before. There

were streaks of white in the King's hair and, as he rose from his chair, his long robe could not conceal the swell of his paunch, but he was a formidable figure for all that.

"Well, what are you goin' to do about it?"

"We are holding it back, Sire, Sir Jarrod and I, with the forcefield that we created, but . . . ."

"I still don't like the idea of your Motherless field. What is my army goin' to do, pray tell? I had to sit the last battle out, but I'm damned if I'm goin' to sit around through this one." There was a flush creeping up Strongsword's neck.

"But Sire . . ."

"Silence Sorcerer!" The words came out in a roar and the King looked at Greylock with blazing eyes. "Warfare has been my life and it has always been the most honorable of occupations. Now I am expected to stand by and settle for a stalemate achieved by invisible fortifications and incredible animals? I'll not have it, my Lord Magician. You belittle me, Sir. You give me a life that is meanin'less and I tell you that I will not have it!" He was shouting and the cords of his neck stood out. The face was flushed and, at the temple, a small, blue worm pulsed and jumped.

Greylock allowed silence to return to the room before he said, in a carefully level voice, "That is not so, your Majesty. The field cannot stop heavy objects. It does not even slow them down appreciably. Their soldiers will be able to get through it and so will ours. It was designed to hold back their atmosphere and to stop the new weapons that the Holdmaster of Gwyndryth and others have described. Not the vehicles themselves, of course, but the flame that they throw.

"I know you think that such protection is unmanly, but, in fact, what the shield does is to even things up. It prevents them from killing us at long range and gives archers and foot soldiers a fighting chance again. It brings back the sporting element that the enemy had eliminated." Robarth grunted, mollified but not convinced.

"Besides, Majesty," Greylock continued, pursuing his advantage, "what other option do we have? We can fight the creatures, but we have never been able to fight their atmosphere. If we drop the shield they will win a bloodless victory."

"I suppose you're right, but I still don't like it," the King said grumblingly as his complexion returned to normal. "Things seem to be gettin' more complicated these days. Justinex seems to understand them, but I can't say that I do. Oh all right, keep the blasted thing up. But find me a way to destroy the bastards, you hear me?"

"As your Majesty commands." Greylock bowed and Jarrod hurriedly followed suit. The Mage turned and left the audience chamber, but Jarrod backed all the way to the door.

"Phew." He expelled a long breath when they were safely outside. "He can be rough, can't he? What brought that on?"

"The unenviable process of getting older. Problems with the new mistress perhaps?" Greylock replied as they moved down the corridor. "It's a bit early for it, but he may well have been drinking and that makes him bellicose. You mustn't pay too much attention to it. He needs to blow up and shout every so often. It makes him feel better and it keeps the Court on its toes. He usually comes round pretty quickly and he doesn't bear grudges.

"Justinex is calmer than his father, but a great deal more stubborn. There are times when I'm tempted to use the Voice on him; on both of them, for that matter. Luckily, the Prince doesn't feel the same way about the forcefield as his father."

When they got back to the compound, Greylock called off the assaults by the elements. As the usual Winter weather returned, the pace of preparation for battle intensified. Squadrons of cloudsteeds took to the skies and men and materiel began to move through the gate in increasing numbers.

Marianna, wearing light armor, her hair caught back in a plain gold war circlet, took to riding Amarine along the camp fires at dusk. She controlled the big unicorn with a silver bit and a silken bridle. She was perfectly well aware that they had become a symbol of hope and she delighted in the role. Naxania, not to be outdone, rode her chariot along the forward lines.

The skies were filled by wheeling cloudsteeds and the ground covered with warcats, their warriors, by cavalry and pikemen and archers. All were drilling in formations that had been old when their fathers were young. The Magicians on the wall carried on their silent and invisible battle. Jarrod remained on the

Causeway long after his tours of duty were over, fighting to push the brackish air back across the violated ground. Hatred of it welled in him and he took to dosing himself and eating with fanatical care. What time off he permitted himself he spent exercising the colts, partly because experiencing a ride through their eyes and muscles always exhilarated and refreshed him. He slept deeply and Marianna rarely intruded.

He was dreamless when the night duty boy roused him and told him that there was trouble on the Causeway. The candle sitting on his clothes press responded to his will and he dressed hurriedly. He grabbed up his Staff. Greylock was at the stables before him.

"What sort of trouble is there?" Jarrod asked over his shoulder as he fetched a saddle from the tack room.

"Don't know," Greylock replied shortly. "Just trouble." He swung up and held his horse in check while he waited. "Not going to take the unicorns?"

"I've got my Staff and we can always send for them if you think they're really needed." Greylock nodded and put his heels to his horse's flanks.

They cantered to the reserves' encampment, were challenged and passed through. They trotted past the sleeping barracks and walked their horses up the ramp to the Causeway. Once on top they tethered the steaming animals at the Southern parapet and approached the four immobile shapes that were the Magicians. They leaned against the forward parapet and stared out. All they saw were the points of light that marked the sentinel fires, but they could feel the strain.

Without waiting for instructions, Jarrod took himself and his Staff to the far end of the line. He and Greylock slipped with habituated ease into the support of the shield. They were immediately aware of the pressure. It was as if a giant slug had come up against a clear pane of glass and was pushing at it with uncomprehending determination, its underside spreading and flattening across the surface. Jarrod experienced the flow of power from the Mage and gradually fed in his own. He held the pattern clear in his mind and made adjustments to keep everything even. Given the structure of the field, he felt like a spider making minute repairs to a gigantic web. Then, as if they were bright

children transferring string games from one set of hands to
another, they took over the skeins and allowed the others to relax
and disengage.

It was a measure of their superior skills that not only could
they hold the lines by themselves, they also had sufficient concentration to spare for speech.

"The thrust is a lot stronger than it's ever been," Jarrod
remarked.

"How long has this been happening?" Greylock inquired.

"About an hour, I would guess," one of the other Magicians
replied. "It's been pushing us back. I don't know exactly how
much ground we've lost."

"You did well to call us," Greylock said mildly. "Now get
back to the Outpost and send up your replacements. Courtak and
I will hold them until they get here. And have Thorden send
word to the King that an attack is on the way."

The two turned their concentration within and were unaware
of the departure of their colleagues as they strained to push the
foreigners' intrusion back. Jarrod became subliminally aware of
the language of the Place of Power and knew that Greylock was
calling on his allies for aid. He groped with his left hand for his
Staff and laid it across his lap. He began the incantation that
awoke the runes and felt them respond. They grew brighter
under his voice until he seemed to be holding a bow of light
and then he fed the extra energy into the screen.

The pressure lessened and then returned in full force. They fed
still more into the web, but the enemy was obdurate. They knew
that the shield was flowing outward and upward, expanding to
accomodate its new resources. It made no forward progress, but
neither did the enemy. They battled thus, in silence and in sweat.
They ignored the urge to break off and Make the Day, but they
could not budge the foreign pestilence.

Reinforcements arrived as light began to seep into the bilious
sky. When the four fresh Magicians had taken their places,
Greylock detached himself and went to fetch his own Staff and
the colts. Jarrod stayed and labored. When the Mage returned
and replaced him, Jarrod broke away wearily, feeling attenuated
by the struggle, and went over and embraced the unicorns. They

sensed his tiredness and his dejection and their presence in his
mind was a soothing balm.

They watched over him while he put nosebags on the horses
and were with him when he rolled himself up in his cloak and
surrendered his body to oblivion. He was ignorant of his surroundings, of the hardness of the pavement beneath him, the
creeping cold and the bugles that called the army into full alert.
He was unaware of the toing and froing of officers and men and
of the King's visit. His spirit was exhausted and he slept.

The armies of Paladine were ranged beyond the Giants' Causeway when he woke. He rolled to his feet in the soft light of
daymoon time and stretched to get the kinks out. He had slept
the clock far down and his body felt as sore as if he had been
involved in a long wrestling bout. Greylock was standing behind
four seated Magicians, leaning on his Staff, and the colts were
watching the goings on, their heads over the parapet. They felt
Jarrod rouse and were trotting toward him before he tried to
communicate. They might have been growing beyond him, but
the ties seemed closer now. They were bored and hungry.

*I can't take you back now, I've got to relieve Greylock. He
must have been manning the shield for at least ten hours.*

*No need. We know the way. We are perfectly capable of
getting back to the stables by ourselves.*

*All right then, but I may need you later if the enemy gets any
stronger.*

We shall always answer your need, was Pellia's thought as the
three trotted off down the ramp. Jarrod watched them go and
then picked up his Staff and went to join Greylock.

He sat down next to the end Magician and let the phrases of
summoning trickle through his mind. He spoke the words aloud
with quiet resonance and the Staff began to glow. By the time
the crooning ceased, he was filled with a feeling of confidence
and all his minor aches were banished. The extra surge he
brought to the forcefield made no difference to the enemy, but it
did enable Greylock to slip out.

"I'm going to go back and get something to eat and take a
nap," he announced, realizing as he said it that he was far more
tired than he cared to admit. It was as well that he was as hale as
he was. The creation of the Staff had depleted him more than he

had anticipated. He had gambled that there would be enough time to recover before the enemy struck and it looked as if he was going to lose.

''I'll send a runner up. You're to call me if there are any major changes. The new contingent is on its way. With this extra burden, we're going to have to work shorter shifts.'' It was easier to keep the weariness at bay when he was organizing things.

Jarrod heard him but remained within his concentration. There was leeway enough for stray thoughts, however, and they were not comforting. Greylock was putting a good face on things and the others didn't seem to sense that anything was amiss, but Jarrod knew the man too well. He was far from his old self. If the enemy attacked in force, the colts and he were going to have to take the main brunt of it. A filament of unease squirmed in his belly. Was he up to it? He began to wish that the colts were with him now. Still, he thought, I've got the Staff.

His Staff was proving to be something of an enigma. It seemed to have protected him from the kind of exhaustion that Greylock was going through. He had been bone weary after the long spell of duty, but felt fine. The Staff, however, hadn't made the difference at the interface that he had expected it to. Perhaps he had somehow failed it? He was conscious of the pricklings of anxiety. They were new to each other, he reassured himself. The Staff felt like an old and trusted companion, but they needed time to adapt to one another. Perhaps a fairly tranquil time like the present would be a good time to experiment. He settled down into the patterns of pressure and resistance and stepped up his involvement.

At about the third hour, when the spirits of men are at their lowest ebb, when the body is well-nigh shut down and doubts creep in to haunt even the most worthy, there was a sudden, dramatic change. Out in the unending blackness sunbursts flowered. The sharp, stinging shock of it jolted Jarrod. There was a cry of pain from one of the other Magicians and the field wavered. Fear quickened his reactions and energy was released into the shield. The hitherto invisible surface lit up under a bombardment of efflorescent color. The effect was spectacular. The darkness turned to day.

It was as if all the Summer lightning in the world had been collected together and loosed. The fowl around Stronta crowed and the birds began to sing. Men and women woke and clung in the special terror that only the unknown can generate and the kina bellowed even though their udders were not full. The light, reflected from the underbellies of the clouds, turned from red to white and blinded those who might have thought of flight.

No time, Jarrod thought as he struggled to hold the shield together. The careful pattern that the Magicians had created and imposed on Nature was warping. No colts; no Greylock. The runewood twitched in his grasp as he repeated the incantation that linked them.

Energy fermented inside him and he gave it to the grid. His mind's eye saw lines straighten and thicken. Another of his organless senses told him that the field was absorbing power from the assault and his shoulders began to ache fiercely as he became a conduit struggling for control.

One by one, he felt the supporting Magicians fall away. He was left alone with his fears and his exultation. What had happened to the others? He couldn't tell. This was his fight now and there was no time left to be afraid. He narrowed the focus of his inner vision and concentrated on the particles of the front. He felt the slick pressure of the dark, shifting, brown atmosphere. His skin would have crawled if he had had a skin.

The bursts of energy that peppered him were stabs of excitement that warred with the slithering distaste he felt. He was diaphanous and indestructible. His Staff, his incomparable Staff, was making this extraordinary empathy possible. With it, all he had to do was to know what he wanted to become and imagine strongly enough and the Staff would transmogrify him. He was Power: he was flight: he was victory.

The real life of the forcefield intruded on his reverie. His surface began to move of its own accord and continued to do so in defiance of his wishes. His new self was becoming difficult to manage. He was so much surface and so little depth. He began to expand and contract like a laboring heart.

Where is my heart? he wondered.

Somewhere, something of him gripped the Staff and raised it. Radiance seemed to stream from its horns and it made his disembodied self more resilient. He was back in control again, but all the elements had been notched higher. The pricks of pleasurable pain multiplied and became a thrilling diversion. He revelled in the sensation until it began to cloy.

There came a point where the pain surpassed the pleasure. He sought to disengage himself and found that he could not. Doubt flooded him and in that instant the forcefield that he had become wrested itself from his control. He began to fluctuate. He called on the Staff, but the answering tide only made the oscillations wilder. He willed himself back into his own body, but the death throes of the field, like the pangs that birth engenders, came ever closer together.

There was a searing flash followed by a ground-shaking boom strong enough to make the great wall tremble. Atop it, part of Jarrod Courtak felt the shifting of the massive blocks. Out at the edge, well beyond the monumental jumble of the Giants' Causeway, the rest of his being surrendered to dissolution.

I'm alive, he thought. I can't feel anything or see anything. Something terrible has happened, but I have survived. Where am I?

Jarrod's body was sitting behind the outer battlements, protected from the effects of the explosion. Tents and horses and stooks of pikes were flattened. Had the Upper Causeway not stood, bulwark-strong, in its path, the damage would have been terrible. As it was, the outer doors, whose sturdy timbers had withstood both time and battery, hung lopshoulderedly. It was an impartial explosion. It shredded the brown churn that hid and nurtured the foe. It left behind an exposed fan of ground, a litter of crumpled white suits and the wreckage of unfathomable structures.

Jarrod floated and waited. He felt warm and safe and good. Something was not quite right, but it was too much of an effort to find out what. His vision detected a swirl ahead and Jarrod gazed at it ravenously. It was marvelously, inventively fluid, yet it did not move. Grain, something said to him, stone grain. He was on the Causeway. The cold pavement beneath him made its presence felt and was welcomed. You are here, it said. The pain proves it. Concentrate on the pain, it said.

He wanted to move his hands and prove to himself that he was solid, but they were anchored. He looked down and took in the curve of quiet symbols that held them. He stared at them for a very long time and then he realized that he was holding his Staff. The warmth of the knowledge coursed through him like his first draught of wine. They found him with a smile on his face. It contrasted oddly with the frozen masks of agony around him.

CHAPTER XXIV

HE WAS A RAPTOR AGAIN, OR AT LEAST HE WAS SEEING THINGS FROM the same point of view that he had had when he had taken over the hawk's body. The Upper Causeway unspooled into infinity beneath him. From his vantage point, he could see the palace far to his right. The curtain that contained the enemy formed a broad border on the left. Tiny figures, in groups and alone, scurried between them. It was all clear and quite remote. Martin's down there somewhere, he thought.

He was stationary and below him the Paladinian army was drawn up for battle. In front of them, sitting on their steeds, were a miniature Robarth Strongsword, his slightly smaller son and Martin. The eyes that were Jarrod drifted down and the details became clearer still. Was it the stillness that made him feel uneasy, threatened? Was the slowly building fear that he was feeling a memory from the last time he had inhabited this body? No, there was something else. He wasn't really flying, he was simply aloft, fixed in the sky like a kite. No, not a kite, he covered far too large an area for that. It was almost as if he was a transparent drumskin stretched across the sky. That, he realized, was exactly what he was and at that instant he was aware of the padded hammers poised above him. The top side of him tingled in anticipation. They struck, soft and slow.

He was being distended, bowing down toward the ground beneath. Each rhythmic beat pushed him closer to the waiting

338

figures. Martin seemed to swing toward him and retreat. The tempo quickened and brought him closer and closer. Any minute now he should be able to reach out and touch her. The idea was intensely pleasurable until he realized that he had no hands, no limbs. If he were forced down too far he would suffocate them all. There was no way to avoid the blows so he tried to stiffen his surface and resist them. The resilience lessened but he felt himself becoming brittle. If he shattered now, he knew he would blow everything below him clear off the face of Strand. Panic and pressure built as he fought to stay whole. He knew that he was going to lose and it was at once thrilling and terrifying. The pulsing quickened and he exploded in a cloud of stars.

There was an interval. He had no idea how long an interval. There was no sign of Martin or of Amarine. There was no sign of anybody. He was alone in a moon-drenched parkland. The grass was rimmed in hoarlight and stands of trees became black and silver forests as he skirted them. Out of the darkness came the Princess Naxania, a creature of the night, all black hair and silver skin. She carried his Staff and Jarrod's heart warmed to her. She had rescued it and was returning it to him.

She sailed across the argent sward, the Staff towering above her, with a set expression which boded no good. She came to rest before him and her eyes were sad.

"I warned you, Jarrod Courtak," she said. "I warned you to take good care of this Staff that I have made. You paid me no heed and now I must take it back."

"But you can't. It's mine," he replied, horrified.

"It was only lent to you and you were not worthy of it. You lost it."

"That wasn't my fault."

"You lost it."

"I did my best," he remonstrated.

"Yes." The syllable was infinitely sad. "And you could not hold on to it. Poor Jarrod." She smiled and began to fade back into the night.

"But you can't leave me," he pleaded. "I need my Staff to get out of here."

"You should have thought of that before," the Princess said as she dissolved. Jarrod sprang despairingly for the Staff and was falling, down and down through the bottomless dark. He woke in a muck sweat.

He lay, ceremented in lethargy, trying to escape. Slowly, he realized that he was alive and then that he was in a bed. He remembered his battle with the foreigners and remembered that he had lost. Lost: he had lost his Staff. He clawed his way out of the bedclothes and looked about for a bellpull. The door opened and Diadra stood framed in it as if he had magicked her there.

"Awake, are you?" She bustled forward and seized his wrist. She pressed for his pulse and shushed him when he tried to speak. She dropped it with an enigmatic grunt, thumbed his eyelid back and peered suspiciously into his left eye.

"How many fingers?" she demanded as she stood back.

"Four."

"Reckon you'll do," she said grudgingly. "And it's a lucky young lad you are."

"What happened?"

"They'll be time enough for all that. What you need now is a little perking up and a great deal of rest. There's a visitor waiting to see you as should put a smile on your face. You called the name out often enough when you were delirious." She sniffed. "You're not to get yourself excited, mind." It was more a threat than an admonition. When she returned, she ushered Marianna in.

"He's very weak yet," Diadra said. "You promise to leave the moment he starts to tire?"

"I promise." Marianna smiled at her and went and put her gauntlets down before she approached the bed.

Jarrod took in the shining hair and the golden war circlet, the mail-clad figure, and knew that Martin was back.

"In bed again, I see," she said, trying for humor in the face of what she saw. She had been envying him for being able to participate while all she was able to do was practice, but there was no way that she could resent this pathetic, old man. "I swear I've never come across such an idle rogue," she added with as bright a smile as she could muster.

Jarrod lay there and bridled silently. He had risked his life and she thought he was malingering. It was unfair. His lower lip quivered toward a pout. He was tempted to remind her of how she had felt when she came out of Interim and into the Place of Power, but he decided against it. It would only make her angry and he couldn't cope with that in his present state.

"I had nightmares about you and Amarine," he said instead. "I'm not too sure about the ending, but I think you both got killed."

"You mustn't worry about us," she said soothingly. "Nothing's going to happen to us. The enemy threw everything they had at us and nothing could touch us." Pride rang in the quiet tones. "She was the only one left standing when the blast had done its work. I was clinging to her neck. I don't remember doing it. It happened so fast that it must have been automatic. When the dust settled, there she was, head high. I'd recovered by then and I was sitting up. When the men finally emerged from under the canvas, there we were." She broke off and looked at him with shining eyes.

"They cheered, Jarrod." She sat down gently on the edge of the bed. "The dawn, the real dawn, was coming up and it was as if there was a limelight shining down on us. It was very weird. I don't know if you can understand this, but, right at that moment, I felt like someone in a legend." He looked into the glistening eyes and saw the reflection of the memory. He nodded.

"You were certainly in the lap of the gods this time," he said gruffly and reached for her hand to contradict his voice. She was surprised by the gentle, dry grip. She found it reassuring and quite sexless. "I know you couldn't help this," he continued, "but I really don't think you ought to risk her again."

"Don't be melodramatic," she replied, with a playful little shake of the hand to stop him getting upset. "What could possibly happen to her?"

"She isn't immortal, you know. When the colts consult that memory of theirs, it's their dead ancestors that they are consulting."

"I think she's the one that verse was referring to," she said matter-of-factly. "You can see it in the way that the troops react to us. When we're with them, they think they're invincible." Despite himself, Jarrod found himself smiling at her. She suddenly seemed very young.

"Don't allow it to get a hold on you. It's very seductive being hero worshipped. I've felt it when I've been out with the colts or when I'm carrying the Staff in public. It isn't real: it isn't us. It's them. It's a combination of the power of the symbol and the need of the people watching us.''

"You're just jealous." She dropped his hand.

"No, I'm not. The verse said 'unicorns.' When we started looking I thought there would only be one, but the verse was right. Whatever the reason is for their being here, it concerns them all and that means that it concerns both of us." He stopped and stared at her. From his viewpoint, the chin was very firm and the look defiant. He felt the argument slipping away from him, but he was too tired to know what to do about it.

Marianna was turning his words over in her mind. He was right and she knew it, knew too that she was going to lose. Jarrod had become a person of importance. So had she, but with him it had gone beyond the unicorns. She looked down at the white hair and the wrinkled face. There was no trace of the callow boy whom she had bossed about in the Saradondas. I'll never be allowed to ride Amarine into battle, she thought, but I shan't give in easily. He's going to understand what I'm giving up.

Jarrod had been kind in his reference to the verse. She knew it by heart and there was no mention of her there. If she foreswore this chance for glory, there was no guarantee that she would ever get another.

"It's been snowing for days," she said, appearing to change the subject. She got up off the bed and began to wander around the room looking at things. "I suppose that's Greylock's way of making sure that those ghastly creatures stay put. The army's pulled back to regroup.

"Has it been a long time?" he asked, propping himself up on an elbow to follow her progress.

" 'Bout six sennights." She disappeared from view, screened by the bed curtains. "I never realized that your Staff was so big."

"Where is it?" There was no mistaking the relief in his voice and it puzzled her.

"Propped up in the corner."

"Is it all right?"

"As far as I can tell. It looks new and shiny to me. It must be a lot of trouble to lug around."

"It's not, actually."

"Well, it must be a lot lighter than it looks or you're a lot stronger than I thought you were."

"Not the way I'm feeling at the moment."

"Yes," she moved back into sight and toward the bed, "I ought to be going and let you get your rest."

"Must you go so soon?"

"I really ought to. There's a war still going on out there, you know, though, thanks to you, it's quiet for the time being." Jarrod wasn't sure whether he was being praised or blamed for that.

"Promise me that you won't put yourself in danger."

"Listen, Jarrod," Marianna's voice was commandingly serious, "everybody around here is doing something, something necessary. You're lying there because, in your own way, you fought the enemy. You haven't seen the results of your handiwork yet, I have. It's frightening to think that someone you thought you knew rather well is capable of doing something like that."

Like what? Jarrod wondered, but she continued.

"Now, you may be blasé about war, living so close to the Causeways, and especially now that you can hurl thunderbolts about, but I've had to cope with it at a distance all my life. It takes my father away every year. I could be dying, but if the summons came, he'd go off to the front.

"All the young men I've ever known went away to fight and when they came back, if they came back, it was all they could talk about. For the second time in my life I was excluded." He watched her face, more open now than he had ever seen it, save in sleep.

"And your father brought you up like a boy," Jarrod said softly.

"He didn't have to force me," she replied defensively. "That's what I wanted." She patted his legs aside and sat on the bed again. "Do you know what it's like to grow up as the only girl? No, of course not, how could you? At first everyone's the same. If anything, you get special attention from the boys. Then one day you're a complete outsider. No warning; no reason. Suddenly all the boys are making elaborate excuses for not including you in games. Nobody could tell me what I was doing wrong. Daddy believed that it was good for me to learn how to fight my own battles and the other grown-ups said that that was just how boys were.

"There was no one to confide in. I couldn't have had a girlfriend if I had wanted one, and suddenly I wanted one very badly. There was nobody of what Lady Myrgan called 'comparable status.' " The words came out with a sarcastic edge. She paused and looked up. "The boys' attitude changed a few years later, just as unexpectedly, and everything was wonderful again. Then it was time for them to go off to the war." She took his hand and stroked it absently with her thumbs.

"I've never known what this thing called battle really is. All I knew was that I couldn't compete with it. Now I'm here," she gave a little nod of acknowledgement, "thanks to you, and there's going to be a battle soon. I can sense it in the excitement of the new officers. You don't have to be a Mage to feel a battle coming on."

She changed tack. "No one thinks that the unicorns are here by accident. Not at this particular time. The army was badly mauled by the new weapons the last time, but now we've got the unicorns, they feel that we can't lose." Jarrod saw the look creeping back into her eyes and sighed inwardly.

"That's just it," he said, rallying his forces for a final try. "Without the two of you, we probably won't stand a chance. If anything happened to either of you, even a minor accident in training, it would be a terrible blow. It's more than just the army," he added earnestly. "That horn of hers is an enormously potent Magical instrument. Just look what it did to Greylock at Gwyndryth."

"I wasn't allowed to look," she interjected acidly.

"He couldn't contain the force." Jarrod hurried past a potential danger point. "He'd purified himself the night before and taken all the proper precautions. What I mean is that we can't risk anything that powerful. We don't know how to take advantage of that horn yet, but it could be that it's what the prophecy was all about." He made a business about getting more comfortable and thanked her when she helped him. He lay back and watched her with a detachment that was new to him.

"Would you be able to live with yourself if anything happened to her?" he asked shrewdly. "If anything happened to her, I think the colts would desert us. I would if I were them, and I've spent a lot of time in their minds."

She was silent and her eyes were elsewhere as she thought of what he'd said. Her emotions wanted to ignore him. The pull of glory and the thrill that proximity to danger brings were strong within her. Her mind, however, agreed with him. She hesitated.

"All right," she said reluctantly. "I'll stay to the rear when the fighting begins." She rose to her feet. "But I'm still going to ride along the lines until then—even the front lines. After all, they're the ones who need the boost in morale most."

"Agreed." She bent down and planted cool lips on his forehead.

"Take care of yourself, Jarrod," she said. "Hurry up and get well. Amarine and I aren't the only ones they need."

"Thank you for coming. I can't think of anybody I'd rather have as a first visitor." She grinned at him.

"You must be feeling better. On second thought, you're obviously not your old self. I could have sworn I heard a compliment and I'm going to leave before you disabuse me." She cocked her head pertly to one side, blew him a little kiss and was gone.

Once Diadra had lowered the drawbridge there was no keeping Greylock out. She ushered the Mage in and stayed to hover until he was settled with a posset of wine. All the while she stared at her two most frequent charges and marvelled that, unless one knew in advance, no one could have said which one was the younger. She understood nothing of what was said. Figures and pressure zone and suchlike. What was important was that her new old man didn't seem to be getting excited or upset.

Jarrod was grateful for the queries. They were technical and needed precise answers and the question of blame never once came up.

"You did well, lad. You were lucky, but you did exceedingly well," was the Mage's final judgement. "The engagement cost us, no doubt about it. We lost four good Magicians, but without you, it could have been a catastrophe. You've learned well and I'm proud of you.''

"Thank you, Sir." Jarrod was warmed by the first overt praise he had heard.

"The King doesn't see it that way, of course." Jarrod tensed for the awaited censure. "We're being blamed for the horses that had to be put down and he says that the forcefield is as dangerous to us at it is to them. Stupid man won't realize what would have happened if the forcefield hadn't been in place." There was bitterness in the deep voice. "He has forbidden me, on pain of exile, to resurrect the forcefield. He's gone even further: he's put the Upper Causeway off-limits to me." The hurt of it echoed in the low-ceilinged room.

"That doesn't make any sense," Jarrod said, struggling to sit up. "He may not approve of the field, we always knew that he didn't like it, but we still need to see what's going on."

"You're being logical," Greylock said wryly. "That's a disadvantage when you're dealing with royalty. I, however, have been dealing with this particular piece of royalty for a long time now," his hands rubbed themselves together, "and I have developed a logic of my own." The conspiratorial glee of the hands transferred itself to the eyes. Jarrod wondered, for an uneasy moment, if his master hadn't been overtaxed.

"Strongsword has no jurisdiction over the Place of Power, right? So he cannot object if we raise a forcefield to protect it." The eyes glittered. "Now," he said, drawing the syllable out like a major-domo, "the field is a delicate and complicated mechanism. It is an arcane construct that few know of and fewer still comprehend. Besides ourselves, I doubt there's anyone who really understands it and, as we amply demonstrated, even we are fishing in the dark. This is a brand new science and there are precious few rules as yet. We're working with unknowns: no one can predict what the enemy will do." He fixed Jarrod with a worrisome stare.

"Who could blame us, then, if it drifted forward? We'd never let it get beyond the Upper Causeway, but should the unthinkable occur, we could give our people some kind of protection."

There was a pleading note behind the words. The man, Jarrod thought, is asking for my approval. His heart went out to his mentor. A Mage, Counselor to the King, was reduced to seeking his approval.

"It's a wonderful idea," he murmured. "I also think it's time that I was out of bed. I want to be there to help you."

"Thank you, lad." Greylock smiled and, for once, the lines seemed to lessen and he looked younger. "I welcome your support, but I don't want you to rush things. You were severely tested and that kind of exertion takes time to recover from."

Jarrod began to chuckle. In his condition it hurt, but he couldn't help himself.

"I'm quite serious about this, Jarrod. You have been through a very punishing time. You have to give your body a chance to catch up."

"I'm sorry," Jarrod spluttered, bringing himself under control, "it just occurred to me that you have exposed me to the Place of Power, sent me off after unicorns and left me in charge of your forcefield and now you're worried that I'll get out of bed too soon."

"I'm right and you know it," Greylock said with familiar authority. "It's true though," he added as he rose, "that I'll need help with the forcefield." He smiled broadly.

CHAPTER XXV

DIADRA MUSTERED HER FULL BATTERY OF COMMANDS, CAJOLERY
and wiles, but Jarrod was out of bed the next morning. *There's a
battle coming.* Marianna's voice reechoed in his mind's ear and
made him deaf to all of the Wisewoman's ploys. Greylock had
sent him away before the last one and he had no intention of
being on the sidelines for this one. When it came down to it, he
admitted, he wasn't too different from Marianna. Besides, Greylock needed him.

He took advantage of the fact that no one had any specific
duties for him to perform to develop a regimen that, he felt,
would hasten his recovery and bring him to battle readiness. He
co-opted his old friend Tokamo and together they took daily,
stamina-building hikes. They exercised and chatted, rode and
remarked on how the Winter clouds made them think of the
ancient stories of sky whales, studied spells and dined together at
Hall. Jarrod had been afraid that his recent notoriety would have
changed their relationship and was relieved and delighted when
he found that it had made no difference.

Despite the pleasures of rediscovered closeness, it was an
eerie period of waiting for Jarrod. His body fleshed out and the
grey receded from his hair to the point that he started consciously
looking for Marianna. He loitered around the stables after visiting the colts, hoping to bump into her. He heard enthusiastic

reports of her activities at Hall each night, but their paths never seemed to cross.

The enemy indulged him by confining their activities to occasional sorties and manufacturing enough of their kind of air to reclaim the area cleared by the collapse of the shield. There was nothing the Paladinian troops could do to counter them. The newly revealed ground was poisonous to them. The official broadsheets tacked up on gates and posts downplayed the possibility of another major attack before the next Season of the Moons, but no one believed them.

Everyone was waiting, making a protective pretense at normal life. It was harder for Jarrod than most because there were meetings between Naxania and Greylock and Agar Thorden to which he was not privy. A year ago it would not have occurred to him that he might be consulted, now he felt excluded. Feet ascended the stairs toward the Mage's room long after he had committed himself to his scratchy sheets, lumpy mattress and slack bedropes. He tried to put faces to the footsteps, but the game didn't stop him from feeling slighted.

The unicorns are here, I'm here and Marianna's here, he thought as he tossed. We ought to be preparing to do something special, something to justify all the faith people have in us, but nobody comes to us with questions or ideas. It isn't right. It isn't fair.

No matter how expected an attack is, it always comes as a surprise. The Battle for Stronta was no exception. The first to be aware of it was a battalion of warcats that was on forward patrol along the white, wooden markers that pegged out the approaches to the new Barrier Lands. It was a routine patrol across a dormant front—routine, until the hot beams stabbed out and impaled them. Then, all that was left of routine was burned away and no creature was left to cry warning.

The Paladinian front lines, dug in some five miles South, were standing down and caught unprepared. The sudden appearance of an unhampered enemy bolted the bowmen. They, in turn, stampeded the pikemen and, between them, they offered the enemy the most enticing of targets. Marianna, caught in the confusion, wheeled Amarine on her hind legs and galloped for headquarters.

There were others who were not so fortunate. Helmets rang on

the icy ground as necks were scythed away. Helms ornamented
with horsehair were dyed a more vivid shade of red. Units
commingled as discipline broke down and the chaos was compounded by the blare of trumpets sounding out conflicting orders. The ring and clatter of falling greaves and breastplates
provided an unwanted tympani. The rout was on and pikes and
hauberks lay abandoned in an obscene travesty of a children's
game.

The abrupt arrival of messengers alerted the Outpost. Greylock sent for Naxania and Jarrod snatched up his Staff and
headed for the stables. He knew that he should have waited for
word from Greylock, but the fear that the colts and he would be
left out proved too strong. There was no time for pentacles or
purifications, but the colts were pure enough for any set of
Powers. He let them out of their loose box and, not bothering
with a saddle, rode Nastrus bareback to the Place of Power.

Habit made him ride to the Causeway side and he dismounted
at the shortest altar. Hooves and feet and the butt of the Staff
made dark tracks in the virgin snow as they crossed to the black
ambiguity of the final stele. It was cold, but Jarrod did not feel
it.

I wish I could take you up there with me, he thought, *I know
I'll need you, but I don't know how to do it.*

*You don't need to. You are much changed and much stronger
than you used to be. So are we.* The remarks came all at once
and then Pellia came clear in his mind. *You should not need to
touch us now for us to act as one. We are here. We shall be with
you.*

Jarrod chanted out the meaningless words he had learned so
painstakingly, careful of the cadence. He rose, somewhat to his
own surprise, into the air. As he did so, the intimations of signs
on the outer blocks grew more distinct. The Place of Power, as if
aware of the threat to its peace, was very much alive. Jarrod was
conscious of it as he floated up. There were currents at work of
which he had no knowledge and, inexplicably, that made him
more confident. He hovered over the smooth onyx top and was
on his own two feet again.

His mind reached out for the colts and they were there. With
his Staff in his hand he had no real need of them to raise the

forcefield, but he wanted them with him while he did it. Nastrus, without explanation, used his mind to change the woof slightly and eliminated the unperceived flaw that had caused the explosion. With the field in faintly auroral existence and the colts supporting him, he felt omnipotent.

He did not see Greylock enter the enclave. He only became aware of his presence when he heard the words of levitation. He saw the curl of the Magical crook first and then the diadem perched on the hair. The revealed Mage was fully accoutered and the designs on his robe shone of their own accord. They found reflection in the glint of battle in his eye. There was pride in his smile as he turned and surveyed the land between the Place of Power and the bastion that was the Upper Causeway.

A league away to the North, the reserve encampment and the more permanent buildings that housed the farriers and the armorers seemed to huddle against the base of the Causeway. To the right, past the corner of the Barracks, he could make out the tall doors that flanked the gate. The parade ground in front of the Barracks had acquired tents for the wounded since last he'd stood there. There was constant movement on the far-off chariotway, but here, behind the wall, it was deceptively tranquil. Greylock knew what it must be like on the far side, but he resented not being able to see it with his own eyes.

"Glad you've got the field up. Good work," was all he said.

"Thank you, Sir. Is there any news from the front?"

"The enemy is burning its way to the gate, King Robarth is apoplectic, his son is riding around being abusive and everybody's blaming everybody else." He sighed. "It's a good thing we're not around or they'd all be blaming it on us."

"Any word of Marianna?" The question popped out before he realized and he suffered the humor of the unicorns as it did so.

"Oh yes. She's haranguing them to make a last ditch stand before the gate. Prince Justinex may prefer machinery to Magic, but he's with her on this. He's about the only one, or so the messenger said. Paladinian soldiers don't like taking suggestions from foreigners, let alone from women. Naxania found that out. At least when she takes over for me at the Outpost, no one says boo to her, not even Agar."

As he was speaking, his ring caught and began to glow. He closed his eyes and started to rock gently.

"You've done something different," he said sharply and disengaged.

"Actually, it was Nastrus who did it. It ought to absorb the backlash when the energy levels exceed the capacity of . . ."

"That may well be." Greylock cut him off. "I don't have the time to work it all out now." Jarrod held his tongue, disappointed by the Mage's reaction.

The two Magicians peered down toward the parade grounds. Their elevation, though modest when compared to the soar of the Upper Causeway, was sufficient to provide an excellent view out over the flat landscape. The marshalling areas were filled with soldiers trying to find their units and there were long lines of waiting wounded around the Wisewomen's tents. A steady file of stretchers bore others away to the star shaped sanctuary that was Stronta. It was a long, heavy trudge around the Great Maze to the East Gate and Errathuel and all his descendants were roundly cursed. The Maze remained timelessly indifferent.

Atop the Causeway, a frieze on the horizon, men hurried and chariots raced. A company of archers ducked and loosed with hypnotic precision. Below them, on the outer side, the uncooperative doors were being wrestled closed against the frantic throng clawing for their last chance at safety. Even those who won through had to run another race, for the portcullis that formed the second line of defense was already unwinching down. The area became a human wine press as scrambling soldiers were caught beneath the stakes. None of the lucky had won through unscathed and many were too slow. The final pair of doors ground together and the bar dropped across them with the finality of death.

There was a brief respite on the Stronta side as trumpets brayed and ragged ranks began to form. Jarrod scanned the distant moil for a glimpse of Amarine and was aware that the colts were avid for the evidence of his eyes. Try as he might, he could not satisfy them, or himself. Too much was going on and the figures were so small. There seemed to be a flickering at the gates and Jarrod concentrated on it, half convinced that it was a figment of his straining eyes. It was not. It was being caused by real flames. It's not possible, Jarrod thought. They can't be here. They were.

Red and orange tongues licked around the hinges and spread to outline the gates in light. The greedy flames grew until the gates were an arch of inferno. It flared to white and then dissolved into whirling cinders. There was an unnatural pause. The whole world seemed to hold its breath. Then, like mushrooms through loam, small white buttons popped through the opening and into a hail of arrows. The first ones fell, plumed over by the escaping brown gasses from their punctured suits, but those who followed got further.

The suited figures continued to crumple and the area of white spread out from the gaping gateway as if the snow itself had turned on Stronta and was invading. The clothyards flew and the foe continued to fall. Spears of light poignarded out sporadically and kept the host of Paladine at bay. Then, using the bodies of their fallen comrades as a barricade, the foe let off a broadside that decimated the disorganized front ranks of the army. Then they were at the Barracks and the hand to hand fighting began.

Both Magicians shook off the paralysis of disbelief and moved the shield forward. It was of no help where the forces were interlocked, but the strange weapons were less effective in that sort of fighting. They contented themselves by establishing a protection through which the army could flee, should that become necessary. In and around the Barracks, points of light flicked on and off. They knew that things were going badly when the lethal fireflies turned on the chariotway atop the Causeway and stopped the threat from their rear. White suits began to boil through the abandoned gate.

Above them, a wing of cloudsteeds circled, awaiting their chance to swoop down from the rear. Lines rayed upward from the roof of the officers' quarters and, one after another, the graceful animals fell. Their riders cartwheeled to their deaths beside them. Jarrod's heart plummeted with the cloudsteeds and he sought to disengage his mind from the colts to spare them the horror. They had fled from him the last time that he had shown them such a sight. Beneath that memory was the fear that they might hurt him again.

The revulsion in their minds was plain, but it was not the lash

that it had been. They had already absorbed the idea that the
denizens of Strand could commit the unthinkable and this renewed proof had a less emotional effect. What he was not
prepared for was the clear feeling that the humans were taking
advantage of the cloudsteeds.

Greylock glanced across and noticed the tears in Jarrod's
eyes. They worried him. The boy had been growing too fast for
him and he was no longer sure he could guess his motives or
anticipate his reactions. Greylock felt the burgeoning of loss and
suppressed it. There was no time for that now.

"It doesn't look too good, does it?" he said briskly. "I think
it's time we girdled ourselves. I take it you can employ the colts
even though they are down there? Capital." He paused to see
what effect he had had, unaware of the irony.

"The Incantation to the Powers first, I think," he continued.
"We are, after all, their guests." Despite himself, Jarrod smiled
at the thought of social niceties being offered to unimaginable
beings in the middle of a battle. "After that, we'll check over
the field." He raised his eyebrows at the young man and Jarrod
nodded. They faced the Barracks and the gate and went within
themselves.

All personal thoughts and considerations were pushed aside as
Jarrod joined his voice in the supplication. As the beautiful,
bass, tumble of nonsense progressed, he felt the response. The
runes on his Staff changed colors as the extra energy flowed
through him. The excitement of spellcasting took over as the
chant built and all weakness, weariness and pain were forgotten.
When they were done, the invisible mesh was strung in a quad-
rant West through South.

They were not a moment too soon. The skein was breached
almost instantly by the evacuation of the wounded and the
Wisewomen. They were quickly followed by units of the army
as they were driven from the cover of the building. Jarrod braced
for the inevitable pursuit, but none came. Off to the Magicians'
right, almost level with the Place of Power, they could see
Robarth Strongsword riding to and fro among the panicking
troops. The eponymous battlesword of his house was brandished and while the wind and the distance obliterated his words,
Jarrod, remembering the effects of the royal rage, was not

surprised by the results. Pikes and hauberks were grounded and squares began to form.

Half a league to the South, the Princess Naxania was ensconced before the windows of Greylock's workshop. Four duty boys sat on the floor behind her waiting for messages to dash and deliver. For them, the battle was a welcome and exciting respite from lessons and routine. The Princess could see the Place of Power from her vantage point, but her eyes probed the heavens.

She pulled herself away from the circling glass and snapped over her shoulder, "My respects to Administrator Thorden and would he have the weatherwards advance the storm so that it covers the area between the Place of Power and the enemy atmosphere. Tell him that it should be primed for discharge." She resumed her post as the boy scurried for the stairs.

Perched atop the megalith, Jarrod began to feel the effects of her order. The air around him seemed to vibrate and the hair on his body rose and itched. He pushed his concentration higher and subdued the manifestations. He looked over to his right where the army was reorganizing and it seemed as if he had transferred his problem to the warcats. They were prowling restlessly in front of the forming ranks, hackles high and tails bushed out.

There was activity to the North as well. White shapes began to emerge from the Barracks and muster into formation. Their numbers swelled, but still they did not fire. The remnants of the Second Warcat Battalion, as if enraged by the foreigners' restraint, loped and then hit their full, flying stride. Their warriors, fleetest of all soldiers, kept pace. They were an eye-stingingly gallant sight. Then the foe struck back.

There had been training sessions devoted to countering the new weapons but nothing seemed to work. Cats burst into flame, blood sizzled and then boiled away. Blackened bodies fell and writhed and the trumpets sang a forlorn recall. Above it all, the sky growled and bristled while the forcefield became spotted with red as it intercepted and absorbed the enemy shots that missed their marks.

Clothyards flew in answer and many found a target, but it was not death enough. The enemy held its fire once more, made cautious perhaps by the memory of what had occurred the last time they had encountered Strand's newest defense. The Paladinian army prepared itself, though whether for attack or defense, Jarrod could not tell.

He slitted his eyes against the growing gloom brought on by the gathering storm. The Upper Causeway was no more than a grey ribbon against the backdrop of the darker air beyond it. There was an ominous lack of movement on the chariotway. His gaze swung back in response from a query from the colts and he scanned the lines for a glimpse of Amarine. The question in his mind had been almost incidental. There was no fear behind it, merely curiosity, and he was reassured by their underlying certainty that nothing bad could happen to her.

There was a flash of white among the front ranks and, once located, the unicorn stood out clearly. She emerged from among the soldiery and took a place beside the scarlet caparisons that singled out the King's charger. A ragged cheer floated back against the wind. She promised to stay out of the fighting, he thought as another rider joined them and ranged himself alongside the Royal Standard Bearer. That would have to be Prince Justinex.

Jarrod's eyes went back to the enemy. They were well clear of the Barracks now, despite the archers' best efforts, and the line was longer and thicker than it had been before. There was still a good stretch of clear ground between the two armies and the forcefield hung transparently between them. The invaders' opening salvo changed that. He threw his concentration back into the shield as the evil flowers sprang into vivid and ephemeral life.

They'll be safe this time, Jarrod thought. They can stay put and let these suited obscenities spend themselves against the screen. The assertion was scarcely made before Nastrus brushed it aside.

Your mind tells us that your King does not trust your forcefield. Our forcefield, Jarrod objected and was ignored. *There are no reinforcements for him to throw into the battle and he doesn't know how many the Others may have in reserve. His only chance is to drive them back now. It's the only way a warrior would think,* Beldun added.

Jarrod felt like arguing, even though he knew that what the colts had said made perfect sense, but he was forestalled by a stepped-up flow from Greylock. Robarth was confirming the unicorns' intuition, but not in quite the way that they had predicted. He was not charging: he was walking his mount forward, followed by Justinex, Marianna and the rest of his forces. He drew rein before the iridescent curtain, stood in the stirrups and raised his broadsword once again. The tableau held until there was a lull in the enemy's fire and the screen dimmed. The blade circled twice and then came down due North.

It was as if all the water clocks of the world had been topped up with cold honey. Pennons, standards and gonfalons streamed toward the invaders in eager agitation, whipped on by Naxania's wind. Jarrod risked a glance at Greylock. There was a halo around the Mage that he had never seen before. He tore his eyes away in time to see the army hurl itself at the fading scrim. He watched as the lines crashed together in mutual shock. Drumfire from gravid clouds underlined the impact.

Trumpets threaded the thunder. Steam and dust rose. The picture dimmed and the details melded into confusion. The wind dwindled and became flirtatiously ineffective. The fighting, the Barracks and the violated gate beyond were obscured. The natural chaos of close engagement, abetted by the escaping effluvium from punctured suits, made it impossible to see what was going on.

One thing was obvious. The forcefield was of no help now and, gradually, the two pulled it back. If the counterattack failed there might still be need of it, so they allowed a part of their minds to keep the field together. The colts, unbidden, ceased to funnel power to Jarrod and, when it was quite gone, he felt a pang of loss, though there was enough still and to spare. The Ring of the Keepers gleamed fiercely in the corner of his eye and the comfort of the Staff was in his right hand. The energy was there aplenty, but there was nothing to do with it.

"What happens now?" he asked.

"The hardest thing of all. We wait." Greylock's voice was flat and expressionless.

"There's nothing else we can do?"

"This is your first major battle, isn't it? Nothing like the songs, at least not for us. No cut and thrust; no feats of physical glory. If we succeed, the army will take the credit and if we fail,

or even if they suffer defeat in spite of our efforts, there is
always the talk of denying us the right of tithe.''

"There must be something. . . .'' Greylock caught the under-
tone of rising hysteria and cut him off.

"We hold ourselves ready,'' he said, plaiting humor, resignation and understanding into his delivery. *I keep forgetting how
young he really is,* he thought.

"At least those bastards haven't used their fire chariots, or
whatever they're called,'' Jarrod responded calmly, unaware that
his reactions were being manipulated.

"That they haven't.'' Greylock's tone was brisk and confident
now. "I suppose it's salutory for us to realize how little control
over events we really have, but it's immensely frustrating. It
almost makes me want to believe in the Archmage's Gods of the
Odds.'' He gave a knowing little chuckle.

"I still feel as if I ought to be able to reach over and smash
them. They wouldn't know where the attack was coming from
and so they wouldn't be able to defend against it.''

"A common Collegium fantasy,'' Greylock said drily. "If
you can't see, you shouldn't act. Basic rule number two.'' Jarrod
eyed the battle, unconvinced. He was in touch with so much
power. It seemed inconceivable that he could not affect the
outcome.

"Never forget,'' Greylock said, as if he had the colts' access
to Jarrod's mind, "that we are the instrument, not the cause.''

"It looks as if our people are beginning to give way,'' Jarrod
interrupted anxiously.

"Looks fairly even to me, but let's see what I can do to
improve the visibility.'' He paused and then began to croon. The
wind picked up and began to blow the skirts of their robes
toward the fighting. Gradually, the swirl of dust and vapor
thinned and dispersed.

They could see now, but that made it no easier. The interlocked lines of combat writhed like a worm in agony. Vicious
clots broke away and rejoined it. Jarrod scanned it avidly, half
hoping, half afraid that he would catch a glimpse of Amarine.
He did not. His disappointed eyes moved Northward and took in
the bare patch of trampled ground between the fighting and the
Barracks.

The ragged aftermath of a roaring cheer snapped them back and his heart leaped. The line was bowing outward and, as he watched, it broke. The little white buttons that were the invaders scuttled for the safety of the building behind them. Jarrod's hungry gaze raced ahead of them and his eyes widened suddenly. Something strange was going on. The Paladinian army was charging, slaughtering the slower moving enemy, but there were defenders swarming around the front of the Barracks.

He squinted in an effort to see more clearly. There was a boil of white suits and then they were gone, leaving something behind. He fought to still his awareness of the energy flowing through him so that he could narrow the focus of his concentration. There were black tubes protruding from the ground floor windows. From his lofty and distant viewpoint they looked like wires, but he knew, without knowing why, that they were tubes and that they represented danger.

Greylock may have felt the same thing, or perhaps he reacted to the flare of alarm that raced through his protégé. Jarrod heard the beginning of an unfamiliar chant, but he was too riveted to the action to pay much heed. He searched frantically for Marianna in that galloping throng, but it was too confused and far away from individuals to stand out. As the distance between the two sides closed, a hedge of flame erupted from the Barracks and rolled across the parade ground toward the advancing Paladinians.

He felt the colts reengage and diverted their force into the shield. He was aware of the pressure of the Magicmaking at his side and wondered, briefly, what Greylock was doing. There was no chance to ask. The fire was growing as it travelled, blazing up as if it was being fueled by the rendering fat of a turning roast. The air danced around it and, in its wake, the world was reduced to char and smoke.

The home forces pulled up at the sight of it and turmoil set in again as those in the van tried to turn and escape. Robarth stood his ground, though his charger was rearing in eye-rolling terror. His bellowing exhortations went unheard or ignored. Even his son refused to hear him. It made no difference. The lofting wave of death was too greedy and too fast. Robarth Strongsword met his end as he would have desired, in the gallant futility of a charge. The wave raced over him and then caught and consumed his son, his friends and his followers.

For Jarrod, everything was moving as if mired in nightmare. The red and yellow curl of flame crept across the earth in a hiss of smoke-stained steam. The distant dolls were slower still. A howl built in him and the Staff in his right hand throbbed in response. He lofted it above his head and held it with both hands, the tips probing toward the conflagration.

There was anger in him, ice-cold and implacable. He felt the colts stir uneasily in his mind and quashed them with an ease that would have flabbergasted him had he had time to think about it. A corner of his consciousness was aware that Greylock was plucking at his sleeve, but he blocked that, too. He gathered the thrum of power around him and funneled it into the screen. Out on the plain, an iridescence glowed into pulsing life and moved North.

"It's too dense!" Greylock yelled at the unheeding, young warlock. "Bring the level down. Let go, Jarrod! Let go!" He flailed at the ecstatic figure, but knew that he wasn't getting through.

The marks of lore around them, ancient already past the reading of man, glittered with a livid, green light. All the symbols of Magic were awake. They rippled winkingly from Greylock's gown and ran the length of both their Staffs. They were incandescent and enigmatic on the surfaces of the menhirs that circled and the light of them sparkled in the diamonds among the age-bleached curls. It was something that Greylock had never seen and he plunged into his chant with renewed fervor.

Jarrod's own song was inarticulate now. Surges of energy crashed through him making him shake from head to toe with the effort of containment. Despite that, his mind floated free and clear as it maintained the designs and thrust the screen toward the elemental enemy. Above him, the heavens flashed and groaned in echo and still Jarrod sang on with hoarse hatred.

The shock of contact buffeted and staggered him. The Staff came down as a support and he clung to it as he fought for air. He steadied himself, mouth open in a manic parody of a grin as his breath sieved in and out between bared teeth. He clawed his way back through the welter of unexpected pain.

Out on the battlefield, the wall of fire splashed skyward and fell back upon itself. Purging himself with a final spasm of ferocity, Jarrod heaved the shield forward and sent the roil of heat and flame rolling back the way it had come.

It gathered speed across the ashes of those it had destroyed and crashed through the pipes that had given it birth. The Barracks slowed it, but did not stop it. It slammed into the South face of the Upper Causeway with such force that the carried blackness of its furnace breath reached almost to the top before it slid away to extinction. Jarrod saw none of that. He stood, leaning heavily on the Staff, with dim eyes and palsied limbs.

Greylock fought his own battles beside him. As Strand's link to the Place of Power, he was aware that something was terribly wrong. He could feel that those who dwelled there were withdrawing and he had not asked them to desist. There was no need of their assistance now, but that decision should have been his. He was mortally tired, but this was a situation that needed exploration. Spreading his arms, he began the Incantation of Summoning even though they were not entirely gone.

Jarrod's sight was baffled by the dancing afterimages of the cataclysm. The colts were no longer with him and the screen was unravelling as the normalcy of space reasserted itself. Power was still blowing through him. The Staff seemed to vibrate between his hands, but he was shaking too hard to be sure. He blinked his eyes to clear them. Bright beads of light petillated across his retinas and the outlines of the closest cromlechs blurred, though the alien symbols on them were still plain. He peered at the smaller slab ahead of him, but its whiteness defeated him.

He risked letting go of the Staff with one hand so that he could knuckle his eyes. The markings stayed crisp but the stones that housed them were becoming indistinct. I'm going blind, he thought. The way that Greylock did after the Conclave. It made him turn toward his master. As he did so, the Mage gave a glottal and despairing cry. His crozier slipped from his hand as he sagged and collapsed. The diadem was jarred free by the fall and shimmied into stillness like a coin spun by a Dameschool boy.

Jarrod set his own Staff down gently and dropped to his knees.
He drew back one of Greylock's voluminous sleeves and searched
desperately for a pulse. His hands were too unsteady and he
failed to find one. He breathed deeply to still the rising panic and
reached out with his mind for the colts. They were there, but he
could not penetrate their bewilderment. He realized, with a wash
of guilt and sorrow, that they were trying to contact their dam.
He tried for a pulse again and again he failed to find one.

He tore the fabric of the robe open. There seemed to be so
much of it, as if it had become too big for the wearer. He
pressed his ear to the flaccid chest. His own blood pounded in
his head and deafened him. He swallowed hard and sat back on
his heels. He went inside himself and calmed the unruly racings.
He lowered his ear to the startlingly white skin and listened with
all his being. There was a beat. It was slow and faint, but it was
regular. Tears of relief robbed him of sight again.

He sat up and stared out over the blackened landscape. Fires
flickered and burned in the Barracks. Flashes of lightning drama-
tized the scene as the storm that Naxania had sent animated the
ashes and underscored the loss. They were gone, all gone. The
warmth and lassitude that were part of the compensation of
spellcasting cushioned him from the worst of reality.

Little by little, the silent bleakness, the skeletons of trees that
had survived the years only to be woken sharply from their
Winter sleep into incineration, seeped into his resistant awareness. Everyone had vanished like the trees. Robarth would wench
no more and there was no longer a need for Jarrod to become a
friend to Justinex. Earls and Farrodmen, warcats and cloudsteeds,
all were reduced to debris. The thoughts spun around in his brain
like the ash devils out on the plain. It didn't really matter
though. Nothing did, except Greylock.

He turned urgently to the Mage and tried to pick up one of the
hands to chafe it. It would not move. He tried to move the body,
but it would not budge. The back of Greylock's head would not
leave the stone to be cradled. He shuffled round the body on his
knees, pushing and tugging, but to no avail.

He looked out again to sidetrack the fear that was welling up.
He stared at the huge blocks of stone that surrounded them. They
were less substantial than they had been and the cabalistic inscrip-

tions were invisible once more. Must be the tears in my eyes, he said to himself and busied himself pulling the lackluster cloth of Greylock's robe into order. He retrieved the fallen crook and the diadem and placed them by the Mage's side.

The elation that had kept him going was almost spent and he knew that he would collapse soon. Was there anything more that he should do? Could do? The faint, residual glow of the Ring of the Keepers caught his eye. Almost in spite of himself, his hand crept out. As if in anticipation of the unformulated intent, the stone flared up and the resulting gust of power whirled his consciousness away.

As Jarrod slumped beside his mentor, the ringstone shone for a moment like a beacon and then winked out. All around, the massive stones bled away to invisibility, leaving a broken circle of deep indentations. In the center, a single monolith survived. Three white unicorns clustered forlornly as its foot and, high above them, two ancient humans lay on its jetty surface. The ring on one bony finger was no more than slag set in gold. Its last fire had been burned out. The heavens roared and the rain began to fall.

CHAPTER XXVI

JARROD COURTAK SWAM UP INTO CONFUSION. HE WAS IN BED, BUT it wasn't his. Too big. Too comfortable for the Collegium. Gwyndryth? His mind shied away from the thought. The hangings were familiar. Then clarity sliced through and he knew that he was in Greylock's room. What was he doing in Greylock's bed? Memory began to seep back and with it came an encompassing greyness of spirit. Something must be seriously amiss with the Mage. Was he dead? No. The denial came instantly. Someone was dead. A lot of people had died. But someone special was gone, someone he really ought to be able to remember. He tried to pursue the train of thought, but slumber forestalled him.

It was dark when he surfaced again and he wondered if they had sealed the windows. The idea startled him. The buckets of damp marl were ubiquitous, but he had never known them to be used. They were more a tradition than anything else. Then why . . . ? Oh yes. There had been a battle and the Causeway had been breached. Depression, like a swarm of bees in search of a new hive, descended on him and he found that he was crying. He tried to brush away the tears, but nothing happened. He began to struggle, but interior darkness rose to match the outward circumstances and he slept again.

Recollection came in sharded scenes that melded with his dreamscapes into a kaleidoscopically unreal whole. He rode his dreams above the Place of Power and looked down on a sixty year old man kneeling over the body of an even older one. He knew that he saw himself. He circled the place with the unnatural detachment that only comes in dreams and heard the puppet that was him keening. He strained to hear the words and swooped closer.

"Marianna, Marianna, my Anna, my Anna . . ." The cry fled out on the soughing wind. At the base of the black slab the colts huddled, tails toward the stinging fall of rain. Above them the figure rocked, words bubbling uncontrollably from the throat.

"Anna," it intoned mindlessly, "Anna, my Anna, Marianna, Marianna. . . ."

The sun was streaming through the windows when next he awoke. He was lightheaded, but he knew that he was lucid. He looked slowly around the familiar room to delay the reckoning he knew he must make with himself. He had often sat on this bed in the past, but he had never looked out into the room from this viewpoint before.

There were the shelves with Greylock's books and scrolls neatly arranged in their boxes. He remembered doing the arranging when he first got back from the Collegium and that seemed infinitely long ago. There was the table where the Mage did his late night experiments. His spectacles lay abandoned on top of the clothes press, the ones that Greylock was too vain to wear in public. He smiled at the only weakness he had ever discovered in his mentor. But Greylock is gone, said his mind. Not gone, just lost for a while, he corrected and the floodgates were open.

He closed his eyes uselessly against recall, but his memory was perfect and implacable. He saw, once again, the charge of the Paladinian army, the faltering of the foe and the empty-mouthed tubes that suddenly vomited the wave of fire that consumed them all. He remembered throwing the shield forward, translated by the forces of the Place of Power and of the unicorns. The unicorns? The unicorns that Marianna and he had found. Marianna? His mind was merciful and took him away to rest.

Jarrod woke again in the nightmoonlight and stayed halfway in dream gazing at the odd artifact on the counterpane. A fragment of map with three sharp mountain ridges and six large, blue rivers crisscrossing on the plain. A remarkable, three-dimensional piece, with each element clear in the silver light. Then he noticed the nails and the fine, dry lines. A hand. His hand? Was he then so old? Had his Magicmaking leached away so much? He struggled to sit up and, though no constraint stronger than a bedsheet held him, could not. He sagged against the bolster and slow tears squeezed from beneath his lids. He was eighteen and would never know a prime.

The morning brought renewed pain and Diadra. Her mute, sympathetic fussing, the washing, the feeding, the plumping of the bolster, only served to make him more aware of the loss of the Mage. He tried to question her, but his vocal chords would not respond to his will. She shushed his efforts at speech and tucked him back into imprisonment, leaving him frustrated and a prey to his memories.

The enemy had been destroyed, but at the cost of the House of Strongsword and with them Marianna; Marianna whom he had loved and been forbidden to possess. Now he never would. She was gone, engulfed in the rolling tide of flame, and Amarine, the unmatchable, with her. A terrible doubt assailed him. What had become of the colts? His anguished mind cast back into the distress that clouded those final moments.

They had been in the Place of Power when it had vanished. They had been standing at the base of the black stele as, one by one, the altars and the ancient cromlechs had faded and disappeared. The backlash of the forces he had tried to control had broken his mental contact with them, but he had no feeling that they had been harmed. Surely such Magical creatures could not come to hurt? But their dam was overtaken and consumed. The reminder seared through him and set him scrabbling for the bellpull. It seemed an eternity before Diadra burst in.

"The colts. What happened to the colts?" His voice was working, but it came out weak, high and cracked, like a badly played recorder.

"Now, now, Sir Jarrod, you mustn't take on so. You'll set yourself back and you've been coming on so well lately."

"Never mind that," he said with the querulous authority of the very old. "What happened to the unicorns?"

"They're all right. They're in the stables and I don't doubt but

Lazla's taking good care of them." She put a cool hand on his forehead and then picked up his stick-thin wrist.

"They can't be all right," he said bitterly, resenting her ministrations, "their mother was killed."

"What an imagination." She used the soothing tones of a nursemaid. "The big one's right there with the rest of them. I've seen her myself." She dropped his wrist and went over to the table. She poured something from a flask into a beaker while Jarrod tried to make sense of what she had said. She was obviously trying to humor him.

"Don't lie to me. I'm strong enough to take the truth." He had meant it to sound forceful, but he only managed to sound petulant.

"It is the truth. Now, drink this up like a good boy. You'll see for yourself when you're up and about again."

"What is it?" he demanded suspiciously.

"It's only mandragore. What you need is rest." She watched as he swallowed and took the beaker back.

"Then the Lady Marianna . . . ?" he asked, not daring to complete the sentence.

"Now you just relax and let the medicine do its work."

"Greylock's dead." It was a flat statement and he hoped it would shock the truth out of her.

"No, he's not," she replied placidly, "though why he isn't is beyond me. He hasn't the advantage of your youth."

"If he wasn't dead, I wouldn't be in this bed, would I?"

"He needs special care and the bed was available. It's a lot bigger than that old cot of yours and more comfortable, so you just thank your lucky stars." She smoothed the sheet and tucked him firmly in. He wanted to argue with her, but the draught was making him too muzzy.

He dreamed of fire and loss and unicorns. He dreamed of women, riding, fighting, arguing and the voice of Princess Naxania pursued him. The words made no sense, but the tone of voice was clear enough. It was regal, peremptory and dismissive and it was impossible to ignore. When he waded out of the aftermath of the drug with eyes slow to focus, she was still there, arms akimbo, looking down at him.

"I do not enjoy arguing with that woman," the figure said.

"She is as bad as Celena. They are all the same, those Wisewomen. No respect for authority."

Jarrod blinked at her. She was too solid to be a phantasm. She towered over him, pale and beautiful, even in annoyance, with the remembered long, black hair. She leaned over and peered at him, the hair swinging.

"Can you understand me? Gods of Creation, but you look awful. Can you hear me? Have you gone senile on me?"

"I hear you, Highness." The words were slow and slurred. He had tried for the inflections of the formal mode, but the intonations came out all wrong.

"Majesty, if you don't mind," Naxania snapped. Ah yes, Jarrod thought, she's the only one left and she always did want to be a Queen.

"My apologies, your Majesty. The mandragore . . ."

"Well, at least you sound sane." She straightened up again. "That is something to be grateful for. It would have been just too ironic after all of Ragnor's insistence."

"Majesty?"

"Oh, there has been a veritable concourse of bunglebirds between Celador and Stronta. The upshot of it all is that I am to inform you that the Archmage has appointed you Acting Mage while Greylock is, um, indisposed." She paused and looked at him, a look devoid of warmth. "I cannot say that I altogether approve. You are, after all, ridiculously young, even though you do look a hundred and five. The Archmage, however, is adamant. I just hope that his faith in you is not misplaced." Jarrod was bewildered by this turn of events, but he reacted to her criticism.

"I'm the one who found the unicorns," he said defensively. "I'm the one your prophecy referred to."

"Not necessarily."

"But Majesty . . ."

"But me no buts, young man. I am your Queen and the prophecy was mine. Was there anything in it to indicate that the person who found them was the one who would 'lead' them?"

"Well, not exactly . . ."

"And you haven't led them anywhere, have you?" She's jealous, Jarrod thought. That's it. She wants to be a Mage as well. It did nothing to dispel the disorientation he was feeling.

"I am the only one they will follow and they were with us at the Place of Power."

"Ah yes," the new Queen was sarcasm incarnate, "the famous 'victory' that Ragnor insists we ascribe to Greylock and to you. Now, I know that prophecy is supposed to be a two-edged sword, the Oracle has proved that often enough, but this is the first time that I know of when a victory is indistinguishable from defeat." Jarrod felt the cloak of depression getting heavier. He said nothing. He just lay there and stared up at her.

"Oh, it is thought that huge numbers of those disgusting things were destroyed, but it is hard to be sure. There is no evidence left."

"But I saw it," Jarrod expostulated. "I made the fire destroy them."

"Did you indeed? And did you make it burn my father and my brother and all those other brave men?" Passion and pain thickened her voice.

"No!" Jarrod tried to sit up, but his arms lacked the strength. "They were already dead. I swear it."

"That is as may be." She was unrelenting.

"The colts helped me and together we threw the fire back at them. Nothing could have survived that. Couldn't that be what the prophecy meant?" He was pleading.

"And where is the Ancient of Days?" she asked. "I haven't seen any Ancient of Days, unless you count Greylock."

"Greylock? Is he all right? I tried to ask Diadra but . . ."

"All right?" The pitch rose on the words. "All right? He is alive, if that is what you mean by 'all right,' but that is all he is. He is stuck on that slab in what used to be the Place of Power. I've tried to release him, but I cannot do it." The words were angry and bitten off. "Thorden sends people to trim his hair and cut his nails. If they didn't grow, you wouldn't know that he was still with us." She stopped and took a deep breath. She saw the stricken look on the dried-apple of a face and compassion returned to her.

"I'm sorry," she said. "I should not have taxed you with this so soon, but you must understand what I, what all of us have been going through.'' She turned her head away and Jarrod saw the glisten of moisture in her eyes as she did so. His own tears welled up in sympathy. Naxania took another deep breath and regained her composure.

"Perhaps, when you are recovered, you will have more success than I. We must hope so.'' She tried for a smile and produced a wan imitation. "On the bright side of things, whatever it was that the two of you did has frightened the Others badly. They have pulled back, atmosphere and all, though don't ask me how they did it. Not just here; all up and down the length of the Causeways. In that, we are very fortunate. There is so much to do, so many posts to be filled and so few men left to fill them.'' There was genuine pain in her eyes and, for the first time, Jarrod noticed the shadows and the chalky look to the habitually pale skin. She rallied.

"Luckily, our Cousin of Arundel has permitted me to borrow the Holdmaster of Gwyndryth to help reconstruct the army.'' Warmth crept back into her voice and the face softened into a slow, introspective smile. She shook her head and turned briskly back to him.

"At any rate, I congratulate you on your promotion, my Lord Mage, and I wish you a speedy recovery.'' She gathered up her cloak. "For the sake of the Discipline and of our realm, I trust you will prove worthy of the honor.'' She glanced at him from the doorway. "Oh, and if I were you, I would dye my hair before making an appearance in public. My people have already had all the shocks that they can take.'' Then she was gone.

Jarrod relaxed and felt as if the weight of the world was pressing him into the mattress. Was he to blame? It had not occurred to him that anyone might think so, but Naxania obviously did. He fought back against the inertia that threatened to drag him down. There was no way to bring the host of Paladine back from the dead and nothing he could do for Greylock in his present condition. The Queen's parting words rankled him. He couldn't do anything for anyone before he did something about himself. It was the only spark of hope left to him.

He maneuvered himself out of the bedclothes and swung his legs over the side of the bed. He pushed his way to his feet, but his legs promptly buckled and he sat down heavily. He grasped the bedpost and hauled himself up again, clinging to it, trying not to get tangled up in the curtains, swaying drunkenly as he tried to keep his balance. He hadn't felt like this since he stepped ashore after the trip on the *Steady Wench*.

He righted himself and then pushed off. The floor tilted treacherously and his legs were made of twine. He flung his arms out and took a couple of wobbling paces. He stood, wavering, trying to gather his forces. His head swam and he felt nauseated. He was trembling and his feet were cold. He took another step and fell. He wanted to cry again but, instead, he concentrated on raising himself to his hands and knees and crawled ignominiously to the chest by the wall. He paused to catch his breath and then hoisted himself up so that he could see himself in the rectangle of polished metal that hung above it.

A gaunt, haunted old man looked back at him. He gasped and shook his head in dismay at the image. The hair was white and close-cropped, making the skull stand out like a momento mori. The eyes were huge and deeply socketed in black, the skin was pallid and wizened. His whole face was seined and his neck was scraggy and creased. There were deep furrows on either side of his mouth and little, vertical lines all along the top lip. His cheeks were sunken and both they and his chin were scrubbled with white hair.

He touched them with a tremulous hand and was appalled once more at how thin his wrist was. His eyes moved down and saw that the hoary stranger was wearing a sleeping robe that was much too big for him. Naxania had spoken no more than the truth. He turned and staggered to the bed, unable to keep a straight line and frightened of falling. Once there, he crawled under the covers and curled up into an aching ball.

He lay thus for a long, self-pitying time until resolution took hold of him. Like it or not, he was a Mage now. It seemed impossible, but Naxania was definitely not the kind of person given to practical jokes. So there it was. There was no time in his life left for this sort of indulgence. If only he didn't feel so weak and affectless.

The Wisewoman had dodged his question about Marianna, so she must be dead. It was entirely possible that Amarine had been able to save herself, but not Marianna. I warned her, he thought.

I told her not to, but she was too stubborn to listen. In any case, it doesn't matter what I look like anymore. His duty was clear. He must regain his strength as fast as possible and then contrive to free Greylock from his imprisonment. Naxania, he knew instinctively, would not help him. She had tried and failed and, if she could not have the Mageship for herself, would prefer someone she thought she could dominate than to have Greylock back. He reached for the bellpull.

"How long have I been like this, Diadra?" he inquired brusquely when the Wisewoman presented herself. She had done nothing yet to deserve his disfavor, but if he didn't assert himself now, he was afraid that he never would.

"About two months, Excellency." she replied, using his new honorific for the first time. Had she been listening at the door? Probably.

"Two months?" He was incredulous. "That long?"

"You were in a very bad way. At first, I didn't think I could save you, but you've come a long way since then."

"I'm sure that I owe it to you and I'm very grateful. Now I have new responsibilities. I shall need to see the herbalist and then Agar Thorden."

"The herbalist is a possibility, though what he could do for you that I can't is beyond me, but it's not time for the likes of Agar Thorden yet," she said firmly.

"You are, without a doubt, the most aggravating woman."

"That's just what the Mage used to say," she replied complacently.

"I am glad that you remember that you are the Mage's personal Wisewoman," Jarrod said quietly, preparing to play his trump card. "What you don't seem to have realized yet is that I'm the Mage now and the Mage gets to pick his Wisewoman, not the other way around." The contest of wills was making him feel better.

"You mustn't excite yourself. You'll work yourself into a relapse." The rebuke was automatic, but the fight had gone out of her. She tucked him in grumpily and left, the picture of offended rectitude. Jarrod lay back feeling ridiculously pleased with himself.

The herbalist came the following day and together they devised a regimen. Jarrod embarked on a surreptitious program of exercises when he felt sure that Diadra would not be looking in on him. She had taken care of him since he was a boy and, while he might defy her, there was no way he could bring himself to replace her. His threat had been idle but effective.

As the days went by, he gained strength and felt that he could handle another showdown. He demanded to see Administrator Thorden, but all she said was, "There's one as you'd rather see first," and smiled enigmatically. When she opened the door again, Marianna stood on the threshold.

"Marianna?" His voice cracked with incredulity. "It can't be—not possible. You're dead." She grinned at him and crossed to the bed. She sat and took one dessicated hand in both of hers.

"Do I feel dead, Jarrod? Do I look like a ghost?"

"Oh, no. It's just that I . . ." The words caught in his throat and the choking sobs overwhelmed him as the reality and the relief hit. She leaned forward and cradled his thin form in her arms.

"There, there," she intoned. "It's all right. I'm here and it's going to be all right." She rocked the antedeluvian baby until he had regained his composure and then offered him a handkerchief. As he wiped his eyes and blew his nose, it was as if an invisible membrane had been broken and the weight, the debilitating feelings of guilt and insufficiency, fled.

"What happened?" he said when he was propped back up against the bolster.

"Well, that's a bit difficult to explain. The easy part is that when the fire came at us, Amarine went into Interim. It's the rest of it that's weird."

"You use that word too much," he said and produced a smile. It was wonderful to see her, an unexpected miracle, but what, he wondered, must she think of him in this condition? He smiled again at the resurgence of his vanity.

"Stop looking so pleased with yourself. Weird was exactly what it was. Amarine took me to the place where all the Lines of Force converge. At least, that's how she described it."

"Described it? You can talk to her?"

"Well, talk isn't exactly the right word. We do it the same way that you and the colts communicate."

"That's wonderful," he said with very mixed emotions.

"Yes, it is. I have to confess to you, Jarrod, that I was very jealous of you."

"Oh, come on."

"Yes, I was. And with good reason. Being a Magician, you could do things that I would never be able to do, let alone understand. Being able to think together with the colts as well seemed so unfair."

"I'm sorry. I never. . . ." She leaned forward and stopped him with a forefinger on the lips.

"That's not important now. Oh Jarrod, the things I learned up there. Do you know what it's been like being back here and knowing that no one but you would believe me, would understand what I was talking about? And Diadra wouldn't let me in to talk to you." She broke off. "This really isn't the time to talk about it, though. I promised that old biddy that I wouldn't stay too long. If she thinks that I've tired you out or upset you, she won't let me back in."

"You can't leave me hanging like this. I'll fret myself into a relapse if you do." She laughed at him and he joined her, though it hurt his chest. It was the first time that he had laughed out loud in such a long time and the pain felt good.

"I'll be back soon, I promise. Besides, I think the unicorns should be around when I try to explain and that'll have to wait until you're stronger."

"You'll come back and see me before then, though?" he asked anxiously.

"Of course I will. I told you I found out a lot up there. That included a lot about myself and I've had a lot of time to think about it since. You don't come back from the grave and feel the same." The last was said lightly, but Jarrod sensed the earnestness behind it. She gave him a long look and her eyes caught and danced the way that he remembered. She leaned forward and kissed him lightly on the cheek, got up and smoothed her gown. No more Martin, he thought.

"Oh, and congratulations on your new position," she said. "I think you'll make a fine Mage, though it's going to be a little difficult for me to curtsey and call you Excellency." She grinned, dropped a curtsey and left him to the turmoil of his thoughts and emotions.

He was stronger and a little more sure of himself when next she appeared, but his image in the looking glass still dismayed him. There was more pepper than salt in the hair, but he still thought that he looked hopelessly old.

"My," she said brightly, as she came toward him, "you're up and you look ever so much better."

"Being in a chair isn't up and I look dreadful."

"Stop fishing for compliments. You look distinguished and I've always liked mature men." He smiled in spite of himself.

"It isn't seemly to flirt with a Mage."

"Is that the truth?" she asked pertly. "And I'd always thought that Mages were men." She drew up a chair. "How are you feeling?"

"Much better, as a matter of fact. Diadra has finally admitted that I can go out in a couple of days."

"That's very good news. Amarine says that the colts miss you dreadfully." The message warmed him and lifted his spirits further.

"I'm glad to hear it," he said. "I was half afraid that they would have forgotten me."

"Fat chance." They smiled at each other.

"Tell me, what's going on out there. That damned woman won't tell me anything and Thorden's too preoccupied to be able to spend much time with me."

"Stronta's still very disorganized. Daddy arrived a couple of days ago and he's going to put the army back together again. He says it's going to be difficult because so many of the senior officers were killed. The ones that are left are all administrative rather than combat. The rest of Strand's all right, though. The enemy shows no signs of moving forward again. At least, that's what Daddy says. I think he and Naxania are going to be married," she added offhandedly. She didn't sound particularly happy at the thought. "After the proper period of mourning and the coronation are over, of course."

"You must be very proud."

"Proud? Why should I be proud? It's ridiculous! She's almost the same age as I am."

"Er, yes, yes I see," he said lamely. "Well, he's certainly going to be very busy."

"It'll be quite a while before the Paladinian army will be ready for combat again. It's a good thing that the other side has abandoned the field for a while. Arundel needs the time to practice new tactics. Daddy's already taught the Umbrians, so they should be safe enough."

"It's never going to end, is it?" Jarrod said wearily.

"Who knows?" She gave him a strange, enigmatic look. "Anyway, Ragnor, so I'm told, is as happy as a kina in a byre. According to him, his vision has been rendered null and void. The future has been changed and Strand will survive. You and Greylock are big heroes. Did you know that?" The mention of Greylock's name darkened Jarrod's face.

"And where did you hear that?" he asked edgily. "Palace gossip?"

"No," she answered, nettled. "There are broadsheets from Celador tacked up all over, complete with pictures of the two of you."

"You must be joking."

"No, I'm not. I'll bring you one the next time I come, though I must admit that your picture doesn't look too much like you."

"It probably shows a young man," Jarrod said acidly.

"I think it's time that I was going." She rose, unwilling to deal with him in this mood. "I'm obviously tiring you."

"No, don't go." His contrition was patent.

"Oh, Jarrod, you mustn't go blaming yourself for what happened to Greylock," she said perspicaciously. "I think he knew exactly what was happening and decided to keep the Place of Power from disappearing entirely. It was a noble and deliberate gesture." She patted his arm. "Now I really must be going. I promised the unicorns that I'd take them for a gallop."

"I'm sorry that I'm such poor company." His voice was stiff.

"You've been through so much, my Jarrod. You really mustn't be so hard on yourself." Her look was tender and it did uncomfortable things to his pulse. "Next time we're together, we'll both be taking the unicorns out. You mark my words." She smiled encouragingly at him and, as it turned out, she was right.

The meeting was not the unfettered gambol that Jarrod had

hoped for. Marianna came to get him and helped him down to the stables. His exercises had not entirely prepared him for the stairs and he felt tenuous by the time he reached the court. The happiness that the colts felt when they detected his approach reached out and more than made up for his chagrin at his continued weakness.

It's so good to have you with us again. Pellia. *You are tougher than we thought you were.* Beldun. *Not that tough, just look at him.* Nastrus. The thoughts broke in all at once and he was buoyed by the affection that lay beneath even Nastrus' sending. He went into their special stall on Marianna's arm, stopped and looked at them.

You've grown so and your coats have changed.

He wants us to stay foals forever, Nastrus remarked with sly truth.

And you're all disgustingly fat, Jarrod retorted.

Whose fault is that? Beldun inquired. *Who hasn't taken us for a decent run in months? Ignore the louts,* Pellia advised.

Jarrod turned to Marianna and saw that she was incapable of hearing them, even if they had spoken out loud. She was bonded with Amarine and he now felt a twinge of what she must have felt when he first established contact with the colts.

A very strange emotion, Nastrus said in his inner ear. Jarrod ignored him, but turned his attention back to the young ones.

You look very handsome with proper horns, and speaking of horns, I want to thank you for your help and support in the Place of Power. We could never have destroyed the enemy without you. The statement was accepted with complacence. There was no false modesty in the unicorns. *I was afraid for a while that we had lost Marianna and your mother. I still don't know how they escaped and I think it's about time we found out.* His mind probed out for the dam and met the familiar blankness.

"Marianna," he called. She came back with a start. "Let's get ourselves comfortable on the hay bales and then you can tell us your story. I'll translate for the colts."

"All right." She gathered her skirt and tucked her legs up. "Well, when I saw that wall of fire coming toward us, I was afraid. Riding Amarine, I'd felt quite safe up until then. Now I knew I was going to die. That didn't matter, somehow. What I heard was your words." Memory made her speech staccato.

"The next thing I felt was cold, bitter cold. It was even more shocking because I had been expecting fire. Then there was nothing." She paused and looked at them one by one. "When I came to, we were in a beautiful glade and I thought, so this is what it's like to be dead. It's really rather nice." She gave a tentative little smile.

"Then a voice in my head said, 'Welcome to the Island at the Center.' That was when I thought that death included madness. 'You're not mad and we aren't dead,' the voice said. 'It's just that you have never been able to hear me before.' Well, you can imagine how I felt."

Hungry, Nastrus said and Jarrod laughed.

"Nastrus says, 'hungry,' " he explained.

"Right. That and scared and happy. Amarine was cropping already, but she stopped long enough to tell me to dismount and pick some fruit for myself. Anyway, when we both felt better and I had overcome the shock of it all, the two of us had a good, long get-together." She smiled fondly at Amarine. "She guided me to The Memory and that was quite a revelation."

"It goes so far back, Jarrod. Too far back for me to take it in, but Amarine explained some things to me. Did you know that the unicorns were created, way, way back, by a race of people like ourselves? Well, more like you, really."

Not in the least like you, Beldun remarked. *Much more advanced. You are greatly degenerated.*

Quiet, Jarrod ordered.

"Anyway," Marianna resumed and then stopped again. "This is going to sound like a child's tale. Well, why not? Once upon a time there was a race that could do wonderful things with their minds—that's what I meant when I said they were more like you—and with their hands." She broke off and giggled unexpectedly. "I sound just like old King Sig, don't I?" Jarrod smiled in agreement. "Anyway, one of the things they did was to create the unicorns. The world they lived on went round their sun, not the other way about." There was amusement in the corners of Jarrod's mind. "And in time, that sun began to cool down. Despite all their cleverness, they couldn't do anything about it, so they started to look for another world to live on.

"That's another thing, Jarrod, there are lots and lots of worlds and some of them are inhabited. At least that's what The Memory said." Jarrod made a mental reservation, but it was banished by the colts, complete with Nastrus' mockery of his assumption that Strand was unique.

"Where was I? Oh yes. They set out in a fleet of, er, of vessels to find other worlds and make them habitable. The worlds they picked were supposed to be empty and they had special equipment to make them livable.

"They picked Strand as one of those places. They made a mistake though. They didn't know it, but they made a big mistake. Strand had an atmosphere that they couldn't live in, so they set out to change it. I don't understand how, exactly, but it's the reason we're so keen on growing things. The Giants' Causeway had something to do with it, too, but I couldn't understand that at all." She came to a halt and looked around at them, as if for encouragement.

"And?" Jarrod prompted.

"Well," she said hesitantly, this is the hard part."

"Take your time."

"The mistake they made was that this world wasn't uninhabited."

"I'm ahead of you. That's where the Others came from. But that would mean that the Others were responsible for the unicorns and I can't believe that."

Humans are so blind, Beldun offered. *Not all of them, just this one*, Nastrus teased. *Hush*, their sister admonished.

"No. That's not it at all," Marianna said. "We are the ones who were planted here. Our ancestors were the ones who created them. Those, those Others are the original inhabitants."

"Never!" The word sprang in shock from Jarrod.

True, Pellia said with finality.

"I'm just telling you what Amarine showed me," Marianna said defensively.

"Pellia says it's true. Then, then . . ."

"We are the invaders and we have just about pushed them out," Marianna finished for him.

"Have you told anyone about this?"

"Come on, Jarrod, who could I tell except you? If you couldn't communicate with the unicorns, you wouldn't believe me, would you?"

"No, I suppose not."

"Ragnor would believe you," she said.

"I don't know about that. It's pretty incredible."

"You must make him believe. We can't let this war go on. Not knowing what we do. That would be totally immoral."

"That's all very well, but how do we get the word across to the other side. They're the ones who do all the attacking."

"We may not have to. They may have had enough. Why else would they pull back so far—and not just in front of Stronta. They can't send us an embassy, so they are obviously trying to send us a message." She paused and smiled triumphantly at her own lógic. "Amarine agrees with me," she added as a clincher.

"Peace," Jarrod said musingly. "Peace for the very first time. Then I was right. We are the ones that the verse was talking about." He leaned over and hugged her impulsively. "Naxania was wrong. It did mean me. And you. You are a wonder." He beamed at her and she flushed under the intensity of his gaze. The colts made their amusement plain in his mind.

"And speaking of wonders," he said, collecting himself, "I think I should like to celebrate by going for a gentle ride on one. Pellia, my dear," he spoke aloud to her for once, "I've never ridden you, but you've grown a lot and I weigh far less than I used to. Do you think you could manage?"

It would be a privilege to be ridden by the Mage of Paladine.

Acting Mage, he corrected.

Don't flatter him, Nastrus thought as Marianna went to get the saddles. *He's puffed up enough as it is.*

The stableboys gathered and gawped as usual as the little cavalcade headed for open country, but it was the new Mage and the foreign woman rather than the by now familiar miracle of the unicorns that drew them. As they rode past the encampment where the new recruits were training, the young men put down their pikes and stared until the figures were out of sight. Then they resumed the exercises that their fathers had mastered, but that their sons might never need. The soft breeze that cooled them promised renewal, rebirth and the joys of Greeningale.

FINIS

ANDRÉ NORTON

☐ 54736-5 **GRYPHON'S EYRIE** $2.95
  54737-3 Canada $3.50

☐ 48558-1 **FORERUNNER** $2.75

☐ 48585-9 **MOON CALLED** $2.95

☐ 54725-X **WHEEL OF STARS** $2.95
  54726-8 Canada $3.50

☐ 54738-1 **THE CRYSTAL GRYPHON** $2.95
  54739-X Canada $3.50

☐ 54740-3 **MAGIC IN ITHKAR** Edited by
  André Norton and Robert Adams Trade $6.95
  54741-1 Canada $7.95

Buy them at your local bookstore or use this handy coupon:
Clip and mail this page with your order

TOR BOOKS—Reader Service Dept.
P.O. Box 690, Rockville Centre, N.Y. 11571

Please send me the book(s) I have checked above. I am
enclosing $_____ (please add $1.00 to cover postage
and handling). Send check or money order only—no cash or
C.O.D.'s.

Mr./Mrs./Miss _____

Address _____

City _____ State/Zip _____

Please allow six weeks for delivery. Prices subject to change
without notice.